## Dedication

My deepest appreciation goes out to all the members of The Fellowship of the Quill. Without your support, encouragement, and constructive feedback, this novel would still be sitting in a computer file somewhere. Thank you.

Chapter One

Alex awoke instinctively, as he did every morning. First asleep, then awake. He didn't have to check his watch or look out the window to judge the position of the sun and guess the time. It was always—six a.m.

Occasionally, he wondered how it would feel to pull the covers over his head, to savor their warmth and weight, and drift back to sleep. Especially on a day like today when cool air, misted with rain, blew through the room. But he couldn't allow such an indulgence. Adhering to his routine was vital.

Downstairs, the clock in the parlor chimed six times.

Beneath his blankets, he slid his hands down his torso, to the hem of his nightshirt, bunched up below his hips. Pulling the shirt to his waist, Alex then moved his hands to his groin and the metal band wrapped around the base of his shaft. By rote, he turned the screw to open the device then eased it off, careful not to prick his tender skin with the jagged teeth edging the outside ring.

Lifting aside his blankets, he slid from his cocoon of warmth and planted his bare feet on the cold wood floor. He leaned toward the small table beside his bed and pulled open the drawer. He tossed the double-ring device inside. It clanked against the metal of another contraption, and he slammed the drawer closed.

*Don't think about it.* He squeezed his fingers into fists, even as he ached to feel the pleasure of those

1

fingers wrapped around his length, his thumb brushing lightly over the tip.

*No,* he told himself as he did every morning, as he did every day, numerous times a day. *Don't think about it.* He crossed the room and shoved the window sash down with a thud.

Moving to the washstand, he poured cold water in the basin and scrubbed his face and hands. On days like this, all he wanted was to give in to the temptations of the flesh.

Doctor Powell had to be wrong. This constant self-denial would surely be what drove him insane, not the pleasure of touching himself.

*Don't think about it.* He added a bit of water to the soap in his shaving mug and rubbed his brush against the bar of cold cream and glycerin. He always felt better after his shave. With his face clean of stubble, he looked less like his father.

One day, he'd like to try sandalwood soap. Mr. Goldman, the head teller at the bank, sometimes smelled of sandalwood or cedar, but it was important Alex continued using plain unscented soap. At least for now.

He pulled on his drawers and stockings, then tugged his nightshirt over his head and finished dressing. Sometimes the mental struggle exhausted him so that all he longed to do was surrender. But that way led to blindness, to insanity, and sometimes even to death. He couldn't allow himself to succumb—not yet. His mother needed him. Nellie needed him.

"Alexander!" His mother's voice rose from the foot of the stairs. "Are you awake?"

He sighed as he buttoned his waistcoat. "Yes, Mother!" Just once, he would like her to trust him. Trust him to get up on time, to follow his regimen, and never—

His hand stilled, his tie hanging from his fingers. Today was Wednesday the fourth.

In the mirror he watched the corners of his mouth draw back into a grin. This afternoon he'd take the four o'clock train to Omaha, then down to Lincoln. He glanced toward the wardrobe where his Gladstone bag sat on the floor. He'd packed last night, making sure all was in order for his trip. His smile widened. Lightness flooded his body, easing the oppressive weight that was his life.

Was this how his father felt every time he took one of his trips?

A shudder rippled through him, quelling his enthusiasm. He swallowed and ran his finger between his neck and the restriction of his celluloid collar.

Turning from the mirror, he packed his toiletries and made his bed, though the effort was pointless. As soon as he left for the bank, his mother would come up and check his sheets for any evidence he'd sinned during the night.

The aroma of fresh coffee wafted up from the kitchen. He inhaled deeply. Soon. One day soon, he'd try a cup. He lifted his spectacles off his bedside table and slid them into the pocket of his waistcoat. Grabbing his Gladstone, he skipped down the stairs. He set his bag beneath the hat rack, left through the front door, and headed out back to use the necessary.

The wet grass pearled in glassy beads on the toes of his polished shoes, but he didn't mind. Today was the fourth. He checked his pocket watch. Less than ten hours and he'd be on the train.

He walked to the barn and fed the horse, then

returning to the house, he climbed the back steps into the kitchen.

His sister stood at the stove, scooping scrambled eggs onto two plates. Spatula in hand she used the back of her wrist to brush aside a tendril of hair which had come loose from her bun.

He raised and lowered the pump handle, splashing water into a basin. "Good morning."

"Good morning." Nellie shot him a quick glance. "Mother just took your breakfast to the table."

His mouth watered as he inhaled the smoky aroma of bacon, and his tongue tingled at the remembered saltiness.

Using a fork, Nellie lifted sizzling strips from the pan. They lay straight across the tines and slid easily onto the plates.

He washed his hands. "Smells wonderful."

"You seem happy today."

Towel in hand, he stepped up beside her, leaned down, and gave her a quick peck on her cheek.

She stiffened and shrugged away.

He folded the towel and laid it beside the pump. "I am happy," he said, then headed into the dining room.

The same breakfast he'd eaten every morning since he was thirteen sat at his usual place, a bowl of oatmeal—no sugar, honey, or cream—a piece of dark bread toasted—no butter, no jam—a soft-boiled egg in a cup, and a glass of water.

"Good morning, Mother," he said coming to stand behind her chair while they waited for Nellie. She entered and set the first plate in front of Mother, and the second at her own place. Fried potatoes, bacon and eggs, and toasted bread spread with butter and raspberry jam filled both plates.

Alex seated his mother then his sister before moving to the head of the table. Mother nodded, and he gave the blessing, thanking God for the food He'd provided, for the hands that had prepared it, and for strength to keep from sin.

Alex had recited the same grace at the start of every meal since his father was killed. He'd done it so often, he could allow his mind to drift, to think about things he dared not share aloud.

If all went well at his meeting tomorrow, he'd soon be free. Mother and Nellie would be provided enough money to live comfortably, and he would be able to experience a breakfast of pork sausages, pastries drizzled with icing, and a large cup of fresh brewed coffee with sugar and cream.

None of those foods were healthy for him. They only accelerated his illness, but soon he'd be able to throw caution to the wind and indulge. Until then, he might as well savor the planning.

"Why are you smiling so oddly?" Mother's voice broke into his thoughts. From the opposite end of the table, her sharp gaze narrowed on his face, and he felt as if he were a rare insect an explorer had pinned to a board.

His grin faded. He needed to be more careful, or she might suspect his trip involved more than just bank business—at least it would if Mr. Lathrop said yes.

"I'm merely happy, Mother. It's a beautiful day."

"It's raining."

He glanced at the dining room window. Raindrops trailed down the panes. Unsure what to say, he delved into his bowl of oatmeal, scooping pasty globs into his mouth as if he couldn't get enough.

Mother and Nellie chatted on about quilting bees and their friends from the Methodist church, as though he weren't even at the table. He picked up his knife and sawed opened the top of his egg. He didn't mind being ignored, because maybe, just once he could sneak a bit of…

"Alex-*ander*. Put. That. Down." His mother's reprimand snapped with the same tone she'd used when he was five. Though petite and fine-boned, she spoke with the strength of an Amazon.

With a sigh, he returned the salt cellar to the table. Nellie snatched it away as if it were made of gold and he a petty thief. Her glare reproachful, she set the china dish out of reach.

Mother raised her chin, her rigid posture snapping her spine straight, reminding him of a crow whose sharp gaze caught a bit of movement in the grass.

After five years, she still wore her widow's weeds, as though Samuel James Worthington had been a man worthy of mourning. Her black clothing, a pretense before the town that she'd loved her husband, and a daily reminder to Alex that he too, might one day become the monster his father had been.

"I think it's time you marry."

"What?" His spoon slipped from his fingers and dinged against the plate. A bit of yolk spattered the polished tabletop.

Mother folded her hands, then slipped them below the edge of the table. "Reverend Clark proposed the idea to me yesterday. His daughter is still unwed, and he would like to see her settled in a godly home."

Alex picked up his spoon and set it on his plate. "I don't believe this is an appropriate topic for the breakfast table."

"Don't be a prude. Your marriage is a perfectly appropriate topic of conversation amongst family."

"All right. I'm not marrying Hester Clark." He lifted his water glass, took a sip, and set it down, placing it so the bottom of the glass precisely matched the faint circular mark in the wood finish. He looked up, meeting Mother's steady gaze. "I don't plan to marry. Ever. I will not procreate Father's bloodline."

Her brow furrowed, and her eyes narrowed. "Then Miss Clark is perfect for you. I dare say she is near past childbearing age."

He shook his head. "No. I'm only twenty-four. She is older than Nell. Her hair is going gray. She's too tall, and her front teeth…"

"That will be enough. If her appearance dissuades you from lustful thoughts, all the better. Doctor Powell agrees."

"*You discussed this with Doctor Powell?*" Heat crept up the back of his neck.

"Yes. He believes one or two intimate encounters a year should be enough to satisfy your manly urges, without contributing to your decline."

Gossip in this town ran rampant, especially regarding the Worthington family. Bad enough, everyone believed his father had bedded every prostitute in the county. Did his mother have to provide constant fodder for the town busybodies? No one would ever forget if she discussed her son with every person she met, as though he, like his father, was a burden she was forced to bear.

Alex was the one who took care of her, put food on the table, saw to it the house was maintained. He was the one who'd left college to take over the massive responsibilities of a failing bank.

Things had to go well tomorrow. Then, for whatever time he had left, at least he would finally be free.

He pushed to his feet and tossed down his napkin, leaving the rest of his breakfast uneaten.

"I will not marry Miss Clark. Now, if you will excuse me, I need to get to the bank."

"Nonsense. You are avoiding the issue. Marriage is the natural course of things. Nellie has been wed these sixteen years."

"And where is Clayton, Mother?"

She sipped her coffee then carefully returned the cup to its saucer. "You know business keeps him away for long periods."

Alex laughed, the sound hollow and maybe, a bit maniacal. "His business? You can both pretend if you want, but we all know what his business is, don't we? And the only time he comes home is when he needs to dodge the Pinkertons or extort money from me."

"How dare you?" Nellie's words were softly spoken, yet harsh and clipped. Something icy flickered in her eyes. "You're nothing but a spoiled boy who knows nothing of life. How dare you presume to judge my marriage? Clayton is a man who understands the realities of this world. He respects me, and we share a mutual affection. So, go to your bank and hide in your office where you don't have to actually see what goes on outside your door."

She returned her focus to her plate and stabbed a piece of potato with her fork.

Alex blinked, startled by the quiet venom in her voice. He'd rarely heard Nellie speak more than a sentence or two. Had he missed something important in her life? When had she become as cold and pious as Mother?

Was Nellie right? Was he blind to the realities around him? His rude behavior, his reference to a cold, rainy day as beautiful, salt on his egg—was it all mounting evidence of the encroaching insanity which would eventually consume his mind?

Mother shook her head and reached out to pat Nellie's hand. "It's not his fault, Daughter. Your dear father also suffered irrational outbursts." She looked past Nellie and glared straight at him.

"This is why you must avoid all stress. Mr. Goldman is more than qualified to look after any banking business in Lincoln. The temptations in such a city will only contribute to an accelerated decline."

A low sound, almost a growl, rumbled in his throat. He didn't need to look for reality outside his office door. His whole damn family was insane. He whirled on his heels and strode from the room.

Grabbing his hat and bag he turned up the collar of his coat and left the house. Walking more than a mile to town in the rain wasn't pleasant, though normally this daily walk was the most enjoyable part of his exercise regimen. Droplets of mud spattered his trouser legs and covered his shoes.

He wasn't spoiled. What did Nellie know anyway except the inside of that house and her church friends?

Marriage! Mother wanted to punish him; that's what it was. Punish him for being his father's son. After tomorrow he'd find his own way to relieve his stress, and it wouldn't be with a dried-up hag like Hester Clark.

The covered sidewalks offered some relief from the

light rain. He strode half-way down Sixth Street and stopped at the corner of Sixth and F Street. In front of him loomed the oppressive brick façade and arched windows of the Farmers and Merchants Bank.

What would happen if his meeting tomorrow didn't go well? How many more times could he force himself to step through these glass-paned, double doors?

He withdrew his key, ascended the two stone steps, and turned the lock. Moving inside, he relocked the door. The click echoed in the cavernous room.

Patches of sunlight gleamed on the polished black and white tiles. The scents of beeswax and lemon were always strongest this time of day. By evening the bank would smell of dust and unwashed bodies. The high ceiling amplified his shuffling noises as he removed his muddy shoes.

Footwear in one hand, his bag in the other he headed into his office at the back of the building. Placing his Gladstone beside the umbrella stand, he set his shoes on the floor to dry, then hung up his hat and coat. Last, he pulled his spectacles from the inner pocket.

Moving around his desk, he sat back in his leather chair and glanced at the wall clock above the file drawers. Almost ten after seven. The brass pendulum swung rhythmically back and forth, *tick-tock, tick-tock.* Eight and a half hours, and he could leave for the train station.

He had some time before he'd need to prepare the cash drawers and open for business. Reaching down, he opened the bottom right drawer. He removed a ledger and a couple of file folders, then lifted the false bottom, retrieving a sheaf of papers, and placed them on the desk in front of him.

Hooking his spectacles over his ears, he squinted at the blurry words of the first line.

He blinked and rubbed his eyes, then shifted the pages until the words became legible. An odd lump, heavy and ominous, settled in the pit of his stomach. No matter how much he tried to deny it, his vision had grown worse.

Tomorrow's meeting had to go well. His ledgers were balanced. His reports and charts, perfect. There was nothing else he could do except present himself as confident and professional.

Refusing to think about the bank anymore, he readjusted the pages and read over what he'd written yesterday. Satisfied, he dipped his pen in the inkwell and with the first downward stroke, he escaped into another place, another era.

\*\*\*\*

The sharp banging of knuckles against glass echoed through the front of the bank. Alex looked up. His gaze shot to the clock. Just two minutes before the hour. *Damn.*

He hastily gathered his papers, shoved them into their hideaway, and with his foot—*Double damn,* he'd forgotten to clean the mud off his shoes—slammed the drawer shut. He rose and dashed to where he'd left his shoes. He jammed his feet inside without tying the laces. Spatters of dried mud dotted the bottoms of his trouser legs a shade lighter than the fabric.

There was no help for it now. He grabbed his still damp coat and slipped it on. He left his office and strode across the lobby as he fastened the top button. Reaching the door, he squared his shoulders, slid back the bolt, and holding the latch handle, stepped aside to allow entrance for the two men who stood outside.

"Good morning Mr. Goldman, Mr. Farley," he said, as if nothing was amiss.

"Good morning, Mr. Worthington," they replied in unison, no doubt wondering why the bank hadn't yet opened.

Alex glanced up and down the street. No sign of his third employee. Frowning, he closed the door. Goldman and Farley stared at him as though waiting for an explanation.

"You are being paid to work, not stand here and gawk."

"Yes, sir." Mr. Goldman hurried to his desk.

A flush crept across the tops of Angus Farley's cheeks. The rest of his blush vanished beneath his graying beard. "I'm sorry, sir." He hurried around to the other side of the teller cages and hung up his hat and coat.

Alex walked toward his office, then stopped in front of Mr. Goldman's desk. "I need your ledgers for this week's deposits and withdrawals."

"Yes, sir, but that will only include Saturday, Monday, and yesterday."

"I am aware. I know what day it is."

"Yes, sir. I'm sorry. I should have that for you in an hour."

Alex gave him a curt nod and retreated inside his office. He closed the door and leaned against it, heaving a sigh, grateful in this odd moment that his father had designed the room for complete privacy.

Brushing his shoes and trousers clean, he sat behind his desk and reviewed one more time the figures he'd need for tomorrow's meeting.

Satisfied he knew every decimal point by heart, he

left his sanctuary to collect the ledger from Mr. Goldman.

But instead of working at his desk, Goldman stood at Bill Warner's window assisting Freida Shultz. Farley helped another customer with two men in line behind him.

Alex frowned and glanced at the clock—nearly half-past nine. Warner was late again.

He stepped back into his office and was closing the door when Warner burst into the bank.

Shaking raindrops off his hat, Warner hurried around to the back of the tellers' cages. "Has the old fart noticed I'm late?"

Alex pulled open the door. "Yes, he has."

Warner's face paled.

"Could I please see you in my office? Now?" Alex retreated behind his desk and stood against the wall.

Warner's heels scuffed against the tile like a recalcitrant child approaching the headmaster. He closed the door and crossed the room. Without making eye contact, he stood in front of the desk, his fingers gripping the rolled brim of his hat, as he shifted his weight from foot to foot.

Alex crossed his arms, hoping to brazen out a semblance of authority. "I received no word you would be late today."

"No, sir. I didn't have a chan—"

"This is the third time in the past month you have been late. If it happens again, you will be let go."

"But I need this job. I have a family to support."

"As do we all. When you were hired, it was with the understanding that the workday started promptly at eight."

"I know that, sir. But it was raining. I needed one of my boys to drive me, but my oldest turned the horse out. They couldn't catch him and we—"

"You should have walked."

"It's raining. I would have gotten muddy, and I know how important appearance is to you. I thought, better I'm a few—"

"I live farther than you and do not present myself in a slovenly manner."

"But, sir I—"

"No, Mr. Warner, I am no longer interested in excuses. Nor do I appreciate the disparaging remark you made maligning my character in front of the customers. This bank represents stability and dependability. Constant tardiness and inappropriate language reflect irresponsible behavior, which is not conducive to the image this bank and its employees present to a community who trusts us with their money."

"What kind of image did your father present to the community? Or you? Everyone knows what you did." Warner stiffened as soon as the words left his mouth.

Alex leaned forward, planting his knuckles firmly on the surface of his desk. "You go too far, Mr. Warner. Present yourself to Mr. Goldman for your final pay. Take yourself back into the rain and go home."

"What? You're giving me the sack for being a few minutes late? I have a family."

"You're not being let go for being late. You're being let go for your comments to me. Comments based solely on idle gossip. You didn't know my father, nor do you know my family. You've no right to demean his name, or that of this bank, to which he devoted so mu—"

Warner whirled around and flung open the door. It

slammed against the wall and bounced back, not quite closing behind him, leaving a hole in the plaster the same size as the knob.

"Where are you going?" Goldman asked.

"I've been fired."

"What? For being late?"

Farley said something, but his place at the teller cage was too far from the office for Alex to catch the specific words.

Warner laughed. "Yeah, maybe if he spent an hour or two with one of Mrs. Green's upstairs girls, he wouldn't be walking around with a broomstick shoved up his ass."

"Mrs. Green's girls kept his father happy," Goldman said. "The man knew how to laugh, and he always treated us right."

"I'm to pick up my pay."

"The old goat's leaving later," Goldman said. "Come back before closing, and I'll have it."

Alex stepped from his office.

The three men froze.

Thank God the customers had gone. Alex walked behind Farley to collect Warner's cash drawer. Their gazes seemed to burn straight into his back. Drawer in hand, he stopped at Goldman's desk, and ignoring Warner, said. "If you're finished socializing, I still need that ledger."

Inside his office, Alex collapsed into his chair. He glanced at the clock and propping his elbows on his desk, leaned forward and buried his face in his hands.

Not even ten o'clock. This day was fast becoming the longest of his life.

Chapter Two

Ivy stood in the center of her room, wearing nothing but her chemise and drawers. She'd finished her morning toilet, braided her hair, and twisted it into a thick bun at the back of her head. Opening her wardrobe, she shoved aside her colorful array of silk gowns, reaching instead for the simple two-piece navy brocade.

After laying the dress across her bed, she took a seat at her dressing table. She pulled on a pair of black cotton stockings, securing them with a pair of pink ribbon garters. Stepping into her sturdy black shoes, she quickly tied them up. Her corset came next then a camisole and her under petticoat. She positioned a padded horsehair roll at the back of her waist to form a small bustle, drew the ribbons to the front, and tied them tight. She layered on a second ruffled petticoat then stepped into her underskirt with its diagonal pleats. Next, she stepped into the overskirt, adjusting the latter so the flat placket was turned to the front and the ruffles flowed from the center back. The bodice came last. A coordinating deep blue paisley, neatly fitted at the waist and hips, with black lace, and mid-length sleeves.

Without the risqué bodice, elaborate decoration, and high cut hem of her usual attire, Ivy only wore this ensemble the few times she ventured into town.

She perched a small blue hat with black feather and ribbons at a jaunty angle on the top of her head and secured it with two, six-inch, pearl tipped, hat pins.

Next, she pulled on a pair of black lace gloves, and finally, reaching into the top drawer of her dressing table, she took out her Derringer. Checking to make sure it was loaded, she slipped it into her black, wool reticule.

Leaving her room, she made her way down the hall, and taking the back staircase, entered the kitchen.

Old Maude sat on a stool chopping vegetables. Steam wafted from a large pot on the stove.

"Good morning, Maude."

The woman looked up. Her smile broad across her wrinkled face. "Mawn'in."

Ivy walked over and slid her arms around the woman. She gave her a quick peck on the cheek and stepped back. "What are you cooking so early in the day?" She swiped a carrot from the cutting board and bit off the end.

"I gots a couple a beef bones, simmerin' in there." She nodded toward the stove. "Lily's feelin' poorly ag'in and cain't keep nothin' down."

Ivy shook her head as she removed a spoon from the drawer. "It's that laudanum she always takes for her headaches. I wish she'd stop. At least cut back."

From the smaller pot set off on the side, Ivy scooped a spoonful of oatmeal and gave it a taste.

"A bit of cream and sugar, would do."

"I knows. You tell me ever' time, but Mr. Walter don't like it like that. Mr. Hiram and Mr. George do, so's I say, they can fancy it up how they likes they own selfs."

"Do you need anything while I'm out?"

"No, but I do thank you fo' askin'. Mr. Hiram done fetched up my order yesterday."

"Then I'm off to Mr. Preston's grocery. He's

opening early today, just so I can look through his new shipment of fruit. I think I'll make some fried apple pies, maybe some turnovers, or raspberry tarts. That'd be nice, don't you think? For the gentlemen."

"Yes'um, they sho do like yo bakin'."

Ivy smiled and walked to the window. The early morning sun bathed the prairie in a glow of golden green. Billows of white floated through the vast blue sky. Only the distant dome of the capitol building to the east, and the irregular silhouette of the city roof tops disrupted the straight line of the horizon.

"Yo be careful out there."

"Don't worry." Ivy slipped the drawstrings of her reticule over her wrist. "I'll be fine." Picking up a basket from the table near the door, she headed out.

Holding her skirt hem off the ground, she headed the mile or so into the city. Yesterday's rain had left puddles in every hoof print and wagon rut along the way.

Where the railroad tracks turned north, on the western edge of Lincoln, Ivy approached a cluster of run-down, single room shacks. The door of the closest shack opened, and a man stepped out, clothed only in his underwear. Standing barefoot on the step, he scratched his belly, then urinated in the street. He looked up and Ivy caught his bloodshot gaze.

"Co'mere, darlin'. I got somethin' for ya." He held his fist near his groin and made a jerking motion.

*Pig.*

A woman, clad in only her chemise, her fingers wrapped around the neck of a liquor bottle, stepped from the shack and staggered up against the man. A few ulcerated sores marred the sallow skin of the woman's cheek and neck.

Ivy hurried past, shoving aside the image of what could one day be her own fate and instead focused on the plan she had for her life. She would not end up like that. Another year and she'd have the money she needed.

Ivy turned down an alley off Tenth Street and followed along the backs of the shops until she reached Preston's Grocery and knocked on the delivery entrance.

A moment later Mr. Preston pulled open the door. "Good morning. Right on time."

"Thank you for letting me come so early."

He gestured toward the side of the room where crates of fresh fruit had been stacked.

"Glad you could make it. My wife and I are taking the train to Wyoming tomorrow, and I had to come in early to check my inventory and order stock."

Ivy reached into the nearest box, lifted out a peach, and raised it to her nose. Fresh and fragrant, she could almost imagine biting into the sweet, juicy fruit. She glanced at Mr. Preston and smiled. "I hear the mountains out west are beautiful."

"We're visiting my wife's sister and her husband. They have a ranch north of Cheyenne, and we've never been."

She set the peach in the box. She'd never even seen a ranch. Town life was all she'd ever known. One day, after she'd saved enough money and opened her own place, she'd be able to travel, visit big cities like New York, Chicago, or San Francisco.

Mr. Prescott extended his hand. "Let me weigh your basket first."

She passed over the wicker container and perused the rest of the crates, smelling and squeezing the fruit as she'd been taught when she was a little girl.

Blackberries, cherries, and strawberries.

When he returned, Ivy filled her basket with peaches.

"What are you going to make with these?"

"Maybe a couple of pies, sprinkled with some sugar and cinnamon."

They left the storeroom, and he set the basket on the scale behind the counter.

He sighed and shook his head. "I don't know what I'll miss more, your fine baking or the pleasures of Daisy's company."

"I'm sure she'll miss you too. I think you're her favorite."

"My boys'll be running the store for the next month. They don't know about you...or me and Daisy." He passed her the basket. "It isn't too heavy, is it? You can leave it here, and my boy can run it over in his cart later this morning with the rest of your order."

"I'm fine. Thank you for letting me come early."

He passed her the receipt for the charges to Madame Beauchamp's account. "Happy to help."

Ivy tucked the paper in her reticule and left the grocery. She carried the basket with both hands, the curved side bumping against her thighs as she walked. She inhaled a deep breath. The air felt so much fresher since yesterday's rain.

Wispy streaks of white stretched across the wide blue sky. Birds chirped from the roof tops. The squishy sucking of horse hoofs in the mud drew her attention to a farmer's wagon and team as it passed by. A scruffy yellow dog, his belly fur coated with mud, darted between two loaded freight wagons then vanished into the alley which led behind Declan's Eatery.

She turned down a side street. This early morning outing gave her a chance to check the window of her favorite dress shop before anyone was about.

A burnished yellow dress with golden brown ruffles that spilled from the waist down the back and around the bottom, hung on a dress form. Fancy, gold whip stitching edged all the ruffles. She didn't own anything in yellow, and the colors would match her blonde and brown hair perfectly. Mrs. Leary had her measurements on file. If Ivy sent a note, requesting the hem be raised, the bodice opened up, and the sleeves capped, she could use some of her savings to pay for it rather than borrow any more money from Madame. Except, spending any of her savings would push her plans back even further. She sighed. Maybe another time.

Moving down the street, she paused to admire the ribbons, gloves, and hats on a low table behind the window at Kempler's Millenary. A brown hat with dark red feathers and copper-colored ribbon would be perfect with her russet and coffee colored gown. Too bad the dress wasn't appropriate for town.

"Well, ain't you a pretty sight on this fine morning."

Ivy swung around. Two men sat in chairs, outside a boot shop. Across the street, a saloon and billiards hall, from which the pair had likely emerged earlier this morning. She searched their faces trying to determine whether or not she knew them or if they were drunk.

"Good morning to you both."

They stood. The taller of the pair stepped toward her. "I remember you, from when you was over in Council Bluffs. You got that streak a blonde in yer hair like a calico cat. Look at you out walkin', all fine and proper." He grinned, revealing a missing front tooth.

Ivy still couldn't place him. She flashed them a practiced smile. "Yes. And how have you been?"

The shorter man moved up beside his friend. Thick stubble darkened the lower half of his face. "We's fine. Is you workin' in Lincoln now?"

The tall man spit a stream of tobacco into the street. "You dumb sonofabitch, she don't remember us. She's puttin' on airs, like she done before. That madam kept her only fer the rich ones, payin' thirty dollars a night. She's one a them look-but-don't-touch. Too good fer the likes a us."

A wave of cold shuddered through her, raising goosebumps on her arms. She shifted the basket to her right hand leaving her weighted reticule hanging from her left wrist.

"Would you gentlemen care to escort me home?" Years of practice kept her voice calm even as her mind raced through a list of possible escape routes along the way.

"Iffin we do, do we get a free one?"

She set down her basket and tugged open her reticule. Slipping her finger beneath her Derringer, she withdrew two brass coins. She extended her hand. "Here take these tokens and present them at the front door. Hiram will let you in."

The taller, toothless man studied the coins in her open palm. "Them ain't no good. They's fer over at that Missus Bow-champ's place. She won't let the likes a me an' Neely in her fancy parlor."

"But that's why I'm giving you these. They're good for one evening with any boarder in the house."

"How 'bout just a quick poke for each a us instead? Two bits."

"Take the tokens. Come by the house this evening. I'll see you're properly looked after."

They stepped toward her. She dropped the tokens back in her reticule and picked up her basket. "I'm making peach pies for tonight's refreshments."

"We don't want no peach pie," Tall-and-Toothless said. "We's lookin' for a little somethin' else sweet."

"You boys know the rules. I can't give anything away."

Neely grinned. As he did, his grimy cheeks pushed upward, squeezing his eyes into slits. "Well, my little calico cat, you ain't exactly givin'. We's takin'."

Tall-and-Toothless stepped in front of her. She eased back.

She'd dealt with amorous fools before and in a light-hearted way could usually handle them, but this time she wasn't sure.

Neely grabbed her arm. Heart racing, she pulled, twisting against his hold. With her right hand, she swung her basket of fruit. The solid weight slammed against the side of his head. Peaches tumbled over him, hit the sidewalk, and rolled into the street.

He staggered back a step but didn't let go. His tight hold kept her from reaching her Derringer.

Tall-and-Toothless yanked the basket from her hand and tossed it into the narrow alley which ran alongside the millenary.

Neely's thick fingers squeezed painfully around the bones of her wrist. "Think you're too good for the likes a us?" He tugged her into the alley.

Ignoring the grinding pressure of his grip, she pulled back until she was almost sitting. Despite digging her heels into the soft ground, he dragged her deeper into the alley.

Neely swung her around and slammed her back against the side of the building.

Toothless grabbed her other wrist and pinned it over her head pressing the back of her hand against the rough clapboard siding.

Neely kept his hold on her other arm.

With both men in front of her, she kicked out, connecting the toe of her shoe with the solid bone of someone's shin.

Toothless leaned in close. The odor of his fetid breath closed off the back of her throat. She twisted her hand inside his grip as she tilted her head and stretched her fingers toward her hat.

With his other hand, Toothless grabbed her chin and pressed his mouth to hers, pushing his tongue against the tight seam of her lips. Jerking her chin from his grasp, she tipped her head, bringing her hat and fingertips closer together.

Her thumb brushed the pearl of her hat pin. Grasping it with three fingers, she slid it free, then jabbed it into his forearm.

"Sonofabitch!" Toothless jumped back as she stumbled forward pulling free of Neely's loosened grip.

Toothless yanked the pin from his arm. "You bitch!"

Darting for the street, she tugged open her reticule and pulled out her Derringer. She whirled around, pointing her little gun. "Stay away from me."

Neely shook his head, "Come-on, Lane, we ain't got time fer this."

Toothless slowly advanced.

Ivy backed up, switching her aim from one to the other.

"You ever shoot a man a'fore?" Toothless asked, his words drawn out in a sneer. A patch of blood soaked the cuff of his shirt. "It ain't so easy as ya think."

Neely moved toward her, a step ahead of Tall-and-Toothless.

Ivy pulled back the hammer and squeezed the trigger.

*Bang!*

Neely staggered back. He clamped his hand over his upper arm. "She shot me!" Beneath his fingers, a dark stain spread through the fabric of his coat sleeve. "The bitch shot me!"

Her knees quivered as she slowly eased herself backward. She nearly reached the mouth of the alley when her foot came down on something. *Crack!* It collapsed beneath her weight. Off balance she fell backward, landing hard on her butt, the basket handle caught around her foot. *Blast!*

Tall-and-Toothless advanced, a frown narrowed his eyes. His lips compressed into a tight line.

She brought her arm up, gun pointed at his chest, but he lashed out with one of his long legs and kicked her arm. The gun flew from her hand and whacked hollow against the wooden boards of the sidewalk. Toothless seized her by the hair at the back of her head. Her hat pushed forward, barely held in place as Toothless yanked her to her feet.

Her chin to her chest, she grabbed his wrist with both hands, trying to ease the pressure on her roots. Biting her lower lip against the tearing pain, she stumbled alongside him as he dragged her past Neely, toward the back of the alley.

Releasing one hand from his wrist, she reached

toward her hat. Her fingers groped over fabric, lace, and feather, searching for her second hat pin.

"Neely! Grab that barrel over there."

Neely scooted between them and the building. Just ahead, behind a growth of thistle, Neely grabbed the rim of the weathered, waist-high barrel. Using his one good arm, he wrestled it from the weeds and tipped it onto its side.

Still grappling with Toothless, Ivy's thumb brushed the familiar smooth pearl tip of her second hat pin. *Finally!* This one had to count.

In one smooth motion, she pulled it free and jammed the long slender needle into his side. She barely felt any resistance through his clothing or skin, until the tip bumped against the solid wall of bone.

She expected him to release her hair. Instead, he drove his fist into her stomach. Ivy gasped, curling into herself. The strain on her roots—agony.

He dragged her forward and all but threw her face down over the barrel. His hand slammed down between her shoulder blades, his weight holding her in place as he leaned over her from behind.

The rigidness of her corset kept her back straight, preventing her from bending naturally over the curve of the barrel. Her hands couldn't reach the ground, and her toes barely touched the dirt behind.

He grabbed first one wrist and then the other, yanking her arms behind her, holding both her hands at the back of her waist with one of his.

The rancid stench of old garbage blended with the sour body odor of Tall-and-Toothless. Ivy gagged.

Toothless pawed at her skirt and petticoats, shoving them up to her waist. His hand pushed apart the opening in her drawers. Warm air brushed over her exposed skin right before his hand squeezed one cheek of her bottom. His fingertips pushed deep into her soft flesh.

She squirmed and struggled, trying to twist away from the pressure of his hand. She attempted to gain some leverage with her toes, enough to roll the barrel forward, but her corset kept her spine straight.

His hand lifted away.

She released a breath.

The slap came down hard. She gasped. The sting of heat rushed through the area. The second slap came down just as hard—more painful against her heated skin.

"Hold still, bitch. Ain't like ya never played rough a'fore."

*Don't panic. Let them do what they want, and they'll leave you alone.*

"I get her after you, right, Lane?"

There was the soft rustle of fabric as she envisioned Lane unbuttoning his pants, opening his drawers.

"Let the lady go."

The male voice was firm, the words clipped, and though the timbre wasn't deep, the command was harsh.

She craned her head around to see who belonged to the voice, but the opening of the alley was behind her, and she couldn't see beyond Lane's too-tall body.

"Get outta here, mister," Neely snapped. "This here is our whore."

"I said, 'let the lady go.' "

"And what are you gonna do about it, Mister Fancy Pants?" Lane released his hold on her wrists. The barrel rolled forward.

She somersaulted over and hit the ground in a tangle of skirts and petticoats. Behind her came the scuffling of shoes and boots against mud and grass, the thud of knuckles to body, and the soft "ooof," of the person absorbing the impact of a punch.

Abrasive laughter filled the alley.

Ivy scrambled to her feet.

"Whacha gonna do with that little pea shooter?" Neely asked.

Ivy glanced around for a weapon. A broken broom handle lay in the weeds alongside the milliner's shop. She darted forward and snatched up the long wooden dowel.

The new voice, soft yet strong, demanded, "Put your guns on the ground and step back against the building."

She whirled around—her broom handle raised.

A tall, thin gentleman in a loose-fitting black suit, sporting a bloody nose and a reddened cheekbone, aimed her Derringer at Lane and Neely.

"You're crazy, mister. We both got guns, and all you got is one shot."

"True." The gentleman shrugged. "But one of you will die with me."

Ivy lowered her broom handle, the splintered tip resting in the grass. Knees shaking, she leaned into the handle for a moment, breathing to calm her racing heart.

The two men gaped at the stranger.

"Let's go," Neely said, pressing his hand against his wounded arm. "Boss will be here next week. He'll kill us if we end up in jail, and this whore ain't worth it."

Lane nodded and inched toward the entrance.

"Hold up." The gentleman raised the Derringer a notch. "You two men accosted a lady in broad daylight. You're going to the marshal's office."

Lane chuckled and shook his head.

Drawing a deep breath, Ivy darted forward and grasped the gentleman's arm. "Let them go. They didn't hurt me."

"Are you certain you've not been injured?"

She nodded, slid her hand along his sleeve, and closed her fingers around both his bloody knuckles and the Derringer. She pressed, and his arm lowered.

"What these vermin have attempted is unconscionable."

Lane and Neely scooted past the gentleman and dashed for the front of alley.

She raised her gaze to the man's face and the darkening bruise under his eye. Despite the blood which trickled from his nose and chin onto his collar and coat, he was several years younger than she'd first assumed, and he had the deepest brown eyes.

He passed her the small gun. "I don't understand. What they tried to do is abhorrent. It goes against God. The marshal must be informed."

She slipped the Derringer into her reticule. Was this man actually that naïve? Was he some kind of preacher? No. He was a halfway decent fighter.

"Thank you for kindness, but he won't do anything."

He drew himself up, shoulders squared. "Such inaction by law enforcement is deplorable. These men tried to violate you."

Surely, he'd heard what they called her. "It's because of what I am. Who I am. I deserve it."

He turned into her. He grasped one of her hands in his and searched her face.

"No. You don't."

The back of her throat closed off. Who was this man? How could he not see what she was? She almost hated to tell him. Not only would she destroy a bit of his innocence, these perfect moments of being protected, of being cherished would be gone.

"I do deserve it. They told you. I'm an upstairs girl... calico cat... lady of the evening. I lay with men for money. *I'm a whore.*"

His mouth quirked up in the sweetest smile she'd ever been given.

"I know."

Her eyes burned for the first time in years. She pressed her free hand against his chest assuring herself he was not a figment of her fantasies.

"Who are you?" she whispered.

"Alex."

*Alex.* She held the sound in her mind, savoring the tone of his voice, the cadence of the syllables.

"I'm lucky you came along."

"I enjoy a brisk constitutional every morning. I was returning to my hotel when I heard the gun shot."

He stepped back. He glanced around then leaned over and picked up his hat. He brushed the dust from the wool felt bowler and set it on his head.

Ivy glanced through the footprints and scuffs in the damp soil. She spotted the pearl tip of one hat pin near the building where they'd held her against the wall.

As she turned, Alex presented her hat. The long black feather now drooped over the side.

"Your hat, miss."

"Ivy."

"Miss Ivy." He pulled a handkerchief from an inside pocket and wiped the blood from his chin before blotting at the blood still oozing from his nose.

She shook her head. "Just Ivy."

He stuffed the stained cloth inside his coat then stepped to her side and offered his arm. "Well, Miss Just Ivy, might I escort you safely back to your residence?"

She placed her hat on her head and scanned the ground one more time.

"Have you lost something?"

Holding up her single pin, she said, "I had another one." She pushed it through the weave of her hat, securing it in place.

"Allow me." Alex walked back and forth over the area, as Ivy waited, her own gaze searching.

A few minutes later he returned to her side. "My apologies. I've been unable to locate it."

"That's all right, I have others." She did, but none were as pretty as these.

He offered his arm. "May I?"

"Thank you. That would be nice."

At the entrance to the ally, he retrieved her crushed basket. "I'm sorry, but I don't believe this can be repaired."

The handle was still intact, so she looped it over her arm though it probably looked silly with the side flattened and the bottom hanging out.

Removing his hat, Alex bent over and filled it with the scattered peaches. He collected as many as fit then offered his arm, and they continued walking.

As they crossed the railroad tracks and strolled toward the large brick house on the outskirts of the city, Ivy asked, "Would you like to come in? I can take care of your shirt for you. Rinse it in cold water before the blood sets."

"Thank you, but I think it best I clean up in my hotel room."

Kathy Otten

They ambled around to the side gate. He held it open, and she stepped through. "Thank you for seeing me home. I hope I haven't kept you from anything important."

"No. As you see, I'm an early riser."

He passed her his hat filled with peaches.

"Are you sure you won't come in?" Lord, the man had the deepest brown eyes and the longest eye lashes.

"No, thank you. I'll just wait here."

Her brow furrowed.

The corner of his mouth pulled up in a wiry grin. "My hat?"

"Oh!" She glanced down surprised the hat filled with peaches was still in her hands. "Yes, your hat. I'll be right back."

She whirled, hurried up the path, and into the kitchen.

Maude stepped from the pantry. "Lawdy, girl, what happened to you?"

"I'll tell you later." She dumped the peaches on the work bench, grabbing at two then a third before they rolled off the edge. His hat in her hand, she brushed off the dust with her fingers and ran outside. She slowed her pace, trying to walk toward him like a real lady. At the gate she passed him his bowler.

"Thank you."

She reached into her reticule, grasping a token between her thumb and forefinger. "Please, take this." She held it out. "Show it at the front door, and Hiram will let you in. You can have me for the whole night for free. We can have dinner, play cards, I can give you a bath, a massage, or we can go to my room, and I can pleasure you all night."

"Thank you." He accepted the token, squinted, then held it at arm's length for a moment, before pushing it into the change pocket of his waistcoat. "I shall consider your offer. Good day." He tipped his hat, then turned and strode down the street toward town.

After several minutes, distance swallowed him from her sight. She rubbed her forehead and returned to the house, confused by this strange sense of loss.

Chapter Three

Alex squirmed on the hard wooden seat. Three curved-back chairs had been positioned along the wall of the anteroom to the office of Felix Lathrop, President, Golden Bank and Securities. Alex uncrossed his legs then recrossed them with his opposite leg on top.

He moved his leather document bag and hat from his lap to the empty chair beside him and checked his watch. Ten-forty-two. He compared it to the wall clock. Ten-forty-four. He snapped his watch closed and slipped it inside the small front pocket of his waistcoat. His appointment was for eleven o'clock. Worried he'd be late, he'd arrived a half hour early.

On the other side of the room, a thin man wearing spectacles and a black suit, sat behind a wide desk clicking away on a typewriting machine. The oblong name plate on his desk read, Arthur Getz, Secretary. Every time the man hit the return lever, he shot Alex another furrowed-brow glance. No doubt the man wondered why such riff-raff would have an appointment with the bank president.

Needing Lathrop to believe Alex was nothing less than an upstanding citizen, he'd worn his best suit and hat, hoping to make a good impression. He hadn't counted on presenting himself with skinned knuckles, a swollen nose, and a black eye.

What if Lathrop asked what happened? Should Alex

explain that he'd been defending the honor of a beautiful lady-of-the-evening? Or should he lie and say he'd come off a horse?

A low growl tumbled around inside Alex's stomach. He should have eaten something more substantial than a piece of dry toast and water. Even a bowl of plain oatmeal would have helped.

The wall clock chimed the hour.

Behind the desk, the secretary rose and ran his hand over his hair, slicked back with pomade. He walked to the inner door and knocked twice on the frosted glass insert.

"Come in," rumbled a deep voice.

The secretary turned the knob and leaned into the room. "Mr. Worthington to see you."

"Thank you, Mr. Getz."

The secretary closed the door and returned to his desk. "He'll be right with you."

Alex picked up his document bag and hat and set them in his lap. He took a deep breath and blew it out slowly. Though his stomach churned, and his fingers trembled, he hoped he'd be perceived as calm and relaxed. Five long, hard years had come down to this one meeting. Things had to go well. He had no other option.

The office door opened.

Alex jumped to his feet. His hat tumbled to the floor, rolled along its brim, then stopped under a chair. He bent to pick it up.

When he straightened, an older man stood before him. Broad through the chest and belly, Lathrop wore a black suit, white shirt and tie, with a matching brocade waistcoat. Thick snowy hair topped his head and curved around his jaw line with fat mutton-chop sideburns, which stretched out to touch the tips of his wide, full moustache.

The man's eyes widened as he no doubt took in Alex's battered face.

Alex opened his mouth, poised to spin an elaborate explanation, then changed his mind. Perhaps it best to say nothing and risk Lathrop assuming he'd been injured while brawling in a saloon.

Alex extended his injured hand. "It's a pleasure to meet you, sir."

Lathrop grasped it, barely glancing at the knuckles, then pumped Alex's arm a couple of times. "Glad you could make it, young man. How was your trip?"

"Quite pleasant."

"Good, good." He gestured toward the door which led into the hallway.

A chill washed through Alex. Had the man changed his mind?

Lathrop moved past Alex, opened the door, and stepped to the side, allowing Alex to pass. "After scheduling our appointment, I deemed it best to include our stockholders. They should all be in the conference room by now."

*Relax*, Alex told himself as he followed Lathrop past other rooms and the staircase which led to the bank on the first floor. At the end of the hall loomed a pair of tall double doors, one of which stood open. Inside, several older men sat on either side of a long table, which ran lengthwise and matched the surrounding wainscoting.

Sunlight lit the space through several windows along two walls. The aroma of lemon polish blended with musky scents of various pomades and aftershaves.

All heads turned their way. Alex hung back, unsure

where to sit as Lathrop moved down the length of the table to the high-backed leather chair at the opposite end.

Alex had practiced his presentation several times on the train and once last evening before bed, but he hadn't anticipated delivering it to Mr. Lathrop, as well as a room full of austere bankers. And he only had one copy of his charts and ledgers.

"Close the door and join me down here." Lathrop gestured to an empty chair on the left side of the table.

Feeling a bit like Natty Bumppo preparing to run a Huron gauntlet, Alex's footsteps fell silent on the thick wool rug as he moved to the designated seat. He placed his hat on the table and laid his bag in his lap. The leather chair far more comfortable than the wooden ones outside Lathrop's office.

Each place at the table had been set with paper, pen, and ink. Thinking his hat would be in the way as he spread out his pages of facts and figures, he set his hat on top of his leather bag.

"What happened to your face, young man?" asked the gentleman directly across the table.

"I..." His bowler slid off his bag. Alex shoved back his chair and leaned over to grab his hat.

*Whack!*

His forehead hit the lip of the table.

He pushed his chair back farther as he rubbed the tender spot, then reached beneath to grab his hat from the floor. Coming back up, *whump,* the back of his head slammed against the wooden underside.

*God, send me to the asylum now.*

The man across the table chuckled. "I believe I can guess what happened to your face." His salt and pepper beard not completely able to hide his wide smile.

Hand on the back of his head, Alex massaged his scalp. A sour taste rose past the lump in his throat. His ears burned. These men were never going to believe his proposal to be credible. They no doubt already thought him the lunatic he would one day become.

A clock on the opposite wall ticked, the pendulum swinging rhythmically back and forth.

"Mr. Worthington."

Alex turned toward the head of the table.

Hands folded across his belly, Lathrop met Alex's gaze, the hint of a smile playing around the corners of his mouth.

"Might I suggest you make use of the hat tree." He gestured toward the door where they'd come in.

"Yes, sir."

Alex stood and set his leather bag in his chair, then walked back down the length of the table. The room remained silent, and he felt the eyes of all nine men were focused on him.

In the corner stood a combination hat and coat rack, with an umbrella stand and mirror. He hung his hat on one of the pegs and stared at his face.

The area around his eye and nose had grown darker and more swollen, looking far worse than earlier when he'd cleaned up in his hotel room. Why would these men ever believe him capable of managing a bank?

More than a year past, Alex had begun sending letters to major financial institutions, outlining his proposal, but Golden Bank and Securities had been the only one to respond.

If this sale was going to work, he had to vanquish the terrified boy inside him. He needed to shift his persona into that of a strong, confident older man, the way he had when he was nineteen years old, walking into the Farmers and Merchants Bank as the new owner and president.

*Don't think about what you look like. Focus on what you need to do.*

He took a deep breath and drew his shoulders back. He schooled his features, putting in place the same mask of chilly detachment he used with his employees, all of whom were more than twenty years his senior.

He turned from the mirror and resumed his seat.

Lathrop proceeded with the introductions. The man with the thick salt and pepper beard who sat across from Alex was a contracts attorney, stockholder, and on the city council. The other five men held various positions in the city and comprised the rest of the shareholders. The remaining two gentlemen on Lathrop's right were the bank's vice president and comptroller.

"I want you to know, Worthington." Lathrop tapped the folder which lay on the table in front of him. "I have a report sent to us by the Pinkerton Agency in response to a request made by this board, calling for an investigation into both your background and your character."

Alex's heart sank. Why even schedule this meeting if they were going to reject his proposal based on what his father had done?

In his mind he heard Reverend Clark declaring repeatedly from the pulpit, *"...the iniquity of the father will be visited upon the children..."* a sentiment Mother drilled into his head every time he deviated from his routines.

And in the same way Alex dealt with boyhood bullies, town gossips, and employees at the bank, he fixed his gaze on Lathrop's face and braced himself to not flinch, to affect instead a façade of indifference.

Lathrop inclined his head with a slight nod toward the folder. "I can't pretend to consider your father as anything other than an incompetent businessman, gambler, and fornicator of the worst kind, who was apparently murdered by an unknown assailant."

Alex shifted in his seat. Did the Pinkerton report mention the rumors, the speculation surrounding the circumstances of Samuel Worthington's death?

"Your brother-in-law is also a man of dubious character. An illusive man, whose business acquiring rare paintings and antiquities is rife with rumor and innuendo. A man whose whereabouts are evidentially of great interest to the Pinkertons."

Alex struggled to swallow against the knot in the back of his throat. True, Clayton was far from an upstanding citizen, and Samuel Worthington was a despicable bastard, but how much credence would Lathrop give to gossip and rumor?

"Your character, however—" Lathrop continued, "—appears to be the complete opposite. According to this investigator, you are a quiet, hard-working, dependable, church-going young man. You are at the bank from dawn till dusk and provide a comfortable home for your mother and sister." He set the folder aside. "Commendable."

Alex slipped on his spectacles, unbuckled his bag, and removed a sheaf of papers. He passed the extra set to Lathrop then expounded on each page of notes. He explained the bank's current interest rates on loans, the monthly totals for accounts receivable, and how many loans were in arrears.

The shareholders' interest appeared genuine. They listened and asked for numbers on funds invested in the community and the gains and losses on the bank's stock portfolio.

Lathrop perused several of the papers, then asked for the interest paid on savings accounts, and the bank's operating and payroll expenses. He made some notes and slid the pages over to the vice president who also wrote some things on a sheet of blank paper, before handing the pages to the comptroller.

The clock behind him chimed twelve times. Alex removed his glasses and rubbed his fingers over his tired eyes.

Maybe his years of hard work and personal sacrifice would finally pay off.

Lathrop glanced at Alex. "When precisely did you assume responsibility for the bank?"

"November of seventy-three."

"And do you have figures for that time, which would have been during the worst of the Panic?"

"Yes, I believe you have them there, beginning on page five." What was he going to do if Lathrop asked for ledgers prior to seventy-three? He wiped his sweaty palm over his thigh. "My father had speculated heavily in the railroad, and when they defaulted on their bonds, we were virtually insolvent. Rather than foreclose on all loans, I used the money my grandfather had left me for college to float the daily cash withdrawals and to buy out most of the shareholders who panicked and wanted to sell.

"I created charts there to show all aspects of the bank's investments, accounts receivable and payable, and monies on hand from that day forward. You can see, where most figures started in the red, the bank is now in the black."

After weeks pouring over years of figures, then creating these charts, Alex had gone to bed each night with aching eyes and a pounding headache.

Lathrop grunted a few times as he read through the material, made notes, and passed the charts down the line.

Alex gnawed on the inside of his lower lip and twisted his fingers in his lap, trying to appear relaxed, hoping he didn't look concerned.

His stomach gurgled.

The board member sitting beside Alex shot him a couple of covert glances as his empty stomach continued to complain.

Even some of those tasteless, graham flour crackers his mother always pushed him to eat would be welcome right now. He didn't want to be caught looking at the clock or pulling out his watch, but he wished his stomach would stop rumbling.

The men murmured and whispered as they passed the papers back and forth and across the table. Were these gentlemen genuinely interested in his proposal?

The clock chimed the hour. Alex's stomach grumbled again.

Lathrop set his pen in the wooden holder, steepled his fingers, pressed them against his chin, and looked at Alex.

"I commend you, young man, for having been able to move your bank from the red, so far into the black. Thank you for providing us with such a comprehensive and detailed look at your finances."

Alex swallowed. His stomach tightened,

expecting…

"But you have provided us with so much material, it will take time for us to go through it all. We need to carefully review, and discuss this, before making a decision."

At least Lathrop hadn't said no. "I understand."

"I see your price listed on this page. I will say your figure appears to be on the high side."

*Be calm. Don't let them see how desperate you are.*

"Yes. However, the Union Pacific and the Fremont, Elkhorn and Missouri Valley railroads converge in our town creating a transportation hub and a wealth of opportunity. The town is growing steadily. Our investments in both farming and small business are what have brought the bank out of the red. If you decide to accept, you will not regret it."

Lathrop nodded. "Yes, our investigator did make us aware of those start-ups as well as the increase in the number of surrounding farms. We shall be in touch. I see you are staying at the Adams Hotel. We will send word once we have reached a decision."

Alex rose. "Thank you, gentlemen, for your time. I look forward to our next meeting."

He picked up his bag, retrieved his hat, and slipped from the room. Once outside, he exhaled a long breath. What if they said no? What was he going to do?

He started back to his hotel. They had to say yes. Alex was holding on to his sanity by a thread. His mother and sister needed an income large enough to sustain them once he was gone. And he'd be hard pressed to maintain his strict regimen for another year. He couldn't do it. He just couldn't.

\*\*\*\*

Ivy relaxed into the corner of the divan and draped one stocking clad leg over the lap of the young man beside her. Her opposite foot slid back and forth over the smooth leather of his shoe, then slid up beneath the hem of his trouser leg, to his lower calf and back down to the thick, wool pile of the parlor rug.

His fingertips skimmed slowly up her silk-clad leg, over the garter that held her stocking in place, then beneath the ruffled edge of her drawers. Mr. Roaming Hands drew lazy circles over her thigh then trailed his fingers back down to her ankle.

One arm around his shoulder, Ivy absently twirled a lock of his hair around her index finger while he rained light kisses over the exposed top of her bosom. What time was it? Too bad clocks weren't allowed. Her first appointment should be along soon, shouldn't he?

Slowly, the moist kisses inched up her neck and along her jaw line. At least the man smelled good, though maybe he'd applied a little too much cologne. When his lips brushed the corner of hers, she gently pushed him back. She pressed her index finger against his mouth and shook her head.

"Now, now, Sugar. You know the rules. No kissing."

He leaned in and nipped the thin skin at the base of her throat. "You're nothing but a little tease, aren't you?"

She toyed with the top button of his coat. She gave him a sidelong glance from beneath lowered lids. "Maybe."

On the love seat across the room, Daisy sat in the lap of a man who whispered in her ear. Every so often she would emit a coy, girlish giggle or a quick shriek of surprise. The *tee-heeing* laughter grated on Ivy's nerves, but some gentlemen loved the illusion of an innocent young girl. So, Daisy continued to make the annoying sound.

Walter played the haunting melody of Aura Lea on the piano. Though Madame required the gentlemen to schedule ahead any appointments with their favorite girl, in the foyer several other gentlemen waited in the chairs placed along the wall hoping for an opening if a scheduled appointment didn't arrive.

In the second parlor, the room opposite from where Ivy sat, Violet and Lily flirted with other customers who sat around tables either playing poker or trying to "buck the tiger," at the Faro table where Georgie dealt cards.

Hiram stood behind the bar taking drink orders as Rachel then served them to the gentlemen. Madame Beauchamp, wearing a fine, green silk gown with lace and layered ruffles, chatted with the men, moving gracefully between the foyer and dining room, where an evening repast had been laid.

Instead of making peach pies this morning, Ivy had had just enough of the damaged fruit to make three dozen turnovers. She'd taken two of the nicest and had Maude set them aside.

The fingers of Mr. Roaming Hands slid a little too high up the inside of her thigh. She flicked his ear.

He jerked his head up, gave her a sheepish grin, and shrugged.

She smiled and shook her head.

The front door opened.

Her stomach gave an unusual flutter. A gentleman entered, but he was too short, too round through the middle. She didn't know his name, but he was a salesman who came through the area every month. He likely had an appointment with Violet, who seemed to be his favorite.

Ivy trailed her fingers down the coat of Mr. Roaming Hands and over the waistband of his trousers, stopping just short of his groin.

He placed his hand on the top of her head and let it slide down, sifting his fingers through her loosed tresses. He toyed with the ends. "How did you get this blonde streak?"

She shrugged. She couldn't remember not having it. A swath of blonde a little wider than the length of her thumb. Unusual, for the rest of her hair was a light, autumn brown. Most of the time she forgot the blonde was there, but the gentlemen found it fascinating, which was probably why Madame had allowed her to stay longer than most. Normally girls were asked to leave after a year so Madame could bring in someone young, and fresh, and beautiful.

Mr. Roaming Hands slid his gropey paws all the way up her thigh. His fingertips had barely brushed her nest of curls when she clamped her hand around his forearm and shoved his arm down. She withdrew her leg from his lap and tucked her foot under her, leaving her bent knee to rest on his thigh.

She shook her head. "Now, Sugar, I don't think you want to give up your appointment with Anémone to spend it with me."

"Come-on, Ivy. Tell me. Do you have a blonde streak down there too?"

She gave him a nonchalant shrug. "Well, I suppose you'll just have to pay to find out."

He leaned into her, scooping his hand around her waist. "Maybe I will. Are you free later tonight?"

"Why don't you save your money and your loving for Anémone? I know you paid extra for her. She'll be ready soon. I'm sure she's picking out the perfect dress, one that will highlight her big brown eyes. Imagine the scent of your favorite perfume on her skin where you'll nuzzle her neck and bosom. And think about those sweet French words she'll whisper softly in your ear."

He leaned away from her. "Damn, Ivy. You got me hard just thinking about it."

"It's nearly time for my first appointment." She stood. "So nice chatting with you, but I need to freshen up." She curled her index finger around the ends of the blonde streak, bent forward giving him an up-close view of her ample bosom, and using her hair like a paint brush, swiped the ends over his nose. She straightened, winked, and gave him a smile. "Enjoy your evening, Sugar."

She whirled around, allowing the skirt of her pink gown, several inches shorter than society deemed acceptable, to billow out, giving Roaming Hands a glimpse of her calves and knees.

In the foyer she scanned the men waiting in chairs. She moved down the hall and checked the dining room where Poppy sat in the lap of a portly man with white hair. As the couple chatted, Poppy finger-fed him bits of cake. Servants cleared dishes and set out more food.

Madame glided through the room, pausing to offer a smile and a word or two.

Alex hadn't come. Both disappointed and relieved, she started back toward the front of the house. She met Rachel coming toward her.

"Your nine o'clock is here," the servant whispered. "He's in the back room washing."

"Thank you. As soon as he's ready you can escort

him up."

Rachel nodded and moved on down the hall.

Before turning to go up the stairs, Ivy ducked into the second parlor with the bar that ran along the wall, just inside the open pocket doors.

"Hiram, I need a bottle of Old Crow and a couple of glasses."

He shook his head, even as he placed them on a small silver tray.

"You should have rung for a servant. You know Madame don't like the gentlemen left alone."

"He's still washing, and this is his favorite whiskey. But I need a favor. I gave a token to someone this morning. He's tallish and thin. A nice dresser, with brown eyes. Oh, and his face is bruised, and he has a black eye. If he comes in and asks for me, please have him wait. This appointment is only booked until ten."

Resting her forearms on the bar, she leaned forward and pressed her upper arms against the sides of her ample bosom. Pushing the mounds together provided Hiram a view of her deeper cleavage as she gave him her sweetest smile. "Do you like my dress?"

"You know I do."

"What color is it?"

He frowned. "Ivy, I hate when you do that."

"I'm sorry. How can I make it up to you?"

"Let me think about it."

"And could you give Mr. Simms to someone else?"

"Now, you know—"

"Yes, I know, but please? Simms doesn't care who he's with, and he can't afford more than half an hour. I know you can shift the appointments around to fit him in." She walked her fingers over his hand and up his arm.

"Please?"

"I'll do it, but only if you promise to make some more of those can-o things you made last month."

Ivy frowned. "Can-o things?"

"Yeah, they were long and open at both ends and filled with some kind of cream."

"Ohhh, cannoli." She shook her head. "The chef at the Adams Hotel ordered that cheese for me special. I don't think I can get it again. How about a custard filled puff pastry?"

"I'll take anything you make, but I want a whole dozen, just for me."

She grinned. "And I won't tell Madame you have them."

He winked. "And I won't tell her you switched clients."

"You're a dear." She kissed the tip of her index finger and pressed it to his lips, then taking the tray, hurried upstairs to her room.

She set the tray on a side table near the bed. Then from the bottom drawer of her dressing table, she removed a bottle of vinegar and a small sponge in a net bag. She soaked the sponge with the vinegar, placed her foot on the chair, hiked up her dress, and inserted the sponge, making sure the string would be easy to grab afterward.

A moment later there came a light knock, and Ivy opened the door, a wide smile on her face.

"Roger, how nice to see you." She closed the door and after taking his hat, set it on her dressing table. She gestured to a pink and red striped chaise in the corner of the room. "Why don't you make yourself comfortable? Would you care for a drink? I brought up a bottle of the whiskey you like."

"Yes, please."

She poured two fingers while Roger removed his coat and waistcoat and laid them over the back of the chair in front of her dressing table.

He accepted the glass, took a sip, then sat to remove his shoes and stockings. Standing, he tossed back the last of the whiskey and stood barefoot in the center of the room as though he didn't quite know what to do with himself.

She poured him a second drink and pressed the glass into his hand.

"Here you are, Sugar."

He sipped from his glass.

She took his other hand and slowly led him toward the bed. "How have you been?"

"I've been busy."

Beads of moisture clung to the beard hairs around Roger's mouth.

As he sat, she searched for a topic. The last time he was here a couple of weeks ago he'd mentioned an argument about... "And how is the curb and gutter proposal going? Are some folks still against them?"

Roger's silvery blue eyes lit up. "Yes." He swallowed the last of his drink. "Many residents are from the early days—before the city expanded. They don't see the need, and the rest don't want to pay for it. I'm part of the committee looking over the bids trying come up with a proposal the residents will accept."

Ivy shook her head. "All those numbers and contracts? You must be the smartest man I know."

She moved close, lifted the empty glass from between his fingers, and set it on the tray. Lowering her gaze to meet his, she smiled and draped her arms over his shoulders.

His gaze roamed over her face.

She stepped back. "Let me help you."

His thick graying beard brushed her knuckles as she undid his tie and tossed it in the direction of his coat. Roger liked her to take charge. Some days he wanted it a little bit rougher than others, but he always wanted it fast.

In his late forties, Roger was a city councilman and an attorney. If she remembered right, he was also on a board of some kind, something to do with securities.

Very much a man of habit, who valued discretion, Roger scheduled one or two hours with her every other Thursday and always arrived through the back entrance.

Ivy slid her palms over his shoulders. Hooking her fingers under each suspender, she pulled them down his arms while she gently pushed him backward across the mattress.

Slowly, she undid the buttons of his shirt and undershirt, then straddling his hips, tugged both garments over his head. She tossed the clothing over her shoulder, letting it scatter on the floor. She trailed her fingertip through the sparse graying hair of his chest, over the soft paunch of his belly, to the waistband of his trousers. Keeping her gaze locked on his face, she gave each button a sharp yank, jerking his hips with each tug. Placing her palm in the center of his chest she leaned over him and slapped his cheek.

His eyes widened. His chest rose and fell as his breathing increased.

"Have you been a bad boy, Sugar?" She scooted backward off the bed then raised her foot and brought it down sharply between his legs, her toes barely missing his groin.

His breath hitched in his throat. His lips parted.

Leaving her foot between his legs, Ivy slowly rolled her stocking down, over her knee, then her calf. Shifting her foot, she pulled off the silky hose. Holding the stocking out in front of her, she pulled it through her loose fist a few times then leaned over him and tied it around his wrist.

Smiling, she did the same with her other stocking.

After telling him to shift around, she tied his hands to the brass headboard. Her skirts hiked up, she straddled his hips, and bracing herself with her hands on either side of him, she leaned down. She kissed his forehead, both cheeks, and nose, carefully avoiding the itchy hairs of his beard. She teased his belly with her fingernails, then sat back.

His engorged member swelled against her, and he whimpered. "Please."

She gave him a light slap. "Not yet, Sugar." She scooted off the bed, then moving around to the footboard, grabbed his trousers and drawers and pulled them off. Taking her time, she undressed, then hung up her gown and tidied the room.

Finally, when his pathetic begging grew too annoying, she poured a bit of clove scented oil onto her palm, rubbed her hands together and climbed onto the bed. She'd barely touched his shaft when he came in her hand and over his belly.

She grinned. "Sugar, you must've been storing that one for a long while."

He closed his eyes and lay still, his mound of stomach rising and falling with each heavy breath.

Ivy climbed off the bed. At the washstand she poured water from a pitcher onto a cloth and returned to clean Roger.

At least she wouldn't have to douche. She untied the stockings which bound his hands to the headboard and poured him another drink. Pulling back the covers, she arranged the pillows then climbed in beside him, pulling him into her arms. Talk seemed to be the main reason Roger came to see her, and since he was paying—

"If we are to be known as a progressive city, curbs and gutters can only enhance that reputation, not to mention the derived health benefits."

"That's so interesting." She trailed her fingers up and down his arm.

"No one actually argues the benefits, they merely want the funds to come from somewhere other than their pockets."

"Hmmm. I'm sorry they can't understand how hard you're trying."

"I am. You're so much more understanding about this than the backward thinking men of the city."

Did he share these concerns with his wife over dinner? Did he even discuss his business with her?

"I spoke to the women at Muriel's church group—"

So, he did talk to his wife.

"—about how much cleaner their hems and shoes would be, but they seemed to want to leave such decisions to their husbands."

"Why? Their good opinions could encourage their men to agree."

"Exactly. You're such a practical girl. It's too bad you're not fit for proper company."

Ivy closed her eyes against the prick of pain. She

should be used to it. She *was used to it*. Why did it bother her now? Alex. That's why. Because in that short time this morning, he'd treated her like a lady, and in her entire life, no one had ever done that.

She'd make it good for him—whatever he wanted, whenever he arrived.

How much time did she have left with Roger? She should have looked at her watch before joining him in bed, but it was tucked in the center drawer of her dressing table.

How long had it been since she'd replied to something Roger said? Quite a while. Maybe he'd think she'd dozed off. *Say something.*

"Fascinating."

"Yes, we all thought so. A remarkable young man."

Ivy kissed Roger's temple. He hadn't noticed her lapse. Except now, she had no idea what he was talking about.

"The whole board thought him an idiotic fool at first, but he knew every fact and figure for the past five years."

"He sounds almost as smart as you."

"Lathrop was impressed. I know what he wants to do, but the rest of us are undecided. We have another shareholders' meeting tomorrow morning to discuss it further."

A floorboard creaked in the hallway.

Ivy stilled, listening for the two light raps on her door letting her know time was up.

Then, tap, tap…tap. She smiled. The extra tap. Her next appointment had arrived. Had Alex come?

Roger rolled out of bed and began dressing.

Ivy threw on a pink silk robe to cover her nudity and

passed Roger his clothes. This time she buttoned his shirt and slipped his suspenders onto his shoulders. He raised his chin, enabling her to knot his tie without his beard getting in her way.

He left a folded bill tucked under the hand mirror on her dressing table.

Looping her arm through his, she walked with him to the top of the back staircase. "It was lovely seeing you again."

He leaned in—his intent clear, but she turned her head at the last moment so his lips brushed her cheek instead. She shook her head. "You know the rules, Sugar. Kissing is too familiar."

He raised his hand and stroked her hair then lifted the section of blonde, forward over her shoulder. "If you ever want to leave Madame Beauchamp, let me know. I can put you up in a place of your own on a nicer side of the city." His fingertip traced her jaw line then slid down the side of her neck, to the deepest part of the V created between her breasts. "You will only have to please me. I'll only visit a couple of times a week. The rest of the time will be your own."

She smiled and patted his chest. "That's a generous offer. I'll think about it."

Once he started down the stairs, she whirled toward her room rubbing vigorously at the lingering tickle where his beard had touched her cheek.

Closing her door, she picked up the banknotes.

At the foot of her bed, she knelt in front of her trunk. Throwing back the lid, she lifted out the top compartment and set it on the floor. Then pushing aside some old dresses, a battered ragdoll and a red notebook, she lifted out a tin from the German Mills American Oat

Company. Prying off the red lid, she added Roger's tip to the banknotes inside. Carefully she counted every bill and coin in the tin. Five hundred, two dollars and thirty-seven cents.

Maybe another year she'd have enough money for her own place. A large, well-built house where the roof didn't leak. She'd be her own boss. She'd choose who she slept with and when. She could keep her beautiful clothes and not have to worry about being old at thirty, trading favors for a bottle of whiskey in a back-alley crib.

Until then, as long as she stayed with Madame, she'd be safe. The rich gentlemen who frequented the house only came here because Madam made sure all her girls were clean. Every month they were given a thorough checking over by both Madame and the doctor.

She smiled and closed the lid. After making the bed, she dressed, choosing a red petticoat which would peek out from beneath the high hem of her favorite lavender gown. A navy ribbon edged the low-cut bodice and trimmed each layer of ruffle. She ran a brush through her hair, letting it spill down her back, and dabbed a bit of jasmine perfume behind her ears.

She pulled on a clean pair of white silk stockings with lace inserts, slid her feet into a pair of heeled slippers, and dashed to the top of the stairs. Taking a deep breath, she placed her hand on the rail and like a grand lady, gracefully descended. As she moved down each tread, she surveyed the waiting gentlemen. At first, she didn't see him. A slight squeeze like spidery fingers tightened inside her chest. She didn't see Simms either, and the tension eased.

Then she spotted Alex—back in the shadows. Though his face was hidden, it was him. Black, pin-striped trousers, long legs crossed, and shoes so highly polished they gleamed in the lamplight.

She smiled and nodded toward the other men as she turned at the bottom of the stairs and moved past them.

He rose, hat in hand, and bowed slightly. "Good evening, Miss Ivy."

*Alex*, her mind whispered. Madame Beauchamp had a strict policy about using a client's name in front of other customers. "Oh, your poor face." She reached up and laid her hand on his cheek.

Chapter Four

The moment her thumb brushed over the tender swelling beneath his eye, Alex was lost. He'd thought her beautiful this morning, covered in dust with her hair a mess, but in this moment with her features softened by lamplight and her brow furrowed with concern, his heart swelled.

Her gaze softened. "I feel terrible," she murmured. "Your eye looks so much worse."

He stepped back, away from the current which radiated from her hand. Yet, the second that contact was broken, he missed its warmth.

"Does it hurt?"

He shrugged.

She frowned. "And your nose. It's swollen too."

"I'm fine. I've received worse."

At the opening to the dining room where the pocket doors had been slid into the wall, she gestured to a servant. They whispered for a moment then Ivy turned back to him and smiled. "Come."

Helpless against the allure of her Siren song, he trailed along behind as she led him up a back staircase and down a wide hall. Wall sconces lit the way, and a patterned runner muted their footsteps. She stopped halfway down the hall and pushed open a door. With a sweep of her hand, she gestured him inside.

Like the dangerous shoals of a rocky shoreline, he was unable to steer away from his destiny.

An innocent floral spread covered the mattress, and

the extra pillows at the headboard invited him to lie down, embrace the luxury, succumb to this need that burned for release, to finally—*No!*

What was he doing here? How many men had lain there with her, naked...bare skin against bare skin? He gulped as a rush of heat washed over him. Surrendering to the lust of the flesh was inevitable, but once he started would he be able to stop?

*Calm down. Think of something else.*

"You look pretty tonight."

"Thank you."

"Your dress matches your eyes."

Her lips turned up in a bashful smile. "My eyes are blue, not lavender, but thank you."

A large trunk sat on the floor at the foot of the bed. An armoire, dressing table, marble topped washstand, and striped chaise filled the rest of her room. Paper with birds on tree branches covered the walls. Drapes with fringe and tassels had been pulled closed over the window. Beneath his feet lay a thick pile rug bordered by a dark band of color.

With nothing left on which to focus, his gaze rested once more on Ivy's face.

A thin, white scar he hadn't noticed this morning curved through the delicate skin between her left eye and eyebrow. He reached out to trace the line with his finger then jerked back gripping the brim of his hat with both hands.

She shrugged. "It's nothing. A small reminder that sometimes men get a little rough."

He stilled. "Someone hit you?"

"It was a couple of years ago when I was working in Council Bluffs. That's why I like it here. Hiram and

Walter protect all of us, even Georgie when he's not...
working." She stood so close, if he took a single step
forward, he could rest his chin on her head.

Gently, she pried his fingers from his hat. He closed
his eyes for a moment as he breathed in the sharp, sweet
scent of her perfume. "Now, no more talk of bruises and
scars." She placed his bowler on her dressing table and
gestured toward the bed. "Please, sit down. Relax."

The tension in his shoulders eased, until he felt her
fingers loosen his tie and pop free his stiff collar.

He took a quick step back and glanced down. Not
only had she undone his collar and tie, she'd unbuttoned
his coat and waistcoat as well.

Heat singed his cheekbones and flooded his groin.
Coming here had been a mistake. He was his father's
son. Weak. A slave to temptation. Alex ached to just
abandon all restraint and finally yield to the desire that
burned his blood, but it was too soon. Lathrop and the
board of directors had yet to reach a decision.

He knew this, yet he'd still come here. He'd been
strong all these years, why weaken now? Even as he
asked himself the question, he knew the answer.

Ivy. There was something about her that drew him.
This longing to see her, to see her smile, to smell her
perfume, to hold her, and feel her body next to his had
become far more tangible than his usual faceless
fantasies.

After dinner, he'd taken a long walk then lain on the
bed in his hotel room trying to deny his need, while that
small brass token burned a hole in his pocket.

So, he'd rolled out of bed and made the late-night
walk. Was this the same all-consuming lust that had
driven his father to similar houses of ill-repute when he'd

been off on one of his many business trips? Had Samuel J. Worthington been so consumed by his insatiable carnal passions that he'd gone too far in his depravity and been driven insane?

"Make yourself comfortable." The warmth of her smile gleamed in her eyes. She made a sweeping gesture with her arm, encompassing both the striped chaise and her bed. "Would you like something to drink?"

"No thank you." Since he'd never had an alcoholic beverage before, this was probably not a good time to start. Soon maybe, but not now.

"Coffee, tea…"

He shook his head. "Thank you, no."

"A glass of cold milk? Water?"

"Thank you, Miss Ivy, I'm fine."

She grinned. "Relax. I'm not going to throw you down and have my wicked way with you." The amusement in her smile faded as something slow and sensual took its place. Her fingers did a slow walk up his chest. "Unless you want me to."

Wrapping his hand around hers, he halted its upward progression while pressing her palm against his heart. His pulse thrummed at the back of his jaw. Mouth dry, he licked his lips as his bollocks tightened and his shaft swelled. This was not good.

His gaze locked with hers "I…"

"Alex," she whispered holding his gaze. "I'm here for you. Whatever you want, however you want it. I can make your fantasies real."

He swallowed. He had to leave. *Make your apologies and go.* "I…" He exhaled a breath. "I…"

She laid her hand against his bruised cheek. "We don't have to do anything you don't want. I gave you the token as a thank you for what you did."

He stepped back away from her touch. Squaring his shoulders, he smiled, but it felt more like a grimace. "There's no need for reciprocity."

She frowned.

"Your thanks are more than enough. You don't need to offer favors in exchange. What I did, I would have done for any lady."

She pressed her lips together and clasped her hands at her waist, her knuckles white. A myriad of emotions crossed her face, disbelief, confusion, sadness.

The lamplight reflected a watery shimmer in her eyes.

A light tap sounded against the door.

Feeling like an intruder for having glimpsed that bit of vulnerability in her expression, he looked away. He should leave. Head back to his hotel before…

Ivy stood at the open door talking to someone he couldn't see.

Piano music floated up from downstairs. Whoever played the classical piece, they played rather well.

Ivy stepped back. In one hand she held a porcelain bowl and cloth, in the other a small plate with two triangular pastries. She bumped the door with her hip, and it swung closed with a soft click.

"Please sit. You look like a horse ready to bolt." She raised the bowl. "I have some ice for your face."

She extended the plate. Two puffy triangular pastries with a shiny glaze. He closed his eyes and inhaled. Sweet and fruity…like…*God, those damn peaches!*

He opened his eyes.

She gave him a grin that lit up her face, and she

nodded toward her bed—that big, comfortable looking bed.

"Come, sit. I won't bite." She backed toward it.

Her smile and sultry voice as powerful as that which lured many a sailor to his death. If he stayed, all his years of celibacy and strict diet would be wrecked on the rocks of gluttony and lust.

She set the plate of pastries beside the lamp on the side table.

He spun around. The door was right there, yet he couldn't seem to make his feet move toward it.

Instead, his hand reached out and grasped the back of her spindly chair. He pulled it away from her dressing table and lowered himself onto the embroidered seat cushion.

*Crack*, or was it a creak? He wasn't that heavy, was he?

Holding the basin at her waist, she sighed. Her shoulders rose and fell. The top of her dress shifted outward to the very edges of her shoulders.

He crossed his legs and clasped his knee, hoping to hide the evidence of his arousal as he stared at the designs in the rug at his feet.

With a soft rustle of silk, she stood before him. Fancy stitching which looked like ivy, twined below a line of ribbon along the edge of her low-cut bodice where the soft mounds of her bosom nearly spilled free. He dropped his gaze to the ruffles at the bottom which stretched into a train at the back. However, rather than brush the floor all the way around, as other dresses did, hers was cut high in front, and when she moved a certain way, the skirt parted all the way to her knees.

Her toes curled into the pile of the rug. Then a silk-clad foot slid up, over the arch of his shoe. Then higher, as her toes slipped beneath the hem of his trouser leg, then glided upward, over the top of his shoe and touched his leg. He reared back, uncrossing his legs, as the chair rendered another crack. He jumped up.

She laughed. "Have you never been with a woman before?"

He glanced around the room seeking something to focus on other than what he assumed would be her amused expression. Heat singed his cheeks. He pulled out this pocket watch and popped open the cover.

"There's no need to check the time. You had a token. You have me for the whole night."

*The whole night?* He wasn't sure he could last. He knew he couldn't.

"Alex, why don't you take this."

She held out the basin of ice. "I'm going to sit there." She nodded her head toward the striped chaise.

He accepted the basin. Unsure where to put it, he lowered himself carefully onto the chair and set the wide porcelain bowl in his lap. The cold immediately seeped through the wool of his trousers.

Ivy moved across the room and reclined on the tufted striped lounge chair. "Why don't you make yourself comfortable on the bed? Those turnovers on the side table are for you. Maude kept them warm. Try one."

She drew one knee up, allowing the skirt of her gown to fall open, revealing her bent leg all the way from her toes up her shapely calf, to her knee.

Leaning forward she loosed the ribbon garter and slowly slid the silky, white stocking down her leg and off her foot.

He gulped, mesmerized. Ivy's foot was nothing like

his, all bones and veins and bits of hair. Hers was fine boned, not so broad. The curve of her arch and turn of her ankle tempted him to touch, to hold it in his lap, run his hand over her smooth pale skin, upward to her calf, over her knee and...

Where were her drawers? Women wore drawers, didn't they? He'd seen them often enough drying on the line.

He jumped up to his feet, poised to dash out the door and straight down those stairs. But, as before, his feet had a mind of their own and instead of taking him to the door, they took him straight to the bed. Slowly, he lowered himself onto the edge of the mattress. The soles of his shoes planted squarely on the floor. The basin of ice held tight in his lap.

Rather than look toward Ivy and that long beautiful leg, he focused on the pastries. Puffed and flakey, his mouth watered. The temptation to taste them as powerful as the temptation of Ivy herself.

"You don't like turnovers?"

He glanced across the room where she reclined, that bent knee gently rocking side to side.

He swallowed, captivated by the rhythmic motion. "They look...look...wonderful. I like them. I think." He glanced back at the plate. "It's only that I don't care for sweets."

"Oh."

Such disappointment filled that soft sound, a wave of guilt washed over him.

Maybe if he broke off a corner and tried it, that would be enough. It wouldn't be sweet. It would be akin to eating dry toast.

She sat up and tucked under her foot. Only a glimpse

of her bent knee now. "I don't want to offer you something you don't like. Let me ring for a servant. What do you want? I can have it brought up from the supper table."

"No thank you, Miss Ivy. I'm not hungry."

She shifted around on the chaise, facing him. She crossed her legs, both now stripped of stockings, and rhythmically bobbed her foot. She grinned. "You know I had the ice brought up to help reduce your swelling, but I intended it for your face not—"

Mortified, he stood and set the basin on the other side of the lamp. He pulled a handkerchief from his coat pocket and dabbed at the beads of sweat forming across his brow.

"Are you...hot, Alex?"

Damn, the way she said hot. What was he doing in the bedroom of a practiced courtesan before he was ready? "It is rather warm in here."

She rose and crossed to the window, her movements slow and graceful. "You might be a little cooler if you remove your coat."

She shoved aside the heavy drapes and pushed up the sash. The drapery fringe fluttered as a cooling breeze swept into the room.

God help him, he wanted to remove his coat. He wanted to remove his shirt, his trousers, his drawers— remove it all. He ached to rip open that teasing gown like a paper-wrapped package, to throw the layers of silk from her body and run his hands over her bare skin, feel the weight of her breasts in his hands, slide his fingers into that illusive, most intimate place. To join himself with her as one, to finally know the reality of this all-consuming need that ruled his life. To make wild, sweaty, fantasy crazed—

—like his father.

Father.

He shivered as nausea churned in his stomach driving acid up the back of his throat. Had his father ever come here—touched Ivy in that way?

No. Father had been dead these five years. Ivy would have been a girl.

*God! No don't think of it!*

Saliva pooled around his tongue. He swallowed.

She moved around the room, cupped her hand around the top of each glass chimney, pursed her moist lips, and blew out the flame of every lamp.

"If we don't extinguish them, every moth and mosquito in the county will be in this room."

Her gown rustled as she moved. The bedsprings squeaked.

He stood near the foot of the bed, waiting for his eyes to adjust. Gradually, her silhouette came into focus where she sat on the mattress.

She patted the quilt. "Come sit beside me. We can just talk if you want."

Like the moth, she was his flame, and despite the knowledge that he should leave, he joined her, the mattress dipping beneath his weight.

The words of John 3:19 rang in his head as they did when Reverend Clark rained them down from the pulpit, as though God himself reviled Alex for who he was.

*"And this is the condemnation, that light is come into the world, and men loved darkness rather than light, because their deeds were evil…"*

Exhausted, he allowed himself to lay back—his feet still flat on the floor—and clasped his hands over his chest. He was so tired of battling the two sides of himself. How evil could it be to lie with a woman who was not his wife?

Breathing deep he inhaled the sweet scent of Ivy's perfume. If he surrendered to temptation, he envisioned her arms wrapped around him, holding him close, the way God intended for man and wife back in the Garden of Eden.

She lay back and rolled onto her side, drawing her knees up, and propping her head in her hand. "Do you have any hobbies? What do you enjoy doing when you're not working?"

He focused on a wide shadowy spot on the ceiling. "I work a great deal."

Her fingers touched the backs of his hands where they lay clasped over his chest. He flinched.

He squeezed his hands tighter and tighter, until pain radiated through his bones and erased the glide of her fingers over his knuckles and wrists.

"I-I manage a bank. Own it actually. Well, my family does."

"A bank. You must be so smart, keeping track of all that money." Her hand slid away.

His breath escaped in a long sigh of relief. "I'm of no more than average intelligence." He flexed his fingers a few times and re-laced them. "Banking is mostly managing columns of numbers and doing basic arithmetic. It isn't all that difficult."

Was that dark circular area on the ceiling above the bed a water stain?

She shifted. Her knee bumped his thigh.

He held his breath.

Her knee eased back. "I still bet you were the

smartest boy in your school."

"No. But I did attend the university here in Lincoln for a brief time before my father passed away."

"Did you always want to be a banker?"

"Ivy, does the roof leak?"

"A little. If there's a hard rain it drips some, but not too bad. I usually just rearrange my furniture, so the customers don't notice."

"You shouldn't have to live with rain dripping on your bed."

"There must be something you like to do when the bank is closed."

"I read."

She nudged his shoulder. "Books?"

He chuckled. "Yes."

"What kind? Tell me your favorite. What's the last book you read?"

He rolled onto his side pulling his knees up, mirroring her position. No one had ever asked him about his books before. Except for Mrs. Lindberg at the Dry Goods and Fine Furniture Emporium, who ordered his books from a catalog she had behind the counter.

"I prefer adventure, like Jules Verne's *Twenty Thousand Leagues Under the Sea* and *The Mysterious Island*, which I'm reading now."

"So which book is your favorite?"

He shrugged. "I like so many for different reasons. But I have read *The Last of the Mohicans* three times."

"You read the same book three times?"

"Yes, I did. It's the second in the *Leatherstocking Tales* by James Fennimore Cooper and takes place during the French and Indian War."

"Well, I don't believe you. You have to be smart. I

never read a single book."

"Not a one? What do you do on lazy Sunday afternoons?"

"We have no lazy Sunday afternoons here. We're open for gentlemen callers every day."

"I'm sorry."

She gave his shoulder another nudge. This one harder, less playful.

"Don't you feel sorry for me. I chose this life. I make my own money, my own decisions. Madame treats us right. She makes sure the gentlemen are clean before they come upstairs. I keep half of everything plus whatever tips a gentleman offers. I get to wear pretty clothes and sleep in a beautiful room."

"With a leaky roof."

She pushed up to side-sitting. "Who the hell are you to judge me? You, Mr. Fancy-Banker, growing up in a nice house with a sister, and a momma and poppa, going to college and reading books. I bet you never missed a meal in your life. Or slept in the cold."

"Miss Ivy, I'm sorry." Instinctively, he sat up and grasped her hand. "Forgive me. I didn't intend to criticize your life choice."

She shifted to face him but didn't pull her hand from his. "What else is there for a girl with no husband and no schooling? Sewing shirts for two dollars a week, or working as a laundress in some mining camp out west? I might as well be here. At least I don't have to worry about some filthy miner taking me in a tent, in the rain and mud, praying he doesn't have the pox."

"Ivy, I apologize."

He released her hand and fell onto his back. "Believe me, I understand. We do what we can in this life, to avoid our destiny, but in the end, what does it matter? It's who we are."

Above, the discoloration that spread out from the center of the ceiling appeared to also bulge from the plaster like a boil.

While his bedroom was always cold, he'd never actually slept in the cold, and while this house might not be a mining camp...

"Marry me."

"Excuse me?"

He rolled onto his side and sat up. He grasped her hand. "Marry me, Ivy."

She blinked several times.

"Live with me. Be my wife for a few months. I'll pay you of course. You would have your days free to engage in whatever activities you like, as long as you are available at ni—"

A pillow came out of nowhere and smashed against the side of his head. It whisked away, giving him barely enough time to bring his arms up to cover his face before it slammed against the side of his head again.

"Wait!" He tried to shove the pillow away, but she hit him again, raining down blow after blow. He had no idea something so soft could hurt.

"Get out!" she cried even as he continued to block her assault.

"Stop, Miss Ivy, please."

"I thought you were different. You bastard, you're just like the rest of them." On her knees, she swung the pillow like a club slamming it against his head, arms, and chest, over and over. "I don't need a protector. I take care of myself."

He grabbed the corner and tried to wrest it from her

hands, but the outrage which enveloped her like a thundercloud gave her the strength to yank it from his grip.

She jumped from the bed and using the pillow like an extension of her hand, pointed to the door. "Get out."

He slid off the bed, and giving her a wide berth, inched his way to her dressing table and put his clothing to rights. Reaching into his coat, he withdrew his wallet and placed several banknotes on the table.

"I've said this badly." He returned his wallet to his inside pocket. "I meant no offense. My offer is genuine. Marry me. Any preacher or church you prefer."

"Just go."

He nodded, picked up his hat, and stepped to the door. Hand on the knob, he turned. "If for some reason you change your mind, I'm staying at the Adams hotel for the next day or so."

He pulled the door open and stepped into the hallway. "It was a pleasure meeting you, Miss Ivy. I wish you all the best."

Her palm on the door, she shoved it closed with a bang and stood in the middle of the room staring.

Why had she done that? Roger Barnes asked her to be his mistress. His offer hadn't upset her in any way. In her line of work such offers were common. So, why had she reacted so badly to Alex?

Because, somehow, she'd expected Alex to be different.

By rote, she walked to the window and keeping in the shadow, watched the alley below. Alex had used the back stairs, and a moment later his silhouette came around the corner and stepped carefully around the clutter which littered the ground. As he reached the entrance to the street, he brushed at the sleeves of his coat and disappeared up the sidewalk.

She moved to her dressing table, and there sitting atop four bank notes was her missing pearl tipped hat pin. She stared at it for a moment, then picked it up and rolled it slowly between her fingers. Even in the dark it gleamed, free from even a speck of mud.

Men didn't do nice things for her. She did nice things for men.

She jabbed the pin into a tattered cushion.

Picking up the money, she touched each note. Generous. Added to what Roger had given her, made six. Nearly a week's rent in one night. At this rate maybe she'd have enough in less than a year.

Alex whatever-his-name-was could keep his proposal. She'd never be anyone's kept woman. Not for Roger and not for Alex. He didn't mean marriage anyway. Not really. Smart, rich men like him didn't marry women like her.

Nothing more than a naïve boy, a virgin even, and she as big a fool as he. Fussing over him, falling for his proper manners, his Miss Ivy this and Miss Ivy that.

Pining over Alex, or any man, did her no good. She'd learned that lesson when she was fifteen.

She rose and glanced at the small bedside table. He never even tried her turnovers.

Chapter Five

Chirping birds roused Ivy from sleep. She opened her eyes then closed them against the beam of morning sun slicing through the narrow space between her curtain panels. She dropped her arm over her eyes.

Madame would not be pleased.

Still wearing her lavender gown, she rolled from the bed and stripped off the garment. Laying it over her trunk, she donned her pink silk robe. At her dressing table, she pulled open the center drawer and glanced at her watch. Nearly a quarter past seven. Plenty of time for a bath before heading to the kitchen to make the custard filled puff pastries for Hiram and the gentlemen who would come by tonight.

Footsteps moved past her door toward the front of the house. Probably Rachel or Annie bringing fresh water to one of the rooms.

She sat at her dressing table and ran her brush through her hair. Someone ran from the front of the house, past her room toward the back stairs.

There might even be enough time to make some pies from the fruit Mr. Preston sent over yesterday.

A few moments later the thudding footfalls of two or three people hurried past her room and continued up the hall. Unusual for so early in the morning.

Ivy pinned her hair to the top of her head and gathered her soap, lotion, and towels. She opened her door and stepped into the hall as Madame and Doctor Fiske emerged from the doorway at the top of the back staircase.

Ivy's brow furrowed as they hastened toward Lily's room at the front of the house.

An odd twist in Ivy's stomach sent a shiver of dread throughout her body. Though she knew Madame would disapprove, Ivy set her toiletries inside her room and followed. Hovering near Lily's open door, Ivy peered around the jamb. Georgie stood near the window, tears on his cheeks. Hiram and Walter hovered near the bed. Lily lay still in the center, the innocence of sleep on her face. Madame stood on one side while Doctor Fiske leaned over Lily from the other.

He listened to Lily's heart then opened his bag and dropped his stethoscope inside.

The door across the hall creaked open, and Anémone stepped up beside Ivy.

"Oh my God, Lily," Anémone murmured. "What did that little fool do?" All trace of her alluring French accent was gone.

Walter sat the limp girl upright and held her as Doctor Fiske tried to pour the liquid from a bottle down Lily's throat.

"What's he doing?"

Ivy glanced over her shoulder. Violet, Poppy, and Daisy peered around her.

"He's trying to make her vomit," Ivy whispered. "I've seen it done before, with olive oil and mustard."

Madame looked back at the girls and with a sharp jerk of her head, silently ordered them to get out. The four of them backed away from the door as Madame strode across the room and closed it in their faces.

"You don't suppose…" Daisy began.

Ivy shrugged.

"You think she did it on purpose?" Violet asked in a soft voice as she stared at the closed door.

Daisy shook her head. "Maybe. I know she hated this life, what she'd become."

Anémone crossed her arms. "She has a daughter living with her mother."

"That only makes it worse for her," Daisy said. "Knowing she can never see her little girl."

Daisy's words were harsh but true. If Lily tried in any way to be part of her daughter's life, Lily would ruin the girl's future and leave the girl with no choice but to follow in her mother's footsteps the same way Ivy had followed in the footsteps of her own mother.

"Still," Anémone continued. "She could have saved her money. Got out." She put her ear to the door.

Daisy gave a harsh laugh. "Get out? No one gets out." She nodded to Anémone. "You don't want to think about how this life ends for us, but after a few years, if we don't die of the pox, all we'll have left is servicing men in a back-alley crib for fifty cents and a cheap bottle of gin. Unless we're brave enough to end it ahead of time, like Lily."

"You're a depressing, little bitch," Anémone snapped.

Ivy eased away from them. Anémone was right. To spend time thinking about things like that was depressing. Ivy preferred to focus on the pretty dresses and the rich men who spent the night and left big tips in the morning. Wasting away at thirty-five from alcohol, laudanum, and disease was not the future Ivy had planned for herself. Besides, she was only twenty.

Violet leaned in, lowered her voice. "Who was Lily with last night?"

Daisy's lips curled as though she'd swallowed something bitter. "That nasty little man, Simms."

Ivy's gut clenched.

Violet gasped. "Do you think he demanded too much? Pushed her over the edge?"

Anémone sniffed, her nose in the air as she turned from the door. "Why is she better than us? We've all suffered that *gros bâtard*. Endured his whippings, being tied up, and entered by the back door. At least with him there's no chance of getting with child." She shook her head and pressed her ear to the door.

"That's right," Poppy murmured. "She ain't no better than us."

Anémone gasped and jerked away from the door. "Lily's dead."

"Father, forgive her," Daisy muttered, hastily making the sign of the cross.

"She made her choice." Anémone shrugged. "*C'est la vive.*"

"They're coming," Violet whispered.

The young women scattered. Ivy dashed for her room. Ducking inside she closed her door and dropped onto the chair at her dressing table.

Hands trembling, she picked up her hairbrush, then set it back down. Lily was dead. Had it been an accident, or had she taken her own life?

The bedroom door swung open. Ivy jumped to her feet.

Madame Beauchamp strode across the carpet, right up to Ivy and delivered a stinging slap across Ivy's left cheek.

"You girl, are finished here."

Despite the impact to her face and the burning in her cheek, cold seeped into Ivy's body like fog creeping under a door. She didn't have near enough saved.

Despite her fear, she lifted her chin and met Madame's narrowed gaze.

"You think I didn't know about your little maneuver last night? You know the rules. No trading the gentlemen. If someone has a token, they get whoever is available. This is not a matchmaking service. If that's what you're looking for, I suggest you join the many desperate females heading west as a mail-order-bride."

Madame stepped back. Her fists planted on her hips. "Now sit down."

Ivy dropped onto her chair.

"I see that look in your eye, girl. Don't you think to challenge me."

Ivy dropped her gaze to the waist of Madame's gown.

"Second. You were free last night, yet you told no one. Unless you are sick, or on your courses, you work." She walked over to the trunk and fingered Ivy's gown.

"I employ servants to fetch drinks and cook. If Hiram wants special desserts, he can pay for them like everyone else."

She turned back to Ivy. "This is my house. Nothing goes on that I don't know about."

Ivy kept her gaze lowered. That was true. No one in the house was above currying favor with Madame. Even the gentlemen callers tended to fawn over Madame in exchange for discounts and special rates.

"And don't think for an instant I will let you stay with Lily gone. She knew my rule about addicts and drunkards. Swallowed the whole bottle after I told her she'd have to leave. Stupid slut, took the coward's way out."

Madame's green taffeta skirt moved within Ivy's view.

"Look at me, girl."

Ivy lifted her gaze to meet Madame's eyes. The deep lines of Madame's harsh life were visible around her eyes and mouth, even through the heavy face powder and rouge she wore.

"I recognize spirit in those big blue eyes. You're no coward. You'll find a new place, in a new town. You'll survive."

Ivy swallowed. "Yes, ma'am."

"I like you, girl, but you broke the rules. I bend them for no one. I can't afford to."

Being tossed into the street was nothing new, but this time it was a surprise.

Madame glanced around the room. "You have until four o'clock when we open for our first callers. Gather your things and come to my office. I will check my ledgers, and we'll settle any debts for gowns, rent, and meals. If you wish to leave any dresses, bring them with you, and I will give you half their used value."

"Thank you, Madame."

Madame nodded and left the room pulling the door closed behind her.

\*\*\*\*

Alex forced his eyes to open wide and tried hard not to blink as the doctor, holding a candle and magnifying glass, peered deep into Alex's eyes. The older man's breath streamed warm against Alex's cheek, and he struggled not to flinch away.

Despite a lifetime of denial and strict adherence to his diet, Alex finally admitted that over the past year his eyesight had worsened.

He wouldn't have bothered coming to Joseph Gibbons, Doctor of Optometry, except it had become harder to read his once precise handwriting. Seeing a doctor in Lincoln afforded him the opportunity to acquire new spectacles without the chance his mother would learn of it.

Doctor Gibbons stepped to the side and blew out the candle, setting it on a nearby table beside the magnifying glass. Next, he had Alex read the eye chart on the far wall, and he easily read the letters on each line.

Next the doctor handed him a card. "Can you read this?"

The first two lines of letters were easy. The following lines gradually smeared into one big blur at the bottom of the chart.

"Don't look so devastated." The doctor patted Alex on the shoulder and took the card.

"When did you get your current lenses?" He gestured Alex toward a wooden chair beside the desk.

Alex lowered himself onto the designated seat. "About six years ago. I was starting college and had trouble reading."

"And there have been no changes since then?"

"No, sir. Not since I first got spectacles when I was thirteen or fourteen."

The doctor moved to a wicker and wood chair, rolling it close to his paper strewn desk. "We often see changes in eyesight with puberty." He stroked his beard. "Do you do a lot of close work?"

Alex glanced toward the window, but dark curtains

had been pulled to block out the sun. Should he mention the other deterioration looming like a specter in the back of his mind? He'd managed so far. As long as he could still see, did it matter? He glanced down, studying the thin stripes in the fabric of his trousers.

Doctor Gibbons pulled a pad from beneath a pile of papers in the middle of his desk. Without looking up he scribbled hastily across the top paper. "You definitely need a new prescription. I imagine you've been getting headaches from the strain."

The doctor reached into one of the cubby holes at the back of his desk and passed Alex a piece of paper and pencil. "I send away to American Optical Company in Southbridge, Massachusetts to have them made. They should be ready within the month. You can stop back and pick them up here or leave your address and I'll send them on to you."

Alex jotted down the bank's address. That way Mother wouldn't learn about his failing vision.

"With the exam, the frames, the lenes, and shipping…" The doctor set his pen in the wooden holder beside the inkwell and passed over the receipt. "A little more than you'd pay through the Sears and Roebuck, but these are good quality frames, and the lenses will be custom."

The cost was a little unexpected, especially for spectacles he wouldn't need for long. He removed his wallet and passed the doctor several banknotes.

A few minutes later he left the shop. Walking up the street, he passed the alley where he'd met Ivy yesterday morning.

Whatever had possessed him to ask her to marry him? Especially before he had an answer regarding the sale of the bank. He'd had no intention to wed anyone. Ever. Had his ability to think rationally begun to fail along with his eyesight?

And never, if he was in his right mind, would he have proposed to a woman who had no qualms about revealing her bare limbs or sliding her toes up inside his trouser leg. A beautiful woman with clear blue eyes and hair streaked with yellow. An independent woman who could hold her own in a street brawl.

Yes, it was a good thing Ivy had kept her wits about her last night, turned him down, and tossed him out. Marriage to an upstairs girl would have lured him straight down the same path to Hell his father had traveled. Except, despite all Alex's efforts, he seemed destined to arrive there in half the time.

A bell jiggled as he pushed open the door of the gun shop he'd spotted during yesterday's early morning walk.

A glass display case nearly spanned the width of the narrow room, dividing the space in half. Behind it, along the wall, were racks of various rifles, below them three shelves filled with boxes and boxes of ammunition. Inside the glass case an assortment of revolvers.

A curtain parted at the back of the small shop. A lanky, older man wearing a black apron, the lower part of his shirt sleeves protected by gauntlets, stepped up to the glass case which separated him from Alex. The scent of gun oil wafted from the man.

"Can I help you?"

Alex swallowed and drew a breath. "I would like to purchase a gun."

"Any special model you're looking for?"

Alex tried to remember some of the makes he'd

heard of—Colt, Remmington, Smith & Wesson…

"These here Colt .44's are popular."

Alex frowned as he considered the weight and length of the barrel. "No, something smaller, but larger than a Derringer."

"What are you going to use it for?"

Alex gnawed the inside of his cheek as he considered a plausible lie. "For protection. I manage a bank and would like something fairly easy to conceal."

The man nodded. "Haven't heard of any bank robberies in these parts lately, but I reckon you never know."

The man slid open the back of the case and set a gun on a towel which lay in the center of the glass top.

"How about this Whitney five shot, .31 caliber cap and ball, pocket model?"

Alex picked it up. The wood grip felt good in his hand, and the weight of the piece was more substantial than Ivy's Derringer.

"Now that there's a later model with the brass trigger guard and safety notch in the cylinder."

"It's fine. I'll take it."

"Would you be wanting anything else, cartridges, shoulder holster?"

"No. I mean, no on the holster, yes on the cartridges."

The man turned and scanned the rows of small boxes. "Yup, that there's a good gun to keep loaded in a drawer under the counter. Never can tell. Good idea to be prepared." He set a thin box on the counter beside the gun. "Holds six cartridges. How many boxes you want?"

"That one is fine."

"You'll need caps too." He set a small box beside

the cartridges. "That'll be thirteen dollars."

Alex removed his wallet and counted out thirteen bank notes. This trip had become far more expensive than he'd planned. Fortunately, he'd taken the money from his personal savings rather than explain to Mother why the household account had been depleted by a hundred dollars.

He slipped the boxes in the side pocket of his coat and unsure where to put the gun, stuffed it into the waistband of his trousers.

"Good way to shoot yourself."

Alex stilled. A chill washed over him. He looked up. "Excuse me?" he whispered through the tightness in his throat.

"I know it ain't loaded but sticking it in your waist like that, it's good way to shoot yourself in the leg or someplace else a little more important to a man."

Alex released a breath. "I'll be fine, thank you. I'm just walking over to my hotel."

****

Stepping through the hotel's frosted, glass paneled door, Alex crossed the lobby and approached the front desk.

A short man with gray hair and hunched shoulders, leaned forward. Behind thick round spectacles, his dark eyes appeared double in size as he peered at Alex. "Can I help you, sir?"

"Are there any messages for room two-o-seven."

The desk clerk gave a slight nod. "Let me see." He turned and moved close to the row of cubbies along the wall behind the desk. Holding out a gnarled index finger, he traced an invisible line beneath each row.

Even from here, Alex could read the oval plate with

the number two-o-seven and see the small white note laying inside.

The old man went right past it. "Two-o-seven you said?"

"Yes." Alex gnawed on the inside of his cheek. Once he abandoned the restrictions of his current lifestyle, how long would it take before he was as blind as this old man?

"Ah ha, here you are." The man retrieved the note then slowly turned and held out the folded paper with a shaking hand.

"Thank you." Alex accepted it, and as he headed to the stairs, he flipped open the note.

Lathrop wished to see him at two.

****

This time Alex was shown into the bank president's office where Lathrop and the attorney Roger Barnes waited.

"Good afternoon, gentlemen." Alex lowered himself into the only empty chair.

Lathrop leaned back in his seat and steadily eyed Alex across his desk. He nodded toward the folder which lay in the center of his blotter.

"After reviewing your ledgers and going over our own numbers, we have a few follow-up questions."

Alex squeezed the brim of his hat and gnawed the inside of his cheek. At least they hadn't said, no. Yet.

Lathrop flipped open the folder and tapped the center of the top page. "Your asking price seems a little on the high side. Since prices tend to go down in outlying areas, we'd like you to explain what comparables you used to arrive at this number."

Alex glanced from Barnes to Lathrop. "Sir, there is

currently only one other bank in Fremont. We're the Dodge County seat and at the junction of Union Pacific and Cowboy Lines. The area is prime for development. Also, Farmers and Merchants Bank is the only bank in two states with a brand new, Hall's vault."

Lathrop pursed his lips and nodded. "I've heard they were the only vaults to survive the Chicago fire intact."

"Yes, sir. I don't have the specifications with me, but from what I recall, the walls are made of steel reinforced concrete. The door is three and a half feet thick with staircase shaped grooves, making it impossible to pry open. It has the Hall Premier combination lock, and it's on a timer, preventing any of my employees from being kidnapped in the middle of the night to open the vault."

"Impressive, son."

"It makes our bank the most dependable and the most secure of any bank in Dodge County."

"That definitely adds to the value." He leaned forward and flipped open the folder. "I don't recall seeing expenditures for installation or any necessary renovations."

"They were minimal, aside from cost of the vault which was noted in the ledger for May of seventy-four. Installation was included in the purchase price. There was a…a small…room…" Alex swallowed and glanced from the hat in his lap to Lathrop. "No longer being utilized, so that space was used to accommodate the new larger vault."

"Very good. We'd like you to stay on in our employ as the bank manager. You're smart and innovative. Pinkerton's man says honest and trustworthy. We'll need someone like that to manage our interests. You will come here once a month with all your books, or we will come there. Sixty dollars a month. How does that sound?"

A swell of saliva pooled around Alex's tongue. He should have eaten something for lunch, but he'd been too nervous. Now he was forced to breathe through the nausea which churned in his stomach

"I'm sorry, sir. I appreciate the offer, I do, but…I'm afraid I will be leaving town."

"Sorry to hear that." Lathrop and Barnes exchanged a long glance.

Damn, had he just killed the sale? Ruined his only chance to see Mother and Nellie settled? Destroyed his only hope of experiencing a real life?

"Goldman."

"Excuse me?"

Alex swiped at the beads of sweat along his hairline. "Arthur Goldman. I would like to recommend him in my stead."

"And he is…"

"He is the bank's head cashier and has been with us since the beginning. He also acted as manager many times when my father was out of town. He oversaw the teller drawers, acted as loan officer, handled accounts payable… He did it all. He's honest and trustworthy and reliable. He's been married for years and has four grown children and—"

Lathrop raised a finger. "Hold up there, son. This bank was nearly insolvent until you took over."

"Yes, but Mr. Goldman had no part in that. He was my father's right hand and though he often did not agree with my father's business decisions, he only did as my father asked. He has continued to be my most valued employee."

Lathrop and Barnes exchange another quick glance. Lathrop dipped his pen in the inkwell and tapped the nib against the rim. "What was that name again?"

"Goldman. Arthur Goldman."

"All right then. Contingent upon the results of further investigation by the Pinkerton's into the character of Arthur Goldman, we are prepared to agree to your proposal—if you are willing to accept five percent less than your asking price. Starting a new branch is a risk for us. We will also be changing from a state to a national charter. If you and your stockholders are in agreement, have your attorney draw up the contracts. Bring them yourself or send them by special messenger. Mr. Barnes will look them over before we sign."

"I'll have them to you next week."

"We plan to come out to see the bank, check your books and see first-hand the growth potential you've told us about. Then contingent on a bank examiner's review of the books, we'll close by the end of the month, and open fresh on July first with the new fiscal year."

"Yes, that will be fine." Alex nodded, every muscle in his body poised to leap into the air and cheer. He wasn't going to haggle over five percent. The thirtieth was three and a half weeks away. This was really going to happen.

Chapter Six

Ivy jumped from the cab, carpet bag in hand, and reached up to pass the driver his fare.

"Ma'am, you best hurry," he said. "Folks is startin' to board."

"Yes, thank you."

In front of the station, a train, the engine facing northeast, waited on the tracks.

"Alll abooaarrdd!"

Puffs of steam shrouded the large iron wheels and drifted over the crowd of people advancing to the waiting cars.

Two burly porters approached wearing dark blue waist coats and railroad caps, the sleeves of their white shirts rolled up over their forearms. One man, pushing a wide, flat trolley, veered toward the back of the cab.

"You takin' this train, ma'am?" asked the other porter.

"Yes." She gave a quick glance at the shrinking cluster of passengers. "Can you please ask the conductor to wait?"

"Don't you worry, we'll take care of it. That your trunk?" He pointed to the back of the cab where his partner lifted her trunk onto the trolley.

She nodded.

"Now you go on inside and get your ticket. We'll get this weighed up for you." He pulled a paper luggage tag from his shirt pocket and passed it to her along with a short, whittled down pencil. "Write your name and where you're headed. I'll meet you inside and Eric here will load this on the train and tell the conductor you're coming."

She scribbled out her name and destination and passed them back. "Thank you, both. You're very kind." She gave the man a quick smile, then turned and hurried up the steps onto the platform.

"Don't be too long," he called. "Railroad don't like to wait."

Inside the nearly empty station, her heels rapped against the hardwood floor echoing throughout the expansive room.

An elderly couple stood in front of the only open ticket window, and she stepped up behind them.

"I'm sorry, sir." The ticket agent apologized to the gentleman. "This train is going to Omaha."

"That can't be right. My schedule says the south bound train will arrive at 4:15."

"Sir, the train south is due at 6:22 p.m."

"This is ridiculous. That must be our train."

Outside the call of the conductor rang out. "Alll abooaarrdd!"

The man who helped Ivy with her trunk came up behind the ticket agent, passed him a piece of paper, and whispered in his ear. The agent nodded and glanced at Ivy.

She reached into her purse and withdrew several coins.

If she were going to save enough for her own place, she'd have to be very careful how she spent her money. Working in a parlor house as nice as Madame's had required Ivy to purchase new gowns and undergarments. To pay for them, she'd borrowed money from Madame.

Though she'd given Madame money every month, standing in her office an hour ago, Ivy learned that because of what Madame explained was interest, Ivy had paid little toward what she owed. Between the loan on her clothes, her rent, and the cost of meals she owed for May and this first week of June, along with the cost of the peaches she'd lost on the street yesterday morning, Ivy had had to pay Madame well over one hundred dollars.

"Sir, this is *not* your train." Irritation sharpened the words of the ticket agent's raised voice. "Could you please step aside? This lady needs to hurry."

The woman nudged her protesting husband away from the window as the agent slid Ivy's ticket under the arched ticket window.

Ivy stepped forward, pushed her money through, and snatched up her ticket. Grabbing her carpet bag, she dashed for the door.

"Miss, wait! You gave me too much!"

"Keep it," she called back.

A gentleman, stepping inside, held the door open as she dashed through and onto the platform. The train inched forward.

She raced for the last car and tossed her carpet bag onto the platform. Grabbing the rail with one hand and hiking up her skirt with the other, she jumped onto the bottom step. Pulling herself up and onto the rear platform, she leaned against the rail and heaved a sigh of relief.

She made it! And without falling and getting dragged beneath the train. She laughed then reached toward her bag. She froze. *Holy Hell, my ticket!*

She stared at her empty palm for a moment as if the ticket was actually there. With a shake of her head, she searched the platform around her feet, lifting her hem to be certain.

Whirling, she searched the place where she'd jumped aboard. There, clearly outlined against the red brick, lay a rectangular piece of white paper, growing smaller by the moment as the train picked up speed.

She opened the door and scrunched down in the last seat across the aisle from the water closet. She unpinned her blue hat with the broken feather and shoved it inside her carpet bag.

The passenger car was less than half full and most sat with their seats facing forward. A group of three men had flipped the back of one seat the opposite way allowing them to easily converse. Several rows ahead of Ivy, sat a woman with a little girl, and in the first seat, the back of a man wearing a bowler hat.

Halfway down the car a man stood, set his hat on the seat, then leaned over and whispered something to the woman beside him. He stepped into the aisle and started her way.

*Mr. Preston!* Ivy scrunched even lower, turning her face into the window.

He continued toward Ivy, pulling out his watch as he moved down the aisle. Fortunately, he had his head down as he returned his watch to his pocket, opened the door of the water closet, and stepped inside.

Maybe as soon as he came out, she'd grab her bag and duck inside before the conductor came through the door at the other end of the car. Scooting lower in the seat, the outskirts of Lincoln flew past her window.

Omaha was a thriving town. She'd have plenty of opportunity for employment. Likely there wouldn't be another parlor house as nice or as expensive as Madame Beauchamp's, but a high-end brothel would do. If Ivy had any hope of opening her own place, she needed tips from customers who had money. She was still young. She was still pretty and years away from overdosing on laudanum or working in the cribs.

Her farewell this afternoon had been as painless as any other goodbye. Daisy and Violet had wished her well. Anemoné had merely shrugged, no doubt calculating the extra revenue she'd earn without competition from Ivy or Lily. Ivy didn't blame them. They weren't her friends. What they did was a job. No one let themselves become attached.

Ivy had learned that lesson when she was six. Later cold reality had driven it home, when at fifteen, penniless and ruined, Ivy had been forced to present herself at Mrs. Astella Harding's Boarding House, ready to work.

On rare occasions someone in her profession did marry, but Ivy was a realist. Gentlemen, like Marcello, like Roger Barnes, like Alex, didn't marry women like her. And she'd be damned if she'd tie herself to some farmer and live in squaller the rest of her life.

No, she'd purchase a parlor house of her own. Someplace grand, only rich gentlemen could afford, where the girls were safe, and she could earn enough to live comfortably the rest of her life.

She pulled a handkerchief from the sleeve of her dress and pressed it against the sweat beading on the side of her neck.

The front door of the car opened. She peeked over the back of the seat in front of her. A short man, wearing a dark blue coat and flat-topped cap, stepped inside. He stopped at the first seat and punched the ticket of the solitary man.

*Hurry up Preston! Holy Hell, how long did it take the man to piss?*

The conductor moved to the next passenger. "Ticket please."

Ivy shoved her carpet bag under the seat in front of her. Dropping to her knees between the seats, she prayed her head didn't show, grateful she hadn't inherited her mother's Norse height.

"Ticket?"

Peering under the seats, she watched the conductor's shiny black shoes move closer. "Ma'am, ticket?"

"My husband has them. He'll be right back. He had to use the necessary."

The conductor continued to the next passenger. "Ticket?" And the next. "Ticket, please."

Would he keep coming if he believed the rest of the seats were vacant?

The door to the water closet swung open. His feet turned as he shut the door.

*Don't look down. Go straight back to your seat. Don't look down. Look at the conductor. Please, don't look dow—*

"Ivy?"

*Hells bells!* She rose to her knees.

"Mr. Preston, how are you?" She flashed her best smile and gathering her skirt and petticoats away from her feet, she plopped onto her seat.

"What in God's name were you doing on the floor?"

"Oh, I was… uh… looking for my ticket."

"On your hands and knee—"

"Ticket," the conductor snapped. He directed his request to Mr. Preston, but glared at Ivy, his brow furrowed, and his lips pressed tight.

Preston removed two tickets from his breast pocket and passed them to the conductor.

He punched a hole in each and handed them back.

The conductor's narrowed gaze drilled into Ivy. "Ticket?"

"I had one, but I dropped it and the train…"

"Young lady, I've heard every conceivable excuse and seen every trick possible to garner a free ride. You can believe I would have checked the water closet."

She smiled. "I really did have a ticket. It's on the platform at the station."

"Rather convenient."

She shrugged and smiled. "It's true."

He shook his head. "I find your excuse somewhat dubious. Ladies of good character do not lie, nor do they crawl about on the floor between seats." He turned to Mr. Preston. "Can you vouch for this person?"

Preston's gaze shifted beyond the conductor's shoulders toward his wife, who had turned in her seat. A tall, thin woman, wearing a muddy brown traveling dress, an ugly maroon hat with an orange ribbon, and a deeply furrowed scowl. No wonder he preferred Daisy.

Preston gave his head a shake. "I'm sorry, I don't know this woman. I merely thought her in need of assistance."

He scooted around the conductor and returned to his seat.

The conductor continued to stare down at her. "Unless you produce a ticket or the means to pay for one, you will be put off at Ashland."

She shrugged. "*C'est la vive, mon ami.*"

Being put off the train wasn't dire. Her trunk would land in Omaha without her. It wasn't that far, and she had plenty to offer any man heading in that direction.

"Excuse me, I can vouch for the lady."

*Alex!*

Ivy's gaze shot to the familiar face of the man moving up behind the conductor. He wore a pair of silver spectacles which detracted from the bruising around his eye and swollen nose.

She grinned at the irony of him swooping in to rescue her once more.

The conductor turned. "You know this person?"

"Yes, the lady and I are acquainted." Lifting his hat, he inclined his shoulders forward in a slight bow and settled his hat back in place. "How may I assist you?"

The conductor cleared his throat. "Sir, there is an issue regarding a missing ticket."

Ivy focused her attention on Alex. "I was running for the train and dropped it." She didn't care if the conductor believed her, but for some reason, she cared what Alex thought.

"There, you see," Alex said to the conductor. "A completely plausible explanation. Now I am certain, at our next stop you can send a wire back to Lincoln requesting validation. If not, I shall pay the lady's fare. A dollar and ninety cents I believe."

The conductor's brow furrowed. "You can be sure of it." He swung on his heels and strode back down the aisle to the front of the car.

Behind his spectacles, amusement danced in Alex's brown eyes. "Good afternoon, Miss Ivy. Might I offer you my protection as you travel?"

"That's nice of you, but I have my Derringer." She raised her arm to show him the reticule hanging from her wrist.

"True. However, I believe your hat pins may serve you better." He gestured toward the front of the car. "Would you care to join me for some pleasant conversation?"

"Yes, thank you." She reached under the seat and dragged out her carpet bag.

He extended his hand toward her bag. "May I?"

"You may," she said passing it over. "And I can pay for another ticket. You don't have to keep rescuing me."

His eyebrows rose toward his hat brim, and he inclined his head. Stepping back, he allowed her room to pass. "Please, after you."

Her back straight and her head high, she marched right past Mr. Preston without so much as a glance. She could get used to this, being treated like a real lady.

When she reached the front of the car, she moved aside as Alex stowed her bag in the overhead rack. He picked up a book with a green cover and gold embossed details which lay where he'd been sitting, then flipped the back of the seat so they now faced each other.

Ivy scooped her skirt to the side and sat in the forward-facing seat. "What are you reading?"

Alex slid in across from her. He ran his finger around the edge of the cover brushing over what looked like a small train schedule sticking out from between the pages. "It's Jules Verne's newest book, *Dropped from the Clouds*. It's the first of three volumes in a series called *The Mysterious Island*."

"What's it about?"

"I'm not very far along." He pushed his spectacles

up the bridge of his nose. "There's a group of men during the war, who escape prison and steal a hot air balloon. There's a storm, and they crash on a strange volcanic island."

"Sounds exciting."

"Yes." He gave a slight nod.

"Your face looks like it's healing."

"It is. You've brought your bag. Are you taking a trip?"

She glanced through the window at the open prairie. "Time to move on." She switched her gaze back to Alex.

A frown creased his brow. "Forgive me for being indelicate," he began, "but do you mean to say you have left the employ of Madame Beauchamp?"

She shrugged one shoulder. "It's not good to stay in one place too long. I thought Omaha might be a nice place to start over."

"I see. And are you pursuing similar employment?"

"Why does it matter?"

"I…I wondered if perhaps you…might consider something different?"

She stiffened, her back rigid against the seat. She crossed her arms and glared at him. "Different as something for a proper lady?" she snapped in a harsh whisper.

He opened his mouth, but no words came out.

"Would you rather I sew shirts till my fingers bleed, for two dollars a-piece, or work twelve hours a day in some factory breathing cotton until my lungs are filled? What does it matter to you anyway? I owe you nothing."

He shook his head. "No, no. Please. Forgive me. That's not what I meant at all."

She blew out a heavy sigh. "Then what are you

going on about?"

"How old are you?"

Her brow furrowed. "Twenty, why?"

He glanced down. Pressing his thumbnail into his thigh, he traced one of the thin gray pinstripes in the fabric of his trousers.

"Are you determined to settle in Omaha? Have you committed to a particular establishment there?"

"Why all the questions?"

"My proposal last night was an impulse. My apologizes for upsetting you, but I thought now, in light of your recent unemployment, that is…if you are perhaps…seeking a change…if you might be open to…if you might reconsider…"

He looked up. A gleam of hope lit his brown eyes, like that of a puppy seeking a home.

She sighed and relaxed in her seat. What was it about this man that drew her? Courageous and confident one minute, shy and uncertain the next. "I told you—I will not be your mistress."

"You misunderstand. I'm offering the protection of my name. A true marriage in the eyes of God."

She blinked. He appeared sincere. "No," she said softly. "God or no God, wedded bliss is nothing more than a life of constant drudgery, tied to a man who'd rather run off to his mistress or an upstairs girl than satisfy his own wife."

Alex paled. He closed his eyes and pressed his lips together as though biting back a sharp pain.

"Alex, gentlemen like you don't marry women like me. Tell me what you really want."

He glanced around as though checking the proximity of the other passengers. "My father," he began, his voice barely a whisper. "Had an insatiable…appetite for…for…"

"Women like me."

"Yes, except that he…" Alex dropped his gaze to his book where his thumbnail now dug into the corner.

Ivy leaned forward to hear his soft whisper above the clacking of the wheels over the rails.

"Certain hereditary factors have indicated that I'm…" He glanced up, looked around. "That I'm destined for the same… end."

She reached across and captured his hand in hers. "Alex, everyone has needs. It's nothing to be ashamed of."

He looked up, meeting her gaze. "Outside of marriage it is. Fornication is a sin. My mother has chosen someone for me, but she is older, and…and…I just can't marry that woman. Hence my impulsive proposal last night."

She squeezed his hand and released it, sitting back in her seat. "I like you, I do, and I wish I could help, but I have plans for my life and being tied to one man for the rest of it isn't one of them."

"But it won't be forever, it will only be a few weeks. I came to Lincoln to sell the bank my family owns. The sale will be final before the end of the month. And I will pay you—half of my portion from the sale. After which, we can go our own way. My mother and sister will have the funds they'll need to live. And, as my wife, you'll have the protection of my name. You'll be able to go anywhere and do anything you wish. You must have dreams."

"Then why marry? We can just pretend."

"Because it's important that I refrain from sin, that I

keep my mind and body pure. If we marry, we'll have God's blessing. My desire to experience…to copulate…with…a woman…so consumes my thoughts, I can scarcely think of other things. And I don't want to experience such…intimacy…tied to a woman like Hester Clark."

Ivy looked away. In the distance a farmer walked behind a horse and plow. A small soddie and corral created a bump in the straight line of the horizon. The man's wife was most likely busy doing laundry, or cooking, or sewing, with a half dozen dirty children clinging to her apron.

The aroma of cigar drifted through the car. Low murmurs of conversation filled the quiet. The gentle rocking of the train, the clacking of the wheels along the rails, all felt obscenely normal in light of this strange proposal.

With enough money she wouldn't have to wait. She could stay, wait for Alex to pay her, then go to Denver or San Francisco. Open the most exclusive of parlor houses. Cater only to men who were clean and willing to pay a premium for healthy, young girls. And she'd be able to choose, on her own terms, the men she spent time with.

Alex leaned forward. "I want to lie with a woman," he whispered softly. "To know the feel of her arms around me, to savor the taste of her skin, to finally experience how it feels to be inside her. But I can only truly know her within the sanctity of the marriage bed."

She glanced over her shoulder. Everyone seemed focused on their own conversations.

"Why me?"

"Because you're beautiful, and you

are…experienced. My mother is determined. If I don't marry you, I will soon be tied to Miss Clark. She will want children, and I won't allow my line to continue. You have the knowledge to prevent that. You understand intercourse can be mutually pleasurable without any emotional attachments. When we separate neither of us will be hurt."

She searched his bruised face. His features were set, and he stared right back, waiting.

"Alex, I like you. You're sweet and gallant, but…" This was the man who'd come to her rescue yesterday. He'd gone back to the alley and found her favorite hat pin. He'd been so adorable last night. Being with him wouldn't be a chore. And Alex was the only man to ever treat her like a real lady.

The clicking rhythm of the wheels slowed.

"Miss Ivy, will you marry me?"

This was dangerous. She liked him, but on some level, she liked most of the men she spent time with. Yet, there was something about Alex that felt different. A shudder rippled through her body, raising goose bumps along her arms.

Steam hissed as the train slowed even more. They'd arrived in Omaha.

Alex picked up his book. "Thank you for joining me. Your conversation made the trip much more pleasant."

She heaved a resigned sigh. She was a fool. Definitely a fool. "Annali Hanson."

His brow furrowed. "Excuse me?"

"Annali. If you're going to marry me, you ought to know my real name."

Chapter Seven

"You live with your mother?"

Alex shifted uncomfortably. He stood with Ivy…Annali—such a pretty name—on the back corner of the platform in Fremont, waiting while the porters unloaded baggage from the train. "Yes, and my sister."

Her blue eyes widened. "Your sister too?"

"I realize it's not ideal, but it will only be until the end of the month."

"Could be a problem, but what the hell…" She shrugged. "I'll stay out of the way. But what about nighttime? Are you going to be all right when we're doing it in your bed?"

He hadn't considered three women in the same house as a problem, but then… "When we do what in my bed?"

She grinned and gave his shoulder a quick push. "Mate, Alex. Come together, a little frig and diddle, you know…have sex. Sometimes things get loud."

He glanced around, relieved they were alone, and no one seemed to have heard her vulgar language. "Loud?"

She laughed. "God, you really are a virgin."

Heat singed his ears and burned his cheeks. "Yes, that fact has already been established. Must you ridicule me for it?"

"I'm sorry. I just never met a man who was."

Amusement lingered in her apology. He turned

away, looking toward the back of the station. "Frank Burgess usually comes around with his carriage when the train comes in. I'll see if I can find him."

"Alex, I didn't mean anything. It's just that you're so different from other men I've met."

"Apology accepted. If you'll wait here, I'll shall return shortly."

He started toward the steps at the end of the platform where a couple of wagons and a buckboard waited, spun on his heels, and came back. "I don't want..." he began. "...anyone to suspect our marriage isn't genuine. If you could curtail the whore house language while you're here, I would appreciate it."

She stiffened. The warmth in her eyes chilled. "Don't worry, Sugar. I know how to play my part in this charade. I've been pretending to care my whole life. You'll get what you pay for."

He nodded and turned, swallowing the lump of guilt which rose in his throat. As soon as the train pulled into the station, he'd felt himself change. The weight on his shoulders returned as if the man he'd been in Lincoln had suddenly withered inside himself. He walked around the building and down the steps. Finding Frank Burgess had only been an excuse to momentarily escape Annali. How could he have just treated her the same way he treated his employees at the bank? What was wrong with him?

He kicked a stone and sent it flying. Damn and double damn, he'd just married a prostitute. Another uncontrolled impulse. At the time it made sense. Now that he was home, the scheme felt like a noose around his neck.

She probably could pretend she cared for him, but could she refrain from vulgarities and innuendoes regarding the intimacies of the marriage bed?

The marriage bed. His current single size would never do. It was barely big enough for him. Mr. Lindberg had a nice double-sized brass bed in the window of his Dry Goods and Fine Furniture Emporium. Was there time to catch him before he closed?

Crossing Second Street, Alex dodged a pile of horse manure and lengthened his stride as he pulled out his watch. Ten minutes past. Did Lindberg close at six or six-thirty? He hurried up Main and a few minutes later, turned east on Fifth. His footsteps echoed his impatience, thudding louder than usual against the wooden walkway.

Although early evening, the summer sun created the illusion of afternoon and a glare slashed across the window glass of the Emporium hiding the interior from his gaze. He cupped his hands around his face and leaned close.

A light shone from the back of the building. He walked around the corner to the front entrance. Despite the 'Closed' sign in the window of the door, Alex pressed down on the thumb latch. Locked. He knocked on the wood portion of the door with his left hand, sparing his still sore knuckles. When no one responded, he tried again, pounding with a little more force, rattling the glass.

He stepped back and studied the shiny headboard with its curved shape and scroll work. It certainly looked wide enough for two. Had Ivy's bed been as wide? With all the pillows and the quilts, he wasn't sure. What would she think about his utilitarian bedding and plain room? Would she want to decorate with floral spreads, thick carpet, and lace curtains?

Where would he put this new larger bed? The only

wall wide enough to accommodate its width without blocking the window was against the wall between his room and Nellie's. How would that work? Annali had said they might get loud.

He hadn't thought about the noise which might accompany the act. Although, looking back to when he'd first felt the stirrings of his manhood and the pleasure of his hand around his shaft, he'd muffled his groans by stuffing one of his stockings in his mouth, but even that hadn't worked. His mother had walked in one morning, and that moment changed his life forever.

He swung away from the window. Anticipation had him growing hard inside his trousers. Images of the bed, of him and Ivy—no Annali. Swedish, she'd told him while they waited in Omaha for the Justice of the Peace, which explained Annali's unusual wide streak of pale hair.

How far down her back did her hair fall? He'd been so focused on those long smooth limbs of hers last night, he couldn't remember the length of her hair.

He'd explore that tonight. But how would he be able to explore anything in that narrow bed of his?

The hotel. He'd get a room at the hotel.

"Who is t'at out t'ere pounding on my door?"

Alex stepped to the door.

"Mr. Wort'ington? Goodness, what is wrong? Come-in, come-in."

****

Several minutes later, Alex left Mr. Lindberg and walked north toward the Occidental Hotel at Sixth and Broad, two blocks over from the Farmers and Merchants Bank.

As he neared the bank, Misters Farley, Goldman,

and Warner emerged from within. Was Warner there only to meet the other two for an after-work drink at the saloon, or had Goldman allowed the man to continue working even though Alex had let him go? Alex stopped. His spine stiffened.

Farley and Warner waited as Goldman locked the door, then the trio hurried down the steps and turned in Alex's direction. Their smiles faded, and they stumbled to a halt. Farley took a step back. Goldman and Warner exchanged glances.

Goldman shifted his gaze to Alex. "Mr. Worthington, sir." A stiff smile lifted the corners of his mouth. "We didn't expect you back so soon."

"So, I see."

Warner's gaze shifted downward, and he shrank back a couple of steps.

Goldman held Alex's gaze. "And how was your trip?"

Alex inclined his head. "Successful. However, there is a matter of some import I need to discuss with you tomorrow—before the bank opens."

"Yes, of course."

"I shall expect you promptly at seven-thirty."

"Yes, sir."

Alex nodded and stepped around them, sensing their judgmental stares boring into his back as he continued toward the hotel.

****

Annali stood on the platform, arms crossed, beside her trunk where the porter had set it. Her annoyance escaped with every harsh exhale of breath, much like the huffs of steam which escaped the waiting train.

How dare Alex speak to her like a child in need of a

set down? And where had he gone after his little spat of temper? The nerve of him, leaving her to stand here like this. What happened to the smiling, gallant gentlemen who'd rescued her yesterday morning and earlier on the train? As soon as they pulled into the station here in Fremont, he'd gone rigid and cold.

Well, she wasn't going to stand here all evening. She marched inside past the rows of benches to the ladies' washroom. Once inside, unfastened her bodice and removed a drawstring pouch from between her breasts. Withdrawing a couple of banknotes, she pushed the cloth bag back behind her corset then rebuttoned her blouse.

At the window, she purchased a ticket back to Omaha. If Alex had wanted her to be his wife, he damn well should have treated her like one. Unfortunately, the next train to Omaha wasn't until tomorrow morning.

Carpetbag in hand, she slipped her change and her ticket into her reticule, went outside, and sat on her trunk. She sighed. Now what? Sure as hell, she wasn't going to sit here all night. She glanced up the street. No sign of Alex. She had enough money for a hotel room, but she'd planned that money for a hotel room in Omaha, not here. Maybe if she smiled and flirted a bit, the hotel manager would let her charge a room to Alex.

"'Scuse me, ma'am?"

Annali swung her gaze to an older man, who hat in hand, had come up beside her. She smiled.

"Name's Frank Burgess, ma'am. Can I take you to—"

She stood. "Ah, Mr. Burgess, that would be wonderful. Alex found you then."

"Alex?"

"Alexander Worthington."

"Young Mr. Worthington, yup. The banker. Know who he is."

"Lovely." She smiled and a hint of pink brushed his cheeks along the top of his gray whiskers. "This is my trunk right here. If you could take that, I'll carry this." She picked up her carpet bag.

Mr. Burgess nodded. "Yes, ma'am." He grabbed one handle and dragged it to the edge of the platform, then went down the steps, hoisted it onto his back, and carried it to the rear of a waiting carriage.

Annali followed. "Thank you so much. I could never have lifted it by myself." She wedged her carpet bag into the small space behind the trunk.

He nodded. The pink stain returned to his cheekbones. "Where to ma'am?"

They moved alongside the carriage, and he offered her a hand up into the seat. He gave the dappled gray horse a couple of pats on his way around to the other side. He climbed up front and looked at her expectantly.

"I'm sorry, I assumed Alex already talked to you."

"Ma'am, I ain't seen young Mr. Worthington. So, where do you want me to take you?"

*Hell's bells, Alex!*

"Can you please take me to Mr. Worthington's house?"

Frank's brow shot straight toward his battered western hat. He gave his beard a thoughtful rub, then nodded, lifted the reins, and made a clucking sound with his tongue. The horse started forward.

As they rode north through town, Annali searched for Alex, but he was nowhere to be seen.

Frank turned the horse west. A few young trees, in the yards of homes on either side, added quaintness and provided some shade for the horse, whose coat showed smears of dried lather around the harness leather.

Outside of town houses grew more scattered. A few minutes later, they stopped in front of a two-story white-washed house with a picket fence. A single chimney rose through the center of the roof which extended outward to cover a porch that stretched across the front of the house.

Frank hefted her trunk onto his back, carried it up the worn path, and dropped it with a thud on the floor at the top of the steps. He stood waiting as Annali withdrew her purse and placed a nickel in his leather-stained palm.

"Thank you, ma'am." He nodded and turned to walk back down the path. He clambered onto the driver's seat and looped his horse around in the road.

Annali watched him for a few moments then climbed the three front steps and approached the door. Her fingers barely brushed the brass key of the calling bell when the door opened.

A petite, small-boned woman stood in the doorway, her scowl as black as her dress. Considering Alex's gangly height, Annali expected his mother would be taller—at least as tall as Annali.

Annali took a step back. Clasping her hands in front of her, she squeezed tight the fingers of her right hand.

"Can I help you?" The older woman's gaze darted to the trunk and back.

Annali drew a breath and smiled. "Good evening, ma'am. Is Alex here?"

The woman's narrowed gaze began a slow perusal of Annali's person. From the top of her hat with its broken feather, to her hands, where the woman's gaze lingered a moment on the gold wedding band, before lowering to the toes of Annali's dusty shoes.

The woman raised her head, her chin tilted up. The warmth which gleamed in Alex's brown eyes was missing from this woman's stony glare. "Alexander is out of town."

"No, he's back. He went to find Mr. Burgess to help me with my trunk, but he didn't come back. I thought he came here." Annali extended her hand. "You must be Alex's mother."

The woman propped her hands on her narrow hips.

Ignoring the woman's glare, Annali lowered her hand and forced another practiced smile. "It's a pleasure to meet you, Mrs. Worthington."

"And who might you be?"

*Hell's bells, where was he?*

"I'm Annali. Alex's wife."

The woman blanched, but otherwise showed no reaction. "My son is not, nor has he ever been— married."

"Mother, is Alexander home?" A younger woman, almost a mirror image of the elder, peered around the first. "I saw Mr. Burgess drive away and— Oh, who are you?"

"I'm—"

"Leaving." Alex's mother stepped back, bumping into the younger version of herself.

The door slammed shut.

Annali stared at the closed door in disbelief. *Holy Hell*! Good thing she had her ticket. Except the train east wasn't due until tomorrow.

She turned away and stood at the top of the steps. Beyond the weathered picket fence, to the right, the empty road stretched past a few scattered houses, toward town. On the left, a few distant farms, then endless prairie. What now? She might as well wait. Alex would come home eventually. She smoothed her skirt and sat on her trunk. Leaning forward, she propped her chin in her hand.

What a day! Lily, Madame Beauchamp, the train. Annali sure could use a drink. She chuckled under her breath as she pictured the expression on the old crow's face if she were to knock on the door and ask for a shot of whiskey.

Where had Alex taken himself off to anyway? She'd been a fool to agree to this easy-money plan of his. She glanced over her shoulder and the curtain of the front window dropped back into place. Maybe she'd just sit here all night and really annoy Alex's mother.

From the direction of town, a horse and buggy trotted along the road. As the buggy drew closer, the dome of a bowler hat on the head of the driver grew more distinct. Gradually, the driver's shoulders and rangy frame became clear.

Nearing the house, the horse slowed to a walk then stopped. Alex jumped from the seat and hitched the horse to the ring of a black post near the opening in the white picket fence. He continued up the path, and when he reached the bottom step, he stopped. He looked straight at her, his jaw set, the cords of his neck standing out above his collar.

Without flinching, Annali met his stare. The door opened behind her.

"Alexander," his mother called. "You're back."

She held his gaze as Alex's mother and sister stepped onto the porch. *Say one word of criticism in front of your mother and sister and I'm going straight back to Omaha.*

His gaze softened. The corner of his mouth twitched, and his shoulders relaxed. He extended his hand.

She placed her palm in his—his skin damp. As he came up the steps, she stood. He laced his fingers with hers and they turned.

"Mother, Nell, may I present my wife, Annali. Annali my mother Harriet, and my sister Nellie."

The women gaped—their eyes as wide as their open mouths.

Annali offered a practiced smile. "How lovely to meet you both."

"Dear Lord, Alexander! What happened to your face?"

"Nothing, Mother. Merely a brief encounter with a couple of ruffians."

"You were brawling? How could you? The doctor has recommended calm and quiet. I knew it was a mistake to allow you to go to Lincoln. Look what has come of it. And now you're married?"

"Yes, Mother. Now, if you will excuse us, I would like to show Annali around and let her freshen up before we head over to the hotel."

Harriet turned her gaze on Annali. "We were just about to sit down to supper. You're welcome to join us Ann."

His fingers squeezed hers so tight he very nearly crushed them. "Annali. My wife's name is Annali. And no, she will not be joining *us*. *We—she and I,* will be dining at the Occidental where I have reserved a room for *us* tonight."

Harriet smiled, but from the way her thin lips pressed together in a tight line it looked more like a grimace. "This is all so... unexpected. You must understand why this... this impulsive marriage, and your outburst of temper concerns me."

"Mother, we will not spend our wedding night apart."

Behind Harriet, Alex's sister shot Annali a narrow-eyed glare.

Alex sighed. "I understand you're concerned, but you needn't worry. I'm perfectly fine."

He turned to Annali. "Do you have everything you'll need for tonight?"

"Yes, in my carpet bag. But what about my trunk?"

"I'll carry it up to my room. It will be perfectly safe."

He tipped the trunk onto its narrow end, hunkered down beside it and reached behind for the handle. With a soft grunt he hefted it onto his back.

Harriet extended her hand, her fingers fluttering. "Alexander don't. You'll strain yourself."

Nellie opened the door then she and Harriet followed Alex inside. The door closed in Annali's face.

*Proper ladies, my ass.*

She whirled on her heels, snatched up her bag, and headed down the path to the back of the waiting buggy. She set her carpet bag beside a black leather Gladstone then walked around to pet the chestnut gelding.

What she should do is take the buggy and go. Let Alex learn how it felt to be excluded, left waiting, and wondering.

Maybe she should go to the hotel for the night, then leave in the morning. But what about her trunk?

Now it was in Alex's bedroom. He said it would be perfectly safe, but somehow, she couldn't escape the notion that once night fell, Harriet and Nellie would somehow break the lock and go through her private things. What would they think about all her gowns with the low-cut bodices and high hemlines? Hell, if they hated her now, how would they feel when they discovered what she really was?

She patted the horse on the neck and finger-combed his mane until Alex came down the path.

"My apologies for leaving you at the station." He handed her up into the seat, walked around, and climbed in on the other side. "When I left you, I had nothing more in mind than to find Mr. Burgess." He picked up the reins and turned the buggy back toward town.

Annali propped the balls of her feet on the dash rail. "When Mr. Burgess introduced himself, I thought you sent him."

"Yes. I met him in town. He mentioned that he took you to my house."

Tension radiated from Alex. His jaw remained clenched and his neck cords tight. He turned his head and met her gaze. "I'm not upset with you. When I saw you sitting on the steps and realized Mother had refused to receive you, I was furious. And the condescending way she spoke to you— Unacceptable. I can understand why you chose not to come inside."

Annali shrugged. "It is fine. Proper ladies always—" *slam doors in my face* "—talk to me that way. If they speak to me at all."

"But you are my wife. Mother has no reason to presume you are anything other than a respectable gentlewoman. She had no right—"

Annali twisted slightly in her seat, rested her hand on his shoulder and leaned close. "Please. I appreciate you coming to my rescue *again*, but let's not talk about it. I've never eaten in a real restaurant or stayed in a fancy hotel."

His shoulder relaxed beneath her palm. A small grin tugged up the corner of his mouth. "You're right. Forget Mother. I've waited years to finally enjoy my life."

Chapter Eight

Alex stared at the food before him. A thick steak, covered high with onions and mushrooms, lay on a white, china plate beside a steaming baked potato. He'd dreamed about food like this for so long, now that it had been placed in front of him, he was afraid to touch it.

He lifted his gaze to Annali. Amusement sparkled in her eyes. The trout on her plate was nearly half gone. "Aren't you going to eat? It's getting cold."

"Yes, of course." He picked up his knife and fork and sliced through the steak. Juices ran from the center. He popped the piece of beef in his mouth, closed his eyes, and chewed. He'd had steak before, but never medium rare or flavored with a mixture of seasonings and slathered with bites of mushroom and onion.

He tried his baked potato next, buttered and topped with sour cream and bits of crumbled bacon. It veritably melted in his mouth. He scooped another forkful, then went back to his steak.

Across the table, Annali chuckled. "God, Alex, the look on your face. Anyone would think you'd never eaten a steak before."

"I have, but never one this good."

"Well, I hope to see that look of satisfaction again…later tonight."

"Look, rolls." He snatched one from the basket and took a large bite before he'd swallowed his piece of steak. "These are wonderful," he mumbled around the bread in his mouth. "So warm and soft."

Under the table, something stroked the back of his calf. Annali's foot! He flinched and jerked his leg away. His gaze shot to her face. Her innocent expression gave nothing away.

Her foot returned. The smooth rounded toe of her shoe slid slowly up and down the back of his leg. She leaned forward, elbows on the table, and propped her chin in her hand watching him through lowered lids. A sultry moue pursed her full lips.

"I'm soft and warm, too," she whispered. "Will you eat me tonight with the same...passion?"

A piece of roll caught in his throat. He coughed, bringing his napkin to his mouth just in time to catch the lump of chewed dough. He grabbed his glass and gulped his water.

He set the glass down with a thud as the young waitress, her white apron spattered with food, approached the table.

"How is your meal?" She smiled as she tucked a few strands of loose hair behind her ear.

"Fine," he squeaked. He cleared his throat. "Pardon me. Thank you, everything is delicious."

He moved his leg again and gave Annali what he hoped was a disapproving glare.

The waitress glanced at Annali then back to him. "Pie and coffee are included with your meal. We have blueberry, blackberry, and apple. Can I bring you a piece?"

"None for me," Annali said.

"And you, sir?" the girl asked as she cleared Annali's plate.

"Do you perhaps have any...cake?"

"No, sir. Just pie. Apple, blueberry, or blackberry."

"Apple. No, I think blueberry. Wait, make it apple, please."

"I could bring both if you like, since the lady isn't having hers."

He smiled. "Yes. That sounds good. Thank you."

She smiled back. "You're young Mr. Worthington, right? From the bank?"

"I am." He'd seen her at the teller's window a few times but couldn't recall her name.

"I'm Esther Burgess. My parents own this place."

He stood. "My pleasure, Miss Burgess." Frank, and his wife Florie, had come in about two weeks ago to discuss a business loan. They'd wanted to build a larger restaurant, but their projected cash flow wouldn't have supported the payments. He'd declined their application but had instead suggested they wait for a suitable building to come up for sale. Until then, he'd recommended they continue saving for a more substantial down payment.

"From the way my parents talked, I thought you were much older." Her cheeks flushed. She took a couple of steps back. "I...I didn't mean they talked about you, only the loan. I'm sorry, I'll get your pie. Congratulations on your marriage. Papa told me." She nodded to Annali, then whirled away back to the kitchen.

"Cake, pie? I thought you didn't like sweets." Annali said as he lowered himself back to his seat and replaced his napkin.

Had he said that? Ah yes, the peach turnovers. She'd brought them for him, but that was before Lathrop had said yes, before Alex could finally allow himself permission to indulge.

"I'm afraid I wasn't feeling well last night."

Her doubt showed in the furrows across her brow.

The other day in Lathrop's office, Alex had struggled with the possibility he might have had to lie about the bruises on his face. Now lies seemed to roll off his tongue with ease.

But with only three weeks before they parted ways, there was no reason to share anything so personal with Annali. Yet part of him wished he could confide—

Esther returned and set down two large slices of pie. They looked wonderful, but his enthusiasm for eating was gone.

****

Once the door of their hotel room shut, Annali turned to face him and rested her forearms onto his shoulders. Meeting his gaze, she whispered, "What would you like me to do for you tonight?"

He pondered how to respond as a myriad of fantasies flashed through his mind. Now that he'd finally given himself permission to lose his virginity, if that was possible for a man, he had no idea what to say.

What would she think of him if he fumbled stupidly through the act, like some green youth?

She was a professional though. She'd pretend. Lying the whole time to make him feel as if he were the best she'd ever been with.

"Come on, Alex, tell me. What do you want?"

He was paying her after all. This way they'd both get what they needed. He closed his eyes to better sort through the mental images. All his blood seemed to flow to his groin, as his shaft swelled with need. Was he really going to do this?

Her deft fingers undid his tie and popped free the buttons of his collar and shirt.

"Sometimes," he whispered. "I dream...of a woman...on her knees in front of me."

Her lips brushed over his jaw. Her hands slid down his chest to his waist. Her skirts rustled. Then her hands slowly undid the buttons of his trousers.

He swallowed—opened his eyes. He stood before her, his shoulders supported against the door, his clothing undone, his engorged shaft exposed to her waiting mouth.

He reached for her, his fingers sliding into her hair to tangle among the pins and upswept tendrils.

Her tongue brushed over his tip, and he groaned. He'd waited so long for this, and now the moment was here, Ivy fully clothed, on her knees before him, taking control, making his fantasy real.

Was this act one in which his father had indulged when he frequented houses of ill repute? Was this how it started for Samuel Worthington, to have his depraved fantasies fulfilled by...*Damn!* Urges so sinful they could never be satisfied in the marriage bed.

Her mouth closed over his shaft, even as its strength began to wane. She looked up.

He jerked his hands from her hair; his fingers snagging.

"Ow." She pulled back. Her hat fell to the floor as her hair tumbled down her back.

She frowned as he tucked himself away and buttoned his trousers.

"What's wrong?" She picked up her hat along with a few scattered hair pins and stood.

"Nothing. It's been a long day, and I'm tired." He

walked to the window, pulled down the shade, and yanked the curtains closed, blocking out the late-setting sun. "I think it best we...get in bed and...go to sleep."

"What? Now? It's not even eight o'clock."

He turned from the window, trying to ignore her confused expression. "As I said, it's been a long day, and I'm quite fatigued."

Walking past her, he picked up his Gladstone and stepped behind the dressing screen.

"All right," she said, her voice light and teasing. "But do we have to go to sleep right away? Maybe we could...play a game or two first."

He set his bag on the luggage rack, then removed first his coat, then waistcoat, draping each over the top of the screen before he pulled his shirt over his head. "I've never been one to indulge in the frivolity of silly games."

Soft thumps, the rustle of skirts and petticoats. He swallowed as he imagined what she might look like in a nightgown. Not flannel, something silky, that clung to her as she moved.

"I think I know a few games you might enjoy."

There was a soft popping sound as Annali continued to undress. Was that the sound of her corset coming off? He was tempted to spy through the narrow space between the panels of the screen. Instead, he focused on removing his shoes and stockings. "No thank you. A good night's rest is all I want."

They'd shared a bed less than twenty-four hours ago. Yet so much had changed during the course of this day. Maybe things were moving faster than he could handle. Maybe they should talk, as they had last night, get to know one another better. He doubted his father had taken the time to know the women he'd slept with.

Alex pulled his night shirt over his head. At least they'd be clothed, not as many layers as last night, but not—

The bed springs squeaked.

Alex swallowed. This would be fine. He dug between his folded shirts and drawers, hunting for his slippers. He and Annali would talk, get to know each other better— *Ouch!* He jerked back his hand, the tip of his index finger bleeding.

He stuck the digit in his mouth as he pushed aside the extra shirt and drawers packed in his bag. The jugum penis. He'd jabbed his finger on one of the serrated teeth of his metal pollutions ring. He'd worn the thing every night for so many years, he almost reached for it now.

No. This was his wedding night. He would proceed as any other God-fearing husband. He would get into bed. They would talk for a bit, then he'd kiss her on the cheek and say good night. Once it was fully dark, he'd lift her night gown, place himself between her legs, and quickly enter her.

There was no need for acts of depravity. He'd be satisfied. She'd be… Was it possible for women to enjoy copulation?

Tying his robe closed, he stepped from behind the screen and looked toward the bed.

Annali lay on her side, covered only by the sheet, her head propped up by her elbow, her shoulders bare.

He gulped. Was she actually lying…*naked*…beneath the sheet? His cock stirred to life. How would it feel to stretch out beside her, his bare limbs rubbing against hers, the heat of her body warming him?

The top of the sheet barely covered her bosom. He'd never seen naked bosoms before, just the teasing outline of their shape beneath a woman's clothes. He'd thought about bosoms many times. Overheard the hushed conversations, the jokes, and laughter from both the other boys at school and the young men in college. The twin mounds were soft and had perky nipples he was supposed to touch and taste.

She grinned. "What are you wearing?"

His gaze followed the line of her silhouette beneath the sheet, to where her waist dipped down, then up over the curve of her hip and down the tapered outline of her thigh.

"Where is your night gown?"

She laughed. "In my trunk. I could sleep in my chemise, but it's your wedding night, so what the hell?" She flipped back the sheet on the empty side of the bed. "Come on, Alex, take your robe off and lie next to me."

He stepped to the foot of the bed. His fingers fumbled with the knot at his waist. In his nervousness, he must have yanked the woolen belt too tight. What would she think of him now? An inept virgin whose fingers tangled in his robe. He was afraid to look her way. Afraid she would be grinning. Finally, his fingers worked free the knot. He slipped off his robe and draped it over the footrail.

"A night shirt? I thought you wanted to have fun."

He stepped toward the empty side of the bed. "I do want to have *fun* as you say, but I want to do things properly."

She grinned mischievously. "Properly is when we are both naked."

No. That was not right. He climbed into bed, and

lying on his back, pulled the sheet up to his chin.

She rolled close. Her heat warmed his entire side. She toyed with the buttons on his night shirt. "I don't understand. It feels like there's two of you. A tall, male version of your mother, laced up tight, rigid, and rude. Then there is my Alex. The man who smiles and enjoys good food, who wants to explore his natural desires. I feel like I'm in bed with the first one, and I don't like him very much."

"I'm sorry you feel this way, but this is who I am."

"What are you so afraid of?"

"Nothing. Go to sleep."

She laughed. "Now? The sun hasn't even gone down."

"I have a book in my bag you might borrow."

"Alex, I told you, I don't read. I never went to school. I can read some. Enough to read signs and follow recipes, but I never read a book."

"Yes. Well, then lie still."

Her hand slid beneath the sheet, lightly skimming over his stomach. The muscles of his abdomen tightened. Her fingers brushed over his hip and down his thigh.

"Stop," he croaked.

She grasped his night shirt and inched the fabric toward his waist.

His skin tingled. His shaft hardened, more rigid and swollen than he'd ever felt before. "Don't."

He squeezed his eyes against the mounting pressure, aching for release, desperate to know how it would feel, terrified of the kind of man he might become. "Stop," he whispered through clenched teeth.

Her fingers wrapped around his length. His hips thrust up, then down. He groaned low in his throat.

Her palm rolled over his tip. "Don't stop? All right, I won't." Warm and slippery her hand slid down his shaft then up, and—

He came—exploding his release into her hand as tremors rippled through his body. Time and place vanished in this pulsating sensation of overwhelming bliss.

Then he was done, spent, washed out, and limp.

"God, Annali, that was…"

She chuckled and flashed him a smile. "I'd say you were saving that one up for a while." She threw aside the covers and rose from the bed. "You should probably take off that nightshirt. It's a bit sticky. I'll get a wash rag."

He'd never seen a naked woman before. Her hair hung to the middle of her back, just above the curve of her waist. She walked to the wash basin with the same confidence she had walking through town. Did a woman's hips always sway like that, or was it because she was a lady of the night, schooled in the art of seduction? His fingers itched to grab her bottom, one smooth white globe in each hand. His shaft stirred.

*No*, he told himself.

Lifting the pitcher, she poured water in the basin. A moment later she turned.

His gaze went straight to her breasts. Round and full, with dark centers. The urge to bury his face between them, to lick, and nip, and taste, slammed into him with such force that he almost groaned as his shaft rose in anticipation.

He rolled toward the window, away from the temptation of her, presenting her with his back. Mother, Doctor Powell, Reverend Clark, they were all correct. Once he opened the floodgate, lust would consume him the way an addict craved opium. He'd never be satisfied. Like his father, he would always hunger for more. How much time did he have before he crossed the line and became as evil and perverted as the man who sired him?

The mattress dipped under her weight. Her knee brushed his lower back. He wanted to roll toward her, bury his face in the nest of curls he'd only glimpsed.

"You're not going to sleep already, are you? I was hoping we could do this again." She touched his shoulder.

He jumped up. His nightshirt tented in front of him.

She lay on her side. Her hair had fallen forward, covering her breasts. One knee was bent, hiding that most private, most tempting area from his gaze. In one hand she held a damp wash rag, with the other she patted the mattress.

"Come here." Her voice low and sultry. "Take off that nasty nightshirt and lay beside me."

He whirled away from the vision of her, and keeping his gaze on the floor, he moved around the bed. Pausing, he snatched the wash rag from her hand and ducked behind the dressing screen.

"Alex, where are you going?"

"Changing my nightshirt." He stared into his open bag. He'd only packed one. What was he going to wear?

"Do you need some help?"

"No!" Had that high pitched squeak come from him? She must think of him as nothing more than a silly virgin schoolboy.

The deep sigh from the bed held a bite of irritation. He had to hurry. Fortunately, as he wiped himself off, his shaft wilted. How was he going to survive the next ten hours?

He had a clean pair of drawers in here somewhere. The thick cotton would cover him from his waist to just below his knees. He pulled them on then tugged off his night shirt, catching a whiff of himself as it whisked over his head.

He balled it up and shoved it under the blood-stained shirt from yesterday morning. His fingers brushed over the metal device he'd pricked his finger on earlier.

"Alex, I'm waiting."

Her sultry sing-song voice urged him to hurry. He tugged a clean undershirt over his head and buttoned it to the top. Stepping from behind the screen, he walked slowly around the bed and eased carefully onto his side, facing the window.

Her hand settled on his waist. He shoved it away. "Stop. Go to sleep."

Several long moments passed. The tension in his muscles eased. His shallow breaths grew longer, more natural.

A hand touched his groin and stilled.

She gasped. "What the hell is that?"

Chapter Nine

Alex shoved her hand away. "Nothing. Leave me alone." She grew so quiet; he hoped that was the end of it.

"Is this what you like? Pain?"

He sighed. "Go to sleep."

"I've had a few gentlemen who liked to be tied up and some wanted to be spanked or switched with a riding crop. But that other…I've heard about it. There are very secret places for men who like pain."

"I don't like pain."

"I never understood it. Is that what you want? Is that why you didn't want an ordinary church-going wife?"

"I told you… I don't like pain."

"Then why are you wearing that…thing?"

He sighed and eased himself carefully to sit on the side of the bed.

The mattress shifted as she scooted up behind. He closed his eyes so he wouldn't see her, but it did no good. In his mind he saw her walking toward him, and his shaft swelled against the inner band of the ring, expanding toward the jagged teeth of the outer ring.

Her hand rested at the back of his head. Her fingers sifted through his hair, massaging his scalp.

"We have all night," she whispered.

All he needed do was turn slightly, and he'd be able to bury his face between her breasts, lean into her, and they'd both be supine with him on top.

She leaned close. Her breath warm against his ear.

"Tell me how you want it." The moist pressure of her tongue slipped over the outer curve of his ear. Heat flooded his groin.

He flinched and sucked a long inhale of breath between his teeth as the sharp points of the jugum device pierced the thin skin at the base of his shaft.

He jumped up, squeezing his eyes tight. This wasn't a good idea. He turned his back to her and slipped his hand inside his drawers, fumbling to turn the screw that unlocked the device.

"What are you doing?"

He slid it off and turned, holding it in one hand.

There she sat, her hair with that swath of yellow falling around her shoulders, watching him, comfortable with her own nudity.

"Is that it? Can I see?"

What did it matter? He shrugged and passed it over.

A slight frown marred the smoothness of her brow as she studied the double rings. "Is this blood?"

He stepped close and peered at the tiny dark dots on the tips of a few shiny teeth.

She swiped one of the points with her finger and held it up.

Heat singed his cheeks and the tips of his ears. How could she sit here totally nude, talking about such intimate matters as casually as one might discuss the weather?

"That's its purpose."

"If you don't like being hurt, why do wear it?"

"To maintain control over my carnal nature, to keep from going blind, from going insane, from becoming—"

Her eyebrows shot toward her hairline. Her mouth dropped open, and she laughed.

His spine stiffened against the pain of the sound. Why had he shared that secret with her? Was this proof of the correlation between sexual release and insanity?

He held out his hand, and she set the device in his palm. "Do not mock me, Miss Annali. I'm not paying you for that."

She stiffened. Her lips pressed together in a tight line. A gleam of defiance lit her eyes, or was it pain?

Had he hurt her? No. She knew what she was, and this was business. No emotional entanglements.

He closed his hand around the jugum, walked around the bed, behind the screen and tossed the jagged ring into his bag. What was wrong with him? He'd dreamed of a night like this for so long, and now that it was here, he was saying cruel things and cowering behind this dressing screen.

"It's still early," he said. "I have some work to catch up on at the bank."

"Alex, I'm sorry. Come to bed. Let me make it up to you. It's your wedding night."

His wedding night. He ran his fingers through his hair. What would people think if they learned he'd chosen to ignore his beautiful young wife and instead slept at the bank? That would add to the gossip tenfold.

He stepped from behind the screen and climbed into bed, staring at the ceiling.

She rolled toward him and propped her head in her hand.

At least the sheet now covered her breasts. "Go to sleep, Annali." He rolled onto his side and stared at the curtains.

The mattress shifted as she moved away from him. Back-to-back, not touching, not speaking. A fine way to start a marriage.

Except this wasn't a real marriage. He'd married her so he could know the pleasures of intimacy while having the blessing of God, and to know the release of an orgasm without any emotional entanglements. So, why was he lying here while his every fantasy-come-true lay inches away?

Because he was Goddamn fool, that's why. A God. Damn. Fool.

\*\*\*\*

Up with the sun, the hotel dining room wasn't yet open so Annali walked beside Alex to the Burgess Café for breakfast.

She enjoyed a muffin and a bowl of strawberries, while across the table, Alex remained subdued, having ordered only a piece of dry toast, a soft-boiled egg, and a glass of water.

"Would you like half of my muffin?"

He tore off a corner of his toast and dipped it in the yolk. "No, thank you."

"Some strawberries?"

"No. Thank you."

Annali poured a bit of cream in her coffee and took a sip. Well, he was in a mood. Probably came from being in an aroused state all night and unable to sleep.

"Wasn't the sunrise beautiful?"

He glanced up. "I hadn't noticed."

"I saw you looking out the window. The whole sky glowed. How could you not notice? Pink and mauve, orange and yellow as high as they were wide."

He ran his fingers back and forth over the edge of the table as though fascinated by the grain. "Forgive me for not noticing the colors of the sunrise, but while you may be used to mornings of idleness, I still have a bank to run, and I've been away for three days."

She frowned. Alex-the-ass was back. She picked out the largest strawberry in her bowl and held it a moment in front of her mouth.

Their gazes met.

She ran her tongue over and around the berry then slid it between her lips and sank her teeth into the fruit. She set the stem on the side of her plate as she swiped her tongue over her bottom lip, licking off the bit of juice which lingered there.

"Stop that," he said, his voice little more than a croaking whisper.

She picked up another strawberry and taking her time, put it between her lips, and took a bite.

"Stop eating those," he rasped. He lifted his napkin from his lap and tossed it beside his plate.

Leaning forward, she propped her elbows on the table and folded her hands together, resting her chin on her thumbs. "Why did you marry me? I thought it was because I'm a—"

"Quiet," he shushed in a harsh whisper. "Don't speak of such things here." His gaze darted around the room.

She picked up a strawberry, put it to her lips, then pulled it away, still holding it between her fingers.

"Two nights, Alex." She brought the strawberry to her mouth, slipped it between her lips again, and slowly pulled it out. "And we didn't even enjoy *such things.*"

She ran her tongue over and around the berry.

"Then when I saw you wearing that—" She bit the strawberry in half.

Alex jumped up, his cheeks red. He came around the

table, grabbed her hand, and pulled her from her seat. His fingers squeezing hers tight, he wove around tables filled with customers and virtually dragged her out the front door.

She trotted behind him back the way they'd come, until he turned abruptly and pulled her into an alley alongside a bank with tall, barred windows.

She yanked her hand from his, rubbing her fingers as she glared at him. "What the hell? You want to talk to me, talk, but don't man-handle me, not unless you pay me extra."

The flush in his face deepened. He ran his fingers through his hair, then glanced down as though he expected to find the hat he'd left at the restaurant. He stepped back and leaned against the brick wall. He closed his eyes briefly then sighed.

"I apologize. My behavior was deplorable. It is only that discussing such… You were eating strawberries… In public… I can't… There is a freedom about you…a confidence. You don't care what others think. I wish I had your strength."

She shook her head and stepped up beside him, leaning her shoulder against the wall. "You're wrong. I do care what people think. I've always been judged. Two days ago, I never would have been allowed to eat in a restaurant like that, talk to a respectable woman like Esther, or stay in a nice hotel. Being with you, having everyone here believe I'm a decent woman… You're right, a proper woman doesn't discuss *such things* in public."

He reached for her hand. "I too have been judged my whole life. I know how it feels to have people stare and whisper behind my back. Perhaps, in that respect, we share some commonality."

"But why? You own a bank. You're a gentleman."

He gave his head a slight shake. "Things are not always as they seem."

He turned toward her. "Regardless, I should not have behaved in such a forceful manner. I apologize. It won't happen again." He raised her hand, and leaning forward, kissed her knuckles.

Releasing her fingers, he checked his pocket watch. "I do have an early meeting for which I must prepare. I also have work piled up from three days away, and I'm short a teller, so I will have to be on the floor if we get busy."

He snapped closed the cover and slipped the watch into the small pocket of his waistcoat.

"Can I help?"

He gave her a quick grin. "I'm not sure the people of Fremont are ready to trust their money to a woman."

"What do you want me to do all day?" She reached up and brushed at some dust on his shoulder.

"The new bed will be delivered today. You might visit Mrs. Lindberg at the Furniture Emporium on Fifth and D Streets. Pick out the necessary bed linens, blankets, and such. The decoration of your room in Lincoln looked nice."

"But the pinks and reds I had in Lincoln may not match with your wall papers and curtains."

"My room has no colors. Choose what you like. I have no preference. There is also a dress shop across the street. Miss Sinek carries a variety of fabrics. You mentioned a need for respectable clothes. The dress you're wearing will be fine for church—"

*Church?*

"—but feel free to choose enough fabric to sew a couple of everyday dresses and perhaps a set of window curtains."

*Sew?*

"Ask Mrs. Lindberg to put it on my account and have everything delivered to my house. There is also a millinery shop a few doors down from there. The hat you're wearing is damaged. Perhaps a new one. You look pretty in hats."

"But this will all be so expensive."

"Don't worry. You like pretty things. I want you to have them. When the sale closes on the bank in a few weeks, I'll be more than able to settle the accounts."

He reached for her hand. "And Annali, the sale of the bank is confidential. You are the only one who knows."

She smiled and pressed her palm against his cheek. "Don't worry. I've been keeping secrets my whole life."

"Thank you." He moved her hand to his mouth and gave her knuckles another quick kiss.

"When you finish shopping, come to the bank. We close at noon on Saturdays. We can eat out then I'll show you around town."

"Now, this is my Alex." She stood on her tip toes and brushed his lips with a quick kiss.

He backed away. His cheeks tinted pink once again. He glanced around and over his shoulder.

Few people were out this early. A buggy and a wagon rattled past; no one seemed to notice either her or Alex standing in the shadows.

"Properly bred ladies do not display affection in public."

So, he was back to that again. "Well, they should.

Maybe then their husbands wouldn't come looking for me."

He walked to the front of the alley and stepped on to the walk, waiting as she came up beside him. "I arranged to have our bags sent over to the house later this morning." He hurried up the front steps and unlocked the door. "Enjoy your day," he said then disappeared inside.

Annali turned and strolled down the wooden walk. She peered into the windows of a butcher shop, a grocery, and a billiards hall, before she came upon Lindberg's Dry Goods and Fine Furniture Emporium. According to the sign hanging in the glass pane of the front door, the store wouldn't open until nine o'clock. She hated to go back to the hotel and wait in the lobby, so she wandered back to the restaurant. She'd fetch Alex's hat and sit at a table enjoying a second cup of coffee as though she belonged.

Every table in the room was full. A few men stood inside forming a line across the front window. Not sure if it was improper for a lady to wait with the men, she moved to a spot on the opposite side of the door.

Esther hurried in from the kitchen, balancing four plates of food. She set them on the table nearest the door.

The man closest to her helped pass out the meals to his friends. "Thank you, miss. Looks good."

She smiled. "Enjoy."

Esther started toward the kitchen then turned back to Annali. "I found young Mr. Worthington's hat. I'll fetch it for you in a minute."

"Hey, Esther," a man called from across the room. "When are you coming to take our order?"

"I can see you're busy. I'll get it."

"Thank you, missus. It's on the table inside the

kitchen door."

"Esther, where's our eggs?"

Across the room, a man held up his coffee cup. Esther headed in his direction.

Annali wove between the tables and pushed open the kitchen door. A wave of heat slammed her in the face. The smoky aroma of bacon filled the space, mixed with cinnamon, and the faint vinegary scent of baking sourdough bread.

Standing in front of a wide black stove, an older woman flipped two steaks which sizzled when they hit the pans. She glanced up. Beads of sweat dotted her forehead. Frizzy whisps of gray hair, curled around her face.

"You're late," she snapped before turning back to grind pepper across the tops of the steaks. "I thought my husband told you. You're to start at four." She grabbed a bowl and basket of eggs.

"Start washing those dishes over there. We need plates."

"Ma'am, I'm not—"

"I can see that. Next time don't wear your Sunday best and don't be late." She set the bowl on the worktable and began breaking eggs."

"But ma'am—"

"Aprons are hanging on the back door. Get busy." Tucking the bowl under her arm, she grabbed a whisk and began beating the eggs. "I need those plates."

Annali shrugged and headed toward the door. She had nothing else to do, and the woman obviously needed help. After setting aside her hat, Annali tied on the apron. Taking a large pot, she drew off hot water from the reservoir on the back of a second stove.

She scraped the excess food into a slop bucket and dropped each plate into the hot water. With a soapy rag she washed the plates, rinsing them in a pan of cold water, before setting them on a wooden rack to dry.

Annali stayed focused on her task, as Esther rushed in and out to leave orders and pick up food. Pots and pans clattered as Mrs. Burgess cooked, and Annali worked her way through the pile of dirty utensils and cookware.

Gradually the rush of customers slowed. Esther pushed through the kitchen door. "Whew! What a morning."

"I've never seen such a busy Saturday." The older woman heaved a sigh. "Good thing your father hired some help. Girl!" she called out. "I'm sorry, I forgot to ask your name."

Annali turned, wiping her hands on a towel. She met Esther's gaze.

Esther gasped.

Annali smiled and shrugged.

"Mama, this isn't the girl Papa hired. Do you know who this is?"

Mrs. Burgess glanced from her daughter to Annali.

"This is young Mr. Worthington's new wife."

The woman's face paled. She staggard back a step, reaching behind to steady herself on the worktable.

"She came in to fetch her husband's hat."

"Oh, dear Lord. Mrs. Worthington, I am so sorry. Please, forgive me."

Annali draped the towel over the edge of the dry sink. "There's nothing to forgive. I saw how busy you were. You needed help. I didn't mind."

"And I ordered you around like a common— Oh, dear Lord. Our loan!"

"Mrs. Burgess, please don't be upset. Truly, I didn't mind. I'll just take Alex's hat and go."

"Alex. Oh, dear Lord, she calls him Alex. Our loan, please, Mrs. Worthington, don't tell him."

Annali headed for the door pausing to reach for Alex's hat. She turned to Esther. "Please tell your mother everything is fine. I didn't mind helping, and I'm sure none of this will affect whatever business your family has with Alex."

Chapter Ten

The bell jangled overhead as Annali pushed open the door of the dry goods store. Rakes, shovels, pitchforks, and brooms hung on the far, left wall. At the end of the center aisle, against the back wall, bolts of white cloth had been jammed side by side within two rows of shelves. In front stood a long, wide table.

A woman emerged from a curtained area behind a counter with a cash register at one end. "Can I help you, *signorina*?"

Annali didn't have her mother's Nordic height, but this woman in a pretty floral print dress of yellows and blues, barely reached Annali's nose.

"I'm looking for bedsheets."

"*Sì.*" She gestured to the variety of white fabrics in varying weights and weaves, from cheese cloth to heavy canvas. "How many sheets you make?"

*Make?*

"I…do you have any made?" Annali searched the older woman's face hoping…

"I am sorry. We do not carry finished sheets."

Maybe she could buy a large piece and tuck it in all around the mattress.

"There is a dressmaker's shop across the way. Miss Jane Sinek. You ask, she maybe hem these for you. How large your mattress?"

"I don't know. But Al—Mr. Worthington purchased it yesterday."

"*Ah!* We think, why young Mr. Worthington, does

he buy this bed? Does he maybe take a wife? You then are his young bride, *sì*?" The woman reached out her hands, her joints swollen and knobby, and clasped Annali's hand. "*Che bello*." She pulled Annali into a hug.

The woman's dark hair, streaked with gray, tickled Annali's nose so that if the woman hadn't let go at that moment, Annali would have sneezed.

The woman pressed her hand to her chest. "I am Mrs. Lindberg."

Lindberg sounded more Swedish than Italian. Annali nodded. "Alex told me you order books for him."

"*Sì*. Young Mr. Worthington, he such a sweet boy. You take away his sadness. No?"

She bent down and pulled a bolt of Holland cloth from the row. Turning, she tossed it toward the table, where it landed with a thud.

Annali hadn't considered Alex to be a sad man. Lonely maybe, or bitter.

The woman flipped the bolt of cloth over, unrolling it as she moved down the length of the table. "And you no believe what they say. Remember, the *polizia*, they find no proof young Mr. Worthington do such a terrible thing."

She measured the cloth along the yardstick fastened to the edge of the table, then pulled a pair of scissors from her apron and snipped the cloth.

What had Alex done? She wanted to ask, but this tiny woman was his defender. She'd never divulge any of young Mr. Worthington's secrets.

Mrs. Lindberg's crippled fingers gripped the fabric and ripped, tearing it straight across, free from the bolt.

"He buy for you the pretty white, brass and iron bed

we display in the window, and the expensive spring mattress."

She returned the bolt to the shelf and began flipping open the white linen.

"Two under sheets you will need to protect that good horsehair mattress he buy. Only the best for his young bride."

Why would Alex spend so much? He knew she wouldn't be here long.

"And linen for pillowcases and two top and bottom sheets. Two Witney blankets, four pillows, a bolster... What have you brought with you, *signora*? Have you embroidered shams for your top pillows? Quilted a comforter for your bed?"

"I...um...no." She glanced down at Alex's hat, still gripped in her hand. "No. Nothing."

The woman looked up. "No hope chest?"

*Hope chest? Holy Hell, what was that?*

Annali had a trunk full of dresses, petticoats, and nightgowns, and with half her money gone, not a lot of hope.

"You have nothing of your mama's?"

Annali shook her head. *Think!* "There was a fire," she blurted out. "In Chicago." Annali and her mother had actually left years before, but she'd heard about it.

"The fire? *Mamma mia!*" The woman returned the bolt to the shelf and began to neatly fold the linen and holland cloth. "No worries, *cara*. Young Mr. Worthington's mother, his sister, they will help you, *sì?*"

Annali laughed. She slapped her hand over her mouth and caught the next short bark of sound in the back of her throat. She coughed.

Mrs. Lindberg came around the table and grasped

Annali's other hand. "You are all right?"

"Yes, ma'am." Annali cleared her throat. "I must have swallowed a bug."

"Then come." The woman pulled Annali to the counter where she set the fabric, then through a wide, open doorway into a large room filled with tables and chairs, sofas, cabinets, commodes, sideboards, and bed frames.

They continued to the back of the room where blankets, pillows, and comforters were stacked. The woman picked out everything Annali would need and assured her it would be delivered along with the bed later this morning.

Once Annali was able to escape Mrs. Lindberg's store, she carried the paper-wrapped bed linens, with Alex's hat perched on top, across the street to the dress shop.

Colorful bolts of fabric filled one entire wall. Captivated by all the beautiful colors, she stared. The pink was pretty. Or the light blue with the lavender stripe. She ran her finger across deep plum satin. It would make a lovely ball gown, off the shoulder, with a scoop neckline, fitted bodice, and a long train. She'd seen a picture of a gown like that in one of Anémone's ladies' magazines.

Annali had never been to a ball, but she could imagine. Sometimes wealthy men took women like her to fancy house parties. Her place in San Francisco or Denver would cater only to those rich men. How much money would she need to open such an establishment?

Alex was paying her half of his share from the sale. She imagined it would be a lot, but would it be enough? She should have asked for a specific number.

A mulberry satin with a floral jacquard pattern caught her eye. In her mind she envisioned it as a waistcoat for Alex. All she'd ever seen him wear was a loose-fitting, high-buttoned, single breasted black wool. This fabric would look wonderful with his complexion, and it could be fashioned in the newer double-breasted style with the deeper, wider, notched lapels.

She could pay for it with her own money and give it to him as a gift. The sudden wave of sentimentality left her confused. Turning away from the fabrics, she headed to a rack of ready-made dresses and focused her attention on finding a practical day dress for herself that wasn't too plain.

Two dress forms in the center of the shop caught her attention. On one a simple blue, violet, and green calico print, with a high neckline and long sleeves perfect for every day. On the other form, a beautiful striped, teal blue gown. The stripes alternated dull and shiny in a vertical pattern except for the underskirt which was horizontal. A row of ruffles flared outward from the waist toward the back, and met two rows of ruffles around the bottom, the stripes of one row angled left the second angled right. More ruffles in the same alternating design spilled down from the center back.

"Can I help you?"

"Yes, how much is this dress?"

\*\*\*\*

Two hours later, Annali left the shop. Miss Sinek had taken her measurements and promised to have the green calico dress altered and ready to be picked up later that afternoon along with the hemmed sheets. A pink and red gingham and the teal satin dress would be ready in a week. Annali picked out a black petticoat to wear under the teal dress and a boring white for the calico. Two waistcoats—one in the mulberry jacquard and the other to match her teal dress—would be ready in a few days.

She winced when she heard the total. How would Alex react when he received the bill? Would he be angry? Some men had no reservations when it came to buying hats and jewelry for their mistress but resented their wife spending money on extra ribbon and lace.

What the hell? She'd likely be gone before he received the bill, and if he went back on his word and didn't pay her, at least she'd come out of the arrangement with something of value.

Alex had told her to buy a new hat, and by the time she left the millinery she'd chosen two. One in black with black feathers to match the dark teal and a plain straw one with small purple flowers for every day. Most of the women she saw wore bonnets, but Annali refused to allow her head to be swallowed up inside an ugly cotton shroud. She didn't spend time in the sun anyway.

After arranging to pick up her purchases later, Annali strolled toward the bank, Alex's hat in her hand. She paused now and then to look in store windows, nodding and smiling when men touched their hat brims. The few women she passed actually continued walking on the same side of the street.

She could get used to this. Happily, she lifted her skirt hem, ascended the bank's stone steps, and opened the door. She stood on the threshold a moment, drew a deep breath, and closed the door.

So, this was where Alex worked. She'd never been inside a bank, but this somber place with its dark woodwork, brass finishes, and teller cages felt grim. Even the patches of sunshine spilling across the tiled floor appeared harsh, streaked with the shadowed lines from the window bars.

Two high, narrow writing desks, their cubbyholes filled with paper, stood back-to-back in the center of the room. A scruffy man in dusty clothes and high boots stood at one desk writing on a piece of paper.

Dividing the width of the room from the outside wall to the center, were three caged windows. Only one appeared open and two women stood in line.

In the middle of the back wall was the imposing door of what had to be the vault. Madame had a safe in the corner of her office, but nothing as impressive as this.

This door—nearly two feet taller than the bank teller—was curved at the top and surrounded by beaded black molding. Fancy red and gold lettering arched over the landscape of a lake. Were there shelves of gold bars, bags of coins, and stacks of paper bills inside? Would Alex let her see if she smiled sweetly?

Shifting her attention from the vault, she started toward a gate within the low railing which stretched from the teller windows to the far wall. On the other side of the railing stood a wide desk, where an older man sat writing in a large book with green pages.

Beyond him was a door with lettering which read, *Private*. Madame Beauchamp had the same letters on the door to her office.

Since Alex wasn't out here, she headed toward that door. She pushed through the gate.

The man behind the desk jumped to his feet. "Can I help you?"

She smiled. "Yes, I'm here to see Alex."

"Alex?" His brow furrowed. He glanced at the hat in her hand. "Mr. Worthington?"

"Yes."

"Do you have an appointment?"

"No, he told me to come by. We're going out to lunch."

"Lunch? With Mr. Worthington?"

She chuckled. "Yes. I'm his wife."

"W-w-wife?" He stumbled to a halt. His mouth dropped open.

Her grin widened, and she pointed her index finger toward the door. "I'll just go on in." Stepping up to the door, she turned the knob and pushed inward.

Alex sat at his desk, writing across a piece of white paper, a small stack of written pages set to the side. His head jerked up. "Get ou—"

Annali froze, her fingers still on the knob.

"Annali, wait!" He shoved back his chair, shooting to his feet. "My apologies. I thought you were—"

She closed the door behind her and stood squeezing his hat brim. "I'll come back."

He removed his spectacles and waved her into the room. "No. Please. Come in."

She eased up to his desk, placed his hat on the corner, and stepped back.

He set down his glasses and ran his fingertips along the edge of his desk. "I did not mean to bark at you. It's only that I prefer to work in private, undisturbed."

She nodded. "I understand. I'll wait for you out there."

"No." His gaze met hers. "You are welcome in my office anytime."

His hand reached out, and taking her wrist, he drew her up beside him. Slowly he lowered himself into the chair pulling her into his lap. His arms wrapped around her waist.

She met his gaze and smiled. He was so sweet. What was he supposed to have done?

Mrs. Lindberg had said something about there being no proof. Was that why he'd mentioned that he knew how it felt to be judged?

She rested her head against his shoulder and sighed.

His chin came to rest against her head as one hand slipped leisurely up and down her back.

"Mr. Worthington?"

Alex jerked back, setting her on her feet as he jumped up.

Chapter Eleven

"What is it?" he called striding toward the door.

"I have Farley's drawer here. Did you still want to cash it out? I can stay and do it if you…"

Alex yanked open the door and snatched the cash drawer from Goldman's hands. "Next time, knock."

"I did, but you… Yes, sir. Sorry, sir."

Goldman turned away, snatching his hat off the hat rack. Alex followed him out.

"Good day, sir." Goldman stepped outside and pulled the door closed behind him.

Alex flipped the sign to *Closed* and turned the lock. When he returned to his office Annali sat at his desk, reading his pages.

"What are you doing?" He strode across the room and dropped the cash drawer on the corner of his desk. Reaching across, he snatched away the pages. "This is private."

Her chin came up, and she glared at him. "You left them right here."

He raised his gaze to the ceiling and sighed. Of course. She was right. He was upset with himself, not Annali.

Goldman likely assumed why Alex hadn't heard the knocking. That Alex, like his father, had been deaf to Goldman's knocks, because he'd been sitting in this same chair, kissing, running his hands up the back of a—

He yanked open the bottom drawer.

"Holy Hell, I can't even read your damn papers. I don't know where Alex-the-Ass suddenly came from, but don't take it out on me."

Their gazes clashed.

She was right—again. He was being an ass. None of this was her fault. He sighed. "I'm not upsct with you."

"Like hell you're not."

"I…I'm…" He ran his fingers through his hair. "I'm angry with…" His hand slid around the back of his neck.

*The sins of the father shall be visited upon the son. The sins of the father shall be visited upon the son.*

"Believe me, this entire situation hasn't anything to do with you. Perhaps I have erred by bringing you into it." He glanced at his hand and the pages he'd unconsciously rolled tight inside his fist.

"Alex, I'm only doing this for the money you promised me. So, I'll pretend and play any gamc you want. But you've got to tell me the rules."

"Fair enough. Pretend to be my loving wife. And in about three weeks this will all be over."

As satisfied as he could be for the moment, he rolled his pages the opposite way to smooth out the curl, then knocked the edges against the surface of his desk to neatly align them, allowing himself those moments to calm down. Maybe this bout of temper was another warning sign. Three weeks and this business with the bank would be over. He'd be free to go wherever he wanted, to do whatever he wanted before—

He lifted the lid on the false bottom of the open drawer.

Annali leaned close. "Too bad you weren't carrying that the other morning."

He stared down at the pocket revolver and the thin box of cartridges. "Yes," he whispered and dropped his pages on top. With the toe of his shoe, he pushed the drawer closed. He straightened and met her gaze.

She rose. Stepping around him, she trailed her fingers across the back of his shoulders.

He swallowed.

She slipped around the desk and wandered the perimeter of the room, her bustle swaying with her hips.

He glanced at the clock. At least eight hours to go.

She passed a wall of shelves stuffed with books, ledgers, and thick tomes on finance and investment. Stopping in front of the file drawers, she tipped her head seeming to study the imperfections in the wall rather than the portrait of President Hayes.

"Is this an old doorway?"

Alex stared at the ridge in the plaster and paint, where it faintly outlined the top portion of what had once been a door made of thick oak and stained dark, like the rest of the wainscoting in the bank. An image flashed through his mind of the room on the day he discovered what had been kept inside.

"Alex?"

"Hmmm?"

"Are you all right?"

"Yes, of course. Just thinking. Bank business you know. Forgive me, what was your question?"

"I asked where the door used to go."

"No place." He pulled the cash drawer close. "A small storeroom. Now that space is occupied by a new, larger vault."

She nodded and reversed her course, continuing back around the room in the opposite direction, trailing her finger along the spines of his books.

"Please." He gestured to one of the two chairs in front of his desk. "I need to cash out this drawer before we can go."

She smiled. "Don't mind me."

At least it was one of her normal, unpracticed smiles.

"Annali, a gentleman doesn't sit if a lady is standing."

She gave a small laugh. "We both know I'm no lady."

"To me you are."

The animation in her face faded, overshadowed by a trace of sadness. "There's no one around. You don't have to pretend."

He gestured toward the chair again. "Please."

Her eyes widened. Stepping back, she pointed toward the lobby. "I'll wait for you out there."

As the door closed behind her, a hollow silence filled the room. He lowered himself into his chair and hooked the side pieces of his spectacles over his ears. Normally he enjoyed the solitude, but now the room felt stifling and oppressive. Tugging at his collar, he drew a deep breath then began counting.

Twenty minutes later, he emerged from his office. She stood gazing out the front window. Noon-day sun spilled over her, leaving her silhouette stretched across the floor.

She turned. A wide smile lit her face. He almost glanced over his shoulder to see who she was looking at, for no one had ever appeared so glad to see him. More than likely, the sunlight had brought that sparkle to her eyes.

Hat in hand, he walked toward her. "Shall we go?"

"I was hoping you'd let me see inside the bank vault when you put the money away."

"The vault has a timer and can't be opened until eight o'clock in the morning, and Mr. Goldman already locked it."

"Then what happened to the money you were counting?"

"I have a hidden wall safe in my office. Why?"

She shrugged.

He leaned against the high writing desk where people filled out their deposit and withdrawal slips. He eyed her thoughtfully. "Do you have funds you wish to deposit?"

She glanced out the window then stepped toward him. "I have some, from the tips the gentlemen leave. I'm saving it to buy my own place." She rested her hand on the desk. "Some place grand…in San Francisco or Denver. Only for rich men. I usually keep it in my trunk, but—"

"Your trunk? With the number of unsavory men in and out of your room who could—"

"I keep it locked." She drew her hand to her side.

"Yet I'm sure you can think of a dozen scenarios in which your savings could be lost. Especially while traveling. A bank is the safest place to keep it. We'll go to the house after we eat and collect your money."

"I have it with me."

He reached out and grasped her hand. "Come." He led her through the gate and around to the back of the teller cages. Pulling open a drawer, he took out a blank deposit form and a small, flat bank booklet. He unscrewed the cap on the inkwell, dipped a pen, and filled out all the information. Glancing up he met her gaze.

She shrugged and began unbuttoning her dress.

He swallowed as the base of her throat was exposed, then more of her chest and finally the lacy top of some undergarment which seemed to push up the twin mounds of her bosom.

She reached between them and tugged free a small cloth bag.

She stared at the bag in her hand as she gnawed her lower lip, then eased back a step. "This is everything I have."

"I understand. Your money will be safe here. Trust me."

Her fingers tightened around the top of the bag. She met his gaze. "Can I? Really, trust you? Mrs. Lindberg told me you did something terrible. Did you?"

He stiffened.

"Tell me the truth."

"The truth," he began, his tone sharp and bitter, "is that whether you choose to believe the gossip or not, none of what happened five years ago has anything to do with you or this bank. Now, do you wish to deposit your money, or would you rather trust it to the whims of fate?"

Her shoulders snapped back, and her chin came up as her lips pressed together.

He sighed. He'd done it again. "My apologies. That was uncalled for." He'd lost track of how many times over the past few days he'd apologized to her. This wasn't who he was, who he wanted to be. Was this further evidence of the encroaching insanity?

Several moments passed as she stared at him, then her gaze softened as the tension in her body slowly dissipated.

"There is something about you Alex. I don't know what it is, or why I should—" She extended her hand.

He hesitated for a moment, almost afraid to believe that she still chose to…

He reached out, and she dropped the bag into his palm. The cloth remained bunched at the top where it had been clenched inside her fist.

That she would give it to him so easily, without explanation, left him awed, that she, a virtual stranger, had enough faith in him to trust…

"That's all of it. Everything I have."

"Thank you," he whispered, lost for any other words. As nervous and apprehensive as he'd been on his first day at the bank, he opened the bag with trembling fingers, the fabric still warm and slightly damp. He shook the contents onto the counter. Mostly greenbacks, some coins, and a few banknotes from Lincoln and Council Bluffs. He carefully counted it all out loud then counted again to be sure.

"Three hundred, forty-three dollars and eighty-seven cents."

The notes from the bank in Lincoln were still good, but he wasn't sure the bank in Council Bluffs still existed. Best to wait and see, but he'd be damned before he'd ever tell her those notes might be worthless. If it came down to his last cent, he'd replace the loss with his own money.

She moved up beside him. "I had more, but Madame Beauchamp said I owed her a hundred and fifty-eight dollars."

"For what?" he asked absently as he filled in the amount of her deposit.

"I owed five weeks rent at eight dollars a week, plus fifty cents for meals. She paid for my dresses when I first went to work there. I gave her money every week, but she said I only paid the interest." She picked up the empty bag and twisted the ties around her fingers.

He nodded, dipped his pen, and continued writing. "What was her interest rate?"

"I don't know."

"Hmmm." He stared through the teller's cage to the street outside. "Seems rather high for a few dresses, even if the interest accrued daily." He went back to his paperwork. "You made a wise decision by leaving her employ."

A few moments later, he slid the form toward her and passed her the pen.

"I just need your signature on the deposit slip and the new account form."

She slowly wrote out her name. Annali Hanson.

"You forgot Worthington."

"What?"

A small smile tugged at the corner of his mouth. "We're married. You legally share my last name."

She glanced at her left hand and the simple gold band he'd insisted on buying.

He passed her the bank book and pointed to her name on the inside cover.

She slid her finger under the letters of his last name. Slowly she copied them onto the end of her signature. "Worthington. Mrs. Alexander Worthington." She glanced up and smiled. "I sound like a real lady with such grand name."

Alex snorted and shook his head. "More like a tainted name."

She frowned. "What do you mean?"

"Never mind." He gave her the bank book and locked everything else in his office safe behind the presidential portrait.

Outside, he placed his hat on his head, offered Annali his arm, and they strolled down Main Street to the Burgess Café.

Nearly every table was full. The Burgess girl wove her way toward them, a stack of dirty dishes in her hands. She grinned at Annali, who smiled back as if the two shared some secret. "There's a table over on the other side," the girl said. "Near the corner."

He cupped Annali's elbow as they wove through the room. At the table he pulled out her chair and nodded to the large blackboard on the wall, on which was written the menu options.

She stared at the board for a moment. "Does that say corn chowder?"

"Yes." He brushed a few crumbs from the table onto the floor. "If you can read the menu, there's no reason you can't learn to read a book."

Her eyes lit up.

He couldn't resist. "We can read together in the evening, if you'd like."

"Yes. I would like."

The girl came to take their order. She reached into her apron pocket then placed two rolled napkins on the table. From her hair, she pulled free a pencil then held it poised over her notepad. "And what would you like? The beef stew or the roast pork meal."

"My wife will have the corn chowder. And I'll have the roast pork with applesauce."

"Green beans?"

"Yes, please."

"And what would you like to drink? Coffee, tea, milk, water?"

Coffee. Should he? How much could he indulge before he felt the effects? He and Annali would be eating at home from now on. This might be his only chance to try it.

When he didn't offer a reply, she turned to Annali.

"I'll have coffee," Annali said. "Cream, no sugar. And could I have a slice of that sourdough bread your mother was baking this morning?"

"And you, sir?"

Should he, or shouldn't he? How did he take it?

"Sir?"

"I'll have the same as my wife."

Annali smiled. She smiled a lot, no doubt a practiced skill from her role as Ivy. Now that he thought about it, how would he know if he was with Annali or Ivy? Did it really matter?

The girl returned with two steaming mugs and a tiny pitcher of cream.

He reached for his coin purse.

"Don't worry about your meal," she said as she set their coffee on the table. "Mama says it's on the house." Her gaze shot to Annali for a quick second.

"Excuse me?" Alex stiffened. His brow furrowed as he searched both their expressions. Something transpired behind his back. That Annali was a part of it pricked at something deep inside. Why should he care anyway? She'd soon be out of his life. No emotional attachments. He was a fool for believing they'd grown closer at the bank. She'd no doubt been using her practiced wiles to gain something from him.

"I will pay for our meal. And you may inform your mother that attempts to ingratiate herself with me in order to sway my decision regarding their loan will not work."

The girl's mouth dropped open. She glanced helplessly at Annali then scurried away.

"Why did you snap at Esther like that?"

He unrolled his napkin and arranged his silverware around an imaginary plate, straightening his fork, knife, and spoon so the bottom edges were perfectly aligned. "I will not allow people to believe they can bribe me with favors to influence—"

"You're leaping to a false conclusion."

"No, it is you who is leaping, casting me as the villain of this narrative because I have refused to accept their offer of—"

"Alex, you're being an ass."

"Excuse me?" His face heated. Even the tips of his ears burned in outrage.

"I helped Mrs. Burgess in the kitchen earlier. They were so busy, and the girl they hired didn't come. So, I helped. A free meal is her way of saying thank you. Why is that so terrible?"

He picked up his coffee cup and sipped. He closed his eyes as a grimace twisted his face, and he forced himself to swallow. He set the cup down and stared at it for a moment. Rather disappointing to discover after years of waiting and longing, that coffee was such a bitter brew.

"Even so." He lifted his gaze to hers. "It creates a perception that others may curry favor in order to garner my approval of their own loans."

"Why does it matter what they think?" She picked

up the small pitcher and poured a bit of cream into her mug. "We know the truth." She reached across the table and added cream to his cup. A bit more than she'd added to her own.

His brow tugged together as he tried to puzzle out her motives. "It's important that I present myself as above reproach."

"Why? People think what they want."

"Please, I only ask that you use better judgement in your language and behavior from this point forward. Everything you do reflects back upon me and therefore the bank."

"Better judgement?" A spark of anger flashed in her eyes. She leaned toward him, her whisper so low he could barely hear it above the conversation in the room. "You are the one who brought me here. You say you want me because of who I am, but who I am doesn't fit in this world. Whatever your reason for this strange game you're playing, you have to let me know what's going on. And don't tell me it's none of my concern."

He'd kept everything locked tight inside him for so long he wasn't sure he'd be able share anything. But Annali was right. He had brought her into his mess of a life, and she had a right to know.

He gave her a nod. "Tonight."

He picked up his coffee and took a second taste. Far less bitter. "Thank you," he said. "Much better."

The Burgess girl brought their meals. Hovering close to Annali, she set down a bowl of soup on a plate, with a slice of bread tucked in on the side. Without moving any closer to Alex, the girl reached across to set down his pork roast meal.

"Thank you," Alex said taking the plate.

She nodded and gave Annali a quick smile before darting away again.

He picked up his fork and tasted a bit of the applesauce. Sweet with a bit of…cinnamon? So many years had passed, he wasn't sure.

"Why haven't you told your friends you're married?"

"Pardon me?"

"The man at the bank. He had no idea we were married."

"He is my employee. My personal life is none of his concern."

Her eyes widened. "Even Mrs. Lindberg at the store where you bought the bed didn't know who I was."

"I have lived my entire life in my father's shadow. I fight daily to combat his legacy, and why it is vital I live my life beyond reproach.

"I told no friends because I have no friends. People in this town circle around me like vultures, waiting for any opportunity to swoop in and destroy me. They have no use for me, except for one thing. Money. Including you."

Annali's whole body stilled. Her nostrils flared, and her fingers clenched into a fist around her spoon. For a moment he thought she would throw it at him.

Then in an instant her whole expression softened. She propped her elbow on the table and rested her chin on her fist. The tip of her tongue slipped out to moisten her top lip before a slow smile tugged at the corners of her mouth. "And men have no use for me either, Sugar," she said, her voice low and sultry. "Except for one thing." She winked. "Including you."

Chapter Twelve

Annali followed Alex through the fence opening, along the path, up the steps, and onto the porch of the small white house. Her fingers clenched around the string which tied together the two hat boxes she'd picked up at the millenary. In his arms, Alex carried the paper wrapped packages of her new dress, the quilt, and the hemmed linens for the new bed.

"Here we are." He shifted the packages in his arms, then turned the knob and pushed open the door.

Her stomach churned. This was it. For the next few weeks this would be home. Despite Harriet's disdain, Annali vowed to endure.

If it became difficult, she'd focus on the money Alex was going to give her. She'd imagine the furniture and wall papers of her very own parlor house. She'd think about the desk of her private office, and a safe like Madame's or a hidden one like Alex had. She'd be a real businesswoman, in control of her life for the first time. Biting her tongue and keeping out of Harriet's way was merely part of the price.

Harriet stood at the bottom of the staircase, hands on her hips.

"Alexander, I trust you are aware of how great a disruption this decision to marry has brought to our quiet household."

Hoping the fierce little crow wouldn't notice her,

Annali bumped against the hall tree as she tried to slip in unnoticed behind Alex.

"Mother, please. We've only just arrived." Parcels in his hands, he nudged the door closed with his foot.

Harriet waved her hand between the top of the staircase and the front door. "Strange men have been in and out all day."

"Mr. Lindberg's sons and the boy who runs errands around town are not strange men."

"I don't care who they are. I wasn't prepared to receive visitors. They tromped up and down the stairs, bumping and banging."

"They only delivered the bed and our bags from the hotel. It couldn't have been too great a disruption."

"I was forced to oversee their every move for fear they would damage the walls. Your sister worried they'd enter her bedroom and go through her things."

Alex inched toward the bottom step, and Annali moving with him kept herself squeezed between him and the wall. More likely, the delivery men couldn't wait to get out of the house, let alone linger upstairs and go through Nellie's things.

"Mother, might we discuss this later? I need to put down these packages, and Annali wishes to rest before supper."

Alex started up the stairs, then paused at the landing allowing Annali a chance to scoot past him. A small stained-glass window spilled patches of colored sunshine across the next level of oak stairs. She shot him a grateful smile.

"And another thing," Harriet continued, marching up the steps right behind Alex. "Why this sudden reckless spending? You have always been so frugal.

These extravagances are quite unlike you."

"Father ran the bank into the ground. We were broke. I had to be frugal."

At the top of the stairs, to the right, were two closed doors. To the left, two more doors. Annali glanced back, and Alex nodded toward the open door on the left. She walked ahead and stepped into Alex's bedroom.

When he'd mentioned his room had no colors, she hadn't quite imagined a monk's cell in a monastery—stark white walls, a bare wood floor, and a curtainless window. No pictures or paintings hung on the walls. No personal items or even a book lay within her view. Even the pitcher and basin on top of the washstand were plain white.

Alex moved into the room behind her and lay the new quilt on top of her trunk giving the room it's only spot of color. He set the pillows and blankets she'd chosen from Mrs. Lindberg's store on the corner of the new bed. The head and footboards of Alex's old bed leaned disassembled against the wall. In front of the bed someone had placed her carpet bag and Alex's black leather Gladstone.

"And why did you need to purchase that costly spring mattress frame?" Harriet stepped into the room right behind them. "What was wrong with your bed?"

Alex sighed and turned.

"I have been sleeping on that old rope bed since I was a boy. It's unyielding and too narrow. Hardly suitable for a husband and wife. And for once in my life, I would like to lie on a comfortable bed and enjoy a good night's rest."

"Look where those men have it positioned. Right in front of the window. Whoever heard of such a thing?"

While Annali wouldn't have chosen to put the bed there, she'd be damned if she'd move it now.

"And that bed quilt. Those bright colors and floral patterns—far too stimulating for your eyes. Soothing brown or gray is far more conducive to your sensitive condition."

"I'm sure it will be fine, now if you'll please excuse us…"

"Alexander, I do not appreciate your tone."

"My apologies for not sending word about the deliveries."

"I don't understand this sudden change in your behavior. This hasty marriage, your wild spending, and these erratic outbursts. You must understand my concerns."

"I am perfectly well." He stepped to the door. "Now, please. My wife and I would like some privacy."

With her chin high, Harriet shot Annali an accusatory scowl, then marched from the room.

Alex closed the door. Harriet's shoes rapped sharply against each tread as she descended the stairs. He sighed and removed his hat.

Annali stepped up to the footboard and cupped the brass, ball-shaped finial atop the corner post. "I don't think she likes me much."

"She doesn't care for me either."

Annali swung around. Her gaze locked on his face. "What? Why?"

He shrugged and moved to the wardrobe. Opening the door, he set his hat on the top shelf. "I look very much like my father."

"And that's a bad thing?"

"Let us forget my family for now and put this bed to

rights." He closed the door and unwrapped the sheets.

Walking across the room, she removed her hat and set it on the hat boxes which she'd placed between the trunk and the wardrobe.

Working in companionable silence, they covered the springs with the extra Witney blanket, put the horsehair mattress on top, then spread out the new sheets and quilt.

Maybe Alex would allow her to purchase some pretty curtains to frame the window behind the headboard and a couple of small rugs to place on either side of the bed. A table and lamp in the corner beside an overstuffed chaise and the barren room could easily be transformed into a cozy refuge. Next time she went to town she'd see if Mrs. Lindberg carried wall papers.

Alex came up behind her, standing so close, if she leaned back even slightly, she'd bump against his chest.

Men usually groped and pawed her so enthusiastically she had to shove their hands away. But she wanted Alex to touch her. If only he would casually rest his hand on her shoulder, nuzzle her neck, or slide his hand around her waist. When he looked at her, did he see a whore undeserving of affection, or a woman good enough to be his wife?

"What are you thinking about, Mrs. Worthington?"

She turned, raising her chin to meet his gaze. Mischievousness gleamed in his brown eyes.

"It feels strange when you call me that."

"How so?"

"I don't know. It feels like…a child's game of pretend, like we're not actually a husband and wife."

The sparkle in his eyes dimmed. He eased back a step. "You're right. Although we are legally husband and wife, any displays of affection are entirely pretense."

She ran her palm over the footboard rail. That wasn't what she meant, but she didn't know how to fix it. Maybe it didn't matter if this—whatever this was—would only last a few weeks. "The bed is beautiful."

"Yes." His gaze roamed over her face. "Beautiful," he murmured. "I saw it and had to have it. An erratic impulse buy."

She nodded and clasped her hands in front of her. "I wouldn't call it that. I understand why you needed it, even if it is only for a short while."

He moved to the side of the bed and sat on the edge of the mattress. "Indeed, purely a practical purchase."

"Do you like the new quilt? It's pretty don't you think?"

He slid his fingers back and forth over the fabric as his gaze locked on her. "Yes, very pretty."

"I think it adds some life to this plain, cold room."

"Yes. Yes, it does, even if it's only for a short time."

When he leaned over to untie his shoes, she turned away and removed her skirt and blouse. She'd been wearing it for days, and she was eager to try on the new dress.

"Feel free to hang your things in the wardrobe. There are a few unused pegs to the right of the drawers."

"Thank you." She glanced over her shoulder. He had removed his coat and sat on the bed leaning against the headboard.

She stepped to her trunk, swinging her hips in such a way that her petticoat swirled, giving him a glimpse of her ankles. She untied the string which held together the paper wrapped around her new dress.

"Annali, come join me."

"Let me take off my shoes." She propped her foot on the corner of the trunk, then raised her petticoat to her knee just above her stocking and leaned forward to untie the laces, ignoring the way the edge of her corset dug into her waist. She did the same with the other shoe, then toed them off and walked over to the bed.

Keeping her gaze fixed on his face, she knee-walked to the center of the mattress then grasped the top of her corset and popped free the first hook. "Do you mind if I take this off?" She popped free another hook. "It's so…rigid."

His pupils dilated as her fingers slowly worked their way down every hook of the undergarment. Then carelessly tossing it over her shoulder, her corset hit the wood floor with a thud. "Much better."

She scooted up beside him. Lying on her side, she draped her leg over his and laid her arm on his chest, toying with the ends of his black tie.

"This is bed is comfortable."

"Yes, it is." He placed his hand over hers, halting her movement. "Please understand, even though this purchase was something of an impulse, it doesn't mean my decision to buy this particular bed was wrong. And even though we'll only use it for a few weeks, I have no regrets."

"Neither do I." She wiggled her hand free and undid the top button of his waistcoat. What would he think of the new waistcoats she'd ordered for him? All she'd ever seen him wear were loose fitted coats and trousers. She couldn't wait to see him in the tailored teal stripe that matched her dress, or the mulberry jacquard.

His fingers wrapped over her hand again, stopping her before she could undo the next button. "Please. There are some things I need to tell you. Things you need to understand before we go down to supper."

Part of her didn't want to understand anything. While not knowing frustrated her, learning the truth might make her care too much, and that could be dangerous. After all, in the end, Alex was only a client.

She followed his gaze to the ceiling where two houseflies marred the perfection of pristine white.

"Alex?"

"I have an illness—"

Her fingers, beneath his hand, clenched the fabric of his waistcoat. She dropped her gaze to his face, but he remained focused on the ceiling.

"—known as onanism. My father also suffered from—"

"O-no what?"

"Onanism. It's…it's also known as self-pollution."

"Pollution? What are you talking about?"

Soft pink tinted his cheekbones. "I thought…you…being who you…would know…"

She shook her head.

He heaved a sigh. "An obsession…with oneself."

"*Alex!*"

"When a man…or a boy…touches… When a man or a boy touches…himself in such a way…that he…that he…"

"Alex, are you trying to say you like to masturbate? That's what all this nonsense—"

He rolled off the bed and paced the room.

Annali laughed. The whole idea was ridiculous. And that he believed—

"I've asked you not to laugh at me." He stood at the foot of the bed, his cheeks flushed, his features hardened.

"I'm sorry. It might be a sin, but every man I know does it."

"Yes, but, men like my father, like me, obsess over the urge to do…that." He paced the room, keeping his gaze averted—away from the bed, way from her.

"They regularly visit houses of ill-repute. For that reason. They can't get enough."

"Alex, please." She pressed her tongue to the roof of her mouth to keep from laughing. A moment later, she patted the mattress where he'd been lying. "Come. Sit beside me."

"You don't believe me because you haven't seen what this kind of obsession does to a man. Blindness and insanity will follow. Insanity that leads an evil perversion of the mind."

She pushed herself onto her knees. "No one believes that anymore. You won't go blind. It's old-fashioned thinking."

He stopped in front of her. "You're wrong. I saw first-hand what that kind of obsession did to my father. He was never home. He used bank business as a ruse to visit gambling dens and houses of ill-repute in different towns. Insanity slowly consumed him, until he became so vile, so very evil he—"

Alex spun on his heels, crossed to the washstand, and bracing his arms on the edge, hung his head.

Scooting off the bed, Annali came up behind him and slipped her arms around his waist, resting her cheek against the middle of his back.

His heart thudded beneath her ear, every muscle of his body tight and rigid.

"Alex," she whispered. "What happened to him, doesn't mean it will happen to you."

He swung around so fast he almost knocked her over. He strode to the bed and whirled to face her. "Don't you see? It's already happening. Mother is right. My outbursts of temper, this inner turmoil, my impulsive behavior, new eyeglasses, not being able to see— They are all behaviors my father exhibited, Except for me, the progression of decline is moving much faster."

"Then why am I here? If you don't want—"

"But I do. Damn and double damn, I do."

He was in front of her in three quick strides. Those long fingers wrapped around her upper arms and yanked her against him. Pupils dilated his gaze bore straight into her heart.

He held her so close, so tight, she was forced to arch her back away from him, tilting her head to meet his searching gaze.

"You are the most beautiful woman I've ever seen." Like a primal animal growl, his words rumbled deep in his throat. "And I want you like I've never wanted anything in my entire life."

Feeling more exposed than she'd ever felt while lying naked beside a stranger, Annali could do nothing more than breathe.

Gradually, the pressure of his fingertips eased, and he stepped back.

Like the moving shadow of a cloud across the earth on a sunny day, the brightness of longing in his eyes dimmed into something dull and detached. "My apologies, Miss Annali, for my aggressive assault upon your person."

She blinked. *Assault*?

He swung around and strode toward the door.

"What? Wait. Alex!"

He stopped.

"What in the hell are you talking about? Assault?"

He slowly turned. "I am a gentleman. You are my wife. I have allowed my carnal urges to gain hold of my better nature and accost you in the same way as those vile men in the alley."

"What? Where have you gotten such wrong-heading thinking?"

He stiffened.

*Hells bells! He was so damned sensitive.*

He turned and reached for the knob.

"Alex Worthington, you walk out that door and... and...you'll be going without your shoes."

When he didn't move, she crossed the distance, stopping behind him. "Don't you dare compare yourself to those two, or your father, or whatever kind of wicked man you believe you will become. They are not you. If I didn't want you to grab mc, I would have...stabbed you with my hat pins."

He turned. A glimmer of hope shone in his eyes. "You're not wearing a hat."

She shrugged. "I want you too."

"Do you?"

"Yes."

"Do you really? Or is it just pretend?"

"Yes. No. I...It isn't pretend."

She stepped closer.

His lips parted. He hesitated, a breath away.

She tried to whisper his name, but no word came out.

He leaned in. His hands cupped her face, his long fingers gliding into her hair.

She wrapped her arms around his waist, sliding her

palms up his back, gently pressing him closer, though he could never be close enough.

She felt herself moving backward. The backs of her knees bumped the side of the bed, and she toppled onto the mattress. His weight came down on top of her, and her breath escaped in a soft whimper. She wrapped her legs around his, enfolding him, threading her fingers through his hair.

"Alexander!" The sharp voice echoed up the stairwell.

Alex stiffened as though he'd been doused with a bucket of cold water.

"Ignore her," Annali whispered.

He raised his head.

She tried to pull him back to her, but he resisted.

"Alexander, can you hear me?"

He rolled off, lying on his back. "Yes, Mother!" he yelled toward the ceiling.

"Will you be finished soon?"

Annali snickered and clamped her hand over her mouth.

Alex turned his head toward her and scowled. "Yes, Mother, I'm coming!"

Annali snickered again.

"Good, because we are having a guest to supper, and he'll be here soon!"

"Yes, Mother!"

"And no dawdling!"

He sat up and leaned forward, resting his face in his hands. "Damn."

She sat up and slid her hand over the center of his back. "What's wrong?"

"I can only assume Mother has invited either

Reverend Clark or Doctor Powell."

He sighed and slipped his feet into his shoes.

"Is that bad?"

She ran her hand up and down following the curve of his back, frowning for a moment as her fingertips traced each bump of his spine even through his shirt and waistcoat.

"Apparently Mother has deemed it necessary to summon reinforcements."

"Reinforcements?"

He finished tying his shoes, then rose and moved to the end of the bed, lifting his coat off the footrail.

"I have to go before she comes up here. Please join me as soon as you can."

## Chapter Thirteen

Mother waited in the parlor. Back straight, she sat in the corner wing chair, like a queen ruling her court.

"My wife will join us shortly." He walked to the corner fireplace and draped his arm across the mantel. "Who are we expecting?"

"Never you mind. While we have a minute, we need to talk." Her hands folded in her lap, she raised her chin, her sharp gaze narrowed on him.

"You married this girl with such haste, what could you possibly know of her? What of her family, that they would allow such a thing?"

"Annali is an orphan."

"An orphan or a woods colt? Are you certain of her parentage? You know of your father's proclivity for houses of ill repute. Years ago, he could have—"

"Mother! Enough!" His fingers curled over the edge of the mantel, gripping it tightly. "I will thank you to keep such a vulgar insinuation to yourself."

She frowned. "You are being unappreciative of all I have done to protect you from both your own folly and from becoming the man he was."

"Mother, just because Annali is an orphan doesn't mean she never knew her father. And the probability of any bastard offspring from Father, is in my opinion, naught."

She gasped. "Alexander, your language."

"My apologies, Mother. Consider it yet another lapse in judgment."

She gave him an indignant little huff. "What properly raised young lady marries a man she doesn't know? I can only question the likelihood that the girl lacks proper morals and cannot be the steady influence needed in your life, which a woman like Hester Clark could have provided."

"I told you I would not marry Miss Clark."

"Then this hasty marriage was done to spite me?"

"No, Mother. I have no wish to spite you. I believe your motives are well intentioned, your offensive comments notwithstanding."

"Then I must conclude your business trip was too stressful and upset your delicate humors, which I warned you would happen. Now you have tied yourself to this person—"

"Annali. My wife's name is Annali."

"Are you certain then, that this Annali is a good match for your sedate lifestyle?"

His fingernails gouged deeper into the polished wood.

"Mother, you have controlled my life for as long as I can remember. While I appreciate your concern for my health, I am twenty-four years old and the head of this household. I am sorry you don't approve my choice of bride, but I am married, and Annali is my wife."

Mother rose, her small chin tipped up adding to her regal air. She clasped her hands at her waist and met his gaze. "I find this sudden forceful tone of yours reminiscent of your father's. I begin to despair that despite all our efforts, we will be unable to save you. Excuse me while I help Nellie with the meal."

Alex released a long exhale of breath as she left the room. He walked to the front window, his hands behind his back, his trembling fingers squeezed tightly inside his fist.

How long did he have before he became his father? How long before the same depravity consumed him? And would he be able to stop himself in time?

"Alex?"

He swung around. She stood inside the doorway, as beautiful in the simple print as she'd been when she wore the dark dress and the hat with the broken feather. How could he have been so caught up in his own maudlin thoughts that he hadn't heard her come down the stairs?

She smiled. "Do you like it?" She twisted her hips, allowing the fabric to swirl around her ankles.

"Yes, it's very nice."

"Do you like the color?"

He swallowed and glanced out the window. The curtains billowed as a sudden gust blew into the room. In the distance a buggy headed in their direction. An ache tightened the back of his throat.

"You don't like it?"

He turned to see what she wore. "It's very pretty."

"Green is different from my usual pinks, blues, and reds."

"I told you I care little for what colors you choose." He glanced out the window. The buggy drew closer. From the shape of the hood, it looked like Doctor Powell's rig. He squeezed his fingers tighter.

Annali crossed the room and slipped her arms around his waist. "What's wrong? You're all rigid and tense."

"I said your dress was pretty." He whirled away

from her, the window, and the approaching buggy. He strode to the fireplace in the corner of the room. "I have lived my entire life pandering to a hothouse of female emotions. I did not expect I would have to dance attendance to yours as well."

"You ass," she snapped. "I'm better off helping your mother and sister in the kitchen."

"No." As she stepped past, he grabbed her arm.

She yanked free from his grip and glared.

"Double damn," he muttered. "My apologies, but they won't like it if you go in there."

"They will hate me more for not offering to help. And the atmosphere in there can't be any worse than it is in here."

"Annali, forgive me. Please, just be patient until the bank sells."

The anger burning in her eyes faded, and then he watched her expression transform as it had done in the restaurant. "No worries, *Sugar*. I'll play my part." She smiled and sat in the wing chair Mother had vacated minutes earlier.

The clinking chime of the calling-bell echoed through the foyer. The sound should have been a welcome reprieve, but the tension twisting his stomach into knots only increased as he opened the front door.

"Good evening, Alexander. Nice to see you, my boy." Doctor Powell hung his hat on the hall tree.

"It's a pleasure to see you, too. Come in." Alex closed the door and gestured the older man into the parlor.

"Doctor Powell, may I present my wife Annali. Annali, this is Doctor Powell, a dear family friend, as well as our trusted physician."

Annali smiled and held out her hand as graciously as any fine lady. "Nice to meet you, Doctor."

A strange knot rose in Alex's throat along with the urge to hug her. She was so sweet and beautiful, and as she said, he was an ass. Only three weeks till the end of the month and she'd be rid of him.

The doctor took her hand and bowed. "Alexander, your wife is charming."

Alex nodded in reply even as he met Annali's gaze. She tilted her chin and flashed a smug smile.

"I heard of your recent nuptials. Congratulations."

Alex nodded. "Thank you." No doubt Mother had been quick to share the happy news, as well as inform the doctor of Lord knew what else. Now the man was here to observe firsthand Alex's erratic behaviors and evidence of his rapid decline. He had to get out of here before he said or did something cruel.

"Excuse me, while I tend to your horse."

He turned and headed for the front door.

Annali watched him go, both irritated and confused by his behavior. His moods were so unpredictable, she felt as she did on a busy Saturday night, moving from client to client, each man with a different temperament, likes, and expectations. Whatever had shifted Alex's mood this time was somehow tied to the doctor's arrival.

The pocket doors on the wall opposite the front window parted. "Doctor Powell," Harriet gushed wiping her hands on her apron. "How good of you to come." Like a shadow, Nellie slipped into the room right behind her mother.

"Thank you for inviting me." He bowed. "And Mrs. Miller, how are you?"

*Mrs. Miller?*

Nellie hovered just inside the frame of the doors. "Very well, thank you."

"And your husband?"

Annali's brow rose toward her hairline. *Husband?*

"Clayton is well. His last letter mentioned business will soon take him back this way, and he'll be home for a couple of weeks."

"How nice that will be for you."

"Yes. Thank you for asking, but if you will excuse me, I need to get back to the kitchen." She scooted between the doors and slid them closed behind her.

Harriet gestured toward the sofa. "Please, Doctor, make yourself comfortable." She sat at one end and the doctor at the other.

"I see you've met Alexander's new bride."

He nodded, his gray beard bumping against his chest. He wore an old frock coat which had likely been the fashion back when he began his practice. Were the doctor's ideas as outdated as his clothes?

Why had the doctor's visit set Alex so on edge? The special diet he flaunted, this impulsive marriage, maybe Alex wasn't telling her the truth. Maybe Harriet was right to be concerned.

Alex was thin, his clothing loose. Had he always been this way or was he getting worse? But he'd made her no promises. He'd wanted time to feel like a man, live his life before—

He'd told her madness, like his father, but she wasn't sure. He didn't behave like he was mad. Nor did she understand how all these things had anything to do with o-no-ism or whatever he called the desire to pleasure himself.

If she'd known how drastically her life would

change that day in the alley, would she have given him the token?

Harriet rose. "Please, Doctor, don't get up. If you'll excuse me, I need to help Nellie in the kitchen."

No doubt a strategic maneuver designed to leave Annali alone to finesse the doctor's questions. "Lovely weather we're having."

"Yes," he agreed. "It's been unseasonably warm."

If he'd been a client, she'd have been sitting in his lap, unbuttoning his coat and waist coat, smiling, and saying, *"Oh, are you getting warm, Sugar?"* Instead, she said, "Yes, yes it has."

"Have you known Alex long?"

*Here we go.*

She and Alex hadn't discussed how to handle questions like this. She glanced out the front window, then the side but didn't see him or the doctor's buggy. There was no help for it now. She'd best stick as close to the truth as possible.

"No, not long. We met when he came to Lincoln."

"Rather a rushed marriage. What of your family? Did your father approve of such haste?"

So, the doctor was trying to find out if Alex had compromised her in some way. Any proper young girl could be ruined by even being out after dark with a man. A hasty marriage would be the only way to save her reputation. "I have no family, sir."

"No one to offer you protection?"

She shook her head. "No, but I've managed quite well by myself."

The pocket doors parted, and Alex pushed them both fully open, revealing the table and platters of food. "Mother says, 'Supper is served.' "

Annali and the doctor rose and entered the dining room.

"It all smells wonderful," Annali commented to Harriet who stood beside a chair at one end of the table. The woman said nothing.

Alex offered his arm and seated Annali in a chair at the opposite corner of the table, then Nellie between her and his mother.

Doctor Powell moved up beside Harriet. "Allow me," he said and pulled out her chair.

Alex seated himself beside Annali at the opposite end of the table and recited the blessing.

Harriet passed a platter of cold fried chicken to Doctor Powell, who lifted a drumstick and thigh onto his plate, before passing the platter to Nellie, who then passed it to Annali.

Annali would have offered it to Alex, but his plate was already filled with a cold chicken breast without any skin or seasoning, plain, cold green beans, chunks of cold potatoes, and a glass of water. Was this the diet Alex hated so much? While everyone else had fried chicken, potato salad, baked beans, buttered bread, and lemonade, he had to choke that down?

At the other end of the table, Doctor Powell scooped potato salad onto his plate. He passed the bowl back to Harriet then raised his gaze to Alex. "I was much surprised when your mother told me this morning of your sudden marriage. I'm curious as to how you two met."

Quick glances darted between Harriet and the doctor. Alex must have seen it as well. He shoved to his feet, grabbing Annali's hand, pulling her up beside him.

"Alexander, sit down," Harriet snapped. "We have a guest." She turned to the doctor. "I would like to apologize for my son."

"No need. I can see for myself the personality changes of which you spoke."

A twinge of sympathy rippled through Annali. She lowered herself into her chair, giving Alex's hand a subtle tug. Though he sat, she kept her fingers wrapped with his, his palm warm against hers. She turned to the doctor and gave him her shyest smile, the one she used when she pretended to be a virgin.

"Oh, you should have seen Alex, he was so heroic. I had gone shopping you see and was looking at some hats in the window of a millinery shop." She switched her gaze to Nellie. "There was a lovely brown one with red feathers and copper-colored ribbon. I thought it would go perfectly with my russet gown, but looking at your dress, I see the hat would've looked better with your coffee color fabric."

"I don't wear fancy hats." Nellie sipped from her glass of lemonade. "I find a cotton bonnet far more practical."

"Oh. If you'd like to try, we could go shopping, and I could help you choose one that would complement your—"

"For goodness' sake." Harriet huffed. "Get on with it."

Alex's fingers tightened around Annali's. She glanced over and winked. The tension in his fingers eased.

She switched her attention back to the doctor. "While I was looking at those lovely hats, I was accosted by two horrid men. They were not gentlemen, I assure you. They pulled me into the alley and...and tried..." Her voice broke on a sob. "Why it's just too terrible to talk about. But Alex came to my rescue."

She turned to him and sighed. "He was so brave, the way he fought them off. A real hero."

"Yes," the doctor said. "I did wonder what happened to your face, my boy."

"He was wonderful," Annali babbled, returning her gaze to the others. "He walked me home, and we talked. That evening he came to the boarding house where I lived to make sure I was all right. Such a gentleman. We talked for hours. The next day I was on my way to Omaha, and we met on the train. It was destiny, don't you think? So, when he asked me to marry him, I said yes. How could I do otherwise? It was meant to be."

"Quite the romantic tale." The doctor cut a piece of fried chicken and popped it in his mouth. "But I wonder how such emotional upheaval has affected you, Alexander. How have you been feeling?"

"I'm fine," he snapped. His fingers squeezed around Annali's hand.

"I understand you fired Mr. Warner the other day. That might be considered a lapse in judgment. He worked at the bank for years."

"My only lapse in judgment, Doctor, was in allowing him to continue in my employ for as long as I did."

"You see," Harriet chimed in, "another example of how drastically his personality has altered. Now you know why I am concerned."

The doctor nodded, stroking his beard. "Yes, yes. I see."

Alex stood, pulling Annali up beside him.

"Then you might as well know I have put the bank up for sale."

Soft gasps whispered through the room.

"If you will excuse us, Mother, Doctor, Nell." Gripping Annali's hand tight, he led her through the kitchen and out the back door.

She stumbled down the porch steps and tripped across the yard. "Hell's bells, Alex? Where are we going?"

"I don't know. Out of that damn house."

Once on the road it was easier, but his legs were so long Annali had a hard time keeping pace without being dragged. Finally, out of breath and with a stitch in her side, she pulled back. "Alex, wait." She leaned over, pressing her hand against her side as she panted.

He stopped and turned. "Are you all right?"

"Fabulous."

"I'm sorry. I shouldn't have dragged you with me."

"Next time…walk slower."

After a minute or so, it was easier to breathe, and she straightened.

His brow furrowed as his gaze searched her face.

She offered him a shaky smile.

He stepped close and wrapped his arms around her, holding her tight.

She relaxed against him, slipping her arms around his waist. If she'd ever been hugged before, she couldn't recall, but if it had ever felt like this, safe, and wanted, and cherished, she never would've wished for the hug to end.

His chin rested on top of her head, and she closed her eyes, her ear pressed close to his heart.

"You were perfect," he murmured, swaying slightly. "But me a hero?" His huff of disbelief tickled her hair.

She shrugged. "You are to me."

He pulled back. "Is that really how you see me?"

She lifted her gaze to meet his. "You did save me from those two men, and you walked me home. You saved me from the conductor on the train. You've made me part of your life, even though you know what I am, and you're giving me the money for a new start. To me that's heroic."

"You're probably the only person in the country to see me that way. Thank you."

"And you're probably the only person in the country to treat me like a lady. Thank you."

He pulled her into another embrace.

"Alex?"

"Hmmm?"

"I'm hungry."

He chuckled. "Me too."

The sound brought a smile to her lips. "Can we go back now?"

They took their time, Alex matching his stride to hers. He said they hadn't gone more than two miles up the road, but Annali didn't think she'd ever walked four miles at one time in her entire life.

They returned to the house the way they'd left, through the backyard. Between the garden shed and small barn, the doctor's bay gelding grazed in a large corral alongside another horse with four white stockings.

"I'd hoped he'd be gone by now." Alex pulled out his pocket watch and checked the time. "Twenty past seven. He should be leaving soon."

Alex collected the horse and hitched him to the buggy, then while he walked the horse around to the front of the house, Annali wandered to the back porch and sat on the steps.

"You see, Doctor," Harriet's voice carried through the house and open windows. "Irrational and irritable. And tonight, his stomach was so upset he couldn't eat more than a few bites of his meal."

"Yes, a bit disturbing. We may have to begin a mild sedative to keep his nerves calm."

Chapter Fourteen

Annali had no doubt who Harriet and the doctor discussed.

"Yes," Harriet said. "I should have taken your advice years ago."

"Your concerns are justified. His outbursts are definitely more frequent and volatile. And we both know what he's capable of when he fully loses his temper."

"He does deny it still."

"That is to be expected. In his delusion, he may have convinced himself he's innocent. But we must keep such a thing from happening again. Which is why it is vital he maintain his regimen and keep calm."

What had Alex done? Was this the terrible thing Mrs. Lindberg had referred to earlier?

Who was the real Alex? The man she met in Lincoln? The man who'd hugged her on the road? Or was he a man slowing going insane? The man whose mood swings and bouts of temper had caused him to do something terrible, but which could not be proven?

"I see Alexander has brought your buggy round."

"Then I shall take my leave. Thank you, Harriet, for a wonderful meal. I admire your perseverance. Most mothers would have surrendered him to the asylum in Lincoln years ago."

"Thank you, Abraham."

They moved to the front of the house and onto the

porch. While Annali could still hear their voices, she couldn't understand their words. A few moments later the buggy clattered away and Harriet and Alex came inside.

"I trust you have calmed yourself?"

"Yes, Mother."

"Then I'm off to bed. Nellie has prepared your bath. And remember church tomorrow."

"I haven't forgotten. It's a weekly event."

"Alexander, your attitude."

"Forgive me, it's been a long day."

"I trust your…wife…"

"Annali, Mother. Her name is Annali."

"Yes, of course. I trust she will be joining us for services?"

"Yes, Mother."

Footsteps receded and moved up the stairs, as a heavier set entered the kitchen. "Annali?"

"Out here."

The screen door squeaked open and banged shut. She glanced up as Alex joined her on the bottom step.

"Do you know, with all the windows open, I can hear what everyone says?"

"I suppose, but without close neighbors, I never really thought about it. Why, what did you hear?"

"Your bath is ready." She shot him a grin. "I can wash your back if you want."

"I thought you were hungry."

"I am, but your bath will get cold."

"I doubt that. Hopefully, it will get warmer."

She frowned.

Alex heaved a sigh. "I take a cold bath every day."

"A cold bath? Every day?"

"Yes, it's part of my daily regimen. Though I do confess, I've skipped several over the years especially during the dead of winter."

She nudged him with her shoulder. "Rebel."

"Doctor Powell is a follower of a man named Sylvester Graham, who is a proponent of cold baths, brisk exercise, bland food, no alcohol, salt, or even pepper, and only water."

"And what's that supposed to do?"

"It's a way to prevent stimulation of the senses which can cause the need to—"

"Pleasure your—"

"Yes. Because, as I've said, such indulgence leads to blindness and—"

"Madness. Your father. Unspeakable evil." She laughed, but the moment of joy faded. What was the terrible thing Alex had done? Should she ask him?

Should she tell him what his mother and the doctor planned? Should she stay out of it? After all, she'd only known him for a few days. Maybe this crazy, restrictive regimen was best for him.

"Come on, let's check the ice box for leftovers." He offered his hand and led her inside.

The oak cabinet stood opposite a table covered with a yellow oil cloth. Alex lifted the latch on the largest of the three doors and withdrew a plate with a few pieces of fried chicken from the tin lined compartment.

She accepted a drumstick and took a bite. It wasn't the best she'd ever had, but it wasn't the worst.

Carrying the plate, he led her into the narrow pantry off the kitchen. A counter hugged one wall with cupboards below. Above, on near-empty shelves, a few dozen jars of canned vegetables and fruit remained. At the end of the room stood a copper hip bath.

She wandered over and trailed her fingers through the water. "It's cold."

"Always."

"Maybe I could take some warm water from the reservoir or heat up a couple of big pots."

He shook his head. "She'll know. She always does. Believe me I've tried many times, especially during winter. I've always been caught."

She took another bite of chicken. "Well, I'd like a bath, and I don't care for cold water."

Back in the kitchen, she stoked the fire in the stove to heat the water in the reservoir along with the water she put in the largest pot she could find. While it heated, she returned to the pantry.

Alex stared down at a pie tin half-filled with berry pie.

"Have a piece," she said.

He shook his head and backed away. "I indulged enough last night."

"Alex, I don't understand how all this denying yourself prevents you from doing—or turning into—anyone."

"It keeps the humors of the body balanced and prevents over stimulation. I've read new literature by J.H. Kellogg, and he supports what Doctor Powell has recommended. Even a recent book by Doctor George Napheys warned that onanism frequently leads to insanity."

Maybe she was wrong, but considering how many women were in her profession and how many men visited each one, she couldn't conceive how the act by itself— "Did your father have the pox? Pox on the brain causes madness."

He leaned against the counter and tugged loose his tie. "Mother and I washed him before laying him out. Aside from a bullet hole in his chest, his body was clean of a single pustule or the faintest rash." He opened a drawer and passed her a fork. "Enough of this talk. I'm sick near to death thinking about it. Have some pie. You didn't get any earlier."

Using the fork, she sliced a small wedge and pushed it into the center of the pie tin. Cutting off a bite-sized piece, she brought it slowly to her mouth and pulled it off the fork. "Hmm, so good."

She cut another bite, and this time waved it under his nose a couple of times. "Try it. The crust is a little heavy, too much lard, but the blackberry filling is good." When he didn't open his mouth, she brought it to her lips and making eye contact, slid her tongue up and around the fork, slowly licking it clean of any fruit.

A pink flush tinted his cheek bones, but the mischievous gleam in his brown eyes vanished as his expression hardened. "You are my wife now. Stop playing your whore's games," he snapped and pushed past her. At the door, he turned. "Take your bath and let me know when you've finished. I'll be in the parlor."

Annali glared at his retreating back. Hell's bells, what an ass. He knew what she was. That's why he married her. Now he expected her to suddenly become someone else? Well, too bad. She could pretend, if that's what he wanted, but pretending would never make a silk purse from a sow's ear.

She added the hot water to the tub, stripped her clothes, and stepped into the tepid bath. A couple of days had passed since she'd last bathed, and she savored the chance to scrub herself free of dust and sweat. She should have gone upstairs and gotten her soap, but instead used the bar left on the holder. She held it under her nose and inhaled. It smelled like Alex—clean and fresh. Natural.

She washed her hair but had to sneak out dripping wet to pump a large pail of water for rinsing. She dried off using the towel that had been left for Alex, then slipping on her chemise, she gathered her clothes then walked through the kitchen, into the dining room, and parlor.

Alex sat asleep in the wing chair. His tie hung loose on either side of his opened shirt front. Her gaze lingered on the column of his throat and the glimpse of hair at the top of his undershirt.

The thought crossed her mind to climb into his lap, unbutton his undershirt, and run her fingers through the dark hair on his chest.

But why? He didn't want her. Not really. So, what was she doing here staring at his neck? Acting like a fool, as stupid and naïve as she'd been when she was fifteen and believed Marcello had loved her and wanted to marry her.

She should get a calendar and mark off the days until she could get her money, get on with her life, and forget all about Alex-the-Ass Worthington. Leaving him, she moved into the foyer and tip-toed up the stairs to his room.

****

The door clicked shut. The sound carried through the empty hall and down the stairs. Alex opened his eyes. *Coward. You're nothing but a damn coward.*

He should have married Hester Clark. He rose and

headed to the kitchen and the tub inside the pantry. For the first time, he hoped the water was ice cold.

It wasn't. As he lowered himself into the tub, came the realization that Annali had sat naked in the same water. He picked up his soap, the same soap that Annali had rubbed all over her body, sliding it around those beautiful breasts. Two soft mounds which could easily fill his hands. Breasts between which he longed to bury his face.

A vague image of Miss Clark wavered in his mind. He tried to latch on to it, to focus on her tall, flat-chested body, graying hair, and horse-teeth mouth, but her likeness was overshadowed by visions of Annali.

For several long moments, she'd stood silently beside the chair where he'd pretended to sleep. Had she noticed his racing heart and his growing need? He'd wanted to open his eyes, apologize for being an ass, but… He was a coward.

He stepped from the tub. Drying off with the damp towel Annali had used, swelled his manhood, now aching to be touched—but only by her.

So why did he always push her away? Why did he spew the anger he felt toward himself onto her? She deserved better. She'd realize it if she learned the truth. But she'd leave then, and it was too soon.

If he marked off the days on the calendar in his office, perhaps he'd be reminded of how little time he had left to redeem himself in her eyes. The least he could do was leave her with a few favorable memories.

Pulling on his undershirt and drawers, he emptied the tub, wiped up the floor, and hung the towels on the line. The exertion helped, and feeling less like a randy schoolboy, he climbed the stairs and entered his room.

Late evening sunlight spilled through the window onto the bed, onto Annali, who sat in the middle of the quilt like an angel enveloped in a glow of warmth. Her hair, still wet, fell down her back and over her shoulder. One leg tucked under, the other bent at the knee, she leaned forward running her hands up and down her leg from knee to ankle smoothing lotion into her skin.

She looked up. Her brow furrowed.

He closed the door behind him. She was so beautiful. When the sale was final, and she was gone forever, would he miss her? Would he still want her with the same aching he felt in this moment?

He crossed the room and opened the wardrobe. Glancing over his shoulder he watched as she dipped two fingers into the jar and scooped out a small dab of white. Slowly, she rubbed it over her other leg.

Giving himself a mental shake, he hung his clothes, taking his time, unsure how to proceed, suddenly conscious of how inexperienced he was compared to her, compared to all the men she'd been with who were likely better at this than he would be.

He shut the door and turned. She sat cross-legged in the center of the bed, toying with her jar of skin cream.

"Alex, why am I here?"

He slipped his hands behind his back, twining his fingers into a gnarled knot. He glanced at his bare feet and their contrast against the wood, his toes as long and boney as the rest of him.

He looked up. "Because you are my wife."

She shook her head.

"Because I wanted to know the pleasure of the marriage bed before blindness and—"

"Yes, you say that, but when I try, you tense up and

push me away. So, why am I here?"

He sighed, fumbling for words, not sure himself—of why. "Because…Because I…I want to… But…I want it to be with Annali. Not Ivy."

The lines in her brow deepened. She cocked her head as her gaze met his. "Annali was a girl. Ivy is who I am now. I don't know how else to be."

He stepped to the end of the bed. "I don't want the woman who teases me with fruit and seductive glances."

Moving around the footboard, he sat on the side of the mattress, facing her, his bent knee touching her bare foot. "I want Annali Hanson, the woman free from pretense, the Annali who hugged me and said I was her hero. The woman who lost her ticket and crawled under the seat on the train to hide from the conductor. The woman who agreed to marry me."

She blinked and dropped her gaze to her lap, rolling the jar back and forth between her hands. "Why didn't you tell me this before?"

He reached out and lifted away the jar. "Because I didn't realize… until I said it."

She raised her head and met his gaze. Moisture glistened in her blue eyes.

He set the jar behind him and leaned close. Placing his hand beside her hip, he braced himself and eased a bit closer.

Her gaze locked with his. Her lips parted with a soft whisper of breath.

She smelled like the glycerin soap he used, smelled like him. He breathed deep, the scent of her skin mingled with his, blending them together as one.

He trailed his finger down the side of her face, brushing a whisp of hair from her cheek.

"You're so beautiful," he whispered.

*So are you*, she wanted to say, but she couldn't make the words come. His brown eyes so mesmerizing, his touch so gentle, she found herself transfixed by him, uncertain how to proceed. Most of the men she'd been with had been kind, but they'd been with her for primarily one reason. Even Marcello had actually only wanted her in order to satisfy his needs. Whispered words of endearment were for him a means to an end.

But in this moment, searching deep into Alex's soft brown depths, she suddenly felt inadequate, as if he wanted something she didn't know how to give.

He laid his hand on her shoulder. Her skin tingled as his palm slid down her arm to her hand. He clasped it with his and laced his fingers with hers.

"My father was a taker. I've spent my life trying not to become what he was. Ultimately, it may be my destiny, but now, here with you, I don't want to take. Tell me what *you* want, Annali. Tell me how to please you."

Her breath caught as her chest tightened. Her eyes stung. She touched his face, the stubble of his beard rough against her thumb as she stroked his cheek. Beneath her fingers his pulse thrummed at the back of his jaw.

"Kiss me," she whispered.

More unsure than she'd ever felt before, she waited as Alex slowly leaned in and pressed his mouth to hers. Gently, he eased her back against the pillows, and she wrapped her arms around him. He nipped and teased the seam of her lips until she opened on an exhaled breath. Their tongues came together, tentative at first, lightly touching and withdrawing. The mint of his toothpowder lingered on the edges of her tongue as their breath mingled warm between them.

She couldn't give him her virginity, but she could give him this. Her kiss. The only part of her left untouched she now shared with him. Alex. Her Alex.

Raw and powerful and inexperienced, his kiss raced through her like lightning, igniting a yearning in her very core, an urgency she'd never felt with any man. His tongue brushed her own as a low groan rumbled in his throat.

His hand slid down her side to her hip and back up, dragging the hem of her chemise with it. Goose bumps rose in its wake, and she squeezed her arms tighter, pressing her fingertips into his back.

She hooked her leg over his. Her heel pushed into the mattress. A soft moan rose in her throat as she arched against him, aching to feel more, aching to be part of him.

His hand slipped over her shoulder. She felt the tugging at the ties of her chemise.

She slid her hands down his back and slipped them beneath his undershirt, savoring for a moment the warmth of his skin, before reluctantly breaking the kiss and tugging the shirt over his head. As he pushed her chemise off her shoulder, her fingers loosed the drawstring of his drawers.

He moved off the bed and shucked that last bit of clothing as she tossed aside hers. He climbed in beside her. With nothing between them, she lay facing him— each exposed and vulnerable to the other for the first time.

His gaze roamed over her, lingering on her breasts. His hand reached out, then hovered for a moment as he shifted his gaze to meet hers, silently asking permission.

She inclined her head, and he touched her, caressing, nuzzling. He glanced up as if to reassure himself that what he was doing was still all right. Such wonder filled his eyes she felt a flash of inadequacy, as if she were unworthy of such adoration.

No, Alex was not like his father. He would never be like his father.

Men had always taken from her, and she'd let them, giving them her body to use. That was fine, but she'd always held a part of herself back, never wholly surrendering. Never once having had the desire.

But in this moment, suddenly all she thought she understood of sex, of men, was turned downside up. She felt as confused and uncertain as she had that very first time with Marcello.

Alex kissed her neck, sucking at the tender skin.

A strange tightness rose in the back of her throat as she sifted her fingers through his hair.

She wrapped her legs around his waist, pulling him closer, holding him tight, as desperate as he to make them one.

His shaft pressed against her, pushing, seeking entrance.

She reached down, her fingers wrapped around the length of him, guiding him to her entrance.

He thrust into her, once, twice… The bed springs squeaked in matching rhythm. Her muscles tightened around him as her thighs clenched and quivered. Her head arched back against the pillow as intense waves of pleasure washed through her. "Alex…"

He stilled. His back stiffened. He thrust again. His head tipped back, and he groaned, deep in his throat. The tension in his body eased, and he lowered himself, resting on his forearms.

"Annali," he whispered. He touched his forehead to hers, then shifted to lay beside her.

She rolled toward him and slid her arm around his waist. Doubts rose in her mind, and she wondered if maybe—somewhere deep inside—she'd accepted his proposal to gain not the money—but Alex.

Chapter Fifteen

Chirping birds woke Annali from a light sleep. With the bed in front of the window, she had only to tip her head to see scattered whisps of white against the pure blue sky of an early summer morning.

Alex had opened the window last night after they'd come together a second time. She didn't mind, for the cooler night air had drawn the stuffiness from the room.

She pulled the sheet over their shoulders and lay her head in the hollow of his outstretched arm, savoring the soft whisper of his breath against her forehead.

He smelled clean, not saturated in the scent of bay rum or vetiver. His hair, as she combed her fingers through above his ear, was soft and silky, not stiff from pomade or limp from grease and sweat.

The rest of the household stirred as Alex's mother and sister moved around in their rooms, then a few minutes apart, they each quietly descended the stairs.

Alex shifted beside her and opened his eyes. A soft smile pulled at the corner of his mouth. "Good morning, Mrs. Worthington."

"Good morning."

He kissed her, then reached out and toyed with the ends of her hair where it had fallen over her shoulder and lay on the mattress between them. "Where did you get this unusual streak?"

"I suppose from my mother. I remember she was

tall, and beautiful, with long blonde hair."

"What happened to her?"

"I don't know. After Mr. Giovani died—"

"Who?"

"Mr. Giovani. He and his wife ran a bakery in Council Bluffs. I worked there."

"You worked in a bakery? Then how... How did you... My apologies. I've been remiss. I should have taken the time before now to learn something of you and your life prior to our meeting in the alley."

She glanced down, studying the small patch of white sheet between their bodies.

He nudged her chin up with his finger, and she met his gaze. "Forgive me, Mrs. Worthington, for my inability to see beyond myself. Tell me something of your family. How old are you?"

"I'm twenty."

He looped his finger loosely around the ends of her hair. "And how long did you work at the bakery before...before you became... Before you changed your profession?"

She smiled. "Thank you for asking. I think most people believe I was hatched, fully grown, lying with a man between my legs."

A hint of pink swept his cheekbones. "I never thought... I didn't believe that you... I... that you had..."

She pressed her index finger to his lips. "Hush. Let me tell you. I remember we lived in a big city. Chicago, my mother told me. I don't know why my parents weren't married. Looking back, my mother may have been my father's mistress. I remember his beard and his brown coat. He gave me a ragdoll for my birthday one year. I still have it in my trunk. Something happened to him though. I think he died. I remember my mother crying."

"I'm sorry." He trailed his fingers up and down her arm, raising goose flesh in their wake.

"That left my mother with a young child and no means. I don't know how we ended up in Council Bluffs, but I was five or six when she gave me to the Giovani's to help in their bakery, and she went to live at a place called Harding House. At first my mother would come see me every week or so, but gradually that stopped.

"Mr. G. and his wife were kind and gave me a little room all my own in the back of the kitchen. Every day, from early morning until late at night, I helped Mr. Giovanni bake breads, cakes, and pastries.

"They had a grandson, Marcello, who worked weekends and summers in the front of the shop. He was charming, and funny, and so nice to me.

"When Mr. G. died the bakery closed. At first, I believed Marcello would marry me. After all we'd done together, I thought he loved me. But all he'd wanted was a bit of fun before he settled down with a respectable woman."

"*What*? Do you mean he violated—"

"No. I wanted to be with him too."

"Regardless. No man has the right to use you to satisfy his— Only a vile, repulsive man of low character would use a young girl in such a way. What he did was unconscionable."

"Alex, I wasn't that young. I was fifteen. He was seventeen. I thought I loved him. I was foolish."

He wrapped his arms around her and pulled her close. "Still, even at seventeen, to take advantage of a young girl in such a way, speaks to the sort of man he will become. If he'd been any sort of gentleman, he would have offered you marriage."

"After the funeral, Mrs. Giovani gave me five dollars, Mr. G.'s old book of recipes, and sent me on my way without references. I went to find my mother, but all Mrs. Harding could tell me was that she'd left years before. I was ruined, but I was young and pretty, and she needed a girl, so I stayed. Better than starving in the street."

"I'm sorry you had no one to protect you."

She ran her hand slowly up and down his arm. "I appreciate the way you always defend my honor. No man has ever treated me the way you do. But sometimes I think you forget what I am."

With his index finger, he reached out and nudged her chin up. "I think... perhaps you are the one who forgets who you are."

He sighed. "You see yourself only as Ivy, but I see Annali. And when this sale goes through, you'll have the funds to go anywhere, do anything, be anyone. You're not destined to be Ivy forever."

She slid her hand down his arm and laced her fingers with his. "And what of you? Are you actually destined to become like your father, or is that the only way you see yourself?"

"It's true."

She reached out and lay her hand on his cheek. Her thumb brushed over his rough early morning stubble. "I don't believe that."

Dropping her hand to his shoulder, she toyed with the hair behind his ear. "One day I'm going to run my own place. Be independent and make my own decisions.

Choose who I want to be with and when. Alex, you're smart. You can go anywhere and do anything."

"It's different for me."

"Why? You must have some kind of dream."

"My life doesn't allow for choice."

"Good or bad, we always have choices."

"Perhaps." He leaned close and kissed the tip of her nose. "But let us speak of more pleasant things. It's a beautiful morning." Tossing the sheet aside, he rolled over to sit on the side of the bed.

"Where are you going?"

"It's time to get up."

"Now?"

From downstairs the clock in the parlor chimed six times.

*Hells bells!* She hadn't been awake this early since her days in the bakery. She'd hoped they could linger in bed a little longer, but the clatter of pots and pans and the scent of coffee drifting up from the kitchen reminded her that morning routines in this household were more rigid than the lazy mornings she'd grown used to over the last few years.

She sat up, and drawing her knees to her chest, wrapped her arms around them.

Alex bent over and picked up his drawers, each bump of his spine starkly visible as he pulled the legs right side out. He raised his arms to slip his undershirt over his head, the outline of each rib clear.

Was there really something wrong with him, or had years of Spartan meals like the one he'd been given for supper, created his boney frame?

Moving to the washstand, he poured a bit of water in his shaving mug.

"Are you getting out of bed?" he asked as he brushed soap over the lower half of his face.

"Eventually. I want to watch you shave."

He swung around, his brush in one hand, his mug in the other. "Why?"

"I'm curious. I've never watched a man shave before."

He grinned. His smile encircled by white. "You can't see much from over there." He turned back to the mirror.

Annali scrambled off the bed, snatched her chemise off the floor, and dropped it over her head as she moved beside the washstand, and leaned against the wall.

He set down the mug and brush and unfolded the razor. Turning the right side of his face toward the mirror, he placed the blade just below his sideburn and drew the razor downward.

"Alexander!"

He winced and immediately pressed his finger to the edge of his jaw.

"Are you awake?"

He tipped his face toward the ceiling as a trickle of pink slid through the soap and down his neck.

"Yes, Mother! We're awake!"

"Don't dawdle. We have church this morning!"

Alex sighed and leaned close to the mirror as he moved his finger away from his face and examined the cut.

"You'd better start dressing."

She glanced longingly at her trunk. "I wish I could wear one of my other dresses."

"The black one will be fine."

"It's navy blue. I'm just tired of it." She moved to

the wardrobe and stepped into her drawers and petticoat.

"I can hardly wait until my new dress is ready." She sat on the trunk and began pulling on her stockings as Alex wiped his face and put his shaving things into the top drawer of the washstand.

"It's a beautiful striped, teal blue with black lace. Maybe the alterations will be finished by the end of the week, and I can wear it next Sunday."

She frowned as Alex pulled on his trousers and tucked in his shirt.

"Have you lost weight?"

He pulled his suspenders over his shoulders. "No, why?"

"I couldn't help notice how thin you are." She wrapped her corset around herself and began hooking the two sides together. "And your clothes are loose."

"Loose clothing is another recommendation. I suppose I've grown used to wearing a size or two larger." He shrugged, slipping his arms through the sleeve holes of his vest.

His too big, boring black waistcoats were fine for the bank, but on Sundays or special days, she couldn't wait to see how handsome he'd look in the new fitted ones she'd ordered, especially the mulberry jacquard.

Once their morning ablutions were complete, Annali followed Alex downstairs, out the front door, and around back to the necessary.

A few minutes later, she walked with him toward the barn on the other side of the garden. They stopped at the corral, where a black gelding with white stockings and blaze nibbled grass around the base of a fence post.

Annali reached through the middle rail and patted the gelding's neck.

"He's pretty. What's his name?"

"Ben."

"I haven't been around horses much. He's friendly."

Alex nodded and ran his hand under the horse's mane. "He's a good horse. We got him when we moved here, just after the war."

"Is he all you have? A horse and the chickens?"

"We had a cow, but she made more milk than we could use. Royd Pederson bought her a few years ago. "He's a widower with four children. That's his place way out there."

Annali turned in the direction he pointed. He stepped up behind her. His arm stretched out over her shoulder. "See that white house with the peaked roof and those two outbuildings?"

She nodded, and he lowered his arm, resting his arm across her chest.

"He and his brother do most of the construction you'll see going on around town. They're also both shareowners in the bank. Which reminds me, I need to talk to them if they come to church."

She turned into him and slipped her arms around his waist.

He kissed her forehead, and they parted. Alex headed toward the barn, and Annali marched toward the house. Drawing a deep breath, she climbed the back steps and pulled open the screen door.

Nellie stood at the stove lifting flapjacks from the griddle onto a platter. Harriet emerged from the pantry, carrying some plates and a small bowl.

"Good morning," Annali said, letting the door bump against her backside rather than bang against the jamb.

Both women turned, but neither uttered a word of

greeting. Not even a nod in her direction.

*Hells bells. This promised to be the start of three fun-filled weeks.* "What can I do to help?"

Harriet set the plates and bowl on the worktable in the center of the room then returned to the pantry. Nellie ladled more batter onto the griddle.

Annali stepped to the sink and using the water already in the dishpan, picked up the bar of soap and washed her hands.

"I can set out the plates for you." She moved to the table and seeing only three, considered whether the missing plate had been a simple mistake or intentional. She started toward the pantry as Harriet came out, carrying silverware, a crock of butter and a small jug of what looked like maple syrup. The corners of her mouth turned down, and her eyes narrowed.

"Where are you going?"

"To get another plate."

"Three is all we need."

Annali swallowed and stepped back as Harriet pushed past.

"Well come along, girl, if you insist. And bring the plates." In the dining room, Harriet set the butter and syrup in the center of the table then began laying out the silverware.

Annali followed behind, setting a dish at each place setting except the place where Alex sat.

Harriet must have sensed Annali's question for she turned and grasped the top of Alex's chair with both hands and raised her gaze to meet Annali's.

"Evidently Alexander hasn't mentioned his condition to you."

"Yes, he has, but I…"

Harriet heaved a long-suffering sigh and slowly shook her head. "This hasty marriage. So unlike Alexander to be impetuous. He tells me you are an orphan. No doubt you saw an opportunity to better yourself by manipulating—"

"Excuse me, but Alex asked me. Twice. And that was because I refused his first offer."

"Regardless, I see Alexander hasn't told you anything of import. I can only imagine he neglected to follow his diet while he was away. That likely caused this wild impulse to marry you along with his newest notion to put up for sale our only means of income."

Nellie entered the room, her gaze darting between Annali and her mother. She set a bowl of oatmeal, a small plate with a piece of toast and an egg cup at Alex's place.

Annali looked at the unappetizing meal and frowned.

"I see that look, girl. Don't you dare interfere into what is none of your concern."

"I'm sorry, but it is my concern. Alex is my husband, and he looks to be twenty pounds underweight. At least give him a larger portion."

Nellie moved up beside her mother. The pair presented a formidable line, which was oddly intimidating, considering the tops of their heads barely reached above Annali's eyebrows.

"Who do you think you are?" Harriet lashed out with all the intent of a rattlesnake strike. "To come into our home, a scheming little hussy from Lord knows where, with the audacity to tell me, to tell us, what is best for Alexander."

Was it better to give in or argue? She'd be gone in a

few weeks. Meanwhile, she'd have to live here with them. Both women glared at her with such malice, Annali acquiesced with a nod. She withdrew into the corner between the window and the doorway into the kitchen.

With their heads high, mother and daughter proudly savoring their small victory walked into the kitchen.

****

Alex took the back steps two at a time. The aromas of coffee and bacon wafted through the screen door as he pulled it open and entered the kitchen. "Morning."

"Good morning," his mother replied from the work table. A pile of potato skins in front of her, she peeled and cut potatoes into chunks before dropping them into a pot of water.

After washing his hands, he stepped up beside his sister, who slid a spatula under the last flapjack and passed it onto a platter already piled high. "Smells wonderful," he said as she set the spatula aside. He leaned over to kiss her cheek, just as she reached forward to lift the platter of flapjacks from the back of the stove.

His lips brushed over her hair.

He glanced around the room. "Where's Annali?"

"How should I know?" She shrugged.

Mother carried the pot of potatoes to the stove. "I took your breakfast to the table already."

"Thank you." He bent and gave her a quick peck on her cheek.

"Go ahead and seat your sister. I'll be right there."

Nellie picked up a second, smaller plate filled with bacon and carried it, and the platter, to the dining room.

Frowning, he stepped through the doorway. Annali stood just inside the room, hidden behind the jamb.

"Here you are." He grinned.

She smiled back, but it was her fake smile. The one that didn't reach her eyes.

He noticed then, the unease, the tension in the air. Moving close, he slid his hand around her waist. "What's wrong?" he whispered in her ear.

"Nothing," she breathed as he captured the word with his kiss.

"Alexander!"

He instinctively jumped back, hating the sting of heat across his cheek bones.

"Have you lost all sense of decorum?" Mother asked, her mouth drawn down at the corners. "A gentleman does not accost a woman in broad daylight in the middle of the family dining room."

He slipped his arm around Annali's waist and pulled her up against his side. "I have not accosted anyone. Annali is my wife."

"Pfff." Mother marched past them to the end of the table and stood beside her chair.

Alex guided Annali toward the chair to the left of his own and seated her first.

Immediately, his skin prickled as invisible daggers hurled toward him from the opposite end of the table.

He pulled out Nellie's chair next then moved to seat Mother, ignoring her narrow-eyed glare. He returned to his place, gave the blessing, and focused on his bowl of oatmeal.

Breakfast with a group of nuns under a vow of silence would have provided a more cheerful ambiance than that of breakfast with the Worthington family.

He'd never been so glad for Nellie to rise and begin clearing the table.

Taking Annali's hand, he laced his fingers with hers. "Let me show you around outside."

She flashed him a grateful smile as they headed out the back door and strolled toward the garden.

"Are you hungry?" He stopped in front of a row of green beans. "I can pick some vegetables for you. I noticed you barely ate half a flapjack."

"I'm fine. I don't usually eat breakfast, and I'm afraid I didn't much care for your sister's flapjacks."

He tugged her hand to his waist, drawing her so close their shoulders bumped together. "Mother used to make them on Sunday mornings, but I haven't had them in years. I imagine Nellie uses the same recipe."

"Old Maude, the cook at Madame Beauchamp's, made them big, like your sister's, but they were light and fluffy."

Alex guided her past the shed and chicken coop.

"And Mrs. G., when she could get ricotta cheese, made these wonderful little pancakes served with figs and drizzled with honey."

Ahead in the corral, Ben nibbled at bits of grass around the bottom of a fence post.

"Was it you who baked those peach turnovers?"

"Yes." She gave him a light shove with her shoulder. "You should have tried one."

"My apologies. I was too much the coward to risk even a bite. Make them again and I will."

She shook her head. "No. My feelings were crushed. I'll never bake them again."

Uncertain, he searched her face. Amusement gleamed in her eyes, or maybe it was a reflection of the sunlight.

She chuckled. "Alex, I'm teasing you. You take

everything to heart. I may have been disappointed that night, but I've had a few hard knocks in my life. It would take a lot for you to actually crush my feelings."

He nodded—hoped she wasn't lying to assuage his guilt. The horse came up to them as they reached the corral.

"I've been thinking... Do you know what I used to love when I was a boy? And I haven't had it in years."

"Let me guess. Custard, mince pie, molasses cookies?"

He shook his head and grinned. "Cake."

Chapter Sixteen

Alex shifted on the wooden pew and discreetly pulled out his watch. Nearly twelve-thirty. Reverend Clark had been droning on and on for over an hour. Beside him, Annali's eyes drifted closed as her chin lowered slowly toward her chest.

He gave her a slight nudge.

Her head snapped up. She blinked and met his gaze.

"How much longer?" Her whispered words barely audible.

He shrugged one shoulder and mouthed. "Fifteen minutes maybe."

A sharp pinch bit his waist. He winced. His gaze swung to his mother sitting on his other side. With her furrowed brow and downturned mouth, she scowled as if she were Aunt Polly and he Tom Sawyer misbehaving in church. Heaving a sigh, he refocused his attention on the tall, thin man behind the pulpit.

"Fornication is sin committed against your own body." The man droned on in his slow monotone.

"1 Corinthians 6:18 entreats us, 'Flee fornication. Every sin that a man doeth is without the body; but he that committeth fornication sinneth against his own body.'"

Beside him, Annali's hand slipped around his arm and slid down its length to twine her fingers with his.

He gave her hand a light squeeze.

"'Marriage is honorable in all, and the bed undefiled: but whoremongers and adulterers God will judge.'"

Alex had long ago accepted that his father had apparently held no fear of God's judgement, felt no shame for the evil he'd done.

"In 1 Peter 2:11, Peter says, 'Dearly beloved, I beseech you as strangers and pilgrims, abstain from fleshly lusts, which war against the soul…' For it is Satan who drives you to commit sin, but God will be your judge."

Alex glanced out the window at the cluster of buggies and the horses waiting in the hot sun, their tails swishing away flies.

He pictured his father standing before the Almighty. And God in his judgement rightly condemning Samuel Worthington to the deepest recesses of hell where he would burn for all eternity.

"For prayer and repentance are the only means to deliverance from the evil in your soul."

*Or a bullet to the center of the chest.*

Annali squeezed his hand.

He turned his head and returned her smile, grateful to have an ally, to not be struggling alone in all this.

"But keep your body and bring it into subjection, lest you should be cast aside."

His daily regimens had helped, but they couldn't stave off the inevitable.

"Let us pray."

\*\*\*\*

Alex found Royd Pederson and his brother heading to their respective buggies near the haystack alongside the church. Taking them aside, he explained he was selling the bank and wanted to meet with them the next morning to discuss the details.

Several minutes later, Alex hitched Ben to the buggy and drove around to the front of the church. Mother and Nell who'd been standing at the bottom of the steps marched straight toward him. So similar in dress and appearance the pair could have passed for sisters.

"Where have you been?" Mother demanded as he hopped down. "The roast will be burned by the time your sister and I get home."

"I hardly think so." He handed Nellie up into the seat then Mother. "You have never in your life burned anything."

"Alexander. I don't know where this new attitude of yours has come from, but it must stop."

"My apologies." He passed her the reins. "I will endeavor to guard my tongue."

"See that you do."

He stepped back.

"And don't dawdle. Dinner will be served at precisely one-thirty." Mother jiggled the reins, and the horse started forward.

He watched the buggy for a few moments then walked back to the corner of the building where Annali stood talking with Hester Clark.

Hester smiled at him, the first genuine smile he'd ever seen from her. "Congratulations on your marriage, Mr. Worthington. I wish you both much happiness."

"Thank you."

Annali exchanged good-byes with Hester then looped her arm with his, and they strolled west, away from the church. Though the town had been laid out in a grid, the streets were still wide and dusty and most of the city blocks were still empty. The church, a board and batten building with a steeple, stood alone on the corner of Eighth and Broad.

"Do you know Hester didn't want to marry you either?"

"She didn't? I had no idea."

"Did you even talk to her about it?"

"No. I wasn't told of the arrangement until the other morning at breakfast, right before I left for Lincoln."

A gust of wind spun up a small dust devil on the road in front of them and lifted the corner of Annali's hat. She slapped it back down with her hand.

He hadn't bought her a wedding gift, maybe she'd like a pair of nice hat pins.

"Hester didn't say, but I had the feeling someone else has captured her fancy."

"Really? Who?"

"I don't know. I'll find out tomorrow morning. We're going shopping."

"You're going shopping with Hester Clark?"

"Yes, why?"

"No reason. I never imagined you and she as friends."

"Don't you think someone like me can have friends?"

"No. Yes… I never thought about it. I…it's none of my concern how many friends you make while you're here. I'm glad you will have someone to help occupy your days, especially since neither Mother nor Nellie appear to be… If you need money, come to the bank in the morning. No need to use your funds."

They stepped to the side of the road as a horse and buggy trotted past.

"Are you sure you don't mind walking?"

"No. I've spent so much of my life indoors I've

rarely had the chance to feel the sun on my face."

"Daily exercise has been the one part of my regimen that I enjoy."

She grinned. "If not for your early morning walk, we never would have met."

"I'm glad I was able to help you."

"You're less scary looking now than you were on Friday. Instead of purple and black, now your eye is more violet and greenish yellow. Still, people seemed to give you a wide berth."

"It's not the bruises. It's because of my father, because of the rumors, and because I hold most of their mortgages. They gossip behind my back, looking for flaws, for the evidence that I will fail." He sighed. "Suffice it to say, people in this town don't like me much."

"Your mother must care—in her odd, overly strict way—if she's trying to protect you."

"I'd like to believe that's true, but sometimes I think she finds pleasure in being the victim. The wife of a profligate and gambler. The mother of a son who—"

"And your sister. Why doesn't she like you?"

"Nell? Why would you think that?"

Annali shrugged. "I've seen girls avoid a friendly kiss when they don't like the man. I've done it myself."

"What are you talking about?"

"Your sister moved away from you this morning before you could kiss her."

"That was merely poor timing on my part. She was trying to get breakfast out."

Annali shrugged. "Girls who do what I do, we don't kiss on the mouth. It's too familiar, but gentlemen will sometimes kiss our cheek or neck, and if they're too disgusting, we shrug them off. I laugh and pretend I was being coy. They never know."

Noon day sun beat down on his shoulders. A trail of sweat slipped down the side of his face. "Strange you should think that about Nell."

"I'm probably wrong. I don't know your sister."

"Until the other day I would have disagreed with you, now…" He stared ahead at the scattered houses and barns sprawled across the prairie in front of him.

"Nellie has always been shy. She's never had any friends and defers to Mother in all decisions, seemingly content to let Mother take that role. Looking back, she has frequently avoided my…touch. And the other morning I said something about Clayton, and she snapped at me. Called me an immature boy. Told me I know nothing of the world."

"Who's Clayton?"

"He's Nellie's husband."

"Her husband?"

"Yes, my apologies for not explaining earlier. Father arranged their marriage when Nell was about fifteen."

"Nellie told the doctor that he's coming home soon. What if he…?"

"You needn't worry that he'll recognize you."

"Are you sure?"

He chuckled. "Quite."

\*\*\*\*

Apparently, Alex was right. He was going blind. What other explanation could there be? Annali had received twenty-seven dirty looks so far over the course of Sunday dinner. Harriet by herself had shot well over a dozen poisoned darts toward Annali, and Alex-the-Ass hadn't said a word.

He sat there oblivious, sipping his water, cutting his beef, eating his boiled potatoes.

The silence grew so crushing, the soft clink of the silverware against the china plates sounded as loud as the clatter of pots and pans in the kitchen of the Burgess Café during breakfast rush.

The moment Harriet and Nellie set their knife and fork across the top of their plates, Annali jumped to her feet, snatching up both her plate and Alex's.

The rest of the family mirrored her movement and popped from their chairs. Harriet stepped around the table and took the plates from Annali's hands.

"No need," Harriet said. "Nellie and I will clear. Sit down. You are a guest."

Annali glanced at Alex, expecting him to say something, even it was just, *Annali is not a guest. She is my wife.* But he remained silent.

She surrendered her dishes to Harriet and slowly lowered herself back to her seat. Alex followed suit. Annali shot him a glare she hoped was on par with one of Harriet's, but Alex stared out the window seemingly unaware.

Beneath the table she stretched her foot toward his leg, but instead of running the top of her foot up back of his calf, she thumped him in the shin.

He flinched. His brow tugged together, and he gave her a blank look as he returned from wherever he'd gone in his head.

"I'm going for a walk," she said and stood.

He rose as Nellie returned with the pies left over from the night before. Behind her came Harriet carrying plates and a pie server.

"Are you off to the bank again?" she snapped.

"No, my wife and I are going for a walk."

Harriet set down the plates and grasped the back of Nellie's chair so tight her knuckles whitened.

"And when were you planning to discuss with me, this idea of yours to put the bank up for sale? I saw you talking to the Pederson boys after service."

"Mother, they own shares, you do not. Father's shares came to me when he passed. But you needn't worry. You will be provided for."

"And your sister? Have you considered her as well in this ridiculous scheme of yours?"

"I have. Nell, there will be funds set aside for you. Clayton however, will no longer receive his monthly…um…stipend…from me."

Nellie gasped.

Harriet hummed softly, like a tea kettle about to whistle.

Alex took Annali's hand. "Now if you will excuse us."

He led her through the parlor into the foyer. At the front door he released her hand. "I'll be right back." He dashed up the stairs.

Loath to remain in the house a moment longer, Annali opened the door and stepped onto the front porch.

How many days were left before the sale was final and she could get out of this town, go to Denver or San Francisco and purchase her own place? She descended the steps and walked to the end of the path. Grasping the top of the closest fence picket, she stared toward town.

There were some nice people here in Fremont, Esther and her family, the Lindbergs, and Miss Sinek at the dress shop. Even Hester Clark. But every one of those budding friendships were based on a lie. If any one of those fine ladies learned who she was, what she was—they'd lift their chins and cross to the other side of the street just as the women had in Council Bluffs and Lincoln.

Behind her, the front door opened and closed. Alex's footfalls skipped lightly down the steps and strode up the path.

She turned. Cradled in his left arm he held a gray blanket and a book.

"Come on," he said, extending his hand.

She placed her palm in his. "Where are we going?"

He led her around the side of the house and toward the small, white-washed barn. "Once the sun moves past noon, there's shade on the east side. And we won't be seen from the house."

Happy to sneak away, Annali helped him spread the blanket, and they sat, leaning against the board and batten wall. He passed her the book.

"What's this for?"

"I promised to help you with your reading, remember?"

"I can't read all this."

He laughed.

She couldn't help but smile. Had she ever heard him laugh? If she had, it hadn't sounded like this—deep, and full, and happy.

"No, not today." His laughter wound down to a few soft chuckles. "I'll help you with the first chapter. Then I thought, we could read the rest together in the evenings."

She ran her fingers down the cover, across the picture of some men in the basket of a falling hot air balloon on the brink of crashing into a stormy sea. She'd heard of balloons but had never seen one. "Can you imagine? How wonderful it must be on a clear day, floating through the sky just like a cloud."

"Yes, that's what I love about reading. You can leave your life and all its burdens and go away to…"

"Is this the book you were reading on the train?"

"Yes. *Dropped From the Clouds*. Mr. Jules Verne writes wonderful adventures, around the world, to the center of the earth, or to the moon. Can you imagine that?"

She sent him a sideways glance. "Is that what you do on Sunday afternoons. Hide out at the bank, away from your family, so you can read your books?"

He shrugged. "Among other things."

"I can understand why you'd want to do that. But why don't you have these books, or those Leather Stocking books, in your room?"

"My books are a secret. The only person who knows about them is Mrs. Lindberg. And now you."

"I don't understand."

"Because novels are over-stimulating."

She shook her head and chuckled. "You deny yourself personal pleasure, but you don't deny yourself books?"

He shrugged. "My father never read beyond the financial section of the paper. As such, I assumed writing and reading books are an indulgence I can allow myself. Please, don't tell anyone."

"I won't, but then where do you keep your books? In the bank vault?"

"Close. I keep them in a cabinet in my office."

She laughed, content to stay here with him for the entire day.

"I love the way you are when you're away from your family. Whenever they're around you turn into such an ass. Like you were at dinner."

"At dinner? My apologies. Old habits I suppose. Mother and Nell usually prattle on about the service and gossip about their church friends. After talking to Royd Pederson and his brother I realized there is much yet to be done.

"I'll be meeting with the other shareowners at ten tomorrow morning. My attorney will need to draw up the sales contract. Then as soon as it's ready I'll take the train to Lincoln and deliver it to Lathrop at the bank. I could send a messenger, but I—"

"Alex." She tipped her head up and met his gaze. "The more you talk the more you tense up."

"—don't want anything to go wrong."

"Relax. Things are going fine."

He sighed, leaned close, and kissed the top of her head. "You're right, but I've waited so long for this."

"You think too much."

"Maybe."

She opened the book and flipped to chapter one. Staring at the page the words blurred together. "What did you mean before when you told your sister Clayton wouldn't get any more money?"

"Clayton is…a…friendly, personable fellow, but he's not above a bit of extortion to get what he wants."

She looked up, meeting his gaze. "What's extortion?"

"He knows a secret about my father. And when Clayton needs cash he comes to me because he knows I guard that secret."

*What secret,* hovered on the tip of her tongue.

If she asked, he'd shut down, and this relaxed, fun Alex would turn into an ass. However, if she waited, it seemed likely he'd share the information in his own time.

She placed her finger below the first word on the page, took a breath, and began.

Most of the smaller words were easy to read, but there were so many unusual words like—*de-scen-ding, bal-last, and o-ver-board*—that she struggled to pronounce most of the first page. But the story grew so exciting eventually Alex took over the read, shifting around so he lay stretched out with his head resting on her thigh and the book propped upright on his chest.

The afternoon waned, and by the time Alex checked his watch, it was time to feed the horse and head inside for supper.

Harriet had prepared a beef and vegetable soup with cold meat sandwiches. Though it was surprisingly quite tasty, any enjoyment of the meal was again overshadowed by an atmosphere ripe with tension.

As soon as Harriet and Nellie began clearing the table, Annali escaped into the parlor and wandered around the room. She stopped to peruse the framed photographs along the mantel.

Alex came up behind her. Slipping his hands around her waist, he yawned and rested his chin on top of her head.

She leaned into him, content. "Who are all these people? I recognize the middle one. That's you."

He chuckled. "Yes, right before I went off to the university in Lincoln. I believe the photographer thought I would look smarter and more studious standing beside that podium."

"Who's the handsome soldier with Nellie?"

"Clayton."

"That's Clayton?"

"Yes. The photograph was taken on their wedding day, back in Kansas City, right after Clayton was forced to enlist because of the Militia Act."

"They're both so young."

"Nellie was about fifteen, and Clayton was around twenty."

"And who are those people in the old tintype?"

"Those are my parents." He yawned.

"That's your mother? Hell's bells, she's young."

"Annali, hush," he whispered.

"Sorry. But she looks like a girl, and your father is so much older."

"She was around fifteen maybe even fourteen."

"She looks more like twelve."

"She and Nellie are both petite and were, if I might be so crass, what are sometimes referred to as late bloomers."

"I'm sorry Alex, but hell. Your father looks like he's thirty."

"Shhh." He glanced over his shoulder. "If I remember correctly, from the birthdate I had put on his headstone he would have been...closer to thirty-three."

"How could she marry such an old man?"

"That's how it was back then. My mother came from a family of ten children. My father was fairly well off, working in a bank. He asked for her hand. It was a good match, and her parents agreed."

He drew a deep breath and exhaled. "They were living in Springfield Missouri then. Nellie was born there. Later they moved to Kansas City, where I was born. My father had worked his way up in banking, and

228

after Clayton left for the war, we moved to Des Moines. My father was a bank manager there. After the war we came here, where my father started his own bank."

"Well, I can see you have his height and slender frame, but even though his beard covers most of his face, I don't think you look like him, and even if you did, I don't believe whatever it was that made him insane, will happen to you."

"As much as I'd like to believe that I…" He yawned. Forgive me, but I seem to be more tired than usual. I must not have gotten enough sleep last night."

"Hmmm. I wonder why that might be." Tipping her head back she gave him a wink.

"Hush. Don't say things like that here."

"She's in the kitchen. How can she hear me?"

"With Mother one never knows how, but she can." He blew out a sigh and stepped back. Rolling his shoulders, he stretched. "If you'll excuse me, I think I'll lie down for a few minutes before I bathe. Will you be all right alone with my mother for a little while?"

"Yes, I'll be fine. If not, I'll come join you. See if I can tire you some more."

"Maybe later." He gave her a quick peck on the cheek and headed up the stairs.

Bored, Annali wandered to a curio cabinet beside the front window. A porcelain ballerina captured her attention. She leaned close to the glass fascinated by how life-like she looked standing on her toes, her arms over her head.

"What are you doing?"

Annali jumped. A mouse-like squeak caught in her throat as she whirled around.

Nellie stood in the doorway, a sewing basket looped

229

over one arm and a dark brown dress draped over the other. She took a seat in the wing chair and placed her mending in her lap. The accusatory glare she sent Annali was every bit as fierce as one sent by Harriet.

Annali backed toward the foyer. "If you'll excuse me, I think I'll join Alex upstairs."

Spinning on her heels, she rushed across the foyer and up the stairs. Relieved to have reached the sanctuary of Alex's bedroom, she closed the door, leaning against it for a moment as she released a tension filled sigh.

Alex lay sprawled across the bed, on his stomach. One arm hung off the edge of the mattress. Soft snores rumbled in the back of his throat.

He had kicked off his shoes and left them haphazardly on the floor. His coat hung from the closest bedpost. He'd removed his tie and collar and left them carelessly beside the pitcher and bowl on top of the washstand.

What was she supposed to do now? Too bad she couldn't whip up some bread dough to let rise or bake that cake Alex wanted. She wandered over to her trunk and picked up the book Alex had left there. As long as daylight streamed through the window, she could practice reading.

Stripping down to her chemise, she climbed into bed and leaning against the headboard, opened the book.

Chapter Seventeen

"Alexander!" Harriet's shrill voice rang out from the bottom of the staircase. "Are you awake?"

Startled from sleep, Annali blinked then threw her arm over her eyes. Why did these people have to get up so early?

Beside her Alex groaned. "Yes, Mother," he mumbled. He tossed aside the quilt Annali had covered him with, then rolled to sit on the side of the bed. Leaning forward, he propped his head in his hands like a man suffering bottle-ache.

"Alexander!"

"Yes, Mother!" he yelled, then moaned. "Damn, I'm more tired now than when I went to bed."

She sat up cross-legged. "Are you all right?" She reached out and rubbed his back.

"I can't get sick now." He stood.

Annali frowned as he dragged silently around the room, changing his clothes and shaving, his movements similar to Lilly's when she stumbled from bed each day.

Until this moment Annali hadn't given it much thought, but had Doctor Powell actually given Harriet laudanum to calm Alex's nerves? Had she secretly dosed his soup last night or was Alex really ill?

****

Alex sat at the breakfast table, his posture rigid, as though someone had laced his corset too tight. Austere in his black suit and perfectly knotted tie, he stared at his food for several long moments and sighed. Picking up his spoon, he dipped it into his oatmeal and brought it to his mouth with the enthusiasm of a child taking a spring dose of castor oil.

He ate a few bites, sipped his water, then set his napkin beside his bowl.

"I'm not very hungry this morning. If you will all please excuse me, I'm leaving for the bank." He stood and left the room.

Annali's gaze darted between Nellie and Harriet, as she tried to read in their expressions some hint which might confirm her suspicion. Either they were innocent or very good at poker.

She stood and tossed down her napkin. "Excuse me." Darting around the table, she called, "Alex, wait for me."

She caught up to him in the foyer as he lifted his bowler from a peg on the hall tree. "I'm coming with you." She dashed upstairs, grabbed her reticule, and hurried back down.

He opened the door for her and put on his hat. At the bottom of the steps, he offered his arm, and she walked with him at an amiable pace all the way into town.

Reaching the bank, he unlocked the door, and they moved inside.

"What are you going to do this morning?"

"If you'll take a couple of my dollars out of your safe, I think I'll walk down to get some breakfast at the Burgess Café. Then I'm meeting Hester Clark for some shopping."

He reached into his coat, withdrew his wallet, and passed her a couple of banknotes. "Take these. You don't need to spend your own money."

"Do you want me to bring you something? You didn't eat either."

He shook his head. "I'm feeling a bit out of sorts."

She folded the bills and slipped them into her reticule. She'd forgotten her Derringer. Oh, well. She probably wouldn't need it here. Everyone believed she was a lady.

"Do you think you'll feel better later? Can we meet for lunch?"

He stepped close and gave her a quick kiss on the cheek. "Go. Have a good time. I will see you at noon."

Before he could turn away, she reached out and grabbed his hand. "Alex, the other night, while you fetched the doctor's buggy, I heard them talking and the doctor told your mother—"

"Can this wait?" He frowned, already pulling his hand from hers. "I have an important meeting this morning for which I must prepare."

"Yes, I'll tell you later." After all her suspicions were just that. There was no proof. Why upset him needlessly?

\*\*\*\*

Annali met Hester at the dress shop after a leisurely breakfast. Her new friend eagerly accepted Annali's advice for hats, flattering dress colors, and hair styling. They chatted as they shopped, and Annali discovered the mystery man Hester liked was Royd Pederson.

"He barely knows I exist," Hester said as they strolled toward the bank. "He's so handsome, and he's one of the few men actually taller than me. He already has children, so it may not matter that I'm too old bear him another."

"He'll notice you now," Annali said as they crossed the street. "Those grays and browns you were wearing absorbed all the color from your complexion. These richer colors you picked will brighten your whole face, and fixing your hair so it's not pulled back in that severe style will soften your features."

Hester stopped and pulled Annali into a hug. "Thank you for helping me. I'm so glad you married young Mr. Worthington. And you don't seem scared of him at all."

Annali chuckled. "Why would I be?"

Hester shook her head. "Oh, no reason. A few unfounded rumors about young Mr. Worthington and…"

They continued up the walk. Rumors. Again. Alex had gotten angry when she'd mentioned what Mrs. Lindberg had said. Why?

"Forgive me," Harriet gushed as they turned the corner onto Sixth. "I'm being silly. After all it's been five years since old Mr. Worthington was mur…died. And…"

"And what?"

"And, I shouldn't say. You are married and know the truth better than me."

"Hester."

"I'm sorry, but his mother often confides in my father and some of us in the Ladies Fellowship Circle, about young Mr. Worthington, his outbursts of temper and erratic behavior."

Annali gasped and tugged Hester out of sight into a narrow space between two buildings. "That's ridiculous."

"Forgive me for interfering, but after Sunday service, my father expressed some concern for you. You're so young, and sweet, and your marriage so hasty, we fear you might be naïve to young Mr. Worthington's true self. That your love may have blinded you to—"

"Hester, stop."

Alex was right. Harriet did tell everyone everything. "You don't need to worry about me. I am not naïve to Alex's faults, nor he to mine. We have no secrets. What I don't understand is if your father is so concerned about me, why in the he— in the world did he want you to marry Alex?"

Hester glanced toward the street and shook her head. "He didn't. He just couldn't say no. Despite her diminutive stature, young Mr. Worthington's mother can be a rather forceful woman."

Annali burst out laughing.

The rigid set of Hester's shoulders eased. She grinned. "I'm glad then for your sake, that the rumors aren't true. I never should have brought it up. You've been nothing but kind. Forgive me."

"Of course. You helped me too, choosing this lovely shawl. I can't wait to show Alex."

They parted with a promise to get together again. Hester crossed the street toward her home, and Annali turned the corner, walking toward the bank.

A little girl with blonde curls, wearing a blue dress, walked toward Annali, both her arms wrapped around a wicker basket. "Good morning," said the girl.

"Good morning to you," Annali replied.

The girl raised her basket. "Would you like a kitten?"

"Oh, you have kittens in there?"

"You want to see?" She moved off to the side where a few chairs had been lined up in front of a boot shop. She set the basket down and lifted away a light green blanket.

Four little heads raised and blinked up at Annali. Three were gray tigers and the fourth gray with a white bib and paws.

Annali reached in and picked it up, holding it close under her chin.

"Do you want that one?" The little girl looked up, her blue eyes wide and earnest.

Mr. Giovani had had a few cats around in the back room of the bakery to keep the mice out of the flour and sugar, but they were wild and though Annali had tried to make friends with them, they would scratch and claw her if she did manage to catch one.

This kitten seemed to like cuddling, and Annali hated to return her to the basket.

"You can keep that one if you want. Papa said I have to give them all away. We have too many."

"I'm sorry, but I don't know if my husband will let me keep it."

"Can you ask him?"

Annali chuckled as she pried the tiny claws from her new shawl and returned the kitten to the basket. It wasn't Alex she feared would say no.

"I'll ask him. What's your name? Where can I find you if he says yes?"

"I'm Sarah." She covered the kittens with the blanket, and they immediately began mewing. "Can you ask him now?"

"All right, he's at the bank right up there. You stay here, and I'll be right back." Annali started walking, and Sarah followed right beside her.

"Can I come with you? My papa was at the bank before. He said I could give away kittens, but I have to stay on this side of the street, and I can't go around any corners. That's the rule."

"Where is your papa? You must tell him where you're going."

Sarah ran ahead, past a few store fronts and pointed toward the roof of a tobacco shop where two men were putting up trusses for a pitched roof.

A tall blond man hunkered down at the corner of the flat roof to talk to Sarah who pointed toward Annali.

"Yes, you can go." Annali heard as she drew close. The man nodded. "You're young Mr. Worthington's new wife."

"Mr. Pederson?" She guessed.

He nodded. "Sarah can go with you. Bring her back here when you're done."

"I will," Annali said. The little girl walked beside her, so trusting, as if Annali was the same as any other woman in town. It felt strange, but nice, this taste of a life she'd never known and never believed she could have.

They met Mr. Farley at the front steps. He tipped his hat.

"Good afternoon, ladies." He held the door and entered behind them.

Instead of sitting at his desk, Mr. Goldman stood behind the first teller window waiting on a frumpy man with white hair.

Annali held open the swinging gate for Sarah to walk through.

Mr. Goldman took a step back from the window and turned toward Annali.

"He's at a meeting with his attorney. He should be back soon."

"Thank you," Annali said. "We'll wait in his office." She opened the door, gesturing Sarah in ahead of her.

The little girl set the basket down, then she and Annali sat together on the floor while the kittens tumbled over each other and climbed into Annali's lap.

Several minutes later, the door opened.

Annali looked up. Her smile faded.

Alex stood silhouetted in the doorway, his face ashen, his eyes widened in horror.

She scrambled to her feet. "Alex?"

"Get. That. Child. Out of here!"

Annali scooped the kitten she'd been playing with back into the basket. Sarah quickly gathered up the rest.

"Come along, sweetie," Annali said, taking the little girl's hand. "Mr. Worthington has a headache. Let me take you back to your papa." She hustled Sarah past Alex whose gaze was fastened on the ceiling. As they moved through the lobby, the door behind them slammed.

\*\*\*\*

Panting, Alex struggled to breathe. His stomach rolled as sweat broke out across his forehead. Pulse racing, he staggered to his desk hoping his knees wouldn't give out.

He reached a trembling hand to pull his chair closer, but his fingers brushed over the arm, and the chair rolled toward the wall. Heart pounding, he lowered himself to the floor.

Drawing his knees close to his chest, he pressed his back against the drawers and leaned forward. His heart hammered wildly behind his breastbone. Pressing the heels of his hands against his eyes, he fought for each shallow breath. Bright white spots flashed behind his eyelids.

*This can't be happening.*

A wave of dizziness washed over him. He gagged, swallowing back the acidic taste of stomach bile grateful he'd only eaten a few bites of oatmeal.

He found himself gathered against something soft, something warm, something safe.

"Alex, what's wrong? Let me send Mr. Goldman for Doctor Powell."

"No," he gasped. "Don't leave." He clenched fistfuls of material, clinging to her desperately, too terrified of dying alone to let her go.

Her hand, warm against his clammy forehead, gave him comfort.

"Shhh," she whispered. "Shhh. Calm, Alex. Breathe."

Gradually, his short gasping pants slowed to match each hush she whispered. The room slowed its spinning as his heart beats settled into a normal rhythm. Still, he clung to her, loathe to let her go.

Her fingers sifted through his hair, calming…soothing.

"Alex." She nudged his shoulder. "Are you feeling better? Can you sit up?"

He sighed and pushed himself off her lap. He leaned back, resting his head against the edge of the desktop. Shakey and embarrassed, he studied the dings and scratches in the wall behind his chair.

He half expected her to run, but she remained beside him.

Mortified that she'd seen him in such a condition, he focused on the wall, counting the hairline cracks in the plaster, refusing to look at her, terrified he'd see revulsion in her expression, or worse pity.

"Don't you like kittens?"

"What?"

"Kittens. Do you like kittens?"

He blew out a sigh and scrubbed his hands over his face. "Kittens? What are you talking about?"

"When you walked into your office, we were on the floor playing with kittens."

He massaged the knot tightening the muscles at the back of his neck. "I didn't see any kittens."

"Hmmm. That's what I thought. So, are you going to tell me?"

He turned and met her gaze. Her eyes glistened. Tears? For him?

"Alex, you can't live like this. Is this what happens every time you see a little girl?"

"No." He tipped his head back focused for a moment on the ceiling. "Only that she was here. On her knees. I could see him—"

Annali gasped. Her hand clamped over her mouth as her eyes squeezed shut.

He reached for her hand gripping it tight, though he couldn't tell whose fingers crushed whose.

She drew several deep breaths and opened her eyes. A stray tear leaked from the corner. She swiped it away. "Is that what you're so afraid of…becoming?"

"Yes," he whispered.

He shoved to his feet. Pulling her up beside him, he wrapped her in a hug.

Her hands slipped around his waist beneath his coat, up his back, to his shoulders. "Are you sure he violated—"

He gently turned her to face the opposite wall which separated the office from the vault. He nodded toward the bookcase, the picture of President Hayes, and the ridge in the plaster, outlining the top of the old door. "Remember when you asked about that?"

"You said it went to an old storeroom."

"I caught him. In there. His trousers down...a...little girl..." He pressed the heels of his hands against his eyes, trying in vain to erase an image forever burned into his brain.

Annali's stepped in front of him.

He'd told her the truth, and she was still here. He pulled her close and rested his chin on top of her head.

"I attacked him. That vile, revolting, evil *thing* who was my father. We fought. Right here. I never in my life felt such rage. I wanted to kill him."

He released a shuddering breath against her hair and tightened his arms around her.

"It was a Saturday afternoon. The bank was closed. I'd come home from college for the Thanksgiving holiday and come here directly from the train. The door was locked, but I had a key.

"Our fight was bad. The office a mess. Both of us bruised and bleeding. I came to in that corner over there. By then it was dark. I dragged everything out of that room—a straw pallet, children's books, dolls, candy—took it all way out back and set it on fire. I returned here, picked up the best I could, grabbed my suitcase and left. I walked to the depot and took the first train going west. I planned to never come back."

"Why did you?"

"The little girl. I got as far as Cheyenne. I couldn't stop thinking about her. Had my father taken her with him, or had she escaped while we were fighting? I didn't know what I was going to do, but I had to find her, see if she would be all right."

"Did you?"

He shook his head and squeezed her a little tighter. "I couldn't get back until the next day. I asked around, but I had to be discrete. The best I could presume was that she'd been on the train, and her family had come into town during a wait to transfer to another line. I can only hope that I stopped him before he went too far.

"Now I wonder every time I see a young lady come into the bank, walk down the street, or sit in the next pew at church. Had she once been…? Does she see me and remember? Does she too believe like father like son?"

Annali pushed away from his shirt front. "Does your mother know? Is that why she so controls every area of your life? Because she's afraid too?"

"No. She doesn't know. No one does. If any of the girls he violated said anything, I've heard naught. Mother believes his onanism caused his obsession for the company of wh—upstairs girls to satisfy his insatiable appetite for intercourse. At least when my father visited one of those places, he wasn't ruining the lives of…"

Annali tipped her head back to meet his gaze. "Alex, I don't know if you know this, but there are places in the cities, dark, secret brothels, that cater to particular tastes…"

Cold washed through him. He set her away from him and dropped to sit on his desk. He searched her tearstained face. Nausea rolled through his stomach again. For a moment his ability to think vanished.

"Most times they're orphans or runaways," she whispered, lacing her fingers tight against her waist. "Girls and boys, even young men."

"Damn," he choked out. "Are you saying…when

my…when he…went to Chicago on bank business, he was… With innocent children?"

She shrugged.

He rubbed his hands over his face. "Everyone believes he was with women, courtesans. Why don't they run away?"

"Some of them prefer that life," she said softly. "Rather than a life of petty theft, hawking newspapers, and going hungry, sleeping in the rain and snow. Some of them have already been violated by family members or others on the street."

"Double damn."

"Madams pay a lot of money to the law for turning a blind eye, and men like your father will pay high prices to get what they want."

"And you…? Have you…?"

She shook her head. "No. My mother didn't leave me on the street. She sold me to the Giovani's. I started in their bakery was I was six."

"Thank God."

"Still, I am what I am."

He reached for her hand. "And if you weren't, you could never comprehend…never understand the weight…" Her hand in his, he drew her forward and kissed her knuckles "You're the only person I could ever tell."

"I thought you said Clayton knows."

"Clayton knows my father embezzled money from the bank to cover his gambling debts. I've been careful to protect the bank's reputation as a trustworthy institution. Clayton understands that and uses it against me."

She lifted her chin and met his gaze. "Alex, you're

not destined to become your father."

He shook his head. "How do you know what I'll become? What my constant desire for physical release, for intercourse will grow into?"

"Desire is normal. But what your father… that's not."

"Exactly." He set her away from him then leaned over and yanked open the bottom drawer of his desk. Dropping his ledger on the desk, he opened the false bottom and pulled out his sheaf of papers and set them aside before passing her an article Doctor Powell had given him by George H. Naphreys from the Journal of Mental Science.

"Read this."

She skimmed over the words, then slowly read,

"*The habit of self-abuse gives rise to a particular and disagreeable form of insanity…*"

"Skip past the part about extreme perversion, down to the bottom where it's underlined."

"*Once the habit is formed… The sooner he sinks into his degraded rest, the better for himself and the better for the rest of the world, which is well rid of him.*"

She lowered the article, her lip drawn tight between her teeth.

"Better the world is well rid of me." He reached into the drawer again, wrapped his hand around the grip of his new pistol and set it on the corner of his desk.

She gasped and shook her head. "No. You can't mean that?"

"I do. Better the world is rid of me now than I wait until I become as loathsome and perverted as my father. God knows I'll do it myself, before someone does it for me."

Chapter Eighteen

A tentative knock on the office door jolted Annali's attention from both the gun and the sick feeling churning in the pit of her stomach.

"Mr. Worthington, sir?"

Alex heaved a sigh. "What is it?"

"Sir, Mr. Goldman has gone to lunch, and we've suddenly become quite busy. If you could take the other window…"

"Coming." Alex locked his gaze with hers. "What it means to me…" he whispered. "That you know the truth…and stayed." He pulled her close, kissed her forehead, and stepped away.

Picking up the gun, he replaced it in the bottom drawer, and using the toe of his shoe, he pushed the drawer closed.

"If you don't mind waiting, there are books in the bottom of that cupboard over there. When Goldman returns, we'll go to lunch." He stepped around the desk and started for the door.

At the last moment he turned. "Annali, I…" Pink stained his cheek bones. "Thank you." Whirling, he fled, pulling the door closed behind him.

Annali stared after him, hardly able to fathom the horror of the secret he shared—the depth of his fear.

Beyond a doubt, his father had been a revolting human being, but having seen how Alex reacted to

Sarah, she couldn't imagine he possessed anything close to the same unnatural obsessions as the man who sired him. There must be a way to convince Alex he was not destined for the same end.

Turning from the door, she paced the perimeter of the room, stopping at the place in the wall where the door had been. She massaged her temples refusing to picture the room or what might have gone on in there. And Alex had to look at that reminder every day.

She wandered back to his desk then sat in his chair. She stared at the wall. Alex must look at that spot a hundred times a day.

If she rearranged his office, she could put that view behind his desk. Yet, Alex was smart. He could have done that himself.

Why did he need to punish himself with the reminder, like one of those monks who wore hair shirts and whipped themselves. Thank God he'd put the gun away, but she still saw it, laying on the corner of his desk, placed there with such finality, his intention clear.

He was only twenty-four. There had to be some way to prevent such a tragedy. What had he determined to be that line, which once reached, would signal his need to end his life?

He wouldn't do anything until after the sale of the bank. Could she convince him by then?

Heaving a sigh, she picked up the thick sheaf of papers he normally kept in his bottom drawer now forgotten beside a green ledger. She set them on the blotter in front of her.

Skipping words she didn't know, she made her way down the page.

*Tentacles of brush tore at the sleeves of his buckskin*

*shirt as he dodged trees and leapt gullies and deadfalls. Sweat trailed down his face and neck as he ran, pushing aside low branches with one hand, his Kentucky Long rifle held in the other. Were they still behind him?*

What was this? Annali thumbed through several of the handwritten pages. A slow grin spread across her face. Alex was writing a book.

A frontiersman out hunting was being pursued by several Shawnee Indians. Trying to out fox them, he entered a creek and created a false trail leading out, then he reentered and headed downstream.

The office door closed with a soft click. Annali looked up, meeting Alex's gaze across the room. He didn't appear happy to see her reading his story.

"You wrote this?"

He walked toward her and reached out as if he were going to snatch the pages away as he'd done in the past, but he hesitated and lowered his hand to his side.

What the hell, she might as well be shot for sheep as a lamb. "Alex, this is really good."

He seemed to study her a moment, as though gauging her sincerity. "You like it?"

"Yes." She returned the pages she'd read to the top of the pile.

"It's just something to do when I have time."

"Well, it's wonderful. Is this what you do when you go to the bank early every morning?"

He shrugged.

"You know what this tells me? It tells me you have hope. That what you believe about yourself, what you think you might become is overshadowed by this. Your dream." She pulled open the bottom drawer. "And between that damn gun—" She nodded toward the drawer. "—and this story, you should pick the story."

He ran his hand around the back of his neck. "You really believe that?"

"Yes." She picked up the pages and replaced them inside the drawer. "And before this bank is sold, I'll find a way to make you believe it too."

Standing, she stepped around the desk as he moved toward her and wrapped her in his arms.

"I never imagined," he murmured into her hair. "On that train, how deeply I...how in awe of you I would become."

They left the bank, her arm looped through his, as they strolled the few blocks to Burgess Café.

"My attorney will have the sales contract ready for me by noon tomorrow. I'm taking the four o'clock train to Lincoln to deliver them. Come with me."

She forced a smile and shook her head. "I'll be fine here."

He stopped and stepped to the side of a gunsmith shop. "No, come with me. We'll get away from this town, from Mother, and have some fun. Maybe go to the theater."

She reached out and adjusted his tie. "I love how you forget what I am. You can't be seen with me in Lincoln. I'll ruin everything." She brushed a bit of dust from his shoulder.

He grabbed her hand and pulled her close. "People see what they expect to see. We'll be fine."

"Alex, you don't realize the risk. My hair. Men know me by this blonde streak. I can't go. At least here I can walk through town as your wife, have coffee at the restaurant. I can visit Hester or the dressmaker's shop without people crossing the street to get away from me or sticking their noses in the air and ignoring me as if I'm no better than the dirt under their feet."

His shoulders sagged and his mouth turned down in a sad sort of smile. He glanced around then leaned down and kissed her forehead. "Do you ever wish it could be different?"

"Sometimes. But this…what we've had this week isn't reality. Sooner or later, someone will recognize me and think they can take what they want. Like those men in the alley. No, I'd rather work someplace where they have to pay to be with me, and where big, muscular men like Hiram and Walter, even George are ready to toss them to the street if they go too far. While I love being here with you in this town, this can't be forever so please—"

"My apologies." He offered his arm. "Then let us enjoy what we have for as long as it lasts." He escorted her down the street and around the corner to Burgess Café .

\*\*\*\*

After lunch Alex returned to the bank, and Annali, notebook and pencil in hand, walked to Lindberg's Dry Goods and Furniture Emporium. The little Italian woman followed Annali up and down the aisles eagerly making suggestions as Annali jotted down prices for an assortment of furniture and linens she might need in her new parlor house. The poor woman more than likely assumed Annali intended to redecorate Alex's current house and would later purchase these things from her store.

Overwhelmed by the enormity of the potential cost, Annali garnered a new respect for Madame Beauchamp's need to squeeze every penny from both her girls and her customers.

Returning to the bank a little before six, she and Alex strolled home as any young married couple might stroll. They chatted about everything from the weather to how fast the town was growing, from Alex's struggle to understand banking to the time Annali dropped a bowl filled with two dozen already cracked eggs on the bakery floor.

Except this time together was something of a holiday from real life, at least her real life. Bittersweet in that while she knew their time would end, much like love, maybe she was better for having known it.

She wouldn't miss family meals eaten in silence. Though tonight Harriet served a cool glass of lemonade along with Sunday's leftover roast beef. While Alex still was only given water, at least a wedge of lemon floated in the glass.

Afterward, as Nellie and Harriet cleared the table, Alex ran upstairs to grab his book.

With her arm looped through his, they wandered outside to feed and pet the horse then settle in behind the barn to read.

With a yawn, Alex stretched out as he had the day before, with his head in her lap. For a moment Annali savored the warmth of the summer evening and imagined she was a normal girl being courted by her favorite suitor. Opening the book and lifting aside the train-schedule bookmark, she read aloud.

Slowly, she worked her way down the page, carefully sounding out each big word she came to, certain she'd mispronounced every one. But since Alex said nothing, she continued.

A fly landed on the page. Instinctively, she shooed

it away. She glanced at Alex. His eyes were closed, his chest slowly rising and falling. She poked his shoulder.

"Alex, what does c-o-n-v-a-l...Alex?" The fine hairs at the back of her neck prickled. She grabbed his shoulder and gave him a shake.

He groaned and raised his hand in a feeble wave before it fell back into the grass. She shook him again. "Alex, wake up!"

She scooted around behind him, shoving at both shoulders, forcing him to sit, but he only fell back against her.

"Alex, you can't sleep out here. You have to get inside and go to bed."

A quiver rippled through the walls of her stomach. *Lily.* Scooting out from behind him, she eased him back to lie on the ground. Coming to her feet, she dashed around the barn then ducked inside. In the corner she spotted a bucket. Snatching it up, she ran out to the horse trough and scooped the wooden pail full.

Water slopped over the sides onto her skirt as she lugged it around the building.

Lying right where she'd left him, Alex slept blissfully on.

Annali upended the bucket, drenching his head and upper body in a deluge of water.

Coughing and sputtering, he swiped water from his eyes and nose.

"Damn! What are you—" He sat up, shoving his hands over his head, shucking his dripping hair back off his forehead. "What did you do that for? Are you trying to drown me?"

She dropped the bucket. "You were sleeping."

"I know." He rubbed his face and heaved a sigh.

"You didn't wake up."

"I didn't feel like it."

"Alex, I think you mother is dosing you with laudanum."

"What? Don't be ridiculous."

"But—"

He reached out, swiping droplets from the cover of his book. "You got my book wet." He picked it up and flipped through the pages giving it a shake or two.

She snatched the bucket off the ground, clenching the rope handle tightly in both hands as she considered. She could swing it and clonk him in the side off his head as she'd done to Neeley with her basket of peaches, or she could… Raising the bucket over his head, she tipped out the remaining bit of water.

"Double damn, what's wrong with you?"

"I wanted to be sure you were awake."

He finger-combed his hair, loosened his tie, and unbuttoned his collar. Glancing up, he shot her a scowl reminiscent of the ones Harriet often shot toward Annali when Alex wasn't looking.

Rolling to his feet he held out his arm, ever the gentleman, despite what she'd done.

She took his arm, and swinging the bucket like a basket, they returned the bucket to its corner in the barn.

"I heard them talking the other night," Annali said. "Your mother and the doctor. About you needing a sedative."

"Mother is a woman who enjoys being a victim. Who constantly reminds me and anyone who will listen, how she has suffered trying to save a son destined to become a gambling, womanizing, reprobate. If she felt the need to sedate me, she would be sure to let me know how she agonized over this difficult decision."

"Maybe it was Nellie."

"Nell would never hurt me. Beside she has no more gumption to think beyond what Mother tells her to do than a mouse trembling in the corner."

Annali glanced up at him as they walked past the garden. Were they talking about the same person? Nellie might be quiet, but a mouse in the corner? More like an alert beady-eyed rat.

At the porch he paused. "This has been a long, trying day. And whether you choose to believe me or not, I am exhausted. You may come upstairs with me or remain down here." He pressed the book into her hands. "Keep reading if you like."

He held the door, and they walked through the kitchen into the parlor.

"Alexander! You're all wet." Harriet glared at Annali.

Alex plucked at the lapel of his coat. "So I am."

"Despite your sarcastic tone, I can only consider this as further evidence of your erratic and impulsive behavior."

"Believe me or not, Mother. I'm too tired to care. Now if you'll excuse me…"

"Excellent idea, change out of those wet clothes before you catch a chill, and I'll call you when your bath is ready."

"I told you I'm tired, and I will not be taking a bath tonight."

"What? Alexander a daily bath is an essential part of your regime. From your recent unpredictable behaviors, maintenance of your daily routine is more important than ever."

"I don't want a bath. I'm tired. I'm going to bed."

Annali glanced from Harriet to Nellie. An evening with these two ladies? No. If Annali spent more than five minutes in their company, she'd more than likely confront them about the laudanum and the dreadful consequences of its prolonged use.

She scooted past Alex, into the foyer, and up the stairs.

Alex followed a moment later, his footfalls heavy on the treads behind her. "How can a dousing of warm water on a summer night, give me a chill and a cold bath in January be good for me?"

Maybe the blinders were coming off, and he'd soon realize there was nothing wrong with him.

Once the door closed, he stripped out of his wet clothes and climbed into bed wearing only his drawers. Pulling the covers up, he rolled onto his side. "G'night," he mumbled.

With nothing to do, Annali sat on her trunk. Maybe she was wrong, and he was just tired. It had been a hell of a day.

Taking the little notebook and pencil out of her pocket, she once again imagined all the rooms in her parlor house and how much it would cost to furnish it.

Sometimes houses were sold fully or partly furnished. That would be something to keep an eye out for. Or she could save money by purchasing used furniture.

Next, she considered her wardrobe. Madame had always dressed in beautiful gowns like those a fine lady might wear. Madame's clothes weren't designed to tease and lure men.

Annali flipped open her trunk, sifting through layers

of silk and linen. Maybe some of these could be altered.

Pulling out her pink gown, she held it up against herself. Maybe a light blush color underskirt and another tier or two of ruffles in the same shade. The bodice would need to be reworked long sleeves added, and buttons that opened down the front.

Maybe Miss Sinek had some magazines or fashion plates Annali could look through to see what the fine ladies from New York and San Francisco were wearing.

But Miss Sinek was a respectable woman. Annali couldn't ask her to rework these gowns. In Lincoln, Madame had someone who did business through the back door late at night and was paid double to make gowns for the girls. Once Alex paid her, Annali could go there.

As she reached to close the lid, she spotted a bit of faded calico and pulled out the rag doll her father had given her all those years ago. She fluffed out Betty Lou's flattened dress. The simple cloth doll had once been Annali's best friend. The friend with whom she'd shared all her fears and secrets in those early years at the bakery. She laid Betty Lou on top of the lavender gown and reached between the dresses and the back of the trunk, her fingers brushing over the book of Mr. Giovani's handwritten Italian recipes.

With so much attention today on Alex's father, Annali wondered about her own. She had no memory of cruelty from him only happiness when he came to visit. Who had he been? What had happened to him? After all these years she'd likely never know.

Mr. Giovani, too, had been a nice man. She ran her finger over the red leather cover. Though she'd been expected to work hard, he and his wife had both been kind to her. Mr. G. had never touched her, even to punish.

She couldn't imagine being a scared little girl and having someone as large and intimidating as a grown man do with her the things Annali did now. She shivered and tried to put images of old Mr. Worthington from her mind, thankful her mother had tried to give her a different life.

\*\*\*\*

Jane Sinek stepped through the curtained doorway into the main shop. "I finished the waistcoats you ordered for young Mr. Worthington."

Annali looked up from an assortment of ribbons and lace, displayed on a rack behind the ready-made dresses.

Jane laid the new waistcoats on the table in front of a wall of shelves stacked with bolts of fabric. "I hope you like them."

Annali joined her. "They're beautiful." She ran her fingertip over the collar of the mulberry jacquard, awed by the workmanship.

Jane smiled. "I enjoyed the opportunity to create something other than women's dresses."

"I can't wait to see these on Alex." Annali picked up the teal stripe, fascinated by the way Jane had covered each button with pieces from the shiny strips of fabric.

"If you have time to try on your gown, I have the alterations basted."

A few minutes later Annali stood on a low pedestal, staring at the respectable young lady in the mirror as Jane checked each area of the sleeves, bust and waist. "Do you like it?"

Annali brushed her hand down the front of the skirt. For a moment the oddest sensation washed over her, as though the refined woman in the mirror was the real Annali Hansson and Ivy had been the façade.

"Yes," she whispered. "It's the most beautiful gown I've ever owned."

## Chapter Nineteen

A half hour later, Annali walked into the bank and stepped in line behind the town marshal, who spoke in low tones to the new teller, an average man of nondescript features, Alex had mentioned hiring. The marshal stepped away and gave her a nod as she moved up to the window.

Whether it was the fact that the teller was new, or that she was Alex's wife, the poor man made two subtraction mistakes in her bank book and dropped a blot on the page when he forgot to tap the nib of his pen against the rim of the inkbottle.

Her money finally in hand, she folded it into her purse and snapped the clasp. With her purse back inside her reticule, she stepped around the teller's area and gave the door to Alex's office two quick taps before she turned the knob and entered.

He glanced up and smiled as he came to his feet. He'd removed his coat. Despite the baggy waistcoat, his spectacles and sleeve garters reflected the very image she held of a hard-working bank president.

"I came to see if we could have lunch before you leave."

He moved around his desk and gestured to one of the two chairs in front.

She started toward a chair, but at the last moment she shifted her direction and sat instead on the corner of his desk.

His gaze went straight to her bosoms, now level with

his big brown eyes. They widened and a flush of pink tinged his cheekbones.

She grinned. Teasing Alex was such fun.

He gestured toward the ledger. "My apologies, but the train leaves in about two hours and Mr. Paxton's drawer from yesterday doesn't balance. If I don't fix this now, it will be even harder to trace any mistakes he makes while I'm gone."

"But surely you have time for a goodbye kiss."

"Annali, this is a place of business. I have to get this done. Now please, you're on my ledger."

"Just a kiss, Alex. How long does that take?"

"With you, 'just a kiss,' won't be enough. We've not…the past two nights—"

"That's your mother and her laudanum."

He shook his head. "Regardless, now that I've…now that we've…I can't stop thinking about…and I want you so much right now if I kiss you, I fear I'll ravish you."

She laughed. "Alex you're wonderful. What would you say if I told you I can't stop thinking about the other night either, and that right now I want you to ravish me."

Red scorched his cheeks and tinged the tips of his ears. "Annali—" He cleared his throat. "The train. I have work to do. We haven't time for—"

"Yes, we do, right here." She patted the desktop beside her. "You just stand between my knees. Or you sit here, and I'll straddle your lap. Or we both stand, you behind me, and I'll lean over the desk."

"Stop it." He shoved back his chair, bolting to his feet. "Godly gentlemen do not…do not…perform their duty…in such a…Annali, this is a place of business, not a whore house."

"I'm sorry. I was teasing you. Just a little." She hopped off the desk. "But one day, before our arrangement is over, I'll show you how much fun we—"

"Stop. You're putting images in my head that are…that are making me…"

Annali stepped close and leaned close to whisper in his ear. "I can take care of *that* for you. You did tell me you dreamed of a woman on her knees…" She lowered her hand to his waist then slowly down to his groin, and the bulge of his hardened shaft.

He groaned, then pushed her arm away. He drew several deep breaths, his gaze locked on hers. "I thought I was clear. I don't want to make love with Ivy."

The bubble of laughter inside her suddenly burst as if pierced with a needle. "You're an ass." She stepped back, bumping against the desk. "Do you know that? I can't forget what I've learned. And I don't want to."

"Then how am I to ever know the difference?"

"Maybe you'll never figure it out, but don't forget you wanted Ivy because you didn't want a frigid virgin. And that wanting doesn't make you your father." She whirled and started toward the door.

"Annali, wait. Please, my apologies. You're right. I'm an ass. Don't go."

She drew a deep breath, and turned.

"I don't wish to fight with you," he said. "Please."

Part of her wanted to storm out the door and leave him to his frustrated state, but the other part wanted to stay, to hang on just a little longer to what was good between them. She walked back to the corner of the desk.

"You're perfect just as you are," he said taking her hand. "And I am an ass. My apologies. Can you forgive me?"

Maybe she expected too much. What did it matter if she forgave him or not? After all, this wasn't—*till death do us part*. This was—*till the sale closes and the money comes through.*

She cocked her head to the side. "I don't know. I hate it when you act like a pompous ass. Then again…I am going to miss your ass."

He made a small choking noise deep in his throat.

"Alex, when you return, we'll have time to explore all the different ways you can find satisfaction."

"Me? Annali, I…" The pink on his cheeks reddened. "I want that for…not just me…for you also."

Her smile faded. Behind her breastbone, her heart gave a little flutter. She blinked at the sudden stinging in her eyes. When had he become so dear?

"Annali—"

She leaned down and silenced him with a quick kiss. "Don't worry about me. Girls like me seldom find pleasure during sex."

"But I thought…"

"I shall see you tomorrow night." She whirled and fled his office…

"Annali!"

…fled the bank, before she could run back to him and… What? Tell him she loved him? What good would it do? She couldn't stay.

None of this was real. Marriage was merely a means to an end for both of them. She'd best remember it and focus on the money—her dream of having her own place. Somewhere far away from him and his big brown eyes and gentlemanly ways. She was being as foolish as she'd once been when she'd believed Marcello had loved her.

She'd best remember it too. Gentlemen like Alex did not marry women like her.

"Annali!"

She stopped and whirled toward the feminine voice behind her.

Hester Clark waved from outside a grocer's shop. "Goodness." She shifted the sack of flour she carried, higher in her arms. "Where are you off to in such a rush?"

Annali glanced up and both sides of the street. Hells bells, where was she?

"You walked past without stopping, even when I first called to you. Is everything all right?"

"I'm sorry. I was wool gathering."

Hester reached for Annali's hand and gave it a squeeze. "As long as everything is all right."

"It is."

"Where are you going? May I walk with you?"

"I'm going to the dress shop."

"Goodness, you're headed toward the city livery. You must have lost your way. Come."

Jane had the waistcoats wrapped in paper and tied with string when Annali came in to pay for them.

A few minutes later Hester held the door for Annali, and they stepped outside. "Please, might you join me for lunch? My father is out for the day making calls, and I would love to have you."

"Only if you promise, no talk about Alex, or Harriet, or Nellie, or even the bank."

"I promise."

Rather than return to an afternoon with Nellie and Harriet, Annali stayed to help Hester make up baskets of food for parishioners who were sick or injured. While Hester cooked up extra chicken and dumplings, Annali mixed together a bowl of blackberries, flour, and sugar, then rolled out the crusts for pies.

After everything had cooled, Hester packed the baskets. A clock somewhere in the house chimed three times. Annali frowned. She'd hoped to stay away a little longer.

"Can I go with you?"

"Yes, I would appreciate your company. Today is Papa's usual day for making calls outside of town, but this morning he rented a rig from the livery and left our horse and buggy for me.

"Afterward I need to drive out to the Pederson's. I have a couple dresses I made over for Sarah. That littlest girl of his is growing so fast. And Mr. Pederson gives me eggs in exchange for mending."

"I met Sarah and her kittens yesterday."

Hester laughed. "Yes, her kittens. I believe she still has one or two left."

They chatted about the weather and upcoming church activities as they rode.

"Will you and young Mr. Worthington be staying in town after the bank is sold?"

*Hells bells! How had Hester learned about that?*

Hester glanced over and frowned. "Forgive me. I assumed you knew. But then young Mr. Worthington doesn't seem the sort to discuss business with a woman, even one who is his wife."

Annali drew a deep breath hoping she appeared unconcerned by the news. "Can I ask how you learned this?"

A bright pink flush highlighted Hester's cheek bones. "Mr. Pederson. I was at his farm to drop off some mending and a dress I made for Sarah. And he asked me my opinion."

Hester's enthusiasm had her nearly bouncing on the seat. "Can you imagine that? It seems he was in a quandary regarding shares he owns in the bank and asked if I thought he should sell or transfer his holdings to the new bank."

She reached out and grasped Annali's hand. "He is so forward in his thinking, to ask the opinion of a woman. Goodness, and to think he asked me."

Royd Pederson had a big mouth. How long before he told someone else, before Hester told someone and Harriet found out? Annali flashed a practiced smile. "I believe Mr. Pederson likes you and only wanted to know you better."

"Do you think so? I'm nearly beyond hoping…"

"Yes, I do."

****

Annali entered the kitchen carrying her package of waistcoats.

Nellie stepped from the pantry holding two plates and silverware. She huffed and exaggerated sigh, returned to the pantry, and came out a moment later with service for three. She kept her gaze straight ahead, passing right by Annali on her way to the dining room.

Harriet slammed a pot lid down on the worktable. "Out all day, spending Alexander's hard-earned money I see. You, no doubt, are the one who has influenced all his recent frivolous purchases."

"This is a present for Alex, bought with my own money. And I spent the day helping Hester Clark make meals for shut-ins." Annali kept her gaze lowered so Harriet wouldn't glimpse the same challenging spirit that Madame had seen. "I'm going to take this up to Alex's room."

"Pfff," Harriet snorted turning her back as she reached to pull open the oven door.

Annali scooted through the dining room, past Nellie setting the table, into the parlor, then up the stairs.

She lifted the lid on her trunk and set Alex's gift on top of her dresses. After freshening up she hurried downstairs to join Harriet and Nellie in the dining room for another meal eaten in silence.

****

The next afternoon, right after lunch, Nellie and Harriet left to meet some of their church friends for a quilting bee, leaving Annali alone in the house. Not that Harriet had invited her to join them, which Annali suspected would have been the proper thing to do, even if Harriet had known Annali couldn't sew.

Once the pair set off toward town, Annali wandered into the pantry, poking through the shelves and drawers.

Alex had done so much for her she wanted to do something special for him. Aside from knowing a thousand and one ways to satisfy a man, Annali knew how to bake.

Years helping Mr. G. had branded the basic recipes on her brain, and while Annali didn't need a recipe to make enough batter for six cakes, being able to divide out the recipe involved arithmetic skills she didn't have.

She rummaged through the kitchen and pantry, hoping to find a cookbook or recipe cards. Harriet and Nellie must have memorized every recipe then burned all the cookbooks so Annali wouldn't be able to use them. Judging from those awful griddle cakes the other morning, burning their recipes might have done the world a favor.

Frustrated, Annali dashed upstairs and grabbed Mr. Giovani's recipe book from her trunk. Since these were his personal recipes, some handed down from his mother and grandmother, hopefully the proportions would be normal. With her limited Italian, if she could find a recipe that had letters which looked as if they sounded like *torta*, maybe she'd have an easier time figuring out the ingredients.

Returning to the kitchen she set the faded red and gold notebook on the table, seated herself on the bench, and slowly flipped through pages hand-written in Italian. He'd had a beautiful voice and his early morning singing as they made the breads, pastries, and cakes for the day made the long workdays happier. His deep belly laughter used to fill the bakery as he talked and joked with his customers. And he'd always called her *Cara* while giving her head a quick pat or her shoulder a squeeze.

Folded and tucked between the pages were recipes clipped from the newspaper. Molasses cookies, gingerbread, and... Everyday Stack Cake. She set the notebook aside, smoothed out the clipping, and perused the recipe.

Humming one of Mr. G.'s, favorite songs, she scooped coal into the firebox. Then in a small bowl, she whisked together milk, eggs, and vanilla. After adding it to the dry ingredients, she poured the batter into two round cake pans. She'd do this for Alex, give something he hadn't had in a long time.

A few minutes later, she checked the oven holding her hand inside and counting until the heat caused her to pull back her hand at the correct fifteen to seventeen seconds.

While the cakes baked, she beat eggs whites for a

large bowl of Italian icing. Later, with the cakes cooling on the windowsill, she washed and dried the dishes, wiped down the table, and swept every speck of flour dust off the floor.

Afterward, she sat at the table on one of the bench seats, smoothing her final layer of icing over the cake. She'd spread strawberry jam between the layers. Too bad she hadn't had fresh strawberries instead.

"Yoo hoo!"

Annali's gaze swung toward the screen door. A woman, older, and taller than Nellie, peered through the screen.

"Are Harriet and Nellie home? I'm Rose Gourley. I live two houses down."

"No. They went to a quilting bee."

"Oh, that's right. Today is Wednesday. I'd forgotten."

Annali stood and gestured to the bench on the opposite side of the table. "Would you like to come in and sit? Harriet has some lemonade in the ice box."

"Thank you. That sounds refreshing." The woman fanned her face with her hand as she entered. "It is rather a warm day." She slid onto the bench opposite from where Annali had been sitting. "You must be young Mr. Worthington's new wife."

"Yes, that's me, Annali." She ducked into the pantry for two glasses then reached into the largest compartment of the ice box for the lemonade. She poured the drinks and returned the pitcher.

Rose raised her glass. "Wishing you many years of happiness."

"Thank you." Thirsty herself, Annali drank the entire glassful then returned to her seat in front of the cake and picked up her spatula.

"It's all over town that he'd suddenly married. I'm a Baptist, don't you know, not a Methodist, so I wasn't able to meet you on Sunday as so many of my friends did. Surprised us all that he'd married."

"Why? He's young and good looking. He owns the bank. I'm amazed no one here had snapped him up."

"It's his father, don't you know. Young Mr. Worthington is very much like him in looks and manner. Though not at all as friendly."

Satisfied the icing was as smooth as she could make it, Annali rolled a piece of butcher paper into a cone and spooned in frosting, half listening as Rose chattered on.

"They say he did it, don't you know."

"Who?"

"He must have told you about it."

"Told me about what?" She sliced off a tiny bit of paper from the point of the cone.

"The rumors."

"What rumors?"

"About his father."

Annali looked up and frowned. "He told me. But he said no one knew."

Rose leaned close and whispered, "No one knows for sure, that's true, but they say it was young Mr. Worthington don't you know."

"Alex?"

Rose nodded and trailed her finger through a faint bit of sugar dust on the edge of the table. "That's what they say. Anyone who saw them that night could see they'd been fighting."

"Alex told me about that too." Was Alex wrong? Had others known the truth about his father?

Holding the piping bag in both hands, she began drawing white flowers and leaves around the side of the cake.

"He did?" Rose murmured. "Did he tell you what happened afterward?"

"Yes, we have no secrets."

Rose gasped. "Oh dear, then the rumors are true. He did do it. He tried to leave town. Did he tell you that?"

"Who? Did what?"

"The law captured him in Cheyenne and brought him back."

Annali looked up. Rose leaned forward slightly, her eyes wide, like a child waiting for Annali to confirm the existence of St. Nicholas.

Alex hadn't said anything about the law bringing him back.

"There was an investigation, don't you know," Rose continued. "The marshal and the county sheriff talked to everyone, but young Mr. Worthington was never arrested. No proof you see. Probably won't be after all these years, so we'll never know. But you say he told you. He did do it."

"Are you talking about Alex? What did he do?"

"Why murder his father of course. You said he did it. The rumors are true then."

"Wait. What?" She nearly dropped her piping bag on the cake. "Alex didn't murder anyone. He only told me his father *had* been murdered."

"Oh dear. He didn't tell you. Thought for a minute there that he finally confessed."

"Confessed? To what? Alex didn't kill anyone."

"I see I've upset you. Very bad of me. I must beg your forgiveness. It's only rumor, don't you know?

There was an investigation after it happened, but there was no evidence. He was never arrested."

*No, not possible.* Then again, he had said he'd wanted his father dead. Mrs. Lindberg, Hester, Reverend Clark, and now Rose Gourley.

Had Alex lied to her? "Are you implying Alex…"

"No. No. I'm only letting you know there are some who believe it. That's why no one will have him, don't you know. Why he's not received in respectable homes. He could snap one day, and—" she pointed her index finger like a gun barrel. "Bam!"

Annali flinched. An image flashed through her mind of the gun in his desk drawer, the barrel pressed against his own temple—

"I don't believe it, of course." Rose prattled on. "Young Mr. Worthington is a hardworking, church going, man. It's just that if he were friendlier, more like his father in that regard, people might be more inclined to believe him innocent of such a terrible crime."

A funny lump settled in her stomach as her chest squeezed tight. Was this the secret Clayton knew about—the real reason Alex gave him money? Was Alex's whole purpose in selling the bank part of a scheme to leave town without drawing suspicion, before anyone learned the truth? Had everything been a lie? Had he used her to further his plan?

"You've gone quite pale, dear." Rose reached across the table and gave Annali's hand a squeeze. "Don't worry." Rose waved her hand with a dismissive flutter. "They're only rumors, and there was no evidence don't you know. I'm certain, now that you're married, people will see there is another side to young Mr. Worthington."

Annali swallowed her doubts and gave her head a

shake. No. Alex hadn't lied. She'd known hundreds of men—braggarts, cheaters, liars, the innocent, the shy, and the controlling evil ones. If the people of this town only saw Alex-the-Ass, then maybe they would believe him capable of murdering his father.

But her Alex was a shy, virtuous, man who'd had responsibility dumped on him at a young age. A man who carried the guilt for what his father had done, who lived a stifling, restrictive life in order to stave off the man he believed he would one day become.

No. Her Alex was not a murderer. Those sweet blushes of his had to be genuine.

"Are you listening, dear?"

Annali blinked and tried to recall what Rose had said.

"Your cake, my dear. It's beautiful. How did you ever learn to make all these fancy flowers?"

"I used to work in a bakery."

"Oh, how wonderful. Though dare I ask, you being a newlywed and so busy...but would you consider selling me a cake? My youngest is to be married on Saturday, don't you know. I was planning to bake the cake myself, but there is still so much to do fitting her dress, baking the food, gathering flowers, and your cake is so beautiful. I will pay you of course..."

*Pay me? For a cake?*

"...one just like this. How much would you charge? Perhaps one large enough to feed fifty people."

Could she? Would Harriet let her use the kitchen? Maybe when Alex's mother saw this cake, she'd realize Annali could be of help, that she could be more than just an unwanted guest.

"I'll let you know tomorrow if I can do it. Then we

can talk more about what kind of cake you want."

Rose left a few minutes later, and Annali began piping a border around the top and base of the cake.

The screen door creaked then banged shut.

"What have you done to my kitchen?"

Annali jerked upright.

Harriet stood hands on hips just inside the door glaring across the room. Nellie looking on from behind.

Annali bit her lower lip. *I will not fight. I will not fight. I will not fight.*

There was absolutely nothing for Harriet to complain about. Except for the bowl and the spatula Annali was using, all the dishes had been washed and put away.

"I made a cake for dessert."

"I did not give you permission to cook in my kitchen."

"But…I wanted to surprise Al—"

"Alexander is not your concern."

Annali set down her piping bag, placed her palms on the table and stood. "Alex is my husband. He is not a pawn to be used in whatever game of martyrdom you want to play."

"You selfish, selfish girl." Harriet marched to the worktable and slammed down her sewing basket. "Do you even care that Alexander can't eat a bit of this? That doing so is detrimental to his health?

"I have struggled his entire life to make certain he does not become the whoremongering, gambling, reprobate his father was. Alexander will not become a man who forsakes his family to run off to bordellos and gaming hells, drinking, and flaunting money in a hedonistic lifestyle that will drive him to madness and leave his family destitute.

"It is bad enough he has tied himself to you. How dare you propose that we heartlessly indulge in such a rich dessert right in front of him?"

"But you eat in front of him all the time."

"How dare you."

"How dare you? You've lied to him his whole life. There is nothing wrong with him."

"It's obvious that he disregarded his entire diet while he was away, and you are the unfortunate result." Harriet leaned in.

Annali braced for a slap, but Harriet reached out with both hands and snatched away both the cake and Mr. G's recipe book.

"Wait!" Annali lunged across the table but wasn't able to grab either item before Harriet whirled and strode toward the back door.

"No! Please don't!"

Nellie moved aside as Harriet pushed open the screen door and stepped onto the porch.

Horrified, Annali watched her cake and recipe book sail through the air, plater and all. They fell to earth at the corner of the garden.

## Chapter Twenty

At twelve past six, Alex turned the key and locked the front door of the bank. He slipped the key in his pocket, picked up his Gladstone bag, and started home.

The day had been unusually warm, and the evening air, rather than cooling the heat of the day, drew beads of sweat across his brow. He removed his handkerchief and wiped his face and neck.

He'd gone straight to the bank from the train, wanting to be certain the new teller's drawer balanced, and all was in order for Lathrop's visit this weekend. The president of Golden Bank and Securities had been pleased with the sales contract Alex delivered and wanted to go over it with both the board and his attorney before signing.

There was a risk that something could still go wrong, but Lathrop planned to come out on the Friday train to look over both the town and the bank's ledgers, before giving Alex a deposit and setting a closing date.

Despite the heat, Alex lengthened his stride happily swinging his bag as he walked. He smiled, not because his plans were falling into place, or that he was hungry and supper would be waiting when he arrived, but because Annali would be there. He hadn't seen her since noontime yesterday, and while he'd been away on business trips before, he'd never felt so eager to return home.

He hurried up the front steps and opened the door. He set down his bag, hung his hat on the rack, and stepped into the front parlor. The windows had been opened and the curtains pushed aside, but no breeze stirred the air. Voices drifted from the kitchen, and he walked through the dining room to find Mother and Nellie their faces flushed as they prepared dinner over a hot stove.

"Is Annali, upstairs?"

Mother glanced his way. "How should I know?" She swiped the back of her wrist across her temple. "Nellie and I returned from Ladies Circle, to find the kitchen in shambles and the entire house heated up as that thoughtless girl tried to bake a cake."

A cake. She'd made him a cake. He glanced around the room. Maybe it was in the pantry. A real cake. He'd probably have to come down late at night to sneak a piece, but if Annali's cake tasted as good as her turnovers had looked, it would be worth the risk.

"You won't find it. That mess wasn't fit for pigs."

A frisson of cold rippled through him. "Mother, what did you do?"

Her gaze narrowed. "Don't you speak to me in that disrespectful tone." She shook her finger at him the way she had when he was five years old. "This is what comes of marrying the wrong girl. An orphan. You know nothing of her family."

"Mother, not that it's any of your concern, but I do."

"Lies, no doubt. A penniless girl conspiring to gain your sympathy."

"Enough. Mother, where is my wife?"

Nellie, standing beside the stove, pointed discreetly toward the back door.

Whirling, he strode across the room and flung open the screen door. It snapped back against the frame with a sharp *bang*.

A half dozen crows stood at the edge of the garden pecking through the tall weeds and grass at blobs of white.

His brow furrowed. Though he knew what he'd find, he strode toward it, needing confirmation with his own eyes.

The crows swooped upward landing along the ridgeline of the shed, leaving him to stare at the scattered remnants of what had once been a white layer cake. Tiny brown ants swarmed over most of the pieces, but on one small bit, a delicate, white icing flower remained intact. A lump closed off the back of his throat.

He nudged a piece of cake with the toe of his shoe. Where was Annali? Turning, the shadowy outline of something square caught his attention. A small notebook lay in the grass. He glanced around to find scattered bits of paper and newspaper clippings. Gathering them together, he placed them inside the book and slipped the book inside his coat.

The cake had obviously not been here long. So where was Annali? Had she marched into town and taken a room at the hotel? Why hadn't he passed her on the road? Why hadn't she come to the bank to tell him what happened?

He should probably head back to town and join her, let her know he sympathized and give her the gift he'd bought for her in Lincoln.

If he angled off from the barn and walked across the open prairie toward Royd Pederson's place, he could catch the road at the halfway point to town. He walked behind the garden and turned at the back corner of the barn.

Annali sat in the grass against the wall, her knees drawn up, her forehead resting on her crossed arms.

"I don't like your mother," she said without raising her head.

He lowered himself beside her, drew one knee up, and leaned against the wall.

"You'll get your suit dirty."

"Yes."

"I hate it when you act like her."

"As do I."

She lifted her head and looked at him. Tears streaked her face.

Annali crying? His strong, confident Annali, her smile gone, her eyes red and swollen. He draped his arm over her shoulders and pulled her close.

"She threw it away. All that work and she threw it away, because none of it was good enough for your diet."

"I doubt that was the reason."

"I'm supposed to be a respectable woman, but I don't think it would matter how respectable I am, I will never be good enough for them."

He rested his chin on her head unsure what to say.

"I worked so hard on it. It's been years since I piped little flowers and fancy swags, but it was so pretty. Rose saw it too. She said it was the most beautiful cake she ever saw."

"Rose Gourley?"

"She came to visit your mother and sister."

"More likely she came to see you." He shuddered to think what that notorious busybody might have told Annali.

"I think you're right. But she liked my cake and asked me to make one for her daughter's wedding on Saturday. She's going to pay me, but your mother will never let me—" Her voice broke.

He sighed. She was right. Mother would never allow Annali in her kitchen.

"Come," he said, pushing to his feet. "I can fix this."

"I will not beg your mother."

"Nor will I." He extended his hand. "We're going into town."

She placed her hand in his, and he helped her up.

He swiped his thumb across her damp cheek. Then hand in hand they walked past the corral to the front of the house and continued up the road.

****

When they reached the Burgess Café, the daughter guided them to what had become their regular table. Alex seated Annali then turned to the girl. "I would like have a word in private with your mother."

The girl bit her lip, her glance darting to Annali, who only shrugged.

"I'll only take a few moments of her time."

"All right." She headed to the kitchen.

Alex followed right behind.

Mrs. Burgess looked up as they entered. Her mouth dropped open. In one hand she held a large ladle. In front of her, a long worktable where several plates of food had been lined up. She blinked then snapped her mouth closed again.

She poured gravy over two plates with mashed potatoes and nodded toward her daughter. "These are ready to go out."

The Burgess girl snatched up the plates and scooted

past him into the dining room.

Mrs. Burgess wiped her hands on her apron and bobbed a quick curtsy. "What can I do for you, Mr. Worthington?"

"I would like to ask a favor."

\*\*\*\*

A few minutes later Alex rejoined Annali, taking a seat across from her. He laid his napkin in his lap and arranged his silverware properly on the tabletop.

Annali leaned toward him, her eyes wide and expectant.

"Everything has been arranged," he said. "You may bake your cake here whenever you like."

"Really?"

He nodded.

"Alex, thank you." She jumped up and stepped toward him around the edge of the table.

He held up his hand.

She lowered herself back onto her seat. "I'm sorry. But wait until later." She smiled that slow seductive smile of hers. "I'll find a hundred ways to say thank you."

A touch of heat singed the tips of his ears. She'd made him a cake. Though he hadn't even seen it, that she'd cried over its loss, touched him. He swallowed and straightened his fork, then his knife and spoon.

He looked up. She was so beautiful. Her hair with its light-color streak, and her eyes, bright with happiness. So completely opposite from the earlier heartbroken Annali.

"But Alex, won't this look like you're being bribed with favors, or influenced, the way you said you didn't want?"

"This is to be a business agreement between you and Mrs. Burgess. If people perceive it differently, I no longer care.

"You may use the kitchen here and their ingredients. If you need something special, purchasing it will be at your own expense. In turn, you shall pay Mrs. Burgess fifteen percent of all proceeds from the sale of the cake."

She frowned. "What does that mean?"

"For every dollar you earn, you will keep eighty-five cents and Mrs. Burgess will receive fifteen cents."

Annali nodded as the Burgess girl approached to take their order.

After a leisurely meal of pork chops, applesauce, and mixed vegetables, Alex took Annali's hand, and they strolled toward home.

"Alex?"

"Hmmm?"

"When Mrs. Gourley stopped by this afternoon, she hinted that you—"

"Killed my father." He sighed. "I knew someone would tell you eventually."

She took a step back, cocking her head, her gaze fixed on him.

"Father and I were each seen after our fight with fresh cuts and bruises. Later his body was found alongside this road, up ahead there, by that scrubby bush. I supposedly shot him then tried to leave town. The marshal questioned me numerous times about the murder and the reason behind our altercation."

"Did you tell them—"

"No." He squeezed her hand a little tighter, and they continued walking. "No. Never. I told them we fought because Father was running the bank into the ground and didn't care that everyone who had loans with us was in immediate danger of foreclosure.

"The marshal telegraphed the state bank examiner to come and look at the books to confirm what I said. While that explained the motive for our fight, they couldn't prove I killed him. I told them I went to Cheyenne to get away for a while, then changed my mind and came back the next morning."

As they walked past the bush, Annali pulled back on his hand.

"Alex, stop." She twisted free from his grip.

"My apologies." He turned. "I didn't realize I'd been—"

Her gaze darted away.

Though fleeting, he'd seen that look a thousand times over the past five years. Doubt.

Naively, he'd come to see her as an ally, the only person to have ever believed in him. He drew himself up, bracing himself against the stab of pain at her betrayal. He'd never revealed so much of himself to anyone, never trusted anyone so...

"I'm sorry." Her voice softened. "You said you wanted to kill him. Mrs. Lindberg, Hester Clark, and now Rose Gourley. They all hint at it, waiting to see my reaction. Wanting to know what I believe."

He focused on the distance, on the small white house and outbuildings where the Lester family lived. He'd rather look toward someone else's life than see his own reflected in the tears and doubt on Annali's face.

He drew a deep breath, squared his shoulders, and met her watery gaze.

"It matters little to me what you believe."

"Alex, I—"

"Our agreement only requires you to pretend to believe me. Pretend to love me. The truth of what you think, or feel, doesn't matter. The sale will be final soon, and we will part ways. Until then all I ask is that you continue in the role I'm paying you to play."

"You goddamn, ass! I'm not going to apologize for having doubts. Blind faith is for fools. Every man I've ever known was a liar. I don't know what it is about you that makes me disregard everything I... Doubt only crossed my mind for a minute. I don't believe you killed him. I don't."

"There's no need to convince me of your feelings one way or the other."

She shook her head and laughed—a quick, sharp sound. "Holy hell, you play the victim better than your mother."

If she'd punched him in the stomach, it would have hurt less.

She crossed her arms and shifted back a step. "Look, we both got dealt shitty lives. I accept it. You wallow in it."

"Wallow?" He crossed his arms before she could see his hands curl into fists. "I wallow. I'm sorry I ever shared my secrets."

He spun on his heels and started walking.

"Alex!"

He stopped and turned back.

"Holy Hell, you're a stubborn ass."

He exhaled a long sigh and shook his head. Two and half hours ago, he'd been happy. What happened?

She moved toward him, stopping just outside arms reach.

He searched her face. The sharp lines of anger had

softened.

"Promise me when this is all over, that you won't use that gun. That you take those pages from the bottom of your desk and send them away to get made into a book. And if you believe nothing else I tell you, believe this. You are not your father, and you will never be like him."

Perhaps she was right—about his story. Before his eyesight grew any worse, he should do something with his novel. He'd been working on it for more than five years, rewriting, changing the plot, moving scenes around. Maybe it was time to say, *Good enough.* Leave behind something unfettered and his alone.

The *caw, caw, caw* of a crow caught his ear.

He locked his gaze with hers. "And you must promise me the same. Instead of your parlor house, open a bakery."

She laughed, the sharp unhappy sound he hated. "Alex, don't you understand that life can never be. One day someone will recognize me, and your bakery idea would be shot to hell. I'd end up right back where I was, working for someone else, a little older, and with no money of my own."

That she believed herself as resigned to her fate as he was to his pricked his heart with a twinge of sadness. The word *wallow* hovered on his tongue for a moment before he gulped it down.

"Annali." He reached out his hand. "My apologies. I had no right to presume that after only a week, you would, in blind faith, take me at my word. And I have no words to express how touched I am each time you tell me I am not destined to become the man my father was."

The corner of her mouth twitched. She stepped

toward him and took his hand.

The warmth of her palm against his gave his heart a little kick of joy, like a cash drawer balancing the first time through.

"I hate Alex-the-ass," she said.

"As do I."

"But there's something about Alexander Worthington that I—"

"And there's something about Annali Hanson that I also—"

"Worthington," she said.

He met her gaze. His heart swelled. "Worthington," he whispered. He lifted her hand to his lips and brushed a kiss over the top of her knuckles.

"So," she said as they continued walking. "Since we both know you didn't kill him, who do you think did?"

Chapter Twenty-one

Instead of going into the house, Annali strolled to the barn with Alex. She sat cross-legged on the dirt floor, while Alex fed the horse. He joined her a few minutes later.

"Alex, your suit." She wrapped a stem of hay around her finger.

"I'm not concerned. A good brushing will clean these trousers well enough. What of your own dress?"

"This calico is an easy day dress. Trust me, if I was wearing something nice like the teal Miss Sinek is making for me, or my blue dress, I wouldn't even be out here."

"Yet, I seem to recall you trying to crawl under the seat of the train while wearing that particular dress."

"That was different. I lost my ticket." She unwound, then rewound the hay. "And I didn't know you'd come to my rescue again."

She slid the coiled hay from her finger and tossed it away before picking up another stem from the floor.

"Alex, I might have doubted you for a minute or two, and I'm sorry, but I don't believe you killed him."

"You just might be the only one."

"What about your mother and sister?"

"They've never said anything to me, and I've never asked. Perhaps because I'm afraid they've accepted the idea that I did shoot him."

"How odd. By them not speaking up for you, it appears to everyone in this town that you're guilty. No wonder they all want to know what I believe."

He picked up a stem of hay and rolled the tasseled end between his fingers. "No one mentions my father's murder aloud. Yet, it's discussed daily through glances and whispers and inuendo, which only makes him more alive than he was before. And that in turn serves as a reminder, especially to me, of what I will one day become."

"No wonder everyone in this house is so miserable. And you've been living like this for five years?"

He brushed the tiny seeds from his knee. "Longer. My father has only been dead for five years. He was a profligate as long as I can remember. I didn't realize how despicable he actually was until that day. Looking back, I can only assume this had something to do with the reason we moved so much."

"That's why it's important that you believe me when I say I believe you."

He grinned. "I believe you."

She shot him a sideways glance. "I believe you do."

"I'm glad you believe that I believe you do."

She laughed and bumped her shoulder against his. "This is silly."

"Yes, it is. But I'm very much enjoying myself." He picked up another piece of hay and spun it between his hands. A quick smile flashed across his face. He was such a different person when he was away from the bank and away from his family.

"I've walked past that bush countless times. Most days I don't even think of him. When I do, I feel nothing except gratitude that he's dead. Personally, I don't care if his killer is ever found."

"Who do you think did it?"

He shrugged. "One of his victims could have told her father, who then dispensed his own justice, never telling a soul in order to protect his daughter. It also could have been someone he cheated at cards. He did gamble when he was out of town. That's how he met Clayton. Or it could be someone he'd foreclosed on at some point. After all this time we'll never know."

"But everyone thinks you did it."

"Let them think what they want. Better that they never learn the truth. And as soon as this sale is finalized, the bank will be in different hands, and I'll be leaving town."

"I just don't understand why this belief about yourself is so stuck in your head."

"It doesn't matter." He pushed himself upright and offered his hand.

Annali placed her palm in his, and he pulled her up. Would she ever be able to convince him that what he'd been told for a lifetime, was a lie? Reaching up she laid her hand on his cheek.

He leaned in and pressed a kiss to the center of her forehead, the tip of her nose, her parted lips.

"Alexander!" Harriet's shrill voice carried all the way across the yard.

Alex stiffened and stepped back. Heaving a sigh, he walked around the buggy to the open side door, visible from the back porch of the house.

Annali stepped up beside him, as he waved to Harriet.

In the dusk of fading sunlight, the old crow stood silhouetted on the top step, hands on her hips like wings.

"Are you planning to stay out there all night?"

"No, Mother," he called. "We're coming." He stepped over the threshold, turned, and held out his hand for Annali as she gathered her skirt, took his hand, and stepped over the board at the bottom of the doorway.

Pulling the door closed, they walked to the house.

As they reached the porch, Harriet stepped aside, allowing room for Alex to pull open the screen door. "Your bath is ready. I hope you haven't completely lost sight of the importance of maintaining your regimen."

"No," he sighed. "I haven't forgotten." He held the door as first his mother then Annali stepped through.

The door closed softly as he came in behind them.

Harriet gestured toward a glass of water on the table.

"Someone drank all the lemonade I'd prepared for supper." She shot Annali a nasty glare. "So, we were forced to have lemon water instead. This is the glass I'd prepared for you, but you weren't here to enjoy it." Another fiery glower fixed on Annali.

"Thank you, Mother. I'll have it later."

Annali flashed Harriet a practiced smile.

Alex's mother huffed a short exhale of breath, squared her small shoulders, and marched from the room.

Alex tugged free his tie as he walked toward the pantry. At the doorway, he turned back. "Come join me. If you're as hot and sweaty as I am, a cold bath will be just the thing."

Annali shrugged and gave him a slow smile, then followed, pushing the pantry door closed behind her.

He lifted a lantern from a peg on the wall of the narrow room. Setting it on the counter, he took a match from the tin on the shelf and struck it on the raw edge of the wooden counter.

Moving toward him, she kept her gaze locked with his.

His pupils dilated in the glow of the match. His breath quickened. Whirling, he raised the chimney and lit the wick, dropping the charred matchstick on the counter.

Reaching toward him, she grasped one end of the loosened tie and slowly pulled it free from his starched collar. She tossed it toward the narrow counter beneath the row of shelves which covered one wall.

He stood motionless while she undid his collar then slowly unbuttoned his waistcoat and shirt.

Her fingers slid to his waist, and she popped his suspenders free from the buttons behind the waistband of his trousers.

He yanked his shirt tail loose and shucked his coat, waistcoat, and shirt, heedless of their condition as they fell into a heap on the plank floor.

While he tugged his undershirt over his head, Annali undid the buttons down the front of her dress.

As he bent over to untie his shoes, her gaze fell to the line of his spine and each bump, clearly visible beneath his skin.

He kicked off his shoes and stepped out of his trousers as she tossed her blouse onto the counter. Moving close, she untied the laces of his drawers as his hands grazed lightly up her bare arms, raising goose bumps in their wake. She slipped her thumbs between the warmth of his skin and the soft cotton of his underwear. Grasping the waistband, she tugged and let his drawers fall to his ankles.

He leaned down and captured her mouth with his as

Kathy Otten

his arms slipped around her back.

Instinctively, her own arms wrapped around him, her palms sliding over the damp skin of his back. She returned his kiss. There was only Alex. The solid form of him, his light musky scent, the breath of him warm against her cheek.

His kiss melded with hers, fierce in its passion and hungry for more. His beard scraped against the soft skin around her mouth, but she could only press her fingertips deeper into the muscles of his back. An aching throbbed from deep inside, driving her to pull him closer, to somehow absorb his body into hers.

A small whimper rose in the back of her throat as his kiss went on and on, as unsatiable in his desire as she was in hers.

He tipped her backward over his arm, and she hooked her ankle over his calf to keep from falling.

Her fingers traced the valley of his spine, the sharp angles of his hip, then slipped between their bodies slowly stretching toward his groin.

He sucked in a sharp breath as she grasped the swollen length of his shaft and slid her hand up then down.

He ended the kiss, lifting his face away, yet still close enough that his ragged breath whispered across her cheek. Tiny reflections of lamp light glimmered in the depts of his brown eyes. Mesmerized, she could only stare, not sure what she was supposed to do next.

"I want you," he whispered. "But I'm sweaty, and I stink." He carefully eased her away.

Her hand shot out to steady herself, and she grasped the edge of the copper tub. Her gaze landed on his swollen shaft.

She grinned and looked up. "Are you sure you want to get into that cold water?"

"Yes," he croaked. He cleared his throat. Turning away, he stepped out of his drawers and pulled off his stockings before easing himself slowly into the tub. His eyes closed for a moment as his breath hitched, then he released a shuddering sigh.

She chuckled. "Shall we see if Sir John can rise above the cold?"

He grabbed the bar of soap and washcloth then furiously rubbed them together.

Keeping her gaze focused on Alex, she reached behind her waist, unbuttoned her skirt, and stepped out of it, taking her time as she folded the garment and placed it on the shelf with her blouse. Next, she undid the tapes securing her petticoat. Letting it fall, she stepped out of it, and kicked it aside, all while keeping her gaze locked on Alex.

He stilled, soap in hand, as his gaze followed her every move.

She untied the bustle roll at the back of her waist and removed her under petticoat. Running her fingers lightly over the lace edging at the top of her camisole, she tugged free the knot of ribbon loosening the garment enough to slip it over her head. Placing her hands at the top of her corset, she slowly popped free each hook.

The soap hit the water with a soft *sploosh*.

She chuckled. The tips of his ears turned pink, and a blush tinted his cheekbones. He was adorable.

Clad in only her chemise and drawers, she propped one foot on the rim of the tub and unlaced her shoe. After toeing it off, she reached toward the ribbon at the top of her stocking.

"Let me," he whispered, his tone low and warm.

She gulped and her heart fluttered. Stepping close she propped her stocking clad foot on the edge of the tub.

Water sloshed as he placed his wet hands on either side of her calf. He pulled free the bow just above her knee and slowly slid the length of black cotton to her ankle.

The sensual glide of his fingers sent a quiver through her body. Men had touched her limbs before. But never like this.

Only Alex had ever caused this rush of warmth to flood her core—caused her pulse to race. Her vision, even her thoughts, suddenly narrowed to only him. She ached to throw herself against him. Craved that same sensual glide of his fingertips caressing every inch of her bare skin.

Placing her hand on his shoulder, he lifted her foot, and he pulled the stocking free.

Stepping back, she hastily shed the rest of her clothing and stepped into the tub lowering herself into the cool water between his bent knees, placing her feet against the back of the tub on either side of his waist.

She locked her gaze on his face, unsure if she should make the next move or wait for him.

He lifted his right leg from the water and rested it along the rim of the tub.

She slid her hand over his shin, ruffling the dark hairs on her way to his knee then smoothed the hair as her hand slipped to his ankle.

He had nice feet.

Thankfully, most of the men she'd been with had left their stockings on. Even then, from many of those feet wafted a sour smell. Of the bare feet she had seen, the skin had been dry and calloused, the toenails yellow and broken.

Not Alex. He took care of himself. His bare foot, propped beside her shoulder, was pale and smooth. His toes nicely formed and dusted with just a few of the same dark hairs.

She placed her foot in the center of his chest, sliding it up and down inching lower each time.

He grasped it with both hands, right before her toes could touch the tip of his shaft. His thumbs massaged deep circles into the sole of her foot.

She closed her eyes savoring this rare sensation, both relaxing and arousing.

His fingers slid up her leg. That earlier desire stirred, aching to feel that same caress of his hands over her entire body.

She opened her eyes. He stared at her, his lips slightly parted, his chest rising and falling. She swallowed, needing more.

Shifting awkwardly around in the tight space, the water sloshed as she first knelt, then leaned forward, sprawling on top of him. She braced herself with her hands on the rim of the tub on either side of his head.

He reached up and cupped her breasts. His thumbs grazed over her nipples already hardened, then he leaned forward, laving with his tongue, first one sensitive nub then the other.

A tingle of longing grew at the center of her core as he nipped and sucked. Needing more, she rubbed against his hardened shaft. A small whimper escaped her throat.

Reaching up he pulled her down for a kiss. She relaxed her elbows, moaning as droplets of water trailed over her shoulders and arms. Their mouths came together, hungry and aching. Unable to get enough, she continued to rub against him, even as tension coiled deep inside her.

Shifting her hips, she lowered herself onto his shaft. A deep groan rose in the back of his throat as he began to thrust.

She raised herself up, clenching the sides of the tub as her breath caught. Her muscles tightened. Spasms rippled through her body, clenching around him. "Holy Hell, Alex," she cried in a release of breath.

He continued to thrust, and another wave of tremors shuddered through her. He groaned as he stiffened beneath her, and his body found its release.

She leaned close and captured his mouth in another kiss, less desperate, more gentle, more tender. She never imagined how powerful a kiss could be. How complete, how connected to him she'd feel. There would never be anyone again who could make her feel this alive, so happy in who she was.

Alex broke the kiss, nudging her shoulders. "Annali, my back hurts and my leg is going numb."

Reluctantly, she eased back to sit on her heels.

He pushed himself up straighter. "Can we try this again in the bed?"

She grinned. "Wherever and whenever you want. That was...so...incredible."

His brow furrowed.

She pressed her finger to his lips. "Don't. Don't you dare ruin it with your doubts."

Shifting a bit in the water, she gripped both sides of the tub and pressed her lips to his. Her breasts brushed over his chest as she rocked against him savoring the brush of wet hairs against her nipples.

His shaft hardened beneath her.

She broke the kiss. "This," she whispered, "is how I know you will never become your father." Bracing herself against the sides of the tub, raised her bosoms closer to his eyelevel and gave her shoulders a back-and-forth wiggle.

"Alex, you find pleasure with these. With women. Don't you see. You will never be like him."

His brow furrowed for a long moment, then he grinned and gave a short bark of laughter. He wrapped his arms around her and pulled her into another kiss.

Just the whisper of his lips brushing over hers sent warmth rushing throughout her body. She surrendered to his touch, craving more from him even as he entered her a second time.

No man, even Marcello who'd said he loved her, had ever touched her heart as deeply as Alex. Some men were tender and caring. Once in a while someone would bring her body to physical release. But nothing compared to Alex.

There was something about him that made her want to be near him, ached for the touch of his hand in hers, and longed for a glimpse of his shy smile.

Playfully, they washed each other, stepped from the tub and toweled each other dry. Annali pulled her chemise over her head, not bothering to tie the ribbon. She gathered her clothes and shoes as Alex slipped into his drawers.

"I'll join you upstairs in a few minutes."

Stepping from the pantry, she set her bundle on the kitchen table, beside a glass of water, then turned back to hug one side of the doorway into the pantry.

Alex, bending to pick up his shoes and stockings,

looked up.

Annali grinned and rolled her shoulder, allowing the loose neck opening to fall down her bare arm. Drawing her knee up, she grasped the hem of her chemise and slowly pulled it up to the middle of her thigh.

*Clunk, clunk.* His shoes hit the floor.

She giggled. "I'll be waiting."

\*\*\*\*

Wearing only his drawers, Alex emptied the tub and mopped the puddles from the floor. The little seductress had worn him out, but he felt happy, lighter inside than he'd ever felt before. Yes! He did like bosoms.

On his way upstairs, he grabbed his Gladstone bag from beneath the hat tree.

Inside, wrapped in tissue paper, was a small gift he'd purchased in Lincoln. He'd spotted it next to a pair of lace gloves in the window of a dress shop yesterday during his early morning walk. Once he'd seen it, he had to have it and as soon as his meeting with Lathrop ended, he'd hurried back to the shop, worried it would be gone before he could return.

He'd purchased gifts before, but none that had called to him as this one had. He'd been eager to give it to her all day, to watch her eyes light up, and to see her smile. Now, as he climbed the stairs, doubt crept in.

His gift was not very expensive. Perhaps she wouldn't like it. Rather than waiting, if he casually presented it to her now, its significance would be lessened, and she'd never know of the boyish hope he'd attached to it. He turned the knob and pushed open the door.

She lay curled on her side under the sheet still wearing the chemise she'd put on after their bath.

"Annali, I brought you a little gift from Lincoln." He closed the door and walked over to the wardrobe, set down his bag and shoes then draped his coat over the valet stand.

"Nothing special. It's in my bag, let me get it for…"

She hadn't moved.

A funny squeeze tightened behind his breastbone as he strode to her side. "Annali, wake up." He reached a hand to her shoulder and gave her a shake.

"Hmmm." Her pillow muffled the sound.

He gave her another shake. Annali never went to sleep this early. "Annali, wake up. What's wrong?" She was fine when she'd left him maybe fifteen minutes ago.

"Hmmm. Stop bothering me and come to bed." Her voice was so soft, and her words so slurred he could barely understand her.

In his mind he suddenly heard himself speak similar words to Annali the other day right before she dumped a pail of water over his head.

How had this happened?

*"This is the glass I'd prepared for you,"* Mother had said earlier as she'd gestured toward the kitchen worktable. *"But you weren't here to enjoy it."*

He swung around. His gaze swept through the room. There, next to the pitcher and basin was an empty glass.

Two long strides brought him to the washstand. He stared at the glass for a moment, then picked it up. Bringing it to his nose, he sniffed. Lemon. Tipping the rim to his mouth he tasted that bit of water at the bottom of the glass. Lemon and the faintest taste of something bitter along the back edges of his tongue.

"Damn." He banged the glass down. "Double damn."

Annali had been right. Now where was it?

He lifted his robe off the hook on the back of the door, slipped his arms into the sleeves, and tied the sash before leaving the bedroom and thumping downstairs. He had to find it before Mother could dose him or Annali again.

He checked through every shelf of the pantry, moving aside jars of tomatoes, green beans, and applesauce, dishes, glassware, and pots and pans. He opened each drawer, sifting through folded layers of rags, dish towels, and cheese cloth. Nothing.

He carried out the same in-depth search of the kitchen, assuring himself that the scent of each spice bottle and jar smelled like the name printed on label. He checked through every nook and cranny. He even dug through the icebox. Nothing.

The sideboard in the dining room was next. Starting with the top left drawer, he systematically sorted through table linens, doilies, and Grandmother's silver. Finding nothing he checked every knick-knack and curio in the parlor. He lifted cushions and looked behind pillows. He searched the depths of Mother's and Nellie's sewing and yarn baskets, pricking his fingers several times in the process.

Nothing.

He stared out the front window into the inky black of night and rubbed his chin. *Where had she hidden it?*

A floorboard creaked. His head came up. His gaze fixed on the ceiling for a moment then he headed for the staircase.

Reaching the top, he approached the door to his right, drew a deep breath, and knocked. "Mother, I'd like word with you."

He counted to ten. "Now, please. I know you're awake."

Bedsprings creaked. Soft shuffling. Then a faint click as the lock turned. The door opened a crack. Mother peered out. Clad in her nightgown, her hair fell over her shoulder in one long salt and pepper braid.

"Alexander, whatever are you about, crashing around downstairs?"

"Where is it?"

"Where is what?"

"The laudanum or whatever sedative you're using."

"I've no idea what you're talking about."

"Mother, Annali overheard you and Doctor Powell."

"That girl." She sniffed.

"That girl is my wife, and as such you will afford her the courtesy and respect she deserves."

"I don't appreciate your spiteful tone."

He braced his forearm on the door jamb above her head. "Get it now, or I will come in and get it myself."

"How dare you! These are my private, intimate things."

"Now, please." He pressed his other hand against the door, and it opened a few more inches.

Mother stumbled back a step, shot him a lethal glare, turned, and headed for her dresser. She pulled open the top drawer and reached inside.

Closing the drawer, she swung around and marched toward him, something clenched in her right fist. She stopped an arm's length away. "I did it to save you from becoming like him."

"By drugging me?"

"By preventing the stimulations of the marriage bed from accelerating your illness."

"I'm twenty-four years old. I'm married, like most men my age."

"Alexander, you don't see it, but I do. How much you've changed. Doctor Prescott saw it too. Reverend Clark, Mr. Goldman, Mr. Pederson…"

"Would you please stop discussing me with every person in town?"

"And now you tell us you want to sell the bank. What of your sister and me? You've provided for us since your father…since you took on his role at the bank. Now you're going to abandon—"

"Mother, I am not going to abandon you. Trust me. You and Nellie will be provided enough with funds to live comfortably the rest of your lives."

He reached out his hand. "Please. Give it to me."

She dropped her gaze to her fist for a moment then heaved a sigh. Closing the distance, she slapped the small bottle into his palm. "Fine."

His fingers curled around it, and he withdrew a step.

Her hand grasped the edge of the door as she stepped back. "Now if you're quite through disrupting the entire household, good night." She slammed the door in his face.

Giving his head a shake, he turned. Nellie stood in the doorway of her room clutching her nightgown to her chest with both fists. She stared at him, her eyes narrowed, her lips pressed tight.

The deep shadows of the hallway must have distorted her expression into what for a moment looked like pure hate.

"My apologies for disturbing your rest."

Nellie gave a quick nod then eased back, enveloped by the shadows of her bedroom. Her lock turned with a soft click.

Inside his room, Alex closed the door and turned the key. His entire family was mad. He hung up his robe and climbed into bed behind the only sane person in his life. Pulling her against him, he buried his nose in her damp hair and breathed.

Only two and half more weeks. Could they make it?

Chapter Twenty-two

"Alexander!" The shrill voice radiated through Annali's skull. "Are you awake?"

Through her closed eyelids, early morning sunlight pierced her skull. She groaned and cracked opened one eye.

The mattress dipped as Alex sat beside her. He wore only his trousers and undershirt. Concern furrowed his brow. "How do you feel?"

His hand rubbed her shoulder. A couple of his fingers slipped beneath the edge of her chemise to touch her skin. A pleasant shiver ran through her body.

"That window needs curtains." She sat up and shoved her hair off her face. Drawing her knees close, she rested her forehead on her crossed arms. "Why do I feel like I had too much to drink?"

"Mother intended that glass of lemon water for me. My apologies."

She raised her head and rested her chin on her arm. "You should apologize. I would never have picked up that glass if my thoughts hadn't been absorbed by that amazing encounter in the bath." The corners of her mouth twitched.

He glanced at the floor, then looked at her over his shoulder. "Amazing?"

She shifted around and crawled up behind him. Draping both arms over his shoulders, she licked the edge of his ear. "Amazing," she whispered.

He leaned back, turning his head, and kissed the corner of her mouth.

"Alexander!" Harriet's voice rose from the foot of the stairs.

He sighed, leaning away from Annali.

"Yes, Mother," he called. "We're coming!" He stood and walked to the washstand where he poured a bit of water in his shaving mug.

Annali scooted to the end of the mattress, looping her arm around the bed post as he whipped his brush around in the mug.

"Do we have to eat breakfast here? Can't we eat in town?"

"I'm afraid not. While I do still need to maintain some semblance of adherence to my regimen, I also need to be mindful of my spending."

Lifting the brush to his face, he rubbed white lather over his cheeks and neck. "Tomorrow afternoon, Mr. Lathrop and an associate will arrive to look things over before we meet to finalize a closing date and sign the sales contract."

He picked up his razor and unfolded the blade. "I'll be putting them up at the Occidental, and I thought it would be nice for us to dine there with them tomorrow evening."

"All of us?"

"I would like them to meet my wife. However, until the contract is signed, I would prefer to keep Mother ignorant of their presence."

"Any meal away from your family is fine with me."

Shaking his head, he sent her a quick soapy smile then shifted his jaw and brought the razor downward from his sideburn to the edge of his jaw, swiping clean a swath of soap and hair.

"I like that you don't have a beard. Men always get food and drink in the hair, and they smell like old tobacco."

Alex made several short, careful strokes under his nose and around his mouth.

"I have one regular customer in Lincoln whose beard is going gray, and the gray hairs are curlier than the rest. I hate when I have to touch it. It feels like bugs crawling over my skin."

Tipping his chin toward the ceiling, he slid the razor down, carefully shifting around the bulge of his Adam's apple.

"He's a nice man who likes to talk. He's smart, like you. Not a banker, but an attorney. And he's on the city council and some kind of securities board."

Alex's hand went still. Slowly he turned. His gaze locked on her, his expression somber, despite the shaving soap which covered half his face. "Do you know his name?"

She laughed and shook her head. "I never share a client's name." But the lack of humor in the precise clip of his words, caused the rest of her laugh to catch in the back of her throat. She frowned. "What's wrong?"

"I need to know his name."

"Alex, I don't give out client names."

"Would his name happen to be Barnes? Roger Barnes?"

"How did you— Do you know him?"

"Yes. Damn." He heaved a sigh, glanced at the floor, the ceiling, then back to her. "He's coming here. Tomorrow. With Lathrop. He can't see you. If they find out— Double damn."

That she'd be recognized one day had been inevitable. Her hope had only been to avoid it long enough for Alex's plan to be realized. Ivy was barely hidden behind this façade of proper lady and wife. That her life could ever be different…well, she wasn't fifteen anymore. No sense pining for something that would never be.

Pasting on a smile, she scooted off the bed and looped her arm around the bedpost. "When you meet them for dinner, apologize and say I was unwell, a female complaint or some such thing."

He nodded. "And your presence here will keep Mother from suspecting that selling the bank is still nothing more than my wild idea. She'll merely assume my absence at dinner to be a normal late Friday evening at the bank."

Annali crossed the room to her trunk and removed a clean petticoat and drawers. "And if she asks me where you are, I'll say the new teller—"

"Paxton."

"Mr. Paxton made mistakes, and you have to fix them."

He swiped the razor over his chin as Annali pulled on her stockings and petticoat.

"Alexander!" Another shriek rose up the stairwell and through the bedroom door.

Annali lowered herself onto the trunk and leaned forward to tie up her shoes. How did such volume come from such a tiny woman?

"Coming, Mother!" Alex called back as he wiped odd bits of soap from his face.

"Stop dawdling and come down here. You know

breakfast is served at half past."

"Yes, coming!" He slipped his mug and razor into the top drawer and wiped up the last droplets of water from the wooden cabinet top.

Annali stepped into her green calico skirt and reached behind to button the closure. Grabbing her brush, she sat on the edge of the bed and worked the tangles from her hair.

Alex donned his shirt, buttoned his suspenders, then picked up his oversized, black waistcoat.

"Wait." She set down her brush and hopped off the bed. "I have a present for you." Moving back to her trunk, she lifted the lid and removed the paper wrapped gift.

He draped his waistcoat over the horizontal brass rail at the end of the bed. "I have something for you, too."

"For me?" Her heart quickened a beat. He'd bought a present...for her?

He shot her a quick half-smile and accepted the package. He untied the string. Then as the paper loosened, he set the gift on the bed and unfolded the paper.

Her gaze darted from the new waistcoats to his face, waiting for him to say...something.

But he only stared down at them and slowly shook his head. Reaching out, he ran his finger over the mulberry jacquard, then set it aside and fingered the lapel of the teal stripe. "They're very fine."

"Do you like them?"

He slipped his arm around her waist and drew her into a hug. "I do. Yes, I do. I...I've never received such a...a striking...such a personal..."

His arms tightened around her. "Thank you," he

whispered into her hair.

Keeping her arm around his waist, she moved beside him. "I hope they fit. Miss Sinek is an excellent tailor, and she thought your measurements to be the same as Mr. Tomkins at the hotel. Go ahead. Try on the mulberry. I thought you could wear it today."

"The mulberry?"

She glanced up.

He swallowed, staring down at the waistcoats.

"Yes, the red one. The teal matches a gown she's making for me. I hoped we'd have a chance to wear them together." She patted the center of his chest. "Put it on. I want to see. When you add your gold watch and chain, you'll look so dashing—"

He turned away. "Let me get your gift." Opening his bag, he withdrew a small object wrapped in tissue paper. "It's nothing of any consequence," he mumbled. "If you don't care for it…"

She accepted the present from his outstretched hand. Sitting on the edge of the bed, she stared at the tissue wrapped object for a moment or two. Was it a bud vase? No. It had what felt like a small dish at the base and a flared, dome-shaped top.

The last gift she remembered ever receiving was the ragdoll her father had given her. Mrs. Giovani had bought her clothes over the years, but they had been a necessity and had been made of plain, sturdy cotton and wool.

That Alex had chosen something especially for her touched her heart as much as the gift itself. She swallowed the lump rising in her throat.

The tissue paper crinkled as she slowly unwrapped a porcelain hatpin holder. Tears stung her eyes as she ran her finger over the thin gilt line encircling the tiny holes at the top. The flowers and leaves painted on the side, blurred together.

Alex shifted in front of her.

A tear slipped down her cheek.

"You don't like it."

She swiped away the droplet and another took its place. "I do. It's lovely."

"I realize it holds little value. You must have been given many beautiful gifts over the years."

She bit her lip and shook her head as more tears silently fell.

"I'd noticed you were using an old pin cushion for your hatpins. When I saw this, I thought to present it as a small token of appreciation...for..."

She sniffed and nodded, wiping both cheeks.

"My apologies. I see I've chosen poorly."

Clenching her hatpin holder, Annali jumped up and threw her arms around him.

The impact knocked him back a step.

"Don't you dare apologize." She sniffled. "It's the most beautiful—" her voice caught, "—gift I ever received."

"You like it?"

She tipped her head back, her gaze meeting his brown eyes and furrowed brow. She nodded.

"But... You're crying."

"I'm happy."

"Truly?"

"Yes. I love it. Thank you." She raised onto her toes and kissed him. Then stepping away, she set the hatpin holder on the back corner of the washstand.

"And the color?"

"Yes."

"You're certain?"

She laughed as she removed the pincushion from her trunk. "Yes, I'm certain." Taking her small collection of hat pins, she inserted them into the various holes on the top of the holder, placing her special, pearl tipped pins toward the back.

"I recalled pink to be your favorite color and conveyed that to the woman in the shop. She assured me the roses are pink."

"Yes, of course they're—" She set the pincushion beside the wash basin and turned. "What do you mean, she assured you?"

"Alexander! Breakfast is on the table!"

"Damn," he muttered, then yelled. "I said we're coming, and we're coming!"

"Need I remind you of the importance of your regimen in keeping your bodily humors aligned?"

"Five minutes, Mother! We'll be down in five minutes!"

He paced the room then stopped by the bed and picked up his black waistcoat. "Please, Annali. Get dressed."

Three quick strides brought her to the end of the bed, and she yanked the old waistcoat from his hands.

"No. What are you not telling me?"

With a snap of her arm, she pointed toward the door, the black waistcoat waving from her hand like a battlefield flag—no quarter asked or given. "Why do you believe them and not me?"

"Annali, please."

He reached for the waistcoat, but before he touched it, she crossed her arms weaving the garment in between.

"No."

He strode to the door, to the bed, to the wardrobe. His back to her, his shoulders sagged. "You want to know why?"

"Yes, I do."

He whirled around. "Because they're right. Reverend Clark, Doctor Powell, Mother—they're all right."

"Alex, what are you talking about?"

"All of it, the bland diet, loose clothing, fresh air and exercise, and...and the denial of self-pleasure. They are right. Adherence to these strictures does prevent that gradual decline into blindness and insanity."

"There is nothing wrong with you." She threw the black waistcoat on the bed. "I thought you believed me last night."

He walked to her and taking her hands brought them to his chest and gave them a light squeeze. "And I do believe you. About that. About how reprehensible I might become, to whom I might eventually become attracted."

She searched his face, trying to make sense of his words. "But..."

"But there are other symptoms which indicate a decline."

She frowned. "What symptoms?"

"Blindness."

She blinked. That made no sense. She'd never seen him bump into anything. He had no trouble reading. Wait. He did wear spectacles. But many people did.

He glanced at the ceiling. "You don't believe me."

"I do, but—"

He released her hands and stepped back. "The day I

met you, I visited the optometrist. It had become difficult to read my own handwriting. I'd developed headaches. The doctor prescribed stronger lenses."

"But that doesn't—"

"Yes. Yes, it does. Self-denial, those metal devices, they prevent…" He walked to the washstand and bracing his hands on either side, hung his head.

"That first time, when Mother walked into my bedroom and caught me… It wasn't my first time. She told me what would happen, Doctor Powell told me… A few months later I had trouble reading."

She sighed. "But Alex…" The idea that he actually believed this overwhelmed her ability to speak.

"Damn and double damn, I tried." He raised his head, and she met his gaze in the mirror. "I started the regimen, I read the literature, but it was still so damn hard. I would hide in the barn or use the soap when I was supposed to be taking a cold bath. Two prescription changes."

"Alex, that doesn't mean… I can't believe your own mother created such a terrible fear when you were so young and has continued to keep you believing it."

He whirled around, snatching up the hatpin holder. "Here." He shoved it toward her so fast, she had to grab it with both hands before the pins scattered across the floorboards.

"What color is that?"

She glanced up, confused by the harsh demand. "White with gold trim, green leaves and pink…"

He snatched up the two waistcoats, one in each hand. "Teal, red, mulberry." He nodded to the hatpin holder. "Pink, green, it's all the same to me. The beautiful sunsets and sunrises that people say are filled with pink and orange and red, all look like shades of the same color as these."

He tossed the waistcoats back on the bed.

Relief bubbled up inside Annali's throat. She clamped her hand over her mouth.

His features hardened. "Are you laughing at me? Damn it, Annali…" He snatched up the ugly black waistcoat.

"No, Alex." She grabbed his arm. "Wait. Listen."

He twisted free and tried to sidestep her.

"Wait!" She darted in front of him and placed her palm in the center of his chest. "Alex, listen to me."

He stopped but fixed his gaze on something behind her.

"When you had your eye examination, did you ask the doctor about the color problem?" She shook her head. "Of course, you didn't. Sometimes, Alex, your stubbornness… Well, if you had, he would have told you that it's caused by—"

His gaze shifted to glare down at her.

She lifted her chin and glared right back. "Don't give me that haughty Alex-the-Ass look. If you'd only listen to people other than your mother, you might learn the truth."

He crossed his arms.

She exhaled a loud puff of breath. "I'm trying to tell you that not being able to see colors is a problem inside the eye. If you'd asked the doctor, he would have told you. You were born with it. You remember Hiram? He tended the bar at Mrs. Beauchamp's. He has the same problem as you. His doctor told him all about it. There is a fancy name for it, but not seeing color is a real condition, most common in men. Nothing you did caused this, and you're not going blind. You were born this way. You've been told lies for so long you believe they're true. Think. Have you ever seen colors?"

In the course of moments, a myriad of emotions passed over his face. The rigid set of his shoulders eased. He opened his mouth, closed it, blinked, and looked away.

The black waistcoat slipped from his fingers. He walked woodenly to the bed and sat. Head bowed, he picked up the two waistcoats.

She moved to stand in front of him.

He looked up, eyes shining. "Which one matches your new dress?"

"The stripe."

He set the teal waistcoat to the side and slipped his arms into the mulberry jacquard.

Placing his hands on either side of her waist, he stood, his gaze searching. "Thank you," he whispered then kissed her.

She expected a quick peck, but Alex pulled her into a tight embrace. She wrapped her arms around his neck, drawing from him as he drew from her, overwhelmed by the depth of what was between them.

Even Marcello's declaration of love hadn't stirred so powerful a yearning as Alex stirred in her at this moment.

No man had ever accepted her as a person, as a woman, the way Alex had, the way Alex did. The urge to cry, *I love you*, swelled from deep inside her, but her mouth was so engaged with his while his hands roamed her back, her shoulders, her arms, she could only sag against him, and preserve the words deep in her heart.

No emotional entanglements. That was the

agreement.

He eased away from the kiss. He cupped her face. "Annali," he whispered. "I...I..."

She bit her lip as Alex seemed to catch himself. He stepped away from her and buttoned his new waistcoat.

He moved to the mirror, ran his hand down the fabric, and gave the fitted waist a tug. "Dashing, you said?"

"Yes." She stepped up behind him, brushed off both shoulders. "Most definitely dashing." She rose on her toes and kissed his ear.

Walking to her trunk, she donned the calico blouse and twisted her hair into a bun, securing it with several hairpins. When she turned, Alex stood before her. His gold watchchain added a touch of refinement to his appearance.

"Annali, this...what this is between us... I...I've never felt..."

She shook her head. "Don't say it. We agreed."

"You don't understand. I believe I might be in..."

She stepped close and pressed her finger to his lips. "No. It doesn't matter, because I am still what I am."

He grasped her hand. "It does. It does matter. Everything is different now. Once the sale is final, we can—"

"No, Alex. Things are different for you, but not for me. Your life was a lie, and now you know the truth. I'm happy I could help you finally see that. But I already know the truth of what I am. For me, this life with you is the lie."

"Don't say that. You make yourself sound cheap, as though you're something ugly and dirty. You're not. You're clever and funny and caring and—"

She pulled her hand from his grasp. "You're sweet for saying that, but it changes nothing."

Turning away, she ran her finger along the edge of the washstand then reached past the basin of dirty wash water, touched the pearl tips of her hat pins, and brushed her thumb over the pink roses. "This past week—this life we've been living isn't real. It's protected by a lie as thin as a soap bubble."

"Annali, please. We're married. When this is over, you don't have to go to Denver or San Francisco."

She turned. "No. There will always be another Roger Barnes. You wanted me *because* of who I am, no emotional entanglements. Remember? So, let's go on as we agreed."

His brow furrowed. He stared out across the room with that same focused look he had while calculating numbers in a ledger. Then he seemed to draw into himself. His shoulders squared and his chin came up. "Fine," he said. "If that's what you want."

Grateful, he seemed disinclined to pursue the subject, she smiled and took his hand. "Yes, that's how it has to be."

He responded with a smile that never reached his eyes. "Then let us go down to breakfast before Mother has an apoplectic fit."

Chapter Twenty-three

Alex entered the final numbers on the pages of the loan contract in front of him.

Frank and Florie Burgess had met with him at ten a.m. to discuss their new plan to purchase an empty dry goods store on Military Avenue where the owner had gone bankrupt.

He dipped his pen in the inkwell.

A dark blob landed on his paper. Without thought, he swiped the side of his hand across the paper. Ink smeared over the page. He flipped his palm up to look at the fresh ink stain, and with the pen still between his fingers, another blot fell. He dropped the pen, and it rolled toward him.

He shoved his chair away from the desk before ink stained his new waistcoat. The back of the chair slammed against the wall with a loud thud as the pen fell to the floor.

"Damn." He muttered holding his hand away as he checked over his clothing.

A quick knock on the office door and, "Mr. Worthington, are you all right?" The new teller, Paxton didn't seem to comprehend that when Alex had said, "*Do not disturb me*," he meant, *do not disturb me*.

Rather than charge across the room, yank open the door and chastise the young man, he pulled open the top drawer of his desk and removed an ink-stained rag. Time to allow Mr. Goldman to manage the new employee. In a couple of weeks this office would belong to him.

"All is well," Alex called as he wiped as much of the black from his fingers as possible.

"Sorry to disturb you, sir. And sir, your wife is here."

He glanced at the clock. Almost two-thirty.

Annali stepped inside, a small basket over her arm.

He walked toward her as she pushed the door closed behind her and greeted her with a quick kiss.

"I brought you some lunch."

"Thank you. I hadn't realized it had grown so late." He went to his desk and collecting the contract pages, he placed them in a folder and slipped them into a drawer.

"Alex, it's such a beautiful day, let's have a picnic." Hope brightened her eyes.

*I can't*, hovered briefly on the tip of his tongue. But why? His work was done. The only thing keeping him in this stuffy windowless room was the fact that he'd never done such a thing.

"Yes. Let's." He stepped across the room, pulled open the bottom drawer of the file cabinet, and withdrew a blanket. "I use this in the winter, when I come in early, and the stove hasn't had time to heat the room."

Taking the basket, he laid the blanket on top and offered his arm. "If you don't mind walking, there's a pretty spot down by the river."

"Do you know I've walked more this past week than I have in my entire life."

He held the door open, and they stepped into the bank.

Mr. Goldman looked up from the open ledger on his desk.

"I'm taking the afternoon off," Alex said. "I'll leave you to close out the drawers and lock up."

Goldman's mouth dropped open. A hush fell over the room. Farley and his customers, the marshal whispering with Paxton, they all turned and stared at Alex.

Laughter rumbled behind his breastbone, but rather than release it, he laced his fingers with Annali's and escorted her from the bank.

He was halfway down the street before the dam burst, and he laughed out loud. Ducking into an alley, he leaned against a building as he pressed his arm to his stomach and tried to stifle rolls of laughter that wouldn't be calmed.

"Alex, what's so funny?" Annali stood beside him, a wide grin on her face.

"Damn," he muttered, trying to draw a steady breath. "Did you see their expressions?" More laughter rolled through him, washing away years of tension. "They looked at me like I'd suddenly sprouted two heads."

Annali chuckled. "They did look surprised, but it wasn't that funny."

He drew a deep breath as the laughter wound down. He pressed his arm against his stomach. "My ribs hurt."

He straightened and rested his forearm on her shoulder. "I have never once in the five years I've been running the bank, come in late or left early."

He chuckled. "Can you imagine Mother's reaction when she hears of it? She'll think me gone completely mad."

"If you keep laughing like that, I'll think it too."

Grabbing her hand, he led her from the alley and

down the street toward the river. "Damn, I feel alive for the first time in my life. And there's nothing Mother can say that will spoil it."

**** 

After a leisurely afternoon by the river, they walked home. In the corral, Ben and two new horses nibbled on fresh forkfuls of hay.

"Whose horses are those?" Annali asked, stepping close to the fence.

Alex came up beside her and draped his arms over the top rail. "Clayton's."

"Clayton? Clayton's here?" She glanced toward the house then back. "Who belongs to the other horse?"

"Flint is the name he goes by. He and Clayton are…what could be referred to as…business partners. He has one or two other men in his employ, behind the scenes, but I've never met them."

He picked at a jagged splinter of wood where Ben had been cribbing on the top fence rail.

"Come," he said taking her hand. "Let's get this over with." They started toward the house.

"Do we have to? No one is expecting us this early."

"Trust me. Mother knows we're here. Besides, wouldn't you rather meet Clayton now rather than grant him more time with Mother and her vitriolic opinion?"

Annali left the basket beside the back steps, then holding tight to Alex's hand, they walked through the kitchen and entered the parlor through the dining room.

The man Annali assumed to be Clayton sat on the couch beside Nellie, and though they held hands there remained enough space between them to fit a small child. He stood as she and Alex entered.

Alex's fingers tightened around hers. "Annali, may

I present my brother-in-law, Clayton Miller." His tone had reverted to its usual coolness as his manner grew abrupt and detached. "Clayton, my wife Annali."

Though shadowed by his close-trimmed beard, Clayton's smile was charming none the less. His hair short and slicked back, he looked to be about five years older than Nellie.

"Alexander, wherever did you find such a lovely lady?"

"We met while I was on business in Lincoln." He guided her to a padded chair near the fireplace then remained, his back straight, as he stood protectively beside her.

Clayton gestured to the man in the corner, looming between the window and the couch. "May I present my business partner, Mr. Garrett Flint."

Mr. Flint nodded. He wore a tailored black suit and silk tie. Standing rigidly, with his hands behind his back, he shifted his weight as if he were uncomfortable with either his clothing, or being here, or both.

"A whirlwind courtship, I understand," Clayton said as he lowered himself again beside Nellie.

Alex grunted low in his throat, or was it a growl?

Clayton grinned. Whether he'd heard Alex or not she wasn't sure. "Congratulations, Annali, and welcome. You are a beautiful addition to our family."

She glanced shyly toward the floor. "Thank you, sir."

*Liar*, she thought. Her simple calico dress was dusty and wrinkled. Her hair was a disheveled mess and might even be decorated with bits of grass.

Clayton's clothing on the other hand was immaculate and well-tailored. He wore a gray, checked jacket and matching trousers. A narrow ruffle of lace peeked from the end of each sleeve and filled the space between his tie and the V of his double-breasted waistcoat. Even his shoes gleamed, despite having ridden here on horseback.

"Ah, brother, I see your wife has had a positive influence on your wardrobe. A burgundy jacquard. A choice as refined and elegant as the lady herself."

And though his appreciative gaze roamed over her, the glint of lust was missing from his eyes.

Her chair creaked. She glanced back. Alex held a white-knuckle grip on the chair back.

Clayton chuckled. "Now brother, you needn't scowl at me like a dog guarding a bone." He raised Nellie's hand to his lips and kissed her knuckles. "You know I have no interest in your lovely young wife. I have my Nellie, who has faithfully endured my nomadic lifestyle and stood by me all these sixteen years."

An exaggerated huff of displeasure blew across the room from the wing chair where Harriet sat. "Enough of your foolish posturing, Clayton." Her sharp gaze narrowed on Alex.

"Alexander, what has happened? Why are you not at the bank?"

"I took the afternoon off in order to take my wife on a picnic."

Annali drew a breath and lifted her chin, bracing herself for another onslaught of Harriet's barbs.

"Surely a thoughtful wife wouldn't be so selfish as to take you from your work."

"It was my idea, Mother."

She snorted. "An activity better suited for a Sunday afternoon. Forgoing your daily responsibilities is further evidence of how your surrender to the lust of the flesh has drawn you deeper into a mental decline."

"Mother, enough. I have not fallen into a decline. In fact, quite the opposite."

"Do you see, Clayton, how this fortune hunting orphan girl has blinded Alex to the truth? No matter how I've sacrificed or how hard I've tried to help him, he has turned his back on his family, just as his father did."

Clayton's gaze darted between Alex and Harriet. "Don't fret, Mother. I'm sure all who know you can appreciate how you've suffered to save your son."

Drawing up her small frame up, Harriet somehow created a regal aura around her. "Yes, of course. If you will excuse me, I need to begin preparations for supper."

Clayton stood as Harriet rose.

"Come along, Nellie," she snapped.

Nellie jumped up and turned to Clayton. "Please excuse me, husband."

"Certainly, my dear." He leaned close as though to press a quick kiss to her cheek, but she turned and hurried away.

As mother and daughter left the room, Clayton returned to his seat and fixed his gaze on Alex. "I wish I'd known you were in Lincoln. My business associates and I were there last week."

"I was quite busy," Alex said in that cold, pious tone his mother used. "I doubt we would have had time to meet."

Clayton shot Annali a quick glance. Mischief gleamed in his eyes. "No doubt."

\*\*\*\*

Annali wore her navy-blue dress to dinner. After taking a stiff brush to the layers of dust around the hem, her dress was so clean even Harriet would be hard pressed to locate a single speck of dirt.

Clayton offered his arm to Nellie and escorted her to the table. "My dear, might I suggest a similar style gown for you." He nodded toward Annali as Alex pulled out her chair.

"A rich color, cut in that same style. A cuirass bodice which drapes at the hip would create for you the illusion of height. I'm sure your new sister would enjoy a trip with you to the dressmakers."

From the opposite side of the table, Nellie's mouth curled up in a slow smile that never reached her eyes. "Yes, sister, we must."

"Of course," Annali replied. "I look forward to it."

Clayton took his seat beside his wife.

After Alex gave the blessing, Mr. Flint, seated on Annali's left, passed her a bowl of glazed carrots. She spooned some onto her plate and extended the bowl to Alex.

He glanced at his plate then lifted his gaze to meet hers. She gave him the slightest of nods. Then, taking his knife, he pushed aside his plain boiled carrots.

Accepting the bowl from Annali, he scooped the serving spoon deep into the carrots.

"Alexander!"

He looked up. "Yes, Mother? These look delicious." He lifted out a spoonful, piled high with shiny sliced carrots.

Harriet gasped as Alex added them to his plate. He passed the bowl to Nellie then accepted the mashed potatoes Annali handed to him.

He dropped a large scoop onto his plate beside the chunks of plain boiled potatoes. "Might someone pass the gravy please?"

Annali dove for the gravy boat at the same time as Nellie, but Annali's fingers brushed the tiny handle first.

Nellie narrowed her eyes and glared. Annali smiled innocently and passed the gravy to Alex.

He poured an ample serving over his potatoes and his portion of dry pot roast.

"Alexander," Harriet snapped from the other end of the table. "I am not amused."

"I didn't expect you would be." Alex set the gravy boat down and cut into his slice of roast.

Tension radiated in waves down the length of the table. Harriet sat rigidly, with her spine so straight, it was no wonder she often appeared taller than she was.

Annali pierced some carrots with her fork. Hoping to diffuse some of the hostility, she asked, "Mr. Miller, you mentioned earlier about business in Lincoln, may I inquire as to what you do for a living?"

"Clayton. You must call me Clayton now that we are family."

"Thank you, Clayton. I understand your business frequently takes you away from home."

"Yes. We travel all over. New York, Chicago, Boston, San Francisco."

"Are you a salesman?"

He smiled and glanced across the table toward Mr. Flint. "Not exactly. I procure rare and valuable items for anonymous collectors."

"And, Mr. Flint, you are partners in this business?"

He nodded. His gaze frank and assessing.

"Yes," Clayton replied. "Flint is excellent at locating those rare items while I do better with negotiations."

*Holy Hell, Flint is a thief and Clayton a fence!*
Annali bit her lip to keep from chuckling. "What a wonderfully fascinating occupation."

He seemed to recognize her grasp of the truth and inclined his head. Glancing away, he buttered a slice of bread and switched his attention to Alex.

"Nellie tells me you want to sell the bank. Is that wise, brother?"

"Of course, it's not wise," Harriet retorted. "It's irrational."

"Now, Mother," Clayton soothed. "Alexander is a predictable, sensible man. I'm sure he'll not do anything impulsive."

She snorted. "If you were home more, you might have lent a measure of stability to this household. Convinced Alexander to annul this farce of a hasty marriage."

"Annali seems an appropriate match for Alexander."

"Appropriate! What do you know? Suddenly wants to sell the bank. Leave us all destitute while he and this money-grubbing orphan girl run off to God knows where."

Alex tossed down his knife and fork. They clattered against the plate. A scowl furrowed his brow. "Mother, Clayton, we are sitting right here."

Clayton met Alex's gaze. "My apologies, brother. Annali."

While Clayton sent his wife occasional smiles, he chatted with Harriet, agreeing with everything the woman said while he lavished her with compliments like a drummer selling tonic.

****

Pink, gold, and orange streaked across the horizon

above line of the prairie as Annali closed *The Mysterious Island* and stood. "Where do you think the nitroglycerine came from?" Taking her hand, they strolled around to the side door of the barn.

"From the same mysterious benefactor who left them other things." He picked up the same bucket Annali had used to dump water on him the other day, and opening a bin in the corner, he scooped several cups of oats into the bucket.

"Who do you think is doing all this?"

He rummaged through a corner of discarded harnesses and grain sacks. "I have an idea, but I don't want to spoil it." Straightening he held two more buckets. One without a handle and the other with a crack down the side.

"Can you please take one of these?"

She set the book on the divider between the old cow stall and the area where they stood. Stepping forward she took the handle-less bucket and followed him out to the corral. He divided the feed between the three buckets and set them out for the horses.

"Were you able to make your cake today?" He leaned on the fence while the horses crunched their oats.

"Yes." She stepped up beside him, and he draped his arm over her shoulders. "Mrs. Gourley had an old newspaper picture of the cake from Queen Victoria's wedding. She wanted me to make one just like it. I finally convinced her three tiers would be fine. I baked them today, and I'll do the final icing and decorating tomorrow afternoon. She can pick it up any time after that."

"Mrs. Burgess was obliging enough?"

"I don't know what you said to her this morning, but she's been humming since she got back from the bank."

"Humming is unusual?"

"Yes." Annali chuckled slipping her arm around his waist. "Normally she's abrupt and snappy in the kitchen. Unless she's worried, then she's anxious and wringing her hands. But that only happens when she remembers I'm married to you."

The soft huffing of the horses' breath mixed with the crunching of their oats. Their tails swished and occasionally one or another would kick at a belly fly.

He looked out over the horses, toward the horizon where wide swaths of yellow, white, and layered shades of some other color stretched across the sky.

"Annali, what you've…done…for me. That I can look at this sunset and know what I see is normal."

"You were born this way. Just like Hiram."

"I think…for so long I was terrified I would become him. Perhaps over the years, it created its own form of blindness."

"I suppose it did."

"You must have dreams…want more than money…more than what you had."

"I love that you care, but don't you see, money is the way I'll have my dreams. My own place. As a madam, I'll be independent. Free to make my own choices."

"That's really what you want?"

"Yes, it is."

Chapter Twenty-four

The house was quiet as they climbed the back steps and entered the kitchen.

He nodded toward the pantry. "Join me in the bath again?"

She grinned. Loathe to sacrifice any chance to be with him, she moved ahead of him. At the doorway, she turned back, meeting his gaze across the kitchen. She crooked the index finger of one hand as she unbuttoned the top button of her dress with her other. She popped free a second button, then a third.

He was across the room in two strides. He picked her up, swung her around, and stepped into the pantry, kicking the door closed behind them.

****

"I have to go back to barn. I left your book out there."

She slipped her skirt on over her chemise and stepped into her shoes, leaving them untied.

Alex had finished emptying the tub and was gathering the towels to hang on the line. "All right. Just slide the bolt on the door when you come back."

A full moon illuminated the yard with dull white light. In the corral, the horses searched the ground for bits of hay, occasionally snorting as they sniffed through the dust.

The side door had been left open casting a stream of

moonlight across the floor. Silently, she stepped over the threshold and headed around the buggy to the back corner where she'd left the book on the half wall of the old cow stall.

Something shuffled in the hay on the other side.

She froze. Slowly she tip-toed forward and ducked down below the top edge of the wall. Cautiously, she peered around the end.

Two men lay naked in the straw, one man between the legs of the other.

Annali dropped back, the half wall between her and the men. She listened to see if they'd seen her, but from the low pants and grunts on the other side, she assumed they were too immersed in their own pleasure to have heard her.

She'd known there were men who preferred to lie with other men. That was why Madame had employed Georgie. Though he rarely left his job as a faro dealer, on rare occasions he did disappear upstairs. And while Annali knew all this, she'd never actually seen it.

Curious, she peered around the corner. The deepening shadows inside the old cow stall hid the features of the two men, but from the width of his shoulders as he arched above the second man, it had to be Flint, leaving the man beneath him to be Clayton.

She eased back and carefully inched the book off the top of the half wall then tiptoed from the barn. She ran across the yard, up the steps and into the kitchen. The screen door banged shut behind her.

*Hells bells.* Did Alex know?

She grabbed the rest of her clothes and headed upstairs.

Would Clayton now come in from his romp in the

hay, go upstairs, and bed his wife? Was he the sort to enjoy the company of both men and women?

At the top of the stairs, she studied the door across from the room she shared with Alex. Did Nellie, with her muddy brown dresses, severe hair style, and cold demeanor, even crave the company of her husband? Did she know his secret? Did she turn a blind eye as many wives did, to their husband's mistress, as long as he was discrete?

Annali entered their room and closed the door. Alex was climbing into bed. She crossed the room to the wardrobe, put away her clothes, and kicked off her shoes.

"Is something wrong?" Alex asked. "You have an odd look on your face."

If Alex knew, he'd never let on. If he didn't know, who was she to tell? Should her own secret be discovered, her life here would be ruined. For Clayton and Flint, it would be worse.

"Where does Mr. Flint sleep when he's here?"

"My old rope bed was set up in the sewing room at the top of the stairs."

"Sewing room?"

"Directly to the right at the top of the stairs. It's a small room over the foyer. Why?"

"No reason. Only curious."

He didn't look convinced, but he yawned and snuggled into his pillow. Annali slipped into bed, and he rolled onto his side and pulled her close.

How would she be able to look at Clayton or Flint again and not think about—

The same way she did with any other man she'd seen naked. Nothing special. Tonight was only so odd because she'd seen it here, where nudity and sex were apparently forbidden.

Alex had a very strange family.

\*\*\*\*

Annali lifted Alex's bowler from the hall tree and passed it to him as they stepped through the door onto the front porch.

A beam of morning sun spilled across Clayton and Flint as they leaned against the railing. Smoke curled from a cigarette Flint held between his fingers. The formal clothes he'd worn last night had been exchanged for rougher western garb, complete with hat, boots, and a gun belt.

He stared right back. Did he suspect she'd seen them? Pulling the door closed behind her, she moved up close beside Alex.

Clayton, wearing the same fine suit he'd worn last night, reached into his pocket and withdrew a silver case. He popped it open and removed a cheroot. He held out the case. Alex shook his head.

Clayton flashed a smooth, easy smile. "That's right. No vices for our virgin boy." He slipped the case back into his coat.

The muscles of Alex's jaw clenched as his hand fumbled to grasp hers. Their fingers twined, and she gave him a reassuring squeeze.

Clayton's gaze darted to Annali, then back to Alex. "Maybe not so much anymore. Hence the new waistcoat and that little show of defiance last night."

"Enough," Alex snapped. "How much do you need this time?"

Clayton winced. "So crass. Perhaps we might discuss this in private."

"No need. I assume Nellie told you I'm through with

your extortion."

"Really, brother. Extortion is such a vulgar word. Can't we consider this more of a personal loan."

"For?"

"We thought Europe would be nice this time of year. London, Paris, Milan. There are also some valuables I would like to collect from my safe deposit box before we leave."

"We? Is Nellie going with you?"

"Now, brother. We both know your sister would never consent to go anywhere without your mother."

"Have you asked her?"

"Will that help?"

Alex shook his head. "I'll never understand why you and Nellie ever married."

"Let's just say that the arrangement was advantageous to all parties involved." He took out his pocket watch and checked the time. "Much like any arrangements between us. Secrets must be protected for everyone's benefit."

"I no longer care. Tell whatever you want to whoever you want. Get your jewels out of my vault. I'm done with this whole business. Find another way to escape the Pinkerton detectives."

Alex tugged Annali forward, practically dragging her down the steps. She stumbled along behind as he marched up the path to the road.

"Pinkertons?" She grabbed onto the fence jerking them both to a stop.

Alex glanced at the fence then back to the porch. "Clayton only shows up here when he needs money or to evade the Pinkertons." His gaze met hers as his thumb brushed back and forth over her hand.

"You said he's only bluffing, so who will he tell about what?"

He glanced off toward town. "You're right. There's nothing he can say that would jeopardize the sale now. Lathrop and Barnes arrive this afternoon. Remember not to come near the bank after three and stay away from the Occidental."

She nodded. "Don't worry. I'm going to finish the bride cake for Mrs. Gourley then stay to help Mrs. Burgess with any chores or baking she needs done."

"Don't tell anyone."

"I won't."

"Especially—"

"I won't."

"Lord knows what she'll do if she finds out."

"What should I tell her when you don't come home for supper?"

"Nothing. I'll send a note later explaining a need to work late."

He pressed his lips to hers. The quick kiss slowly grew more consuming. His arms wrapped around her. Her blouse pulled tight as he clenched fistfuls of the fabric at her back.

Eagerly, she embraced the freedom of his open show of affection and matched his every nibble and stroke of his tongue.

After several long moments, he broke the kiss. Her gaze locked with his dark brown eyes. She chuckled. "Alex the virgin, my ass."

He placed a quick kiss to the end of her nose, then walked backward onto the road. He waved.

Laughing, she waved back.

Then he turned and headed toward town, a light

bounce in his steps.

She gripped the pointed tips of the fence pickets and watched him fade into the distance.

"Alex Worthington, I love you," she whispered.

The impact of that spoken truth didn't surprise her. Maybe somewhere deep inside she'd known since that morning in the alley. The when didn't matter. Only that loving him must remain her secret to protect, even from Alex.

Turning, she started up the path. Flint leaned against a support post watching her. Clayton, too, seemed focused on her approach, but his gaze lacked the hawk-like intensity of Flint's.

As she climbed the steps, Clayton withdrew the cheroot from his mouth and casually stepped toward the door, blocking her way.

Her chest tightened as her gaze shot to his face. His expression remained cool.

Flint, still against the rail, narrowed his gaze.

Clayton smiled. "You are an unusual woman, Annali. The streak of blonde in your hair doubly so. I do wonder where Alexander managed to find such a...perceptive and mysterious...young wife."

Annali stilled as her pulse thrummed against the back of her jaw. Did he know? His poker-face gave nothing away. Gathering her courage, she shrugged.

He gave her a slow nod. "As I said, mysterious. And I'd like to believe discreet as well. Perhaps none of us are truly who we pretend to be."

Clayton chuckled. His features softened. "However—" He gestured toward the road. "—young husband yonder also has a few secrets of his own."

Annali glared at him. "Alex told me everything."

Clayton raised his eyebrows. "Apparently there is more to your relationship and more to my brother-in-law than the naïve boy I believed him to be."

"That's right. You don't know him at all." She whirled and hurried down the steps.

She could do without fetching her hat and reticule.

\*\*\*\*

"Oh Lord, such a cake." Hands pressed to her cheeks, Florie Burgess *oooed* and *aaahed* for several minutes. "Learned to do this in a bakery you say?"

"Yes, ma'am, back in Council Bluffs."

"Esther, come see this. Darcy, you too."

Darcy, the young woman washing dishes, wiped her hands and tossed the dish towel on the corner of the sink.

Esther set the coffee pot on the worktable and joined her mother and Darcy beside Annali.

"Lordy, a true work of art, wouldn't you agree daughter?"

Esther flashed Annali a quick smile. "Yes, Mama, it's gorgeous."

"And such a steady hand."

Annali's hand had been anything but steady when she arrived earlier. Clayton's innuendoes had had her hands trembling all the way to town, and she'd had to practice piping on a cutting board for nearly an hour before she felt confident enough to recreate the roses, swags, and lattice onto the actual three-tiered cake.

Did Clayton know her secret? Would he use it to threaten Alex? Put Alex's sale at risk in exchange for the money he needed for Europe? Or was he bluffing? Evidently, he was good at it, for Alex had been paying him for years. But if Clayton knew her secret, she well knew his.

"Mrs. Worthington?"

Annali blinked and glanced around. Esther had left the kitchen, and Darcy had returned to the sink.

"I'm sorry, wool gathering. If it's all right with you, can I put this in that pie safe over there, out of the way, until Mrs. Gourley comes for it?"

"Anything you wish. Your husband has approved our loan." She lightly clapped her hands together. "We are putting this place up for sale and moving to a larger building on Military."

Yes, the loan Mrs. Burgess had so feared was in jeopardy the day she put Annali to work washing dishes.

"Before you go, Esther is serving orders. Could you please take the coffee pot and refill cups? It will only take a minute."

"All right," she said, eager to keep busy. Pot in hand she stepped into the dining room. Mr. Paxton sat at the back corner table chatting as usual with the town marshal she'd seen him with before. The two men leaned close over their meal, engaged in a hushed conversation which stopped as Annali approached.

Mr. Paxton blinked even as a frown crossed his brow. "Mrs. Worthington?"

She smiled. "Coffee, gentlemen?"

Paxton's gaze darted to his companion, then he withdrew his watch and checked the time. "None for me, thank you. I have to get back to the bank."

"I need to get back to work as well." The marshal picked up his hat and stood along with Paxton.

The bank teller nodded to Annali, "Good day to you, Mrs. Worthington," he said and followed his marshal friend to the door.

\*\*\*\*

As the mid-day rush thinned out, Annali hung her apron and walked toward the Methodist Church intending to help Hester Clark with whatever church project needed doing. At the corner of Main Street and Sixth Avenue, she waited for a team of mules pulling a freight wagon to pass.

The pounding of a hammer echoed between the buildings. Across the street, a man nailed boards into the frame of the new roof over the tobacco shop where Sarah Pederson hawked her basket of kittens. And standing in front, hammer in hand, was Royd Pederson, chatting amiably with Nellie and Harriet.

Mr. Pederson had spilled the secret about the bank to Hester Clark. Was he now telling Harriet the same? Would she confront Alex? Could she spoil the sale?

Before they spotted her, Annali stepped into the street, walking beside the wagon as it moved, keeping it between herself and Alex's family. At the Farmers and Merchants bank, the wagon continued past, and Annali darted behind the wagon and around the corner at the end of the block.

Afraid to risk being seen, she waited. A young boy came her way, kicking a tin can along in front of him.

"Excuse me." She pulled her coin purse from her pocket. "I'll give you a nickel if you'll deliver a message for me."

He eyed her suspiciously until she held up the coin.

"Go into the bank and tell Mr. Worthington that Mrs. Worthington has an important message for him and she's waiting…" She pointed toward the back of the building. "…behind the bank."

"Got it." He snatched the coin from her fingers and darted inside.

Annali turned and froze. Three men came toward her, or rather the bank, from the direction of the Occidental Hotel.

*Hell's bells!* She whirled and darted down the alley. Leaning against the back wall, she prayed the men hadn't seen her as clearly as she'd seen them.

Taking several deep breaths, she waited for Alex. He'd be upset that she'd come here, but he had to know that Royd Pederson had a leaky mouth, and Harriet might be at this very moment be on her way to ruin everything.

The approaching footsteps were nearly silent in the grass as someone rounded the side of the building. She turned.

"Ivy, what are you doing here?"

Chapter Twenty-five

*Damn.* Alex had specifically told Annali, *"Don't come anywhere near the bank or the Occidental after three."* Yet there she'd stood, bold as brass, right on the corner, even as his brain worked frantically to deny what his eyes had seen.

Lathrop had been rambling about housing costs and mortgage rates, so engrossed in his opinions he hadn't seemed to notice the young woman who was there then gone.

However, Roger Barnes had no such problem. He excused himself before they reached the bottom step, apologizing for his sudden need to water the weeds out back.

*Double damn.* Alex's instincts had been correct. The sale was going to fall apart. His one chance to get out from under— Why had she come here?

His mind spun with plausible explanations while he struggled to elicit murmurs of agreement to Lathrop's observations on the future of the national economy.

As he and Lathrop entered the lobby, a young boy squeezed between them and darted out the door.

Lathrop wandered around the room checking over everything from the plaster ceiling to the pattern of tiny octagon tiles on the floor.

"Excuse me, sir." Goldman stepped up beside him and whispered. "It seems your wife is waiting for you out back with an important message."

*Damn.*

"Nice little bank you have here," Lathrop said as he approached.

Whatever Annali had to say would have to wait.

"Now I'd like to see that new vault you installed."

"Certainly. Right this way." Alex opened the gate in the railing and gestured Lathrop toward the area behind the teller cages. "And sir, may I present Arthur Goldman, the bank's head teller and cashier officer. Mr. Goldman, this is Mr. Lathrop, president of Golden Bank and Securities."

Lathrop reached out and the two men shook hands. "Goldman, eh? How apropos. Young Worthington here has given you his highest recommended for the bank manger position."

Goldman straightened and squared his shoulders. "Yes, sir. I would be very interested in the post."

The front door of the bank opened, and Roger Barnes hurried to join them.

Alex hung back, leaning on the counter as Goldman, Lathrop, and Barnes examined the door and the interior of the new vault. His breath caught each time Barnes opened his mouth, expecting at any moment, mention of the whore waiting behind the bank, but Roger said nothing.

What had Annali told him? Did the man suspect a connection between Ivy and Alex? Annali was excellent at pretending; maybe Barnes had no idea. A flicker of hope brightened that looming shadow of dread.

Alex pushed open the office door. "Gentlemen, shall we continue this meeting in my office?"

****

Annali gasped, mentally scrambling to switch into her old persona. She smiled. "Why Mr. Barnes, what a surprise. I never expected to see you."

"Ivy, are you working here now? I tried to request you on Thursday and was told you'd left. I was given a girl named Daisy. She talked too much and giggled like a child. Are you coming back?"

She patted his chest and toyed with the lapel of his coat. "Sorry, Sugar. I'm heading west. Denver or San Francisco maybe."

He touched her hair and ran his thumb over her cheek. "My offer still stands. I'd be pleased to take care of you."

"No, thank you. I want to see a bit more of the world."

He sighed. "Were you on your way into the bank? Can I help you?"

"I was going to exchange some of my bank notes for coin. You go on ahead. I'll just wait until all the customers are gone."

He drew her into a quick hug and stepped back. "I'll miss you, Ivy. Take care of yourself."

She smiled. "You too."

As soon as he turned away, she scrubbed furiously at her cheek, erasing the tingle left from the brush of his beard.

"Hey, Sugar."

He turned. His brow raised expectantly.

"Next time, ask for Violet. She'll know how to give you what you need."

He gave her a nod and disappeared around the corner.

She sagged against the brick wall exhaling a long

breath. That was close. For a moment she'd almost forgotten how to be Ivy. A week and a half with Alex and her mind had nearly erased her past.

**\*\*\*\***

"Everything seems in order," Lathrop said. "Why don't we meet with your lawyer now, and we can sign the sales agreement."

Alex could only nod, still expecting Barnes to speak up.

Lathrop held his cigar over the ashtray and tapped off the powdery gray end. "I have a bank draft for the deposit with me. We'll set the closing date for the twenty-eighth, contingent of course on any issues our Pinkerton man might find. Then we'll be ready to open with the new fiscal year."

Again, Alex barely managed a nod.

"You've been unusually quiet, young man," Lathrop said as they stepped from behind the teller cages.

"Mr. Worthington has a new wife waiting for him," Goldman said.

Alex's gaze shot to Goldman's face. His statement seemed innocent enough, but was there an underlying meaning? Had Barnes said something of which Alex was unaware?

"I would love to meet your wife," said Barnes. "Will she be joining us later for diner?"

"No, I'm afraid she's feeling under the weather today."

As they started for the door, it opened.

Alex's stomach sank like a rock in a pond.

"Alexander," Mother snapped.

Goldman scurried off behind the teller cages as if he were a frontiersman escaping a band of raiding Iroquois.

Mother's narrowed gaze swept over Lathrop and Barnes and landed on Alex. "I would like a word with you."

She marched right past them straight into Alex's office.

"My apologies, gentlemen. Something seems to have upset my mother. I should only be a few minutes if you would care to go on ahead." He turned to Goldman. "Would you kindly show these gentlemen the way? I'll lock up and join you shortly."

"Yes, sir."

Was that a glance of pity Goldman shot him as he hurried to join the others on their way out the door?

Alex drew a deep breath and headed into his office. After closing the door, he crossed his arms and waited.

Hands on her hips, Mother glared at him. "Who were those men?"

"What are you doing here?"

"I forbid you to sell this bank."

His fingers dug into the muscle of his forearm, rather than fulfill his sudden desire to throttle her.

"There is nothing to forbid. When Father's shares in this bank came to me, I became the majority shareholder. I am selling my shares to Golden Bank and Securities. We're on our way to Mr. Dayton's office to sign the contract."

She strode to his desk then whirled around.

"This is madness. I'm certain Doctor Powell and Reverend Clark will agree with me."

"I don't care."

"You've lost all rational thought. Erratic behavior, outbursts of temper. I've tried, but you are clearly out of control."

"Out of control?" He exhaled a short bark of laughter. The sound rang hollow through the office. "Look what you and Doctor Powell and Reverend Clark nearly drove me to."

He strode to his desk and yanked open the bottom drawer. He lifted the false bottom, reached under the sheaf of manuscript pages, and pulled out his pistol.

He slammed it down so hard against the desktop, his mother flinched and jumped back a step.

"Do you know what this was for?"

She glared first at the weapon, then up at him.

"I bought it in Lincoln last week. You and Doctor Powell and Reverend Clark had me convinced. I thought I was going blind. That my decisions were impulsive and irrational. Indications of encroaching madness. I was destined to become as vile a human being as my father. So, I planned to end my life with that." He gestured to the gun.

Her brow furrowed.

"The possibility that I would shoot myself doesn't even upset you." He laughed, but the sound resonated hollow and sad. "No, because you could still play the martyr. Poor Harriet Worthington, the humble widow, who despite all her efforts couldn't keep her son from the same madness that consumed her husband. A liar, a gambler, and a fornicator. A man who neglected his family and his business. A man you and everyone else believe was murdered at the hands of his own son."

He grabbed the pistol, dropped it in the drawer, and pushed it shut. "That's why you've refused to accept Annali. You feared she would show me everything I believed about myself, everything *you made me believe* about myself, was a lie."

He shook his head. "I'm sorry for you, Mother. You've played the victim so long, it's all you know how to be."

Her nostrils flared as she drew in a sharp breath. Her chin rose a notch as her eyes narrowed.

He pressed his fingers against the desktop, pushing harder with each word until his knuckles turned white and his fingertips red.

"That's why you don't want me to sell. You need the bank to keep me under your thumb. It's over, Mother. Go home."

He walked across the room and opened the door. "Now, if you will excuse me, I have a sales contract to sign."

\*\*\*\*

With nowhere to go, Annali started back to the house. She doubted Alex would risk meeting her now that Roger Barnes had seen her. To avoid both the bank and the hotel, she walked south on Main, planning to turn west after a few blocks.

Lost in thought, she nearly bumped into a woman coming out of a butcher shop.

"Mrs. Worthington!" Rose Gourley exclaimed, a shopping basket looped over one arm, a paper wrapped parcel inside. "Just the person I wanted to see."

"Mrs. Gourley," Annali replied, grateful for an excuse to prolong her walk back to Alex's house. "Your cake is all finished."

"Wonderful!"

"I used the kitchen at Burgess Café. Come, I'll show you."

"How very convenient. I'm a Baptist don't you know, and the church is quite nearby."

They walked past a few shops and turned down a narrow alley to come up behind the restaurant.

"Transporting the cake from here tomorrow morning will be so much easier. James, Lou Ella's intended, is Lutheran, don't you know. But he's such a dear, he agreed to a Baptist ceremony."

Frank Burgess sat on the side of the loading platform at the back of the restaurant. He spoke with two men who stood with their backs toward Annali.

"We'll stop by my house on the way home," Mrs. Gourley continued. "Mr. Gourley will pay you."

Frank looked up as they drew close. The taller of the two men turned.

Annali gasped as their gazes met.

Tall and Toothless grinned. "Why looky who we have here."

His friend, the shorter one, turned. His eyes widened, and he rubbed his upper arm.

Though she kept focused on them, she sensed Rose Gourley's shrewd gaze absorbing the tableau before her.

Annali drew a breath and raised her chin in the same superior manner as Harriet. "Excuse us, gentlemen."

With Rose Gourley right beside her, Annali attempted to skirt around the men as she headed toward the steps of the platform.

But Toothless moved in front of her.

"Here now!" Frank Burgess pushed off the edge of the platform and strode toward Annali. "These here are ladies. Get on outta here. I got no work for ya."

"Ladies?" The shorter man laughed.

"Ladies a the evenin' ya mean," Tall and Toothless said. "Ain't that right, Neeley?"

Rose Gourley exhaled an indignant huff.

Frank Burgess stepped forward and offered his arm. Rose latched on and nearly dragged Frank to the bottom step. But instead of going inside, she stood on the platform beside the screen door, watching.

Annali attempted to follow. "I'm afraid you gentlemen have me confused with someone else."

But Toothless stepped closer. "Ain't no mistakin' that stripe of yeller hair."

*Damn!* She should have pushed past Clayton this morning and fetched her straw hat with the green and purple flowers. Perched at a jaunty angle atop her head, the hat would have completely covered her blonde streak.

"Is you working here now?" Toothless reached out as if to touch her hair, but she jerked back.

"You men leave her alone," Frank snapped, striding toward them. "This here's a lady. Wife of the owner of the Farmers and Merchants Bank."

"Gettin' a bit above yerself ain't ya?" Neely laughed.

Annali stepped around them and took Frank's arm, hoping neither Frank nor Rose Gourley believed their accusations.

"Do that rich banker know ya make yer livin' on yer back?"

Rose gasped and darted inside, the screen door slamming behind her.

Frank swung around as they reached the bottom step of the loading platform. "Get on outta here, or I'll be fetchin' the law."

Toothless laughed. "Ya sound jest like that fancy pants gent who stopped us whilst we was havin' some fun with this feisty calico cat."

A frown marred Frank's brow as his gaze locked on her face.

Heart racing, her mouth went dry. "They're lying," she whispered. She swallowed and cleared her throat, scrambling for the words that might salvage her perceived reputation. "I worked in a bakery. I lived in a boarding house."

The two men laughed. "Miz Bo-champ's fancy parlor house, ya mean," Toothless said. "Damn, ya stabbed me with yer hat pins, an' shot Neely here."

She never should have left this morning without her reticule and the Derringer she kept inside. She would have gladly shot either of them again if they so much as touched her.

"That rich banker ya married wouldn't happen to be that same fancy pants gent?"

Frank eased his arm from beneath her hand.

From behind the screen door came another gasp as the silhouette of Rose Gourley whirled away and vanished into the depths of the kitchen.

"You best go home, missus," Frank said stepping away.

Reality hit like a rock shattering a window. Pain radiated in all directions. She'd always known discovery was inevitable, but she never considered what she would do or say when it happened—or anticipated how much it would hurt.

She raised her chin and stiffened her spine, drawing herself tight against the hollow aching, the way she had when her mother abandoned her, when Marcello rejected her, and when Mrs. G. tossed her to the street.

There was nothing left to say.

She offered Frank an apologetic smile. Then

squaring her shoulders, she turned and walked from the alley.

Marching up D Street, she glanced over her shoulder several times, but Neely and Toothless hadn't followed.

How long before her secret spread to Mr. Lathrop? To Roger Barnes? To Alex? Had she cost him the sale?

On Eighth Street, she passed the Methodist church and the small white house where Hester Clark and her father lived. Just the other day, she'd been sipping tea in their parlor as if she'd belonged.

She'd deceived everyone, but maybe this pang in her chest was not for the ruse, but for the loss of a life she was never meant to have.

Several minutes later, she slipped around to the back of the barn and sank into the grass. The aromas of fresh bread, onion, and bay leaf wafted from the kitchen. Annali's stomach growled, but she'd be damned if she'd go into that house and share a meal with any of them.

Orange, pink, and gold spread low across the western sky when Harriet's shrieking carried through the open windows. What was going on? Had Harriet learned Annali's secret? Who was she screaming at? Where was Alex? Did he hate her now? Is that why he hadn't come to find her?

Gradually, the sun slipped below the line where the prairie met the sky, and the pewter glow of moonlight spread over the landscape. Low male voices rumbled inside the barn. She focused on their tones trying to discern the timbre of Alex's voice, but there was only Clayton and Flint who had no doubt returned for another romp in the hay.

That meant Harriet and Nellie had gone to bed, and the back door would still be unlocked. She slipped around the barn and dashed past the chicken coop and garden. At the back porch she removed her shoes.

Drawing a deep breath, she tiptoed her way through the house and up the stairs to Alex's room. If Harriet or Nellie heard her, they never made a sound.

## Chapter Twenty-six

Alex never would have found his way home if not for the long daylight hours of June. He reached out, grabbing a fence picket to steady himself as he lurched through the opening.

Staggering up the path, he tripped on the bottom step. He sat for a minute waiting for the handrail to cease shifting back and forth. He tugged loose his tie, unfastened his collar and the top buttons of his shirt.

Not once during dinner had Barnes even hinted at seeing Annali, or rather Ivy. So, when Lathrop suggested they celebrate the signing of the sales agreement with a few drinks, Alex joined them.

He'd intended to have one beer and leave. After all, one beer couldn't hurt, even if he'd never had alcohol before.

Across the table Lathrop made a risqué comment about women.

Roger Barnes laughed. A droplet of beer glistened in his beard. The same beard Annali hated so much. A man with graying hair and a substantial paunch, whom Annali had seen naked. Had lain beside—herself naked. Bare skin next to bare skin, her hands gliding over Roger's body, touching him in the same intimate ways she touched Alex.

He'd ordered a second beer, followed by a glass of whiskey. But imbibing in another round did little to obscure the images burning in his brain. Before he could lunge across the table and drive his fist into Barnes' jaw, he'd said, *"Good night,"* and stumbled from the saloon.

Once the porch handrail stopped moving, Alex grabbed on and hauled himself to his feet. He staggered through the front door.

"Where have you been?" Mother demanded from the shadowy corner of the foyer.

He pressed his fingers to his temples and rubbed. "Not now."

"You're drunk!" she shrieked. "How dare you? After all I've done to keep you from becoming just like him! This is how you repay me? Randy young bull! I should have had you castrated that first time I caught you touching yourself!"

All he wanted was to fall into bed and sleep for a week. He leaned his shoulder against the wall at the bottom of the stairs. *Damn, that was a long way up.*

"Married a whore and sold the bank! I will again be ridiculed and pitied."

"I'm certain…you'll enjoy it."

She snatched a porcelain shepherdess from the small table beneath the mirror. "Get out of this house!"

The figurine flew straight toward his head. He ducked, and it shattered against the wall. "Enough!" He winced and grabbed the banister. "This is my house."

"And take that filthy Jezabel with you!"

"Jessa… Who?"

"Your whore! That scheming, money grabbing Jezabel you married!"

His eyes ached, and his head hurt. "Not…your business." Grabbing the banister, he focused on placing one foot in front of the other, ignoring Mother's tirade.

At the top he turned and opened the door. His gaze fell on the narrow bed and staggering forward, he sprawled face down onto the mattress. He closed his eyes, and as the room gradually stopped spinning, he snuggled into the pillow and sighed.

****

Gray predawn light spilled through the window above Annali's head. She'd dozed fitfully all night. How long before Roger Barnes heard the gossip and put the pieces together? Maybe he already had. Had the sale fallen through? Is that why Alex hadn't come home? Did he hate her now?

She'd always known her deception might be discovered. What she hadn't expected was for Alex to abandon her. He'd known what she was that morning in the alley, and yet he'd treated her with respect. But now, not even a note to let her know what happened.

She rose, stepped over to her trunk, and flipped open the lid. Moving to the wardrobe she took out her blue dress and lay it across her lavender gown—a favorite, but like her, not fit for society.

After slipping into her green calico, she pinned her old blue hat with the broken feather over her hair, packed her carpet bag, and tied her hat boxes together.

She picked up her hatpin holder and touched her finger to the pink rose, before putting it in her carpet bag and swiping away a stray tear.

They'd agreed from the start—no emotional entanglements. If her foolish heart was broken, she'd no one to blame but herself.

She slipped her Derringer into her reticule, picked up her carpet bag, and threaded her fingers through the strings around her hat boxes. Grabbing the handle of her trunk, she dragged it to the top of the stairs. Behind her a bedroom door opened, then softly closed.

She started down. *Bang.* The back end of the trunk dropped and slammed against the stair tread. *Bang.* Annali moved down another step. *Bang.* She turned the corner at the landing and stepped down three stairs. She tugged the handle. *Bang, bang, bang,* all the way to the bottom.

The tin corner pieces scraped gouges in the wood floor as she dragged her trunk across the foyer. She smiled, certain Harriet winced with each thump and abrasive drag against the floor. Annali continued out the door and down each step of the porch. Neither Harriet nor Nellie emerged from their rooms to say good-bye. Not a peak from Clayton or even Flint. She dragged her trunk down the path and through the gate. And not even a glimpse of Alex.

****

*Bang! Bang! Bang!*

*Damn. Who in the world is hammering this early in the morning?* Alex rolled toward the wall, pulled the pillow over his head, and went back to sleep.

****

Sweat trailed down the sides of her face, forcing her to stop less than a half mile from the house. Sitting on her trunk, she pulled a handkerchief from her sleeve and wiped her brow.

The clip clop of horse hooves and rattle of buggy wheels approached from the west. Odd for someone to be out with the glow of pink barely peeking above the prairie.

The buggy grew closer. Dr. Powell drew back on the reins and stopped beside her.

"Good morning, Doctor." She flashed a practiced smile as if it were no matter to be sitting on a trunk alongside the road at dawn.

He studied her for several moments. "Are you waiting for someone?"

She shook her head. "No."

His shoulders rose and fell as he exhaled an exaggerated sigh. "Can I take you somewhere?"

As much as she wanted to refuse, she rose. "Yes, please. It's kind of you to offer."

He stepped down and handed her onto the seat, then collecting her baggage, dragged everything around to the back of the buggy. There were a few grunts and groans as he hoisted her trunk onto the back.

A minute later he climbed up beside her. He pulled a handkerchief from his coat pocket then blotted his forehead and neck.

"Oh dear," she said. "I hope it wasn't too heavy for you."

"No, no. Quite all right. Rather warm start to the day though."

"Yes, it is."

He gathered the reins, and the horse moved forward. "Are you headed for the train station?"

"The Union Pacific, please."

"I believe it's for the best that you're leaving."

So, he must have heard the gossip before he'd gone on his house call.

"Alexander can resume his regimen and realign the humors in his mind and body."

"Doctor, I know you meant well in your advice to Mrs. Worthington. But Alex isn't going mad. He isn't going blind. And he isn't his father."

At the train station, the doctor pulled up alongside the open door of the freight entrance. A porter dashed outside and lifted the trunk onto a flat cart with wheels.

Doctor Powell offered his hand to help her down. "Have a safe journey," he said and climbed back into his buggy.

With nothing left to say, Annali walked inside and checked her bags. Exchanging the ticket to Omaha that she'd bought on her first day in town, she purchased a ticket to Denver—the closest city where men had money.

On one of the long bench seats, lay a dime novel with a torn cover. She picked it up, took it to the farthest corner of the station, and settled in to wait until the bank opened and she could collect her payment.

****

"Alexander!" The shrill demand pierced his skull. "Are you awake?" Incessant pounding followed, whether it radiated from the door or inside his head, he wasn't certain.

He groaned and rolled onto his side, nausea churning his stomach.

"Alexander, the morning is half gone. I won't have it!"

"Go away!"

A few minutes later, the door opened. Footsteps crossed the room, and the bed ropes groaned under the weight of another person.

Alex peered through half open lids.

Clayton sat with his legs crossed, his hands folded in his lap. A bemused smile teased the corners of his mouth.

Alex threw his arm over his eyes. "What are you doing here?"

"A better question might be what are *you* doing here?"

Alex moved his arm and looked around. "Damn."

Clayton chuckled. "Yes, poor Flint was forced to sleep in the barn. Better him than me. He's a much hardier sort and preferred a pillow of hay to Harriet's bitter diatribes."

"What do you want?"

"As your mother so kindly pointed out, the morning is half gone. It is now—" he pulled out his watch and popped open the cover, "—ten past the hour."

"What hour?"

"Eleven."

"Double damn." Alex groaned and shoved Clayton off the bed. He swung his feet to the floor. His stomach lurched.

"You look a little green, brother. Would you like me to fetch the chamber pot? Let me know, because I don't wish to be splattered with any of your vomitus if you can't hold it down."

Alex rested his head in his hands as he sorted through foggy images and tried to make sense of the previous evening.

"Your normal bland breakfast of eggs and dry toast might be just the thing for you right now."

"What do you want?"

"Now that you're awake, there is that small matter of a personal loan we discussed yesterday."

"I already told you, no."

"Initially, yes, but then you added the qualifier that I ask Nellie to join us. I am happy to say she has agreed."

Alex looked up. "Nellie *wants* to go to Europe? Without Mother?"

"Yes." Clayton lowered himself onto the spindly seat of the chair in front of the sewing table. "I was quite surprised myself. She even smiled. First for everything I imagine."

Alex rubbed his forehead. Maybe his brain was too muddled to comprehend properly, but Nellie smiling, wanting to go to Europe?

"Ask her yourself. At this moment, she's in her room getting her things together. Your mother even supports her decision. Wife should be with her husband and all that." Clayton glanced at his watch again. "Brother, it is coming on quarter past. Most inconvenient for you to choose last evening to imbibe for the first time. But may I stress the importance of our need to expedite this loan and retrieve my belongings from my safe deposit box."

"Damn, Clayton, just say it. Pinkertons."

"Very well. My associates spotted a man at your bank, talking to the marshal. If we are going to ride to Omaha in time to catch the train to Chicago, we will need to leave soon."

Double damn, the deposit for the sale was in escrow until Friday the twenty-eighth. The only cash available would come from closing out his personal accounts and the bank closed at noon.

He rose and started for the door. "Let me clean up and talk to Annali."

"She's not here."

"What?" Alex spun around. The room tipped, and he grabbed the door jamb to steady himself.

"She packed her things and left this morning."

Alex dashed to his room and flung open the door. Annali's trunk was gone. Her side of the wardrobe empty and her hatpin holder missing from the washstand. He walked to the bed and dropped heavily onto the mattress.

What had Mother been ranting about last night? *Filthy, vile, whore?*

Damn, their secret was out. But how, and who?

Annali had told him this could happen, but somehow in his naivety or maybe his ignorance, he hadn't believed it. Just as he'd conveniently blocked from his mind— until last evening—the reality of what Annali's profession actually required her to do night after night.

Clayton lounged in the doorway. His expression glowed with amusement. "Astonishing. You actually married her?"

"How did Mother find out?"

"Evidently, your lovely wife was recognized at the Burgess Café."

By whom? Alex had been with Roger Barnes all afternoon. If not him, then who?

"And your neighbor down the road was with her."

"Rose Gourley?"

Clayton shrugged.

"Double damn." Alex shot to his feet. "I have to find Annali." As he darted for the door, Clayton blocked the way, stopping Alex with his raised hand.

"Please, time is ticking."

"Fine, I'll withdraw what cash I have in my personal account and return."

"No need. We'll meet you at the bank as soon as my wife is packed, and Flint has the horses ready." Clayton stepped aside as Alex dashed from the room and down the stairs.

\*\*\*\*

The knob on the office door turned and Annali,

sitting in Alex's desk chair, glanced up as the door pushed inward several inches.

"Mr. Worthington?" Goldman's voice drifted through the partial opening. "Sir, are you all right?"

"Yes, of course."

"I ask only because you've been absent all morning and your attire is—"

"None of your concern."

"Yes, sir. I'm sorry, sir." Goldman cleared his throat. "Sir, we've had no customers since eleven. I had Farley and Paxton close out their drawers and go home."

"Fine."

"Sir?"

"What is it now?"

"My wife's niece… the wedding. May I—"

"Fine. Go."

"Thank you, sir. Oh, and your wife is waiting in your office."

The door pushed fully open, and Alex stepped into the room. His hair stuck out at odd angles. Morning beard shadowed his jaw, his shirt tail hung untucked, and wrinkles distorted the usual precise creases in his trousers.

"Alex, what happened to you?"

He heaved a weighted sigh. "Clayton said you left."

"Not yet." She stood. "But where were you last night?"

He closed the door and strode across the room to the bookcase and the presidential portrait which hung on the wall. "My apologies. I fell asleep in the sewing room."

*The sewing room?* Now that her secret was out, he no longer wanted to share a bed? Her teeth clamped down on her bottom lip as she grasped the edge of the desk. A stabbing pain lodged in the center of her chest. Once again, she'd been a fool.

He reached out and swung aside President Hayes revealing the small wall safe. He turned. Deep furrows knitted together across his brow. "You're leaving?"

"Yes, on the two-twenty train. We both knew this could happen. I was recognized."

"Mother informed me. I'm surprised you didn't hear her screaming when I arrived home."

"It was those two men from the alley."

"The men from the alley? In Lincoln?"

She nodded.

"Damn," he muttered, rubbing his hand around the back of his neck. "That means they're…"

"What?"

He shook his head and returned to the safe, turning the dial back and forth. "Nothing to concern you. They'll all be gone soon."

She flinched. Her breath caught for a moment, as she eased back a step. Alex-the-ass was back. She clasped her hands in front of her, rubbing her palm with her thumb.

With the safe open, he carefully counted a small stack of bank notes leaving a tray of coins then shoved the money into a canvas bag slightly larger than the bills. Swinging around, he approached the desk.

He tossed down the sack which landed with a thump in front of her. Reaching across, he snatched a piece of paper.

Her gaze dropped to the canvas bag stamped Farmers and Merchants Bank. Her stomach tightened. Was this it then? Her payment?

No emotional entanglements. That's what they'd

agreed from the start.

He dipped his pen in the ink well and scribbled a quick note across the paper. Whirling he strode back to the safe and put the paper inside. He closed the door, gave the dial a spin, and flipped the portrait back in place.

The wall clock began its soft chiming of the noon hour, precisely matching the chime of the clock in the lobby.

Alex dashed from the office.

She'd assumed Alex felt as she did, that what they'd shared had meant something deeper, something lasting, something like love. *Stupid fool!*

She crossed her arms, hugging herself tightly as she focused on inhaling each breath through the painful tightness in her chest.

Alex stomped back into the office with the fading reverberation of the twelfth chime.

He stopped near the desk and rubbed his fingers over temples. "The vault is locked." He nodded toward the bag. "That will just have to be enough."

"For my services." She lifted her chin and met his gaze. "As we agreed."

## Chapter Twenty-seven

Alex's head jerked back. If she'd slapped him, it couldn't have hurt more. Was this it then? Had any of what they shared meant anything to her?

She stared as if expecting him to… What?

Had the past week really been just a business arrangement? She was a professional after all. No emotional entanglements. That's what he wanted.

Wasn't it?

She'd fulfilled her part of the bargain now she expected him to fulfill his.

He drew back his shoulders and raised his chin. "Unfortunately, the timer on the vault has been activated. Let me know where you settle. I'll wire a transfer to your new bank for the funds you deposited here plus what I owe you from the sale."

"That will be fine."

He glared at her across the desk. "Damn it, Annali, or should I say Ivy? Is that all I was to you? Another faceless client?"

"No. It was never like that with you. But you know what I am. It's what you wanted. Marriage just tied it up in a nicer bow."

He laughed, but the hollow pain inside his chest wasn't funny. Nellie was right. He was a naïve fool. He knew nothing of the world outside the walls of this bank and the imaginary realms of his books and stories.

He crossed his arms over his chest. "Tell me then, if it wasn't like that, who shared my bed? Annali or Ivy?"

She stiffened for a moment. Her eyes widened. Then, a slow, sultry smile spread across her face. That same damned impassive smile which never reached her eyes.

She set the money on the desk, reached up, and unpinned her hat, placing it beside the bag.

"Why, Sugar, I was whoever you wanted me to be." She sashayed around the desk and dropped her hands on his shoulders, toying with the hair at the back of his neck. "Lady of the night, ready to fulfill your deepest desires, or banker's wife eager to satisfy her husband with a quick romp at a picnic by the river."

She moved her hands to the top of her head, then with a couple of quick tugs, released her hair from its pins and her tresses tumbled down her back.

His heartbeat quickened.

"Aw, Sugar, we pretended for a while, but in the end we are what we are in this life."

Reaching out she grasped his hand. "Now, I know you want it. One last time." She moved backward, a siren luring him to the rocky shore at the front of his desk. She shoved aside his name plate, pens, and ink bottle.

An ache in his groin grew as his shaft swelled beneath the wool of his trousers. Grasping her upper arms, he jerked her against him. Maybe she stepped into him. He didn't care. A primal urge to claim her blocked all, but his need to make certain that no matter where she went or who she was with, she would never forget him.

Her palms slid up his back as he nuzzled her neck, nipping and sucking the tender skin. Grasping her waist, he lifted her effortlessly onto the desk. He cupped her jaw as she arched back, her fingertips digging into his shoulders.

His thumbs brushed over her cheeks as he moved to taste her lips, but at the last moment she dipped her head so his lips brushed over her forehead instead. Puzzled by the slight rejection, he eased back, meeting her gaze.

She smiled, but it held a nuance of calculation, as if to remind him that despite all he did, she was the one in charge.

Her gaze locked with his. "How do you want it, Sugar? Fast?"

She grabbed the front of his waistband and jerked. His thighs slammed into the edge of the desk.

"Or, slow?" One finger touched his cheek and trailed down his throat to tease the hair at the top of his open shirt. At the same time her other hand slipped free each button of his trousers. Her fingers stole through the opening in his drawers, wrapping around his length.

He gasped as she freed his straining shaft.

Grasping her hips, he yanked her to the edge of the desk. She pulled the hems of her skirt and petticoat to the top of her thighs and wrapped her legs around his waist as he slid his hand over her knees past the ruffled edges of her drawers. Locating the opening, he pressed himself against her entrance.

She leaned back on her elbows arching her hips as he pushed into her. She watched him with bored disinterest, the usual luster in her eyes missing.

But desire consumed his ability to think beyond this moment. Closing his eyes, he gripped her hips and thrust deeper, and harder, and deeper. He came in pulsating waves of release. Years of stifling any sound of climax produced the softest of huffing breaths, and he was spent.

He collected himself as she patiently waited. Easing back, he withdrew a handkerchief from his pocket and passed it to her.

"Thank you, Sugar." She attended to herself then passed it back.

Hopping off his desk, she shook out her skirt and brushed at the a few wrinkles. Gathering her hair, she twisted it into a quick knot and pinned her hat in place. Reaching back, she picked up the money sack. With a slight tilt of her head, she smiled. "And now you know the difference."

She jammed the money inside her reticule but couldn't pull it closed. Whirling away before he could see her tears, she left the office, closing the door behind her. She'd almost declined the money not wanting to sully all they'd shared into merely a business transaction. But despite the yearning of her heart, in the end that's all this was—an elaborate job—but a job none-the-less.

As she reached the front door, Nellie and Clayton crossed the street and approached the front steps. Annali gave a hasty swipe to the dampness on her cheeks, then slid the bolt and let them in.

Nellie gave Annali an odd, appraising look.

Clayton smiled. "Good day, sister. Is Alexander here? He promised to collect my money."

*His money?*

She blinked as a pinch tweaked inside her chest. Alex had gathered this money *for Clayton*? The pinch in Annali's chest twisted tighter. Alex hadn't intended to pay her off and send her on her way. Stupid. Stupid. Stupid.

Her heart gave a little flutter. Maybe there was still a chance.

She had to give this money back.

Clayton paused to search her face then flashed a secretive grin. "I see now why he was detained."

The door opened again, and Flint stepped inside. Then right behind him came Toothless and Neely.

Every muscle in her body tightened. What were they doing here? Wrapping her arms around her waist, Annali eased away from the door.

Toothless grinned, moving toward her. "Looky here. Reckon ya did take up with that fancy pants gent."

She brought her reticule to her waist. Before she could squirm her fingers to the bottom and the grip of her Derringer, Flint shot Toothless a deadly glare.

Toothless dropped his gaze and locked the front door.

"Clayton." Alex's voice carried across the lobby. "Bad news, I'm afraid. The vault has a timer, and Goldman locked up early today. The door can't be opened until eight in the morning."

Clayton's amiable features hardened into something cold and menacing. "Now brother, you wouldn't be lying to me now, would you? I have close to five thousand dollars' worth of diamonds and other gems in that safe deposit box." With a jerk of his hand, he waved Neely forward. "I'm not leaving without them."

Alex eased cautiously up beside Annali. "Why don't you wait in my office?" he whispered.

He took her arm and escorted her toward the dividing rail. Tension radiated from his hand all the way up her arm. Her gaze shot to his face.

Leaning forward, he held open the swinging gate. "My gun," he murmured faintly. "Can you load it and get it to me?"

Heart pounding, she nodded and stepped through the gate.

Alex met her gaze and turned back toward Clayton.

At the office, she glanced over her shoulder. Neely swung over the railing and headed for the vault as Alex walked toward Clayton.

Annali closed the door. Dashing to the desk, she dropped to her knees, pulled open the drawer, and lifted up the false bottom. She slipped her hand beneath the pages of Alex's story and withdrew the pistol, a tin of caps, and a box of paper cartridges.

She pulled down the loading lever beneath the barrel then opened the box. Hands shaking, she tore off the excess paper, then shoved the cartridge and ball into the first chamber. After pushing the loading lever back up, she hurriedly repeated the process for each cylinder. Fumbling to open the box of percussion caps, she dropped it, scattering the tiny brass orbs across the desk. Hastily, she gathered up five and pressed them onto the end of each chamber.

Jamming everything back in the drawer, she pushed it closed and jumped to her feet. Whirling, she stepped toward the door and froze, shoving her hands behind her back.

Nellie stood inside the doorway, like some ethereal being silent and staring. "Where are you going?"

"No where."

Nellie closed the door. Her hand disappeared into what looked like a side slit which many women had in their skirts. Withdrawing a revolver, she aimed the barrel straight at Annali.

"Put it on the desk and stand over there." She pointed toward the far corner. "I can't let you shoot

Clayton."

Annali set Alex's pistol on the corner of his desk and eased backward into the corner.

Nellie slipped her gun into what Annali assumed was a large pocket which tied around Nellie's waist and hung hidden beneath her skirt, then walked to the desk and picked up Alex's gun.

Nellie glanced around the room. "I've never been in here. Father used to bring me to his office when we lived in St. Louis. He had dolls and toys in a closet. We'd play special games." A tight smile twisted the corners of her mouth. "How old were you?"

Annali bit her lip, unsure of the question.

An odd gleam lit Nellie's eyes. "Your first time. How old were you?"

"Fifteen."

The word lingered in silence for several long seconds.

"Seven," Nellie whispered.

Annali gaped as a slow cold seeped through her body, like falling into an icy pond, gradually turning her limbs numb until there was nothing left but to drown. Her knees buckled, and she dropped to sit on the floor.

What she'd chosen to do with Marcello and others had been her choice. But seven! And Nellie was so petite she couldn't have been any bigger than Sarah Pederson. To be forced—

Annali clamped her hand over her mouth as the nauseating reality slammed into her stomach with the impact of a punch. Holy Hell, did Alex know?

"I'm going away," Nellie said. "Clayton invited me. Come with us."

*What?* Annali blinked. "But you hate me."

"That was when I believed Alexander had married someone as naïve and judgmental as every woman in this town. But you were crying when we came in. I know Alexander forced himself on you."

An odd light in Nellie's eyes raised the hair at the back of Annali's neck. "Why me?"

Nellie raised one shoulder in a negligent shrug. "Because you know how it feels to be...violated. Repeatedly. To feel such revulsion for the touch of a man, for the sight of that...*thing*. To envision taking a knife in hand and cutting—" She smoothed back a stray whisp of hair. "I would appreciate the companionship of a woman with whom I can talk, a woman who can sympathize."

"And Clayton—?"

"Is different."

Annali choked back the urge to laugh.

"I see you understand. I offer him the pretense of respectability, and he leaves me to myself. You can do the same for Mr. Flint."

Annali's mind raced. "I don't have money for such a trip."

"I'll speak with Clayton. He has reached an agreement with Alexander to secure our funds. Alexander might be ignorant of the world around him, but at heart he can be something of a hero. He won't leave me penniless."

Annali swallowed the acid rising at the back of her throat. Reaching up, she grabbed the corner of the bookcase and stood. The solid weight of her Derringer at the bottom of her reticule bumped against her thigh. Could she get past Nellie in time to give the small weapon to Alex?

\*\*\*\*

Once Annali had disappeared inside the office, Alex swung his attention back to Clayton and the others. Flint gestured Alex toward the floor in front of Goldman's desk. "Sit there."

Slowly, Alex lowered himself onto the tile, extending both legs and crossing them at the ankle. "If you'll wait until tomorrow morning, I'll be able to open the vault."

Nellie wandered over and pushed through the gate, standing over him. She'd been so quiet he'd forgotten she'd come in with the others.

His mind scrambled for a plan in which he might overtake them as soon as Annali retrieved his gun.

Neely stepped from behind the teller cages and settled himself on the low railing which divided the lobby from the employee area. "Boss," he said. "Fancy Pants is right." He pulled the makings for a cigarette from his vest pocket. "That there's a Hall's Premier. It's got a timer on the lock, and stair-stepped grooves in the door. Cain't pry it open, nor punch the lock through the door." He struck a Lucifer off the edge of the counter and lit his smoke.

"Nitro would work, but we ain't got time to boil any dynamite." He drew on his cigarette and exhaled a cloud of gray. "Iffin we even had some."

The tall one stared at the vault and rubbed his chin. "Could we get a half-dozen sticks, I could set charges around the door and blow 'em all at once."

Clayton shook his head. "Too messy and unpredictable."

Flint shrugged one shoulder. "Maybe it works. Maybe it don't. Either way, once she blows, we need to get outta here fast."

Clayton paced to the window, staring out for several moments. Turning, his gaze bore down on Alex.

"Damn, I need cash and that safe deposit box. I swear to God if you're lying…"

"Alexander is much like Father," Nellie said suddenly, a peculiar gleam in her eyes. "And he frequently lied."

Clayton strode toward them from across the room. "My dear, why don't you wait in the office with your new sister. See what she's doing in there all alone."

Nellie gave Clayton a slight nod then stepped around Alex's legs and entered the office.

Had Annali enough time to find and load his pistol? What if Nellie caught her? He could tell Clayton about the money Annali had taken, but there was barely two hundred dollars in that bag. Although turning it over might keep them from blowing up the bank. But damn it, Annali deserved something for having been dragged into this mess.

He sighed and looked up. "Clayton, this is ludicrous. Take your men and go back to the house. Wait till tomorrow. I'll empty my personal accounts, and you can retrieve your jewelry."

Clayton turned toward his men. "Lane, go to the hardware store and purchase some dynamite. Charge it to Alexander Worthington. Tell the clerk you've been hired to remove several tree stumps and boulders from the property."

"But it'll come back on me, and they'll know what I look like."

Flint strode across the floor, grabbed Lane's arm, and shoved him toward the door. "Sonofabitch, go or you'll answer to me."

As Lane scrambled out the door, Flint turned toward Clayton. "I'm going to move the horses from the alley out back."

"Good idea," Clayton said. "A couple blocks east, toward the cemetery, they should be safe enough. But can we get to them without being caught?"

"We played it close before," Flint said. He headed out the door.

Alex traced a pinstripe in his trouser leg with his thumbnail. If Annali could get past Nellie with his gun, he might be able to get the drop on Clayton and this other fellow. Annali could go for the marshal before Flint and Lane returned.

Alex met Clayton's gaze across the room.

The man gave a negligent shrug and straightened his shirt cuffs. "You see brother, whether this works or not, we must be on our way. Fortunately, though, the Pinkerton detective doesn't know we are aware of his presence. So, for now I'll have to ask you to wait in the office with the women until we can decide what to do with you."

Mind racing, Alex rose. He glanced toward the window, hoping for a passerby to try entering the bank.

Clayton made a quick shooing motion with his hand.

Alex scowled then headed to his office and opened the door. Tension hit him in a wave as palpable as the silence that filled the room.

His attention fell immediately on Annali in the far corner. Her fingers knotted at her waist, she chewed her bottom lip, her gaze fixed on his sister.

Nellie stood to his right, in front of a bookcase over which hung the clock. *Tick-tock, tick-tock*, each ominous second echoed through the room.

Her pupils were dilated, and an almost maniacal gleam lit her eyes as her lips pulled up in an odd, twisted smile. In her hand she held a gun. His gun. His gaze shot to Annali.

She gave him the barest shake of her head.

He looked back to his sister. "Nellie? What..."

"Alexander, Mother's perfect precious son."

He frowned. "Excuse me?"

She gave a quick snort of laughter. "Everyone thought it so sweet how Father used to bring me to the bank with him."

Alex's spine snapped straight. He sucked in a deep breath as his whole chest squeezed tight.

"God... Nell," he choked out. "What are you say... Did he... I..." His throat closed off as every muscle tensed. *No, it couldn't be!* Pain radiated through his heart, and he struggled to keep down whatever tumbled around inside his stomach.

That revolting image forever burned in his brain of that little girl in a pink dress, kneeling in front of his father. That Nellie had once... *Oh God! How many times?*

He reached out to steady himself on the bookcase. "I... Damn, Nell, I didn't know."

"Of course, you didn't. Mother's whole life is about protecting you."

He shivered—barely able to comprehend. His own father... A ball of acid rose up in the back of his throat. He swallowed, struggling to make sense of this, to find words to— "Nellie, I...I'm so, so sorry."

"Alexander needs his daily exercise. Alexander can only eat these foods. Alexander must take a daily bath.

But for me, she closed her eyes and played ignorant to those nights Father came to my room."

Alex curled his trembling fingers into fists. His nails gouged into his palms as he fought the urge to drive his fist into the wall the way he'd once smashed it into his father's face, his stomach, his ribs, pummeling the man over and over again.

"Mother won't admit it, but you're just like him. Trying to kiss me all the time. Looking. I saw the way you stared at me in the hall the other night. You wanted to touch me just like he did."

Alex shook his head. "I could *never*." His stomach roiled. "*You're my sister!*"

"You should have seen his face when I pulled out my gun—" She wrapped both hands around the grip. "—and pointed it at him."

Blood pounded in his ears, roaring like wind. He couldn't think. Slowly realization cut through the fog. "*You killed Father?*"

Nellie chuckled. "Of course I did. He begged. Told me he loved me, that I was special. I cocked my gun—"

*Click.* Nellie's thumb pulled back the hammer.

"Wait!" Annali stepped forward. Her hand raised. "Wait. Nellie, I have money." She angled her reticule, the top of the canvas bag visible.

Nellie's eyes widened.

"Take it and go." Annali eased carefully toward the desk, tugged free the bag, set it on the corner, then backed away.

Nellie moved sideways, keeping the pistol aimed at his chest. Snatching the money, she shoved it into her skirt.

"Please," Annali said. "Take the money and go."

"Come with me. Don't you see. Alexander is just like Father. He uses you for his own pleasure."

Alex kept his gaze fixed on the gun barrel and Nellie's finger on the trigger. There had to be a way to take the gun without getting shot.

"I should have killed him sooner. It was so much easier than I anticipated."

Alex's gaze darted to her face.

"He stared up at me the whole time he lay dying beside that bush. I watched until his eyes went blank, then I walked home."

She raised the barrel of the gun an inch. Her expression hardened.

Was she seeing him or Father? Did it matter? He lunged forward shoving Nellie's arm up as he slammed her back against the bookcase.

"Annali, run!"

*Bang!*

The sound reverberated painfully through his ear as bits of plaster rained down on his head. Screeching, Nellie struggled against his hold.

The office door slammed back against the wall. "What the hell's going on?" Clayton charged through the threshold, Neely right behind him.

As they pulled him off Nellie, Annali dashed toward the lobby.

"Grab her!" Clayton yelled.

Chapter Twenty-eight

Snatching up her skirts, Annali raced to the front door just as Flint stepped through. She shoved past the startled man, who stumbled into Neely.

The confusion gave her extra seconds as she crossed the street and raced down the boardwalk toward the courthouse. Close behind, Neely's footfalls thudded a quick-paced cadence.

A couple of blocks ahead, on the opposite side of the street, she spotted Mr. Paxton walking in her direction. She raised her arm and waved, hoping he'd notice her desperation.

Poised to dash across the street, a man rounded the corner and slammed into her. She staggered back a step.

Tall and Toothless stood before her, gripping the handle of a canvas bag.

She spun around. Neely. Whirling, she darted for the street, but a strong hand gripped her arm, dragging her back.

"Where the hell are ya goin, ya feisty little she-cat?"

She swung her reticule up and whacked him alongside his head.

Unaffected, Neely hauled her between two buildings.

Toothless followed.

She glanced over her shoulder. *Where did Mr. Paxton go? Had he even seen her?*

"Ain't no one comin' to save ya." Toothless shoved her against the side of the building as Neely yanked her reticule from her wrist.

"What ya got in this little bag of yours? A rock?" He tugged wide the gathered top and peered inside.

"Looky here." He withdrew her Derringer. "It's that little pea-shooter she shot me with."

She stepped forward, shoving him with both hands. As he stumbled back, she dashed toward the street. A strong hand grabbed her collar and dragged her back. "Ya ain't goin' nowhere ya little she-cat, 'ceptin' back to the bank." He pulled both arms behind her back. "Neely, get rid a that hat and them damn pins."

Neely reached up and yanked her hat from her head, taking with it several of her hair pins, freeing her tresses to tumble down her back.

Toothless released his hold on one arm and wrapped his fingers in a hank of hair, pulling so tight, he pulled her head back.

He leaned close to her ear. "I reckon ya still owe me a tumble." His sour breath wafted to her nose, and she swallowed against the acidic burn rising in the back of her throat.

"Lane, ya got no time. Flint'll kill ya if ya keep the boss waitin' on that dynamite."

With a man on each side, they started back to the bank.

Annali searched the street, but no one was out. Each business and store front they passed had a sign in the window. *Closed for Wedding, Out to Lunch*, or *Back at One*. Had Toothless found the only business open at lunchtime, or had he just broken in and stolen what he needed?

Neely shoved her up the steps of the bank and through the door. She stumbled, catching herself on the high desk in the center of the room.

Clayton stood in front of the railing, holding a gun aimed at Alex who sat on the floor, his back against the spindles. Blood oozed from a cut at the corner of his mouth, and his eye had begun to swell. Another black eye when the first hadn't quite healed. Their gazes met. She looked away hating that she'd failed.

Neely dragged a chair from the front window to the teller cages. "Caught her running off and wavin' at that Pinkerton man." He pushed her onto the seat.

*Pinkerton man?* Her gaze shot to Alex. *Mr. Paxton? Holy Hell, did Alex know?* He didn't look surprised. A flicker of hope ignited in her chest. Maybe Mr. Paxton had seen her.

Toothless pulled a length of rope from his bag and tossed it to Flint, who then tied Alex's hands behind a spindle of the railing.

Toothless slipped behind the teller cages. The canvas bag hit the counter with a clank. Neely joined him, and they each pulled out a hammer and chisel. Steady pounding began near the vault.

Clayton joined Nellie near the customer desk in the center of the room. "I think it would be safer, my dear, if you wait with the horses near the cemetery. I don't want you hurt when the dynamite goes off."

Nellie nodded. "Yes, of course." She waved Annali forward. "Come."

A frown wrinkled Clayton's smooth brow. "What? No. She stays here."

"But she's coming with us."

"My dear, she just tried to go for help."

379

Annali crossed her legs, exposing a generous view of her ankle. "I wasn't going for help. I was going to the train station. I have a ticket in my bag."

"Boss."

Clayton turned as Neely tossed him her reticule. "Alexander told you to run, and you ran."

"Of course I did." She smiled. "I don't want any part of this."

Clayton reached into the embroidered black bag and withdrew the ticket. "Two-twenty train to Denver." He shoved it back inside and tossed her the reticule. He glanced toward Flint standing behind Alex.

Flint shook his head.

Annali drew a breath. "You don't understand. Alex paid me to be his loving wife." She leaned back in the chair, her elbows on the arms, pushing her bosoms forward to strain against the buttons of her blouse. "I plan to open a house in Denver, but I need money. Alex wanted to impress some bankers in Lincoln and avoid marriage to a woman his mother chose. Meantime, we had a little fun. Now the bank is sold, and I just want to leave."

Clayton stepped toward Alex. "Is that true? You paid her?"

Alex's brow furrowed in that way he had when he worked over his ledgers. He glanced at Clayton and shrugged.

Clayton chuckled. "We wondered how you got a woman so savvy to marry you." He turned to Flint who inclined his head with a nod.

Annali stood.

"Wait," Clayton said. "Still, there was something between you two. I saw it."

She inclined her head. "Looks like you believed it. Maybe Alex did too. Forgot what he hired me for."

Her gaze fell to Alex and the dusty, mulberry jacquard waistcoat. "Alex-the-ass. Naïve little virgin boy." She laughed aloud.

Alex flinched. His jaw tightened.

"Aww, Sugar, the secret's out. I'm done pretending I care."

"There, you see," Nellie said. "Alexander has always been blind to what's right in front of him." She started toward the door. "We'll be waiting at the horses."

Annali whirled and scurried outside behind Nellie.

****

She was going for help. Wasn't she?

When they dragged her back earlier, the tall one said she'd waved at the Pinkerton man, but Annali couldn't have known who Paxton was. She claimed she was trying to get to the train station. She'd said she planned to leave, but he hadn't realized she'd already bought her ticket.

Alex twisted his wrists back and forth inside the rope. Despite his desperation, his bonds were too snug.

She'd called him a naïve little virgin boy and laughed—in front of everyone. The pain of that barb still throbbed like a dart inside his chest. Had the past week only been a game of pretend?

He wrapped his hands around the bottom of the spindle twisting, pushing, and pulling but it wouldn't break. Turning slightly, he rocked forward and slammed his shoulder against the spindle, but it held fast.

Nellie was right. He was naïve. Nausea churned in his stomach. Nellie was always so…quiet…so shadow like. He should have guessed. Especially after he discovered what vile a man his father... And Clayton. Alex always wondered why Nellie agreed to marry him. Now it made sense.

Hammering around the vault continued as Clayton's men created cavities in which to place the dynamite.

If anyone should've known, it was Mother. Where did her husband go when he wasn't in her bed? Had her years of silent denial made her more despicable than her husband?

*Damn, and double damn!* He slammed against the spindle again and again. And Annali. He'd believed at least she... She was gone. What did any of it matter anymore?

His shoulder throbbed, overwhelming the ache in his heart. As she'd said, he knew what she was. He was the one who'd gotten caught up in the lie. *Stupid, naïve fool!* He leaned forward and threw himself back.

*Crack!*

He froze. He hit it again.

*Crack!* The spindle snapped off at the bottom. Quickly, he slid his hands down the length. Once free, he wiggled the ropes under his butt. After a bit of contorting, he drew his tied wrists under his ankles and over his feet.

"She's ready to blow," the tall one said as he struck a match and lit the fuse. "Take cover!"

Clayton and Flint ran for the office. The other two hopped over the railing and hunkered down on the front side of the teller cages.

Alex jumped to his feet and raced out the front door.

\*\*\*\*

Annali matched her stride with Nellie's short brisk pace. In a few minutes they reached the cemetery where

Ben and four other horses stood tied to an iron fence, their tails swishing flies.

"Nellie, wait." Annali drew a breath. "I'm sorry, but I can't go with you. Thank you for asking, but I won't live my life pretending to care for Flint."

A shadow of sadness slipped across Nellie's face.

"I'm so sorry for what happened to you," Annali said. "But you have your whole life in front of you. Don't let your father ruin that too."

Nellie wrapped her hand around an iron picket and turned toward the rows of gray headstones lined up in front of her.

Annali eased back a step.

"Wait." Nellie swung toward her and withdrew a gun from inside the folds of her skirt.

Annali froze.

"Take this." Nellie extended her arm.

Easing forward, Annali accepted the gun—Alex's gun. "Thank you."

"I understand now. You were stealing it for protection. Like me, you never go anywhere without a loaded pistol."

Annali tugged open her reticule and pushed the gun inside.

"I would advise you however, to sew yourself a nice size pocket to wear beneath your dress. Much easier to reach than from inside a reticule."

Annali nodded. She stepped back. "Goodbye, Nellie."

"Goodbye…sister."

Whirling, Annali snatched up her skirt hem and ran south toward the railroad tracks. At the corner of Fifth Street, she glanced back but couldn't see Nellie. Turning west, Annali ran along the street parallel to the bank. Ahead people milled around the tables and chairs filling the yard beside the Baptist church. Rose Gourley stood near the table with the wedding cake, and beside her, chatting as if they were best friends, was Harriet. Despite the presence of Alex's mother, Annali ran toward the party hoping to find help before—

*Kaboom, boom, boom, boom!*

The explosions rang out in rapid succession. She shrank back against the front of a tonsorial parlor, as the earth shook, vibrating up through the planks of the boardwalk and rattling the windows. A thick gray cloud rose into the sky. The wedding guests lifted their faces toward the billowing smoke.

*Alex!*

Racing past the wedding party, Annali turned the corner and ran north toward Sixth Street.

From inside the smoky cloud engulfing the area, excited male voices rang out.

"Throw down your guns!"

"That one's getting away!"

"Get him!"

"Where'd he go?"

"This way!"

Gray haze drifted toward her as she approached the alley behind the livery. She skidded to a stop as the figure of a man ran toward her.

Too tall for Alex. Her stomach muscles tightened. She dropped back and ducked behind a stack of crates.

Instead of running past, his footfalls slowed, and the man ducked into the alley, apparently with the same idea as she, to hide behind the crates.

She jumped up to run, but he grabbed her arm,

yanking it up behind her back as his other hand clamped over her mouth. He pulled her up against him, backing them against the barn as two deputies ran past the alley entrance.

"Yer gonna help me get outta here," he whispered, pulling her along the back wall of the barn toward the corral.

A single set of footsteps thudded against the boardwalk near the front of the livery.

She struggled against the grip Toothless held on her arm. She squirmed and kicked at his shins. Unable to access her pistol, she let her reticule dangle from her wrist as she reached up to pry his hand away from her mouth. Grabbing his pinky, she wrenched it back, until... He jerked his hand away.

"*Hel !*"

His hand slapped back over her mouth holding her head against his chest. "Bitch!"

He dragged her backward. In his hand a gun aimed at her head. Behind them several horses snorted, trotting closer to the barn.

From behind the crates someone yelled. "Let the lady go!"

"Stay back or I'll kill her!"

She blinked, trying to focus on the end of the alley where the crates were piled. The heads of two deputies poked above the height of the crates. At the corner of the livery, another man peeked around then ducked back out of sight. Was that Alex?

Toothless shifted his arm and fired a shot in their direction.

"Where the hell are the horses?" he snapped, his voice close to her ear.

"At the cemetery."

"Sonofabitch!" He glanced over his shoulder then maintaining his hold on her, backed himself through the rails into the corral, dragging her with him.

"Let the lady go. Throw down your gun, and you won't get hurt."

Toothless fired another shot.

Behind them the restless horses snorted and trotted anxiously back and forth.

Toothless exhaled a soft *oof* as something knocked him to the ground sending Annali to her knees.

*Alex!*

She scrambled back as the two men rolled on the ground, fighting for control of the gun. But Toothless was bigger and stronger. The horses circled the corral, hugging the fence. As the deputies ran forward, the pair on the ground flipped over again with Alex landing on top struggling to force away the barrel of the gun. With the deputies' line of sight hampered by the fence and milling horses, they wouldn't be able to see the gun aimed at Alex.

Annali reached into her reticule, wrapped her fingers around the grip of Alex's pistol and pulled, but the hammer snagged on the top of the reticule. The pair rolled over again with Alex on the bottom. Terrified the gun they wrestled for would go off any second, Annali cocked the hammer, aimed, and pulled the trigger, sending the bullet through the bottom of her reticule into the side of her nemesis right below his raised arm. He stilled for a moment, his eyes wide, then his arm fell slack, loosening his grip on the gun. Alex grabbed it and shoved the taller man away. Dropping back, he sat on his heels exhaling long shaky breaths.

Annali locked her gaze on Alex.

He gave her a single nod.

She nodded in return. Aside from a few additional cuts which may have been from the explosion, he seemed fine.

The two deputies climbed through the fence.

"He dead?" asked one.

"Someone fetch Doc Powell!" The older deputy yelled to the growing crowd of townspeople and wedding party guests.

Alex rolled to his feet and passed the gun to the older deputy. Then stepping around the wounded Toothless, Alex reached down. She placed her hand in his, and he drew her upright. Her knees trembled as their gazes met.

"Thank you," he whispered. Hand in hand, he walked with her to the fence and helped her through the rails.

The crowd swarmed around them all talking at once.

"Blew the bank all to hell."

"She shot one of her paramours."

"Lucky he ain't dead."

"Can't believe he married her."

"She was in on it from the start, don't you know."

"Just like his father. Easily led by his…"

"Alex—ander!"

Alex's fingers squeezed hers as Harriet pushed her way through the crowd. "The bank is destroyed? What about our money? What has your reckless behavior brought us to?"

"Mother," Alex raised his voice above the whispers and murmurs. "The money is fine. The vault is slightly damaged but withstood the explosion."

Harriet's chin came up. Her shoulders squared. "No

doubt your rash decision to sell the bank has now come to naught." She aimed a nasty glare at Annali even as the corner of Harriet's mouth twitched in what Annali assumed was a smile of triumph.

The crowd surged forward, each person talking over the other.

Annali released Alex's hand, easing to the outskirts of the crowd. She glanced back, but Alex was focused on a group of men all talking at once with Harriet at his side.

"Ma'am?" The younger of the two deputies asked. "Ya all right? Did that feller there hurt ya?"

"I'm fine," she said turning from the crowd.

"Marshal's over at the courthouse with that Pinkerton man. He wants to talk to ya."

Grateful to escape the crowd, Annali nodded. Whether the deputy was nervous or naturally talkative, his non-stop chatter kept her from thinking about how close she'd come to losing Alex.

"Probably got 'em all locked up by now. Ya sure ya ain't hurt? Good thing ya flagged down that Pinkerton man." They walked west on the south side of the street.

"Least ways we caught 'em 'fore they got away. 'Cept for that one ya shot back there. Too bad we didn't make it 'fore they blowed up the bank." He slowed his steps as they passed.

The front and a portion of the alley side wall had been blown into the street. Glass, bricks, pieces of wood and chunks of plaster littered the boardwalk and street, reaching the opposite side, forcing them to step over and around the scattered debris.

No one would want to buy the bank now. Alex was trapped. He'd have to rebuild then try again. She couldn't stay. Her presence would only hurt him.

The town marshal had an office inside the courthouse alongside that of the county sheriff. He seated her beside his desk, poured her a cup of coffee.

"Can I see your gun?"

She reached into her smoky, charred bag and set the pistol on his desk. "It actually belongs to Alex."

The marshal picked it up and checked the chamber. "Whitney five shot, .31 caliber cap and ball, pocket model. Good for close range. Lucky it isn't as deadly as a .44 or .45." He passed the gun back to her, and she shoved it into her reticule.

He pulled a notepad from is desk and dipped his pen in the inkwell. "Now why don't you start at the beginning and tell me everything that happened."

He took careful notes as she told him about Clayton, Flint, Neely, Toothless, and the robbery. The only parts she left out were any hints about the relationship between Clayton and Flint, Nellie's disturbing past, or that she'd killed her father. After all this time why destroy Nellie's life any further?

The older deputy entered the office and stepping around the desk, whispered something in the marshal's ear. Then he nodded to Annali and left.

"Seems the fellow you shot is going to live."

She shifted in her chair and nodded.

"One more thing," the marshal continued. "You say you left Mrs. Miller at the cemetery with the horses."

"Yes."

"How many were there?"

"Five."

"You're sure?"

"Yes, one for each person."

He sighed and set down his pen. "It seems Mrs.

Miller and one of the horses is gone. She's not at home, at church, one of the hotels, or shops in town. It seems she has taken the money you gave her and fled town."

Chapter Twenty-nine

The train whistle blew a second time. Alex extended his stride. His body, bruised from the explosion, twinged with the impact of each footfall against the wooden walk. Wrestling with the outlaw hadn't helped.

"Mr. Worthington!" The tiny woman waved at him from the open door of the Dry Goods and Fine Furniture Emporium.

"Good day, Mrs. Lindberg. Is there something I can help you with?"

She reached out a fluttery hand. "You are all right, *sì*?"

He nodded. Yes, thank you. If you will excuse—"

"The bank."

"Lots of damage, but your money is safe."

"Such a thing! In our little town. How sad this world."

He glanced toward the station. "Please, Mrs. Lindberg, I'm in a hurry."

"But your gift. It is ready for you. Come." She gestured toward the interior of the store.

"I get it for you now."

****

He drew a fortifying breath, crossed Second, darted between two wagons, and dashed around the end of the station.

Puffs of steam engulfed the wheels as the engine

slowly pulled the train west.

Drawing a deep breath, he raced for the last car.

The engine picked up speed.

As the brick platform ended, he jumped. His fingers wrapped around the handrail, clenching tight as his feet lost touch with the ground. Pain tore through his shoulder. He hung suspended for a moment then swung himself onto the bottom step. He dropped onto the platform, drawing short, heaving breaths, keeping his painful arm pressed to his side. Slowly he stood, and taking another deep breath, opened the door.

He spotted her at the front of the car, her face tipped toward the window.

Grasping the back of each seat, he pulled himself along, making his way forward, ignoring the soft whispers and odd looks.

As the train picked up speed, he grabbed the brass rail which ran along the overhead storage compartment to steady himself against the rocking.

She looked up.

He searched her face for even the hint of a smile—one that sparkled in her eyes and lit her features. Prickles of apprehension skittered over his skin. "You lied...at the bank. You haven't been pretending to care. Only Ivy calls me Sugar."

She scooted close to the window leaving him room.

Wincing, he lowered himself into the seat. "You call me Alex"

His hand found hers, lacing their fingers together. At least she didn't pull away. Grassland swished by outside the window. "Annali, I love you. I know you don't love me, but in the corral...when you looked at me. I thought...there's still something between us, but you left. Why?"

Her thumb brushed back and forth over his knuckles. "Alex, you're wrong. I do love you. I've loved you since that day in the alley. You treated me like I had value."

"Have value. You have value, Annali."

"You never once made me feel like I was a piece of merchandise put on earth for your pleasure." She pulled her hand back to her lap. "Until this morning."

The pain in her voice hurt worse than the throbbing in his shoulder. "You're right." He pressed his thumbnail into his thigh and traced the thin white stripe of his trousers. "I'm an ass. I believed I was better than other men because I made you my wife. But I'm worse. I took from you. I doubted you. And in the end threw money at you. Can you forgive me?"

She looked up. Tears glistened in her eyes.

"Please stay. All my plans blew up with the bank." He sent her a shaky smile. "At least Mother is happy."

Annali's lips twitched. "I'm sure she is. Did you find your sister?"

He shook his head. "If I had any money, I'd hire Paxton to go after her."

"Nellie will be fine. If she needs anything she knows she can count on you."

"She hates me."

"She hates men, but she told me you were something of a hero." She nudged his shoulder with hers. "I agree."

Heat singed his cheekbones. "I'm not. But I've realized now that you gave me something precious— something you gave no one else. You gave me your kiss."

He reached inside his shirt and withdrew a small,

flat parcel tied with string. "It's nothing special," he said passing it to her. "You said once that my story showed I had hope. That I could be someone better than who I believed."

She pulled the string and unfolded the paper. "I thought I lost this."

"I found it the other day, near your cake. I gave it to Mrs. Lindberg. She translated them into that composition book."

"Thank you. I..." She opened the book and flipped through the first few pages.

"You couldn't read them, but you kept them. Deep inside, you hoped too."

Her finger slowly traced the words, *La Ricetta* on the old notebook.

His pulse thrummed at the back of his jaw. "The Burgess' are purchasing a new building on Military Avenue. That leaves their current restaurant for sale. You could have your own place, but it would be a bakery."

She smiled sadly and shook her head. "As lovely as the idea is, no one will buy from me. I won't be allowed in church, to eat in a restaurant, or go shopping. You'll be shunned. People will change banks."

"No, if we go on as we have, people will begin to doubt what two bank robbers said."

"Alex, we can't pretend it isn't true. If not them, there'll be another Roger Barnes."

"People see what they expect to see. Stay, Annali. I love you."

She sighed, staring at the recipe book for several seconds. "You've never even tasted my baking. How do you know this will work?" She raised head, meeting his gaze.

He leaned close and cupped her jaw, his fingertips grazing her ear as he pressed his lips to hers. "Those peach turnovers looked wonderful," he whispered.

Her soft laugh filled the space between them. "All right, I'll stay, but I won't live with your mother."

He grinned. "The Burgess' lived on the second floor."

The front door of the car opened. The conductor stepped through and approached. "Tickets."

Alex turned to Annali, capturing her gaze. "Is it too late to crawl under the seat?"

**A word about the author...**

Kathy is the published author of multiple young adult and historical romance novels and short stories. Her novel A Place in Your Heart was a Northwest Houston Romance Writers of America Lone Star Historical Winner and her novel Lost Hearts a Utah/Salt Lake Romance Writers of America finalist.

Recently Kathy became an Author Accelerator certified fiction book coach and now helps clients bring their writing vision to life.

She also teaches classes on writing craft both on-line and in person at workshops and conferences.

When she's not writing, she enjoys walking her German shepherd through the woods and fields near her home or curling up with a good book and her cat.

Contact Kathy at: kathy@kathyotten.com

Website: www.kathyotten.com

Thank you for purchasing
this publication of The Wild Rose Press, Inc.

For questions or more information
contact us at
info@thewildrosepress.com.

The Wild Rose Press, Inc.
www.thewildrosepress.com